THE WATCHER'S DISCIPLE

BOOK TWO OF THE SACROSANCT RECORDS

M. N. JOLLEY

To everyone who's helped me to tell this story.

CONTENTS

Chapter 1	1
Chapter 2	13
Chapter 3	25
Chapter 4	39
Chapter 5	52
Chapter 6	65
Chapter 7	78
Chapter 8	90
Chapter 9	108
Chapter 10	121
Chapter 11	133
Chapter 12	145
Chapter 13	159
Chapter 14	171
Chapter 15	184
Chapter 16	197
Chapter 17	210
Chapter 18	225
Chapter 19	237
Chapter 20	249
Chapter 21	261
Chapter 22	271
Chapter 23	282
Chapter 24	297
Chapter 25	309
Chapter 26	321
Chapter 27	339
Chapter 28	352
Chapter 29	366
Chapter 30	383
Chapter 31	397

Chapter 32	410
Chapter 33	423
Acknowledgments	431

CHAPTER 1

Do the Watchers bless the kind and good?
  Do the Watchers bless the faithful?
  Do the Watchers bless the wise?
  No.
  The Watchers bless only those who will make the difference.
  • Speaker unknown

THE CABOOSE WAS ON FIRE.

This, by itself, did not leave David overly concerned. From the sound of things, it wasn't a particularly big fire. The train's crew was of course equipped to handle these sorts of emergencies. Not to mention, there were thirty two cars on the train, which meant barely three percent of the train as a whole was on fire—nothing to worry about.

Still, David was worried, because there were people riding horseback outside the train, and they were the ones who had *set* the fire.

"Should we do something about that?" Adelyn asked, pulling her head back inside, her hair a stir from the wind as she shut the window up. "Looks like a lot of them, and the fire's not getting any smaller."

David pondered her question. It still baffled him a bit that she would defer to his decisions. The girl was his apprentice, at least until she found someone more capable to teach her magic, but that tentative authority only extended as far as her training. She didn't need his consent to fight bandits.

If he had to give her an answer, though, he was leaning towards 'No'. Normally he would throw himself into the fray without a second thought, but he had lost his voice, and with it his magic. Besides which, he had to think of Adelyn's wellbeing.

The guard in their car had promised that the riders were in no danger, and David believed him for as long as things didn't get too far out of hand.

Peeking out the window, he watched as one of the riders raised a glass bottle with a flaming wick hanging from one end, chucking the whole cocktail at the train. It hit a cargo car, viscous liquid splashing across the side of the compartment and catching ablaze.

Maybe the train's guards would be able to stop them, but it wasn't going to be fast enough. Pushing aside his misgivings, David nodded at Adelyn, got to his feet, and gestured towards the back of the train.

Adelyn stood after him and followed behind. Her cavalry saber—a good blade, made of royal steel—hung in a sheath on her waist. To the casual onlooker, that'd be the most worrisome thing about her besides her height and her strong, work-hardened body. David knew the truth.

A train employee wearing a flat cap and a blue jacket raised a hand as they approached. "No passengers back this way. Your luggage is safe, don't you worry. Besides—"

The Watcher's Disciple

He continued talking, but David paid the words no mind, digging in a pouch on his belt to fish out his badge. Holding out the silver, he waited for the guard to read and let them through.

"You're David?" the guard asked, squinting at the inscribed words.

David nodded, counting off seconds in his head. This was taking longer than he wanted—those riders weren't going to sit idly by and wait for him to show up.

The guard paused, glancing up from beneath the brim of his hat. "And why do you feel the pressing urge to go check on your cargo just now?"

David wanted to scream. *Does he not see the riders? The fire?* It was obvious, he only had to glance out the window. Staring at the ceiling in frustration, David turned to Adelyn, so she would explain.

"We're going to help with the bandits," Adelyn said. "What's the problem?"

"And why couldn't he say so himself?" the guard asked, still holding the badge.

Gritting his teeth, David began drumming his fingers in a rhythm, a release for all the nervous energy building inside him. He'd made up his mind to get into the action, and now this guard seemed determined to keep them on standby until the whole train had been torched.

Adelyn bit her lip and looked at David. "He can't speak."

"Yeah?" the guard asked, sizing David up with a glance. "Is he simple?"

David's face burned at the question. The loss of his voice had been his own fault, the result of his own incompetence, and he hated the reminder of his failure almost as much as the way it left him impotent.

"No," Adelyn said. "He—"

The train shook. David leaned to the side, looming over a few travellers so he could open the window beside them and take stock of the riders. Peering out, he saw a rider-less horse galloping adjacent to the locomotive. Quickly making a sign to Adelyn, David explained what he'd seen, and she in turn translated to the guard.

"Someone's gotten onto the engine!" Adelyn exclaimed.

The guard looked past David nervously, peeking out the window, and finally stepped aside.

Adelyn started to run forward, but David caught her shoulder, flashing his hands in a quick sign. 'Someone needs to protect the engine.' The bandits couldn't be allowed to stop the train.

Bobbing her head in agreement, Adelyn said, "I'll go. Do you need a weapon?"

David shook his head, putting a hand to his hook for emphasis. The blade was not ideal in all situations, but as the name suggested, the crook at the end of its length made it ideal for disarming opponents. It wouldn't be worth a pin if it came to protection against gunfire, but that's what magic was for.

Except, he remembered, he couldn't use magic. Without his voice, he could do no more to cast spells than any other man. If Adelyn made him a shield he could fuel it with spirit, keep it alive, which would serve, but...

He turned, to see Adelyn had already begun her flight towards the front of the train. She had to travel up through more than twenty cars, and had no time to waste.

Without a voice, he couldn't call out to stop her. He could yell and make noise, but not articulate, and he had no desire to shout out a voiceless cry for help.

"Are you just gonna stand there?" the train guard asked.

David shook himself out of his self-pitying stupor. He'd have to go without a shield.

Pushing past the guard, he stepped outside, moving carefully between train cars. They were moving straight, but wind and force whipped at him. If he made a misstep, he'd be crushed under the train's wheels in a heartbeat. Magic wouldn't protect him there, even if he could cast spells.

He ran through a stock car first, passing his own horse in a blur as he ran to the far door, unbuckling the strap that kept his hook in place. Gripping the hilt, he took comfort in its familiar weight as he slammed into the far door and heaved at its handle. As he passed to the next car, he looked to the side and saw another rider-less horse keeping pace. At least one more bandit had made it onto the train. Taking a breath, David jumped the gap to the next cargo car, not wanting to lose any precious seconds.

One man and one woman, both in matching blue flatcaps were in that car, holding rifles and crouched behind boxes. They heard him and turned, raising their rifles, taking him for a bandit.

David shook his head and lowered his hook. It was obvious he wasn't attacking them—he'd come from the wrong direction—but they probably wouldn't realize it. He needed to show them...

My badge.

Feeling a fool, David looked back over his shoulder, realizing he'd left the silver badge in the hands of the guard.

"Drop the sword!" one of the flatcaps yelled, and David turned back to them. He dropped his hook.

The next cargo car was burning. David couldn't hear the fire crackling over the roar of the train, but he could see the flickering red light coming in through gaps in the far door.

"Who're you?" the other flatcap asked. "What are you after?"

He signed with his hands, hoping one of the flatcaps would understand. 'I am a friend. I am here to help.'

They shared a look, and David groaned quietly in frustration. He pointed emphatically, trying to make them understand.

Another of the fiery cocktails crashed through a window, glass exploding inward both from the pane and the bottle itself. Clear fluid sprayed out and burst into a ball of fire behind the two guards.

The flatcaps dove to the ground, covering their heads, and David didn't bother waiting to see what else they would do. It was only a small fire and their clothes hadn't caught, they could evacuate. He scooped up his hook from the ground, charging over and past them. It took a second to scramble over a pair of heavy boxes to avoid the fire, but he encountered no other obstacles as he got outside and hopped from car to car.

The door to enter was locked, handle catching as he tried to slip into the next car. He peered in through a slit window and saw a trio of people, searching through the boxes. The fire was raging on the windows and roof, but it hadn't yet made it inside, giving them time to find what they were looking for.

Stepping back as much as he could, David looked at the door. Heavy steel. Breaking it down would be the next best thing to impossible, and he didn't have time for all that brute force.

He examined his options. The train wasn't going all too fast—falling off it would be no worse than falling off a galloping horse, if the horse was ten feet tall and riding over rocky terrain. The windows on the side were too small for a man to fit through, but there were plenty of metal bars and pieces jutting out from the side of the otherwise wooden car. He had on black gloves that would keep his hands from being cut up, so he could climb without risk of self-harm.

Assuming he could make it safely to the other end of the cargo compartment, the door would surely have to be unbarred. It would be his way in.

He holstered his hook and reached up, standing on his toes to grab the lip of the car. One hand closed easily, grabbing on tight, but his left hand had difficulty finding purchase. His thumb was the source of the issue—having lost the original, he'd replaced the digit with a brass prosthetic. It could lock closed or stay open, adequate when holding a sword or a hook, but it only got him so far when climbing.

One good hand would have to do. He heaved himself up, feet pushing off of the handlebars meant to help travellers move safely from car to car. Shimmying sideways, he used his mental awareness to guide his feet.

He knew where the metal was without seeing or feeling it. He had no voice, but he was still a sorcerer. His spirit sense—his ability to feel the magic in the air—was as strong as ever. By releasing a bit of power into the air, he could sense how the world around him reacted to that energy. Air was too faint and weak, but metals all reacted strongly to the power, and the steel bars which jutted from the side of the train shone like a torchlight to his awareness.

Coming around the corner, a buffet of wind nearly threw him off the car. He clung tight, gripping the side of the train for all he was worth as the wind tried to rip him free and send him tumbling to the ground. The sound of the wind was deafening, and he could smell smoke wafting from the other side of the car.

There was another flaw in his plan which he had overlooked. Wood splintered and flew from an inch to his side as a bullet smashed into the wood. One of the riders whooped and hollered, voice barely audible over the wind, and another bullet ricocheted off of the metal ridge David was standing on, making his footing vibrate.

Mentally swearing, David abandoned his thoughts of climbing across the train. Heaving, he raised himself up, flailing his legs to try and push off anything they could find purchase on. Another bullet managed to graze his leg, but the wound was barely a scratch and he ignored it, heaving one more time and rolling to the top of the cargo car.

Lying on his back, he panted and caught his breath for a moment. He could feel spirit, stored in the necklace around his neck, and realized he'd filled it out of reflex when he heard the gunfire. Wasted energy. Now that it was spirit, he couldn't convert it back to physical strength.

He couldn't stay where he was. Though his profile was low and shielded from gunfire, the fire had spread to the roof of the car, flickering low and hot, only kept from roaring by the wind. Besides which, he had a job to do.

Rolling onto all fours and coming up in a crouch, David looked at the fire. It had spread across the roof, a five-foot wall of burning wood that was still slowly growing. These sorts of flames had once been his plaything, a toy for him to manipulate, but now he'd have to navigate it like any other man.

The only other obstacles on the roof were two low steel bars, one on each side of the train, raised a foot off the ground. The intent was to provide a point to hook onto, so that cranes could load these cars onto ships. For David, they created small hurdles he'd have to jump.

David rushed forward, keeping his head low to provide a

smaller target to the gunners on horseback, praying to the Watchers that he'd make it through this.

It was necessary to build up speed to leap over the fire, but that could kill him if he made the jump and couldn't stop. Too little momentum, he'd burn. Too much, he'd fall. Trying to gauge the speed perfectly, David made it to the edge of the blaze, kicked off, and leapt.

He fell. One of his feet caught the iron bar, and he landed flat on his face, tumbling towards the end of the car without any grip or handhold to slow himself. This was never something he'd practiced for, and so he had to improvise, making a plan in the half second before he slid off the edge.

In the time it took his heart to beat twice, David spun himself around, ripped his hook free from where it was clipped to his belt, lashing it out and timing the motion. Both hands holding tightly to the grip, he waited, feeling out the world around him, closing his eyes to shut out distractions. Time was moving slowly, but he only had one shot and it had to be perfect or he'd fall headfirst into the gap between train cars.

His hook caught on a metal outcropping at the end of the car. The jolt was jarring, and he nearly lost his grip. Gritting his teeth, David hung on as the steel weapon swung, taking him in an arc that turned him around and sent him flying feet first into the car's unlatched door. It kicked inward violently as he finally lost his handhold on the sword, falling into the car and landing on his back. It was the second violent tumble he'd had in ten seconds, and his bones ached and head rang as he stood to look around.

The three bandits were staring at him. All wore vibrant green wraps over their faces and heads, leaving only eyes to look out a tiny slit, and their heavy riding leathers and clothes made age and gender ambiguous. David took stock of their weapons immediately, readying himself for the fight —two had revolvers in holsters and crowbars in hand, which they were using to search through boxes. The third only held a huge staff.

No. No, no, no—

The third bandit raised their staff, and David charged in before they could shout. The tingle of spirit in the air was apparent as they filled the staff with energy, preparing to cast a spell. They let David grab the staff, not thinking it would matter, but as he sucked the spirit out of the weapon they swore in surprise, shouting, "Wizard!"

The other two bandits had been content to let their magic user handle the intruder, but now that it seemed the fight might be on equal ground they pitched in. One raised a revolver, which David kicked away, and the other swung their crowbar, an attack that missed narrowly. If it had been just the two of them, David would have been fine, but he had to keep the bandit wizard occupied or else they'd take him with a spell and that would be the end of David Undertow.

The bandit tried charging their staff again, but David had a hand on it now, and every ounce of spirit that flowed in was promptly sucked out before magic could be unleashed. They let go of their staff, letting David take it and stepping back so they could cast a different spell unimpeded.

There was only one hope David could see. They were a magic user, which meant they could feel the spirit David used, same as he did theirs. Raising a glove, he poured spirit into it, silk thread stitched into runes that he'd added years before. He put out his hands in a gesture of attack, going for intimidation, hoping to get a reaction—

"Stop!" the bandit wizard called, raising his hands—the voice seemed male—in a pacifying gesture. "We don't want to fight you!"

Keep him talking. Don't let him realize you're impotent.

David raised an eyebrow and looked between the three bandits, their disguises making them interchangeable in his eyes. He was not an expert at conveying meaning with body language, but that was a simple enough gesture.

The sorcerer continued, trying to talk down the situation. "We're not trying to hurt anyone, the fire is only to be frightening. You're a passenger, yes?"

David nodded. That seemed safe—even if he had his tongue, he would have still nodded in response to a question that simple.

"Then we have nothing against you," The wizard said, voice slightly muffled and hard to hear behind their mask. "Leave us be, we'll be gone in a moment."

David hesitated. He seemed so... genuine. Like he truly didn't want to hurt David, nor anyone else. The other two bandits got back to work, cracking open boxes as the flames crackled around the train car, and for half a second he almost backed down.

What are they stealing?

The question popped into his mind, and once asked, he couldn't set it aside. Boxes of luggage had been busted open without care or concern. Most of the train's freight would be pedestrian. Clothing, a few small valuables, perhaps a little coinage, but if that wasn't what the bandits were going for, then what else would they want?

"Found it!" one of the bandits exclaimed, her voice clear in the confined space. The box she'd opened was full of opaque white blocks wrapped in thin paper, and it took

David a couple seconds to realize that he was looking at a crate full of blasting jelly.

His eyes widened at that realization. If these bandits got ahold of explosives like that, there was no telling what they would be able to do with it. That left no choice but to fight —he couldn't back down and let them get away with that prize. David tensed, ready to leap forward and resume the melee.

He wasn't fast enough. The bandit wizard threw out a hand and yelled a word, hitting David with a clumsy wall of force. As a magical attack, it was weak, but David had no defense against it and went tumbling backward yet again. This time, his head struck something hard before he could slow his flight, and his landing was accompanied by blackness.

CHAPTER 2

I went out with my hunting party today. Six ships, almost two hundred sailors, twice again that many harpoons. With what trouble we've had lately, we weren't about to let another one slip away.

We took down the bloody beast, sure enough, but it put up a fight for the abandoned. One of our ships was all but lost, we had to tow it in. More men than I have fingers are hurt, but Watchers be praised, nobody killed this time. It's a big one, too. Old. And I could swear the damned thing was looking at me when we finished it off.

Gives me the chills, that.

- Journal entry, written by a sailor on a thulcut hunting ship

"I'll go," Adelyn said, heart pounding in her chest. "Do you need a weapon?"

She watched David as he shook his head and gestured to his hook. Confident he would be okay, Adelyn turned to run at a breakneck pace up the train car. The door handles were great iron wheels that had to be spun to unlatch, and she grabbed the first of many, turning it heavily and swinging it open.

Running inside a moving object was not something she was used to, but she'd gotten her sea legs the day before when they'd boarded their first train. Now that she'd had a day of practice, she could manage it without falling flat on her face.

If the train kept running, at least. They weren't far out from the city, but that was assuming they weren't on foot.

Nobody cared to stop her moving between passenger cars. After opening the door she started at the wind whipping up outside, but after steeling herself she grabbed a handle, opened the next door, and kept moving.

She wanted to conserve her strength, so she'd be ready to fight by the time she made it to the engine, but that would only serve her if she made it in time. If the bandits managed to stop the train before she arrived, her efforts would be fruitless. With this in mind, she ran at full speed, deciding to catch her breath at the final car if she had the time.

Twenty four train cars was a long run. She could have run the distance flat in half a minute, but having to stop every fifteen feet to throw open a pair of doors before accelerating again added to the length of her flight significantly, throwing off her pace, and the shaking of the train car beneath her feet kept her run unsteady.

Taking in a big gulp of breath, she reached the last passenger car. After that, it was one crew car, then the engine.

The door to the crew car wasn't locked, but as she seized the handle and tried to turn it, she found it stuck. Someone had jammed the other side. Putting her face up to the window, she could see two figures inside, and they were on the ground, blood staining their uniforms.

Adelyn swore. She'd been too late to help them, though judging by the train's continued movement, she wasn't too late to save the engine.

"Okay, gotta open this door," Adelyn muttered, looking it up and down. The whole thing was solid steel, except for the glass window, two panes with air between them for insulation.

Perfect.

She raised her hand to the glass, feeling it out for a moment, then began to work her magic.

Spirit slipped out of her and into one of the silver bracelets she wore—each had its own effect, but the one she chose was made to manipulate air.

David had recommended runes to control wind, but she'd been adamant. She wanted something more versatile, something that could be used in situations besides combat. When they'd had the bracelets made, she'd had runes of air inscribed instead.

"Fell gild," Adelyn intoned, mentally picturing what she wanted to happen as she spoke the spell into existence, a whisper of spirit releasing from the bracelet.

Between the two panes of glass, the air began expanding, swelling against the glass from inside. It was a tiny gap between the panes, and the air had nowhere to go, so the pressure built.

Adelyn stepped back and, a second later, the glass shattered. She could have punched through it with a strong enough spell, but the trick with the air had conserved her strength and broken the glass clean, leaving few shards sticking in the door. Sticking her arm through the gap, she felt around for the handle and found that a crowbar had been wedged in place to keep it from turning.

Grasping it in one hand, she pulled the crowbar free, then tried again to turn the handle from her side. It spun open.

Running into the crew car, she knelt by the first of the two people in uniform. A young man, barely older than her, his blue vest stained so much with blood that it looked black. She put her finger to his wrist, but felt nothing.

Biting down on her lip, she checked on the next employee, a woman a couple years older. She had a gunshot in her belly, and when Adelyn moved to check her pulse, she moved.

"Lords!" Adelyn started, jumping backwards in shock. Once she overcame the surprise, she leaned back in. "Are you okay?"

"P-peachy," the woman stammered, shaking her head. "Just taking a nap on... on the job. Don't tell my boss."

Adelyn gave a light chuckle, then pulled up the woman's shirt to look at the wound. "Did the bullet come out the other side?"

The woman shook her head, and for a moment Adelyn was relieved, then she said, "Can't feel much below my belly. Dunno."

Adelyn looked down at her. She was in rough shape, and Adelyn's knowledge of healing magic was rudimentary at best—she only knew the generic word for healing.

A part of her considered that this was all pointless if she didn't stop the bandits. That was priority, not this one woman.

Abandon that. I'm helping her.

"I'm going to cauterize this," Adelyn said. It was the best help she could offer. "Okay?"

The woman nodded, face pale. In fact, all of her was pale, the color in her had bled out onto the floor.

Adelyn drug her fingers through the blood, feeling the spirit there. The blood wasn't fresh and much of the power in it had leached away, but it was still enough for her to charge the second bracelet on her wrist, the one carved with runes of heat and light.

With a word, the air in her hand grew to searing temperatures, a ball of coalesced heat that would burn anything on contact.

Manipulating the air, she put her hand over the bloody wound, wrinkling her nose as the smell of burning flesh and iron filled the air as the blood sizzled. The woman's back arched in pain and she groaned, but within moments the wound had sealed, skin and muscle blackened to a char.

"Roll over," Adelyn said. When the woman shook her head in protest, Adelyn took her by the side with her free hand and rolled her forcefully, looking to see an exit wound obscured by sticky blood.

Repeating the cauterization, Adelyn let the woman lie back. It was no great surgical procedure, but it would hopefully keep her from bleeding out.

"Stay here," Adelyn instructed, feeling foolish. She didn't know what advice would be good. *Should she sit up? Try to stay awake? Sleep?*

Whatever the answer, Adelyn didn't know it. Taking what scraps of energy remained in the blood, she left the woman whimpering in pain and stood to go find whoever'd done this and pay them back in kind.

She peered through the glass slit that stood between her and the engine. In stark contrast to the rest of the train, which was steel and iron, the engine was built from bronze and brass wherever possible. It ran on spirit, and so steel would have trebled the energy cost as it sapped away available power.

Rather than simply having a door going inside, the engine's entrance was on the side, with a narrow metal grate to walk on. There was a handrail, but it was the only thing to protect from the wind whipping around the train car.

Three people were standing on that narrow grate, wearing riding leathers, bright bandanas, and hats over their heads to make them indistinguishable. One was working at the engine's door with a crowbar, trying to pry off the handle, while the other two seemed to argue with wild arm gestures, each holding their own crowbars ready. The bronze door was standing well against their struggle, but they seemed to be making some level of headway.

Throwing open the door in front of her, Adelyn poured energy into the third bracelet around her wrist—the one for force. She didn't bother with subtlety. Throwing out her hand like a slap, she called, *"Shtap!"*, and struck one of the bandits across the face with force.

The bandit was thrown backwards, clutching the bronze rail for support as Adelyn jumped the space between her car and the engine, so that she was on the same narrow metal grate as the bandits.

One of the bandits yelled something ineloquent and anatomically improbable as they saw her, stepping back and clutching for a weapon.

Adelyn couldn't help but smile at that, as she poured power into the rune of air. The wind was dangerous, it would make it possible for any one lucky shot to throw her from the train, so she stopped it. With a few words and an outpouring of power, she froze the air around them, making the wind still—or, rather, creating a barrier of air that would resist the wind for a few moments.

The bandits tried to gather against her, but they couldn't bring their numbers to bear, and were forced to fight her one at a time. Adelyn drew her father's cavalry saber, the ripples in the metal shimmering as she blocked an attack by the first, kicked hard, and sent them stumbling back into the second as they managed to recover from her initial magical slap.

She poured spirit into the runes of heat around her wrist, trying to precisely work magic while fighting the pair of bandits—the third was still working at the engine's door while they fought. Her focus was distracted by the crowbars swinging at her head, but she did her best, mumbling magic words beneath her breath.

As the bandits took turns parrying her away, she let one catch her in the left arm, intentionally taking the blow so that it would draw blood. It was her bad arm, anyways, and she needed the extra power. Her magic was consuming spirit too fast for her to sustain on physical strength alone, so she used the spirit in the blood as a supplement, filling the heat runes again and again, not caring how much of the power was sapped away as she worked the magic.

Seeing the hit as an indication of success, the bandit who'd struck cheered, moving in more aggressively. Adelyn was forced back a few steps and forced to sidestep into the bronze rail, making it shake and tremble.

She could parry and defend well enough, but she was no master. Though she was armed with a well-crafted blade and they had only a steel rod with a sharp bit at the end, it was still a fight she wouldn't be able to easily win on skill at arms alone.

One hard blow nearly knocked the blade from her grip, and she felt a bit of wind graze against the gash on her arm. She threw a quick spell of force at the nearest bandit to distract them for a moment, dropped to the ground, grabbed the grate with both hands to brace herself, and kicked as hard as she could at the bronze rail that kept the four of them from falling to the ground.

Though she was strong, she didn't have the power to kick down solid bronze bars. That was why she'd been working her spells, channeling heat through the runes and focusing it as close to the base of the rail as she could, heating each bar to the point of losing its strength.

As she kicked at the base of the rail, the hot bronze sheared, coming away from the train, and in the same moment, her spell protecting against the wind broke apart. Gales of wind suddenly rushed back against the side of the train, staggering the trio of bandits. They tried to catch themselves against the rail, but the rail was now tumbling on the ground below.

Two bandits fell from the train, hitting the dirt and rolling in heaps. Adelyn neither knew nor cared if they were okay, though she assumed they were not. A fall from that height at that speed was not something to be walked off.

The third bandit only stood by virtue of clutching to the door they'd been trying to pry open. Adelyn staggered to her feet, leaning against the train so that she wouldn't come to the same fate as the bandits, facing off with the last one.

The bandit gripped the door with one arm, holding out the crowbar, shouting something that Adelyn couldn't make out over the wind. Before she could stop the gales a second time, though, the door swung in from behind the bandit and they were pulled backwards, yelping in surprise.

They might have managed to catch their feet, but before the bandit could try, a large bronze wrench smashed into their head, sending them spinning to the floor. Adelyn looked to see the conductor, an aging man with a healthy beard, holding the tool.

He dropped the crowbar and waved at her, a gesture saying to come in, and Adelyn rushed through the doorway, getting out of the wind.

"There's more out on horseback." He kicked the downed bandit for good measure, then looked at her. "Stay on your guard."

"Do you know what they're after?" Adelyn asked.

The conductor shook his head. "Local trouble, likely. I just keep the engine running."

"I'll fight them off," Adelyn said, walking to the front of the train, where narrow windows let her look out and see a handful of bandits still keeping pace on their horses. Checking back through the window of the door, she saw that more had peeled off to help their fallen friends.

"You're a peace officer?" the conductor asked, watching her.

Adelyn shook her head, finally giving herself a moment to relax now that she was sure there was no immediate danger. "A helper."

Standing back, she looked around the engine room. Two great brass teardrops hung from the ceiling, rocking slightly as the train rolled. Those would be the batteries, storing spirit for the train to run. Cables ran from there to a large engine block, which would turn the wheels outside.

"How good are you with all that magic?" the engineer asked.

"Good enough to fight off some bandits," Adelyn said, chewing her lip. "Why?"

The engineer hesitated. "'Cause they were saying if I didn't open the door, they'd go get their sorcerer and have him open it for them."

Adelyn tensed, first in alarm, then in fear. She couldn't fight another sorcerer, not of they had significant experience.

Another thought made her alarm grow. If they didn't have their sorcerer at the engine, that meant—

"David," She said, running to the door. If he fought a sorcerer, he was almost as certain as she to lose.

Skirting the unprotected walkway, she began her flight back down the train. Her legs were sore, her body was tired from all the running, but she carried herself faster than she had coming up the train to begin with.

The doors moved with frustrating slowness, creaking as she threw one open, crossed between cars, and threw another. She sucked in air to keep herself going, wishing she hadn't been so careless in the fight—she'd been cocky, wasted spirit on something flashy when she should have been more conservative.

She passed by the guard who'd given them trouble before, into the cargo compartments, past two more train employees who were busy putting out a fire that had spread on the ground. She shouted an explanation at those two and hoped that they wouldn't try to stop her, sprinting to the next car.

Hitting a door that was blocked, she didn't go for any fancy tricks with air pressure, simply slamming through the window with a wave of power, stuck her arm inside, and threw open the door.

The car's walls were on fire, and smoke was billowing in through windows that had shattered from heat. She saw no bandits, only a body on the ground, limp and lifeless, blood oozing from a wound on his leg.

"David!" she cried, running to his limp form. Rolling him over, she shook him, trying to elicit a response.

"Uh?" David mumbled, eyes blurry as he came to. Seeing her, he started, looking around the train car wildly.

"We have to get out of here," Adelyn said, pulling him up. His leg could support him, but he walked with a pronounced limp, and seemed too weak to hold his whole weight. He accepted her support only grudgingly, perhaps embarrassed to need her help to walk.

As they stumbled, he had to stop to gag and retch, overcome with nausea from the effort to limp away. He panted, waiting until he was sure he wouldn't throw up before he straightened and held out trembling hands so that he could sign, 'Did they get away?'

She didn't know who he was talking about. "I didn't see anyone when I came in."

Once they were in the next train car, one with only a burning roof, he stopped to look out the window, mouth moving slightly as he counted the riders who fled away from the train.

He pounded his fist against the glass in frustration, then winced and waved his hand in the air in discomfort. After a second to recover, he punched the window again, and Adelyn had to pull him back.

"We kept the train running," she said. "We did our best."

She felt spirit, and realized he'd drawn energy into the rune around his neck. Frowning, Adelyn put a hand to his chest, where the necklace was, but he pulled away from her.

"You're fine, I think you just need to lie down."

He shook his head, but let her help him continue walking forward, to the car with the two train employees.

They straightened upon seeing him, and one reached for a rifle that was leaning nearby, but Adelyn said, "He's not any danger. He was trying to help."

To help emphasize, David put up his hands and sat down.

"You sure about that?" one of them asked, adding, "And who're you?"

"A friend," Adelyn explained, putting her own hands in the air.

They approached, raising a rifle to be safe. "You one of them?"

David had his head in his hands, so Adelyn answered for both of them. "No. We're passengers trying to help."

"What happened in there?"

"I don't know," Adelyn said.

"Is he okay?" the one without a rifle approached, putting a hand on David's shoulder.

David jerked away, looking up at them. The welt on the back of his head was plainly visible, and he seemed too little of a threat to be concerned with.

"We're gonna have to arrest you, anyways," The first said. "If you're really nobody, it shouldn't be any trouble."

"Are you peace officers?" Adelyn asked, raising an eyebrow at the two of them. Last time she'd had to deal with peace officers, it hadn't gone well.

The two employees eyed each other, then one said, "Technically, no, but—"

"Then that's fine. We surrender."

CHAPTER 3

BANDITS ROB TRAIN
   Two heroes prevented total disaster, but bandits escape
   A passenger train coming into the city was attacked yesterday by a pack of bandits on horseback. One security guard was killed, and several more were injured defending the engine. Total disaster was averted when two travelers took it upon themselves to aid in the defense, saving the engine and protecting the passengers until the train reached the city and the bandits were forced to flee. One bandit was taken into custody, his name has not been released.
   Though the heroes remain anonymous, city Sheriff Cara Flintwood told us that one was a veteran in town to give offering for Eatle's Day. The sheriff was also unwilling to speculate about the nature of the bandits, but implied that they were part of a Watched cult in the city, and an investigation is underway to determine who their accomplices may be.
   Continued on Page 7
   •Front page article, "Azah Gazette"

. . .

"And why were you coming into the city?"

Adelyn crossed her arms, staring at the peace officer sitting across from her. She had specifically surrendered to a group of non-peace officers, and yet here she was, sitting across from a middle aged woman with a lords-damned gold sheriff's badge pinned to her white outfit.

When Adelyn refused to respond, the sheriff sighed, rubbing her forehead. "Look, Adelyn, you can answer my questions and we'll let you go, or we can sit here until one of us dies of old age."

"Abandon that," Adelyn said, glaring. "I saved that train, I'm not going to sit here and—"

"*I know,*" The sheriff sighed. "We've got an eyewitness that saw you fight off the bandits, another says you saved her life. I just need you to answer a couple questions for the record."

They'd neglected to take her silver bracelets, apparently not realizing that Adelyn could use them as a weapon, so she didn't feel intimidated in the slightest. If push came to shove, she could leave whenever she wanted, but it would be messy and draw a lot of attention, and she'd have to leave David behind.

He had been incoherent and struggling to stay awake when they arrived at the train station, so while Adelyn had been shuffled along to an interrogation, he'd been taken to a holding cell to rest. She had little hope of finding him if it came to a fight.

The sheriff sat back, looking Adelyn up and down, and said, "I should mention that your friend's case isn't looking so good as yours."

That made her sit up straight. "Is he that badly hurt?"

She shook her head. "Not from his hurt. Accusations of aiding the bandits, though, that's a bigger deal."

Adelyn gritted her teeth. "He was trying to help you."

"Oh, now you're talking to me," the sheriff said. "Okay, explain what he thought he could do against the bandits. You, I understand, but he's just a regular man. Am I expected to believe that he would try and fight the bandits all on his own?"

"Yeah," Adelyn said, adding by way of explanation, "He's handy with a blade."

"You think he could fight a few people at once?" the sheriff asked. "That's no small feat without powers like you've got. He couldn't have been going back there for some other reason?"

"He got knocked out fighting the bandits!" Adelyn exclaimed. "What more do you need?"

"His wounds will heal," The sheriff said. "Might be a trick. Do you know what faith he keeps?"

Adelyn tripped on that question, raising a suspicious eyebrow. "Why do you ask?"

The sheriff shrugged. "Trying to put together some pieces."

"He's Divine," Adelyn lied. It seemed a safe guess. If his religion had the chance to get him into trouble, she would tell the safest fib possible, and most of the continent seemed to be Divine. She couldn't remember exactly what those beliefs entailed, but that was fine as long as she didn't claim to be one of them herself.

The sheriff looked at her. "But you're not."

"Why do you say that?" Adelyn asked.

"You don't seem to mind throwing around magic," The sheriff explained. "Not many Divine witches, these days."

"Oh," Adelyn said, filing that information away. It seemed to fit with what she knew, but her memory on

Divine beliefs had been fuzzy lately. "Well, I'm Tarraganian. But I'm not a witch."

The sheriff raised an eyebrow. "We saw—"

"I'm a sorceress," Adelyn explained before the sheriff could correct. "I use my magic to help people." Normally, she'd say something about not wanting to be affiliated with the Thirteen Wizards, a group who'd massacred whole cities wholesale in the war, but she couldn't rightfully say that now that she knew David's history.

"Sure," The sheriff said, sitting back in her chair. "And why were the two of you coming to the city?"

Adelyn crossed her arms and sat back in her chair.

The sheriff sighed. "Look, I'm just trying to get some leads. We're not the bad guys. These people have been giving us an abyss of trouble since we set up here."

Chewing her lip, Adelyn asked, "These people? You know who did it?"

"Not exactly," The sheriff said. "We know the general type, but we don't have any names. It's these 'Watched', they act as though they can do whatever they please. Not all of them are bad, mind, but spotting the troublemakers from the good ones is something even Eatle would struggle with."

"So what do you want from me?" Adelyn asked. "Sounds like something that a couple strangers can't really help with."

"We want to know why your friend is still alive," the sheriff said, finally being straight with her question. "They could have killed him, easy as spitting."

"Ask him," Adelyn replied flippantly. "I wasn't there."

"If he's up to something, he won't tell us. How well do you know him?"

"David's not connected to anything going on here,"

Adelyn said. "Ask that bandit we knocked out, if you don't believe me."

The sheriff sat back in her chair. "He's even more tight-lipped than you. We only want answers."

"I don't have them." Adelyn wondered how this woman was the one in charge. "I don't know what's going on."

"Then why won't you talk to me?"

Adelyn sighed, rubbing her forehead a moment. "If I answer all your questions, you'll let me and David go?"

"Unless you really were working with them and you're playing some long game that I can't cipher."

"Swear it on your gods?" Adelyn asked. It was the best she could do to try and ensure honesty. "Eh... Eatle is justice, right? So swear on him."

The sheriff nodded agreeably, a hint of a smile playing behind her gruff expression. "I swear on Eatle, I'll play you fair."

Adelyn's chair creaked as she sat back in it one more time. "Okay then. Ask away."

"Why were you coming into the city?" the sheriff asked.

"Trying to find a way to return David's voice," Adelyn said. "There's supposed to be a few sorcerers here who know about healing."

"Too many sorcerers, if you ask me," The sheriff quipped. "You know the person you're coming to see?"

"I don't," Adelyn said. "His name is Harrington, I think. David's met him, but doesn't know him well."

"How'd he lose his voice?"

Adelyn hesitated. That was a long story, and not one that she much wanted to recap. "Do you want the long version or the short version?" She asked, to cover her hesitation.

"Short version, for now."

"He gave lip to the wrong guy, lost a fight while I couldn't help him." It was true enough, even if it left out some important details.

"And how'd you two meet?"

That was something she didn't need to be vague about. "My home town ran into some trouble with raiders, I hired him as muscle."

The sheriff scratched at her nose, thinking for a moment. "You know his history?"

Adelyn had to think back on what she knew, and what she could say without arousing suspicion. "Born on the coasts, I think. Fought for the president in the war."

"You know what regiment?" the sheriff asked.

"No. Like I said, you can ask him."

The sheriff chewed on that for half a minute while she thought about it. "You mind translating?"

...

They kept David in a holding cell at the train station for five hours. He didn't complain. He had stayed awake long enough for them to escort him from the cargo car to the cell, slipped his hands free of the knots, found a clean patch on the floor, and laid down to continue his sleep.

His head had ceased pounding when he woke, though his back and side were sore from sleeping on stone. Someone was standing in front of the bars of his cell, and he stood, happy to see them.

"David," Adelyn said, relief plain on her face. "Are you alright?"

David shook his head, signing his response. His right hand was sore and stiff from punching the window, but he did his best. 'They had a wizard. I lost.' It was embarrassing, but he wasn't going to hide the truth from Adelyn. 'What happened at the engine?'

"No wizard up there, thank the Lords," Adelyn said.

"Three bandits were trying to get to the controls. Two of them were dealt with, we knocked out a third."

David stretched his arms. 'You were not injured?'

Adelyn shrugged. "Just got a scratch, nothing to be worried about. They want to ask you a few questions, I volunteered to translate. I think they like me, since I caught one of the bandits." She leaned in, adding in a whisper. "Do you want me to lie for you?"

David hesitated at the question. He'd made a vow never to tell a lie. He regretted that vow—it had caused him endless headaches, trying to manipulate the truth without speaking outright falsehood—but he wasn't about to break it. It meant much awkwardness in concealing his history, though, which is why Adelyn had asked.

If they asked him about his history, David would have to tell the truth, or say nothing at all. If he revealed who he was —the Blue Flame, one of the Thirteen, one of the worst killers in living history—then they would want to keep him for further questioning. His actions had been legal, tolerated by the government since he'd been fighting for their side, but that lenience wouldn't protect from future legal action.

That's where Adelyn's offer came in. She had not made a vow to speak only truth. If they asked a question that would be awkward for David to answer, he could communicate the truth, and she could lie about what he'd said. No vows would be broken, and no secrets would be revealed.

'Yes, please,' he signed back.

"Great. I told them you were a veteran in the president's army, by the way, but not anything else."

David was thankful for that. That was one less lie he'd have to worry about.

Raising her voice, Adelyn called, "He's awake!"

Two people walked in, a pair of peace officers. One woman with a sheriff's badge on her lapel, another younger man with a ring of keys. He held those up, opening the cell, and gesturing down the hall.

"This way. We just have a couple questions, then we can get all this sorted."

David nodded, following the two peace officers down the hall and into an office. It wasn't a true interrogation room, merely a few chairs arranged around a table. They sheepishly pointed to one of the chairs, and David sat.

"Can we get you something to drink?" one of them asked.

'Do you trust them?' David signed to Adelyn, right hand beginning to ache from all the movement.

"Some water, please," Adelyn said, before signing back. 'Not a lick, but they promised to let us go once we answered their questions.' She'd taken to the signs like a fish to water, learning them even faster than David had, and her hands flowed smoothly as she talked.

The peace officer who'd carried the keys stood to go get the water. Without a name to attach to him, David noted him down in his memory as 'Keys', a simple mnemonic that would ensure David didn't forget his face. Keys left, shutting the door behind him.

The sheriff spoke, looking between Adelyn and David, unsure who to address. "Can we get your name, please?"

"I told you his name is David," Adelyn said.

"Sure." The sheriff glanced at David. "Is that what I should call you?"

He nodded, adding in a sign to Adelyn, 'Why are we lying to them?'

'Because I trust peace officers less than I trust the undesired,' Adelyn signed back. The last word wasn't a perfect fit

—she was referring to the Pariah, a religious figure she believed in, but there was no sign for the Pariah, so she'd improvised. 'I promised to talk to them, but I'm not telling them anything I wouldn't tell to a stranger.'

"What're you saying?" the sheriff asked, looking between the two of them. She didn't seem concerned, only contemplative.

Addressing her, Adelyn said, "He was asking if anyone was hurt."

"A few of us," the sheriff replied darkly. "One death. It could have been worse if you weren't there. Did he see the face of anyone?"

David signed out his response, and Adelyn repeated honestly, adding her own comment to the end. "No. They all wore masks and clothes over their whole bodies to cover any distinguishing marks. Same as the people I fought."

She waved her hand for them to continue, prompting, "Was there anything identifiable besides their faces?"

Adelyn repeated honestly, still not seeing fit to lie. "One of them was a sorcerer."

He expected surprise, but the sheriff only nodded at that. "Any distinguishing trinkets, markings on their clothes, something that you might remember?"

David shook his head. No translation necessary for a simple 'No'.

Keys reentered, setting a glass of water on the table and sliding it over. Despite having not actually asked for it, David took the glass and drank deeply, water spilling out of the corner of his mouth and staining his cotton shirt.

"He says they had a sorcerer," the sheriff said, as her counterpart sat down. "Nothing else to go on, though. Any word on what they took?"

Keys shook his head, but David quickly signed an

answer, taking Adelyn by surprise. Adelyn signed for him to repeat, and he did, explaining what he'd deduced.

"Explosives?" Adelyn asked, out loud. "Are you sure?"

Nodding, David signed to confirm, and explain what he'd seen.

Adelyn looked at the peace officers, translating. "He says that the bandits opened up a box of blasting jelly while he confronted them."

"Eh..." The sheriff looked over at Keys, and though she didn't say anything, her expression apparently conveyed the message that she intended. Keys turned to head back out the door, moving quickly.

The sheriff made a note. "Okay, a couple more questions. Do you keep any faith?"

'I'm of the Watched,' David signed.

"He's Divine," Adelyn translated immediately.

She was ready to lie about that, David thought, curious.

"Great." The two train employees conferred for a moment. Finally, the sheriff asked, "How long are you going to be staying in the city?"

Adelyn answered without needing to translate. "We don't know yet. However long it takes to restore David's voice, I guess."

The sheriff hesitated at that, but ultimately agreed. "Where will you be staying? In case we need to ask you anything else."

"Don't know yet," Adelyn said, without waiting for David to speak. "We were going to find an inn or a boarding house. Can we let you know once we find it?"

"Eh..." Again, the sheriff hesitated, chewing the inside of her cheek as she thought about it. Deciding something, she pushed up from her chair, nodding. "Sure. Be sure to tell us right away, though?"

Adelyn didn't have any objections left. "Of course. Is that everything?"

"For now. Like I said, if we think of anything else, we can ask you later. If you think of anything important, ask for Cara. That's me. We've got your personal effects in the other room, you can pick them up on your way out."

David stood, signing to Adelyn. 'Did they find my hook?'

Adelyn paused and shook her head.

'Did you ask?' David asked, feeling his heart sink. He'd had that weapon for most of a decade, it would be a shame to lose it.

'I can't,' Adelyn signed back. 'I will explain later.'

David frowned, but followed her out of the little room. He didn't like being out of the loop. Anxious, he started tapping his fingers against his leg, but the motion shot pain up through his fingers.

Grunting, David held up his hand pulled off the glove to look. He knew it was bruised and hurt from punching the window, but still winced when he saw that two of his fingers were swollen and red.

"David!" Adelyn exclaimed upon seeing the injury. "Why didn't you say your hand was hurt?"

David signed back. 'I am fine. Signing doesn't hurt too terribly.'

Adelyn chewed her lip, but didn't argue, for which David was grateful. He wanted to get somewhere private so they could talk, not get involved in an argument over how badly he needed a doctor.

They collected their luggage, and Adelyn took a moment to make sure that her money was still all secure and accounted for. She had good reason to—they'd brought a sack full of Beor silver, worth at least a couple gold pieces all told. Getting it exchanged for regular currency was a nuisance, but it was a bag full of silver regardless of the denomination.

The whole station up until that point had been enclosed, under a roof and kept inside walls with shuttered windows, the sort of structure that didn't give a good sense of where you really were. So, when they stepped outside, Adelyn got her first real view of the city.

She stood, dumbstruck, mouth agape. "I... I knew you said the city was big, but... this is..."

David grinned, allowing himself to feel a bit of satisfaction at her shock and stupor. She may have known what was going on with the peace officers better than he, and she may have had the magic that David currently lacked, but for just that moment he got to be the one who was in the loop while she was left to stand, baffled and surprised.

He felt guilty a moment later. Adelyn wasn't trying to show him up or belittle him, and it was unfair to take glee in her confusion. To assuage his guilt, he filled her in on what he knew, so she wouldn't be baffled any longer.

'At last census, this city is home to almost one hundred thousand people,' he signed, after getting her attention. 'It's the largest port city in the world.'

Adelyn looked at him, then back out at the city. "I know, but... *wow*."

David looked at the city, trying to see it how she did. They were at a vantage point, looking down over the rest of the city. The ocean was faintly visible on the horizon, with ships like little dots in the port. The city had no real layout or plan, buildings had been made and then rebuilt after fire or war tore them down. The city's central spire stuck up like a stone knife raising out from a sea of wooden boxes, and the great Church of the Divinities could be seen like a block of white marble nestled between ports and docks.

The smell of seawater overpowered all else, and even from their raised position, they could hear the shouts and calls of people, selling wares from rolling carts, building new houses atop old ones to make room for new citizens, cooking up meals to sell to passersby.

It was big, yes, but David couldn't see anything else to gawk at. It was merely a port city, like one of a dozen others on the peninsula.

"I thought Maise was big," Adelyn said. "But that was just some barracks and warehouses. This is a *city*."

David nodded in agreement. She wasn't wrong. 'We should start moving,' he said. 'I would like to find a place to stay.'

He kept an eye out for pickpockets as they walked. It would take an immensely skilled hand to draw from his own pockets, but Adelyn wasn't used to being in a city where she had to watch her possessions at every moment, and so even with his warnings, she might be taken unawares.

'My hook,' he signed, once they were far enough from the station that he felt safe. He had to sign it twice, as Adelyn was gawking at their surroundings and didn't see the first time. 'Why could you not ask about my hook?'

Adelyn paused, glanced around, and signed back rather than speaking aloud. She didn't want anyone else to be a part of the conversation, then. 'They think that the bandits were all Watched,' Adelyn explained. 'You might have seemed guilty by association.'

David tapped his hand against his leg in frustration, regretting it as the pain in his fingers flared up. 'Hooks are not used exclusively by Watched. I-'

"It's called a *Watcher's hook*," Adelyn said aloud, interrupting him. She could do that easily—it took a lot longer for him to sign than it took for her to talk. "They'd have been suspicious."

David sighed. 'And the peace officers?'

"Peace Officers as a lot are terrible," Adelyn said, seeming to forget that David was an officer himself. "But these ones specifically wanted to charge you with collaboration. I had to argue them down. If they'd known you believe in the Watchers, they'd have kept you locked up for sure."

'Thank you,' David signed, his hand starting to ache from all the conversation. 'I need to rest. I can find a new hook tomorrow.'

CHAPTER 4

A certain man went walking one day, up to the highest peak in the realms of man, to beseech Falla for power.

"Grant me your boon, Falla," he said, looking out upon the whole world from the mountain's peak.

Falla, taking interest in the man, humored him with a question. "And what will you give to me for such a trade?"

"I have nothing to sacrifice," the man said, "For you want for nothing. To Garesh I could give my weapons, and to Amel I could give up my crops, but as lady of the air I have nothing you could desire."

At that, Falla laughed. "Is there nothing you could think to give me?"

Pondering, the man gave an answer. "Only the air in my lungs, but in doing so I would truly be sacrificing myself to Ansire, for without the air I would certainly die."

Falla considered this, and then gave her answer. "I will give you my boon," she said, "And I will give you this gift further. Until your dying day, you should never want for another breath of air."

The man began to respond, but his voice left him in that

moment, gone with his air. And so, though he was given power from the gods, he was unable to corrupt that power for heretical means by uttering spells or oaths. By this, he became the first true priest of the gods who did not twist their boon for his own gain.

•Divine parable. Two notes: First, it is unclear what mountain is being spoken of here, because the border between the realm of man and the realm of dragons is ill defined and unclear. Second, the ending of this parable has changed in recent years. Older versions told this parable as a warning against asking too much of the gods without offering an equivalent sacrifice, but this telling instead turns his punishment into a boon, as part of the recent dogmatic push against the use of magic by Divine believers.

"Aaaaah," David vocalized, keeping his mouth open wide so that the physician could look at the injury. A little metal rod clicked against his teeth, and the werelight glowing in his mouth tingled with spirit that made him want to gag.

"Just a moment longer, if you please," The physician said, muttering a spell that changed the hue of the werelight and adjusting the rod slightly.

Another second passed and he retracted the metal rod, wiping spittle off the mirror at the end. David pulled the spirit from the werelight in his mouth, ending the spell and the accompanying tingle.

The exam room was sparse and simple—a water basin and faucet set into a counter, a long table for patients to sit or lie down on, a row of shelves with poultices, bandages, and herbs, a few books in a glass display shelf with a locking door. Most of the medicines were kept on shelves in the front room, tonics and ointments that would be sold to anyone looking, the stuff back here was for surgical use only.

"I can patch up that gash on your leg, and clean up your hand," The physician wizard said, standing back and removing his gloves. "Healing fresh wounds like that? No problem. This, though... this will be tricky."

"Please, Harrington," Adelyn said, addressing the physician. "You're supposed to be the best. Surely there's something you can do."

"I never said it was impossible," Harrington chided, washing his hands at a small basin as he spoke. "But it's tricky. I don't suppose you have the rest of the tongue?"

David shook his head, sitting up from the exam chair and crossing to the basin. Once Harrington was done washing his hands, David spat, cupped his hand under the faucet, and took a short drink.

"Tricky," Harrington repeated, drying his hands. "I will have to do some reading, it may take me some time. I know of a case where someone regrew three fingers, but they were weak and stiff. Do you have a place to stay while I look into it?"

David nodded, and Adelyn filled in. "We found a boarding house near the coast."

"It may take me some weeks," Harrington said. "You should find yourself something to do in the meantime."

Adelyn cleared her throat. "David said something about you having a magic school, yes?"

Harrington paused, eying her for a moment. "There's two of us here, girl, it's hardly a school. I sometimes take on an apprentice or two, but I haven't the time right now. We've got a library, we work our hardest to learn and share our knowledge with those we trust."

Chewing her lip, Adelyn asked, "Can I use your library?"

Sighing, the physician checked his pockets. "One moment." He left the surgery room, walking to the front for a moment and returning with a ring of keys. Turning to the glass shelf, he unlocked it and opened the door to access one of his books, only then answering Adelyn's question. "I don't let just anyone with a lick of magical talent use our library. Tough times, these days."

David frowned, signing out a message to Harrington.

"What's he saying?" Harrington asked. Adelyn looked at David, and he repeated the signs so that she could translate.

"He says, 'I can vouch for her'," Adelyn said.

Harrington pursed his lips. "Sure, David, but... that might not carry far with the other owner."

David signed, and Adelyn translated again, adding her own diction to the question. "What's that supposed to mean?"

Sighing, Harrington flipped through his book, licking his thumb to help turn the pages. "Never mind. I'll talk to her, ask if she will let you read under supervision." Standing, David began to move his hands to ask another question, but Harrington cut him off. "Sit back down, David, let me heal that leg."

Gritting his teeth, he complied. Harrington flipped to a page showing a specifically arranged set of runes. Sacrosanct was nigh illegible when written out properly, at least unless David had the time to sit down and examine the runes for a while. In spite of that, he knew what they were going to be for. Healing spells were universally kept in books, because the magic rarely needed a huge amount of spirit to get it going, and the format of a book allowed many complicated spells to be written out in a compact space.

Raising a hand to David's leg, exposing where he'd rolled up the torn pants, Harrington began chanting a spell.

The spirit flow was tangible in the air, and David closed his eyes, savoring the feeling of the magic as it healed his leg.

He couldn't have cast a spell like that on his own, voice or no voice, but he could appreciate the artistry. Flesh reknit and skin healed with incredible speed, stretching itself over the injury and leaving no trace of the original wound.

"That's what I want to learn," Adelyn said, watching the spell. She wouldn't be able to feel the intricate movements of the spirit, but anyone could watch and see his leg heal.

David signed, waiting for Adelyn to translate for him. "He says, 'What are we supposed to do while we wait?'"

Harrington shrugged. "Visit old haunts. You lived here, right?"

David shook his head, and Adelyn translated for him, "He grew up on the coast, but not here."

"Then visit the coast. Ride a thulcut, I don't know. How's that leg feel?" Harrington stepped back, waiting.

David stood, walked on it a moment, and nodded in approval. The healing had gone properly, his leg felt good as new.

"Go for a walk. See a magic lantern show. Come back in a couple days, I'll know more about your voice, and about whether she can see the library." Harrington said. "I'm dreadful sorry about the situation, wish there was more I could tell you."

David knew he couldn't have expected more. This was better than a flat 'No'. Digging in one of his belt's many pouches, he drew out a few rectangular silver coins, proffering them to Harrington as payment.

He shook his head, glancing at the coins with a raised eyebrow. "What are those? Ingots?"

Adelyn filled him in. "Beor silver. It's a long story how we got it, but the metal's real."

Harrington apparently believed her, dropping the subject and flipping to a new page in his book. "Before we talk payment, let me get a look at that hand."

...

The boarding house provided ample room for two people to train. The bedrooms were small and sparse, but it came with a comfortable common room that provided almost thirty five square meters of space, at least once David had moved all the furniture into the kitchenette. Plus, they were on the ground floor, ensuring that nobody would complain about the sound of footsteps banging.

'That was good,' He signed to Adelyn, watching her form as she moved through a few defensive stances meant for unarmed combat. It had occurred to him that morning that sword and magic training, while well and good, could be well supplemented by a knowledge of hand-to-hand techniques. 'Would you like to practice it with a sparring partner?'

Adelyn shook her head, walking to the kitchen and climbing over an easy chair so that she could get to the sink, pouring herself a cup of water. "I think I've had enough hand-to-hand training for today."

'Okay,' David signed. That was fine. It was supplemental, after all—he could resume teaching her something else.

He'd gone back to Harrington every morning since they arrived, but Harrington had no updates. The physician only told him to wait, told Adelyn that the library was still closed to her, and that they should leave and return another time.

So, David had settled into training. There was much he could teach Adelyn, and if he was being honest, the time to work on his own form and style with the sword was a welcome breather. A couple more days of magic lessons, then they'd go back and see what Harrington had to say... again.

Once Adelyn had set down her cup, David signed to her. 'Would you prefer to work with the sword or with magic?' He would prefer the sword—teaching her magic reminded him of what he lacked—but she could pick.

"David," Adelyn said, her tone making it clear that something was amiss. "We've been here three days, and you've done nothing but teach me how to fight."

'I've taught you more than just combat magic,' David pointed out, arms moving as he signed. 'Isn't that why you came along? To learn magic?'

Adelyn shook her head. "Yes, but—David, you promised me a magic school, not a stuffy apartment and secondhand knowledge."

'I am teaching you everything I know,' David signed, frowning.

"But that's not what I came here to learn!" Throwing up her hands, Adelyn said, "You're great at fighting, sure, but I don't want to learn how to fight, I want to learn how to heal, how to fix things. Can you teach me that?"

Grinding his teeth in frustration, David signed, 'I was wrong about the school, I'm sorry. This is the best alternative I can offer.'

"It's not the same," Adelyn said. "And if I'm not going to be learning what I came here for, I thought I'd at least get a chance to go out, see the sights. We're half a mile from the coast and I haven't even seen a ship since we got here."

'You can go out, I'm not stopping you,' David signed.

"By myself? I'd never find my way back!" Adelyn said. "But that's not the point. Don't you want to go... I don't know, do something?"

David blinked. They were doing something. She had to

mean something besides what they were doing currently, so she probably meant exploring the city. 'You could go see the docks, if you wanted a break,' He offered, after a moment of consideration. 'It's impossible to get lost on your way there, you just head due south. It's a straight shot, and as long as you remember the street name you can find your way back.'

"David," Adelyn said, flatly. "That's not what I'm talking about."

David frowned. He started to tap his fingers against his leg, but needed them to be able to respond, so quickly stopped. 'Then what?'

"I think you need to go out, get some fresh air," Adelyn said. "You're cooping yourself up in here under the pretense of teaching me."

He didn't need his hands to shake his head 'No', so resumed the drumbeat against his leg. What was she getting at? He only wanted to teach her, and to practice himself, to improve their collective skills.

Adelyn sighed. "Okay, I'm going to go see the docks. Will you take my advice if I give some?"

'That depends on the advice,' David said.

"Go for a walk. Get some air. Don't wait around for me to get back." Adelyn walked to her bedroom to retrieve her coat—a new one, bought only a couple months ago. The early planting season weather wasn't unbearably cold, but the coat was still necessary to be comfortable.

'I'll think about it,' David said. It was honest—he would. He had no intention of taking her advice, but he would dutifully consider it. She would be back soon enough, and he could get back to teaching.

He waited a full hour before growing impatient.

How long does it take to look at boats?

He'd meant it as a quick excursion for her to take a

break—it was only a fifteen minute jog to the docks, perhaps twenty five minutes if she took it slow. From there... what would she even do? The ships were all just ships. Some a little bigger, some a little smaller. Once you'd seen a few, there was nothing exciting about them.

She should have returned, unless she was dragging her feet, or unless she was in trouble. She could handle herself in a dangerous situation—she was a sorceress, after all—which meant she was dragging her feet. Maybe she'd gone to look at the great Church of the Divinities that was nearby, even to a Tarraganian like Adelyn she could still appreciate the craftsmanship that had gone into the building.

Retrieving his own jacket, David resolved to go look for her, to ensure that she was okay. Besides, he could genuinely tell her he'd gone for a walk.

Locking the door behind him, he walked onto the dirt street, a surprisingly shady road considering it was still midday. Spindly wooden houses stuck up on the sides of the road, meaning that this dirt path only saw sunlight at high noon. The air smelled like salt, and David could hear shouts and calls from blocks away, echoing into a familiar melody that reminded him of his childhood.

Inhaling deeply, he struck out in the direction of the docks, taking a precise but irregular route, turning left at the end of the road, turning right as soon as he could, zigzagging towards the coast.

It felt strange to walk unarmed, but he still hadn't found the time to buy a new hook, and carrying a sword in the city would make him fairly conspicuous.

It was a chipper day, despite the gloom of the many sunless streets. The sky, where visible, was shining blue, and the cool mist that hung in the air was not so thick that it blocked his view. He could navigate with his eyes closed, anyways, because the rats nest of power lines that ran up and down every street were leaking so much power that his spirit sense was half on fire.

He heard someone gushing praises for a street vendor a few blocks down and, feeling lively, he struck a path down that way. Stopping at their cart, exchanging some coins for a thin strip of thulcut meat wrapped around a stick.

The meat wasn't exactly cheap. Thulcuts were powerful beasts that took a great effort and many ships to bring down, but they were also massive creatures whose flesh would not spoil for months, and so the meat wasn't exactly expensive either.

The kebab was dipped in a nutty sauce and rolled in dried fruits that helped neutralize some of the acidic tendencies of the meat, and as he gnawed at the snack, he couldn't help but feel a little nostalgic. It was a trick to chew on the meat, and he could only taste it at the back of his throat, but whoever'd been gushing about the quality, their recommendation had proven true.

Still, his good mood couldn't last. He heard shouts that were discordant with the sounds of working men and women. Angry shouts. Hateful shouts, even.

Smelling smoke, David looked around for the source. Flickering torchlight was plainly visible a street down at a T intersection. He walked that way, tentative at first, taking the last bite of his kebab.

As he saw a crowd running down that road, he picked up his pace to join them, making it onto the tail end of the mob, some fifty people, a few carrying torches, more carrying bats or crowbars or steel rods. Few had anything that would qualify as a real weapon, but that didn't make the mob any less dangerous.

David followed and watched, curious where they were

going. This was not something he was familiar with—mob justice had been rare, even unheard of when he was a kid. Though the peace officers had been willing to turn a blind eye to smuggling and petty crime, they wouldn't sit on their hands in serious cases, and anything that would rile up a mob this big was certainly a serious case.

He wanted to ask what was going on, but didn't expect anyone to be able to sign, so couldn't. He had to follow, wait, and see.

The mob continued, and David followed, effectively joining them so that he could observe. Their shouts, now audible, were not clear enough for him to understand their purpose—cries of "Let's get him!" and "He's going to pay!" were not enough for him to decipher their intent.

After half a dozen blocks, they arrived in front of a spindly building, identical to the dozens around it. Each of its four stories seemed to be built without consideration for the section beneath or above it, and all the stairs were built on the outside front of the building, implying they'd been retrofitted to allow more rooms to be built atop the old ones.

Someone in the crowd shouted, their voice loud and clear. "Ezra Fisher, you get your sorry hide down here and face justice!"

A second passed and someone stuck their head out from the second floor door, calling something back that David couldn't distinctly hear. Pushing his way forward, David tried to get a better look at the man.

"We know you ain't got a back door!" a woman shouted. "Don't make us come up there and get you!"

This time, when Ezra called, David could hear it clearly. "I didn't do nothin'!"

"We know it was you, Ezra!" someone else shouted.

"Someone saw you runnin' out the same night we found the body!"

"I'm telling you!" Ezra shouted, his voice high and reedy. "I didn't do nothin'! I don't know what y'all saw, but it wasn't me!"

Near the front of the crowd, now, David saw that the leader was carrying a length of rope, a loop tied at one end meant to hold someone's neck. His hands were strong and callused, a fisherman or sailor who'd worked with knots his whole life.

"Kid killer!" someone shouted from the crowd.

"Now, let's be reasonable about this!" the leader called, waving his noose back and forth like a pendulum. "Option one: You can come along, nice and simple, and we'll give you a clean hanging, bury your body proper, make sure your family knows what happened to you."

There was a lengthy pause. The sound of the low fire was audible when nobody was calling back and forth, and Ezra's fear was visible on his face in the flickering torchlight. People on the stories above were sticking out their heads, looking down at the commotion but unwilling to get involved.

"I want my body burned!" Ezra finally shouted. "And I ain't got no family!"

"Option two!" the leader called, ignoring Ezra's comment. "We come up there, truss you up by your feet, and then throw you naked over the front of a hunting ship. You'll get to dangle there, in the sun, until the thulcuts get you!"

In response, Ezra ducked back inside and a second later flung something big and heavy out the door and into the crowd. David didn't see what it was, but he heard somebody shout as it clipped them on the arm and they smashed into the ground.

Someone with a twitchy army returned fire. Their torch left their hand, flying in a wide, high arc. David's eyes widened, and someone shouted "No!" as the torch landed, touching down on the stairway leading to the second floor.

The torch flickered there for a moment before the wood stairway caught, burning brightly as the fire spread out.

"Get the fire brigade!" the leader shouted, turning to the crowd. "Someone, get the fire brigade!"

"Let him burn!" someone else shouted.

"And everyone else?" the leader repeated, turning to push through the crowd to get the fire brigade himself. Still, he stopped, adding, "Don't let the killer leave!"

David watched him go, then turned silently back to the building, watching the fire spread up the stairs.

CHAPTER 5

Sheriff Flintwood: Why don't we start with you telling me your name?

[Subject does not respond]

Flintwood: We have you on the train, with a weapon, caught red handed trying to break into the engine compartment. Whether or not you give me your name isn't going to change your sentencing.

[Subject does not respond]

Flintwood: We know you're not mute, engineer heard you shouting while you took a crowbar to the door. Just give me something to call you.

Subject: Henry.

Flintwood: You have a last name, Henry?

Subject: No.

Flintwood: And I'm going to guess that your first name isn't really Henry, is it?

Subject: No.

Flintwood: Well, it's a start. How about I get you something to drink, Henry, and you can explain to me what you were doing on that train?

•Excerpt from interrogation with prisoner caught attempting to rob Azish passenger train

DAVID FOUND himself running forward before he could determine all the reasons why it was a bad idea. He had no magic, no way of putting out the fire, he didn't even know the layout of the building.

Those thoughts crossed his mind, but were secondary to his goal. People were inside, he had to help.

There was no way to be certain how many people were inside, but David thought he had seen a couple faces on both the third and fourth floor balconies. Even assuming they were the only people in the stack of homes, that meant five people were about to be burned alive if they couldn't get out.

The stairs leading up from ground level were now raging, so David leapt as high as he could, grabbing the edge of the second floor landing, grunting as he pulled himself up. He had to swing one leg up and drag his body onto the platform before standing, at which point he found himself face to face with Ezra.

"I'm not comin' with you!" Ezra said, stumbling back into the doorway behind him. He had a bundle of rope slung over one shoulder, and from so close a distance, David could clearly see that he wasn't more than twenty five and couldn't have weighed more than a large set of dictionaries.

David shook his head, trying to think how he could communicate his goal. The fire was starting to billow smoke, and it wouldn't be long before the landing he stood on would be untenable.

Someone shouted above them, a cry for help. A high, weak voice. A child.

Ezra's head snapped in that direction. "You can kill me later, we've gotta help them!"

Easy enough, David thought, standing aside as Ezra ran out the door and pounded up the stairs to the third floor. He followed him, assuming the man had a plan, fire nipping at his heels as they pounded up the shaking steps.

"No goin' back that way," Ezra commented, looking down.

David thought he may be able to slide down a support banister, but that might not be an option for everyone else. The child he'd heard might slip and fall, and he didn't know if everyone here was able bodied and strong enough to make such a climb before the fire spread further.

Pointing at David, Ezra said, "There's a couple lives inside here, I'm going to get them. Get 'em all from upstairs to come on down. I got a plan."

David hesitated for a moment before he turned to obey. Ezra claimed he had a plan, which meant David only had to worry about doing whatever he called for. Simple enough.

Feet pounding on the stairs, he felt them shake as some fire-weakened boards below him collapsed under the stress. The fire was spreading *fast*. He made it to the fourth floor landing and saw that the door had been closed. Trying the handle, he found that it had been dead bolted from the other side.

There's no time for this. He had on gloves, so there were no qualms about sidestepping the door and driving his fist into the window. It hurt, but nothing cut through the leather to his hand.

Someone cried out from inside, and he climbed in through the broken window, only to sense someone rushing him with a steel blade.

He dropped and rolled, glass shards shredding a pant

leg and the skin underneath as he got away from the attacker. As he raised into a defensive posture, though, he saw that it was a little girl, maybe six years Adelyn's junior, holding a kitchen knife.

Immediately, he dropped his posture, putting up his hands. Smoke was starting to come in through the window. He needed to get her to come with him, fast.

The girl held up the knife, grasping the handle in all ten of her fingers, rusty end pointed straight at David. "Are you Divine?" she asked confidently, certain that her knife meant she was in complete control of the situation.

David shook his head, hands still raised. There was no time for this, the fire would be to them soon. Glancing around the apartment, he saw nobody else—they were in a sitting room, part of a kitchen was visible from around a walled off section, no doubt a bedroom. It was just the girl, then.

"Grandpappy says not to trust nobody who's Divine," The girl said.

David pursed his lips. He could take out his notepad and write a message explaining the situation, but that would take time, and it assumed the girl could read. He had to act quicker than that.

Lowering his hands, he stepped forward, reaching for the girl. She swung with the knife, but it was a clumsy attack that he could have dodged in his sleep. He grabbed her hands, took away the weapon, tossed it into the kitchen, and picked her up by the arms and began carrying the child outside.

She screamed and bit him, digging her teeth into the flesh of his arm. He grunted in pain, but couldn't pull her head away from his arm without giving her the opportunity to wriggle away. Awkwardly using his elbow to unlatch the door from inside, he kicked it open, dragging the child kicking and screaming out the door.

"Lemme go!" the girl screamed, beating at his arms with her tiny hands. He ignored her, carrying her flailing body down the steps and pulling her into the home on the third floor. Smoke was coming up the stairs in billows, and much of the porch was on fire.

Kicking the door shut behind him, David looked around until he spotted Ezra. He released the child, so the other man could explain the situation.

"Lala?" Ezra said, looking at David with wide eyes.

"Ezra!" the girl cried, running to him. "That man—"

"He's a friend," Ezra told her. "I told him to get you. We have to leave, the fire brigade won't get here in time."

David looked around, and quickly spotted what Ezra was planning. The back window had been opened, and the rope Ezra had brought was tied to the stove and dangling out, providing an escape.

The girl, Lala, eyed David suspiciously and said, "He smells funny."

"Where is your grandpa?" Ezra asked, looking around. Straightening, he looked at David. "An old man lives upstairs. Did you see him?"

David shook his head. He had only seen the girl, though his search had been anything but thorough and he'd all but forgotten to feel out the spirit in the apartment.

Ezra swore, running to the door, but as he threw it open a plume of fire roared up, forcing him back.

"Lala, climb down the rope," He said, looking around.

Confused, Lala started to protest. "What about—"

"Don't ask, do it," he said, pointing the girl towards the window before settling his stare on David. "We've gotta get him out of there. I can't walk through fire. You?"

David shook his head, watching Lala run to the window and start down the rope.

"I can't free climb so good," Ezra said. "And the couple who live here already got down. You're gonna have to go up."

David nodded emphatically, rushing to the window and looking down. Two frazzled looking men were standing around near the bottom of the rope, and Lala was almost down. He could see now that the rope had been tied with knots every couple feet, acting as ladder holds to make it easier to go up and down.

The moment Lala's feet touched the ground, David pulled the rope from off the stove, wrapping it around his waist and knotting it tight. He was no dock worker, so he made a basic granny knot, but he doubled it and made it snug so it would stay in place.

Sticking his head back out the window, he looked up, gauging where he would have the best handholds. The dilapidated architecture worked to his advantage—there were plenty of vestigial outcroppings and bits of unnecessary design jutting out, letting him climb quickly up the back of the building.

Reaching the back window, he tried it and found that it, too, was locked shut. He tried to punch the glass, but had no leverage, and the weight of the rope dangling from his waist made him start to waver.

Hand grabbing out, he found four solid grips, holding tight so that he wouldn't fall. That fall would kill him for certain, as well as the man inside who would be left without an escape route if David failed.

Taking a breath, he locked his left arm around a support beam meant to keep the roof in place, planted his feet on a small lip where the old roof had been before this fourth story was added, and drove his fist into the glass.

Again, his glove protected him from shards of glass, but he felt something in his hand fracture at the impact. He was not used to punching out windows, and his hands weren't having it without protest.

He could see smoke inside the apartment, and once he awkwardly clambered around the shards of glass to crawl inside, he covered his mouth with a hand.

Nobody was in the building that he could see, but the walled off room was still unexplored. Approaching, keeping his breath shallow, he kicked in the door, smoke billowing into the room behind him.

An old man sat kneeling by his bed, wrinkled hands crossed over his chest, lips muttering in prayer. David could only make out a few of the words, but they were distinctly Sacrosanct.

He tensed for a moment, thinking that the man was preparing magic, then realized there was no sense of spirit or energy tingling, only smoke and heat from the growing fire. The old man was praying.

Approaching, rope dragging behind him, David grabbed the old man by the shoulder. He started and spun, startled to see David.

"Who—"

David shook his head, pointing at the door. *No time to argue.* He couldn't manhandle the grandpa down like he had the child, but the grandpa also hadn't threatened him with a knife, so it was possible he would see reason.

"The fire brigade? You came?" the old man asked, surprised. "I prayed, but—"

David shook his head.

"My granddaughter. Where is La La?" He spoke the girl's name with long, stressed vowels, almost two separate words, and David finally recognized it as the Sacrosanct word for 'Faith'.

Gesturing with a hand, David started to pull the old man out, but before he took two steps the rope snapped tight around his waist and yanked him backwards. He was thrown to the ground and dragged bodily towards the window, the rope's knots chafing against shards of glass as it was pulled from the building.

David tumbled and slammed into the wall beneath the window, feeling the rope around him tighten further, then go slack. A second later, he heard a cry of pain outside.

Standing with a groan, he looked out and saw Ezra, lying on the ground and clutching at his leg.

He tried to climb down, David thought, feeling an ache in his belly where the rope had gone taught. Ezra had hung on long enough to drag David back, but lost his grip when David's torso hit the wall and came to a sudden stop.

Coughing, the grandpa approached from the bedroom, looking around. David didn't know what to do except wave him over and point out the window.

"You expect me to climb?" the old man said, eyes wide. He didn't look up to it—while he may have been young and fit once, he was not any longer. The calluses had gone from his hands, and most of the strength from his limbs. If he lost his grip even for a moment, he'd fall for certain, and that would be a death sentence as sure as staying in the fire would be.

Thinking it through, David grabbed the rope and began heaving it up, creating a loose coil on the ground behind him. Once he had the whole rope up, he passed it to the old man, making a gesture with his hands.

Mercifully, the old man understood. Taking the knotted rope, he wrapped it over his chest and around his armpits, moving with the skill that only decades of practice could give. He knew knots, better than most men knew their own hands, and quickly fashioned a harness around his chest.

The smoke was so thick by now that the old man didn't bother responding, so he could keep his own breath shallow and sparse. David took up the rope, opened the window so the grandpa wouldn't have to climb through glassy shards, and helped him down.

He lowered the man faster than was safe, but there was no time for caution. Fire was roaring into the apartment, and the smoke was so thick that David could hardly breathe. The knots, meant to provide handholds, only got in the way and kept him from smoothly running out the line, and he had to go hand-over-hand to keep them from catching on the window frame.

Heat was beating at his back, and so David planted one leg against the window frame and worked faster, lowering the grandpa to safety as quick as possible without simply dropping him. His gloves, cut by the glass shards, began to fray and rip as the rope slid against them, but he had no time to worry about that.

The rope went slack as the old man reached the ground, and David wasted no time going for the knot around his waist so he could tie down the rope and climb down himself. His tight granny knot evaded his grip, pulled so tight when Ezra had tried to climb down that David couldn't find purchase to undo his handiwork.

He pulled off his frayed gloves to try and attack the rope with bare fingers, more dexterous without the leather in the way, but it was no good.

Curses would have been echoing in the kitchen if he could have voiced them. Free climbing down the building while smoke turned the windows into chimneys was going to be a chore, and much slower than with the rope.

Watchers, I need—

He blinked and glanced down as his sixth sense nudged him. A kitchen knife was on the floor by his feet, an old rusty bit of steel that had been brandished at him a couple minutes prior.

Seizing the blade, David cut frantically at the knot he'd tied around his waist, strands of rope fraying and pulling apart as he cut. The fire was all throughout the living room now, there wasn't a second to wait, he had to get the rope free.

With one final slice, the knot came undone, and the rope began sliding around his waist. He caught it before it could fall out the window and wrapped it around the leg of a coal burning stove, repeating his granny knot.

Coughing violently, David tugged once to ensure the knot was secure, and all but leapt out the window, rappelling down the side of the building.

The rope burned as his hands slid down it, and again the knots that were meant to provide purchase only dug against his skin and caught, slowing his progress. He wore gloves almost constantly, so his fingers had no calluses to resist the rough strands of the rope that scraped against his skin.

A story from the ground, the rope dropped. Either the fire had burned through, or more likely the knot had come loose, and David fell the last ten feet to the ground.

He knew how to take a fall. He bent his legs slightly, letting them fold and rolling backwards as he hit the ground, head tucked forward, arms thrown out to slap against the ground and absorb the shock. It hurt his already aching body, but children often jumped down from trees higher than that. He would live.

Ezra was leaning against the wall, pant leg rolled up to

show swollen flesh around his ankle. Lala and her grandfather were locked in an embrace, and the other couple that had been rescued were nowhere to be seen, having fled or gone to retrieve help.

"Abandon me," Ezra said through gritted teeth, taking deep breaths as he looked up at the billows of smoke. "But this *really* hurts."

David nodded. Whether it was a break or merely a sprain, it looked nasty.

Glancing at him, Ezra added, "You gonna hang me now?"

Shaking his head, David leaned against the building. He was tired and sore, and his lungs burned from the smoke inhalation. Fingers drumming against his leg, he looked up at the building, taking deep breaths to recover his strength and clear his lungs.

Flame was now visibly coughing out the window, and it wouldn't be long before the neighboring buildings caught as well. He could only hope that the fire brigade would arrive soon, and that someone else had evacuated those before they became inhospitable to human life.

The alleyway they were in was dimly lit, like all the streets of the city, but on top of that it was muddy, and trash littered the corners, blown around and then left wherever they finally got stuck. This was not one of the better parts of town, to say the least.

Ezra coughed, wheezing in pain as the jolt made his leg shake. "Well, you…"

He trailed off as he looked down the alley, spotting a few people coming down. Half a dozen in total, two carrying torches, the others with makeshift weapons.

David looked at them, then back at Ezra. They wouldn't

care that Ezra had just helped save four lives, they wanted him dead.

Sighing, he straightened. His ankles hurt, his chest hurt, his stomach ached. The palms of his hands were bleeding, his fingers ached and might have been fractured, his breath was stifled by the smoke sticking to his lungs. Still, he couldn't leave a helpless man to be killed. Maybe Ezra had done something terrible, maybe not. An angry mob operating on rumor and outrage wouldn't be the group to make that call.

Sinking into a low stance, David held out his hands in fists, fingers aching as the tender flesh and bruised bones protested the idea of further action. He planted himself against the small mob, ready to take them all on.

"You're not gonna fight them, are you?" Ezra asked. David looked back to see that his eyes were wide, though he couldn't be sure what that expression meant in this context. Shock? Awe? Surprise?

David nodded, starting to turn back towards the six, who had spotted him and were coming their way.

"Here," Ezra said, digging in one of his pockets and pulling out a white bandana. He tossed it to David and added, "Put it over your face. So they can't identify you."

It wasn't a bad idea, so David complied, pulling the bandana over his mouth and nose. His eyes and hair would still be visible, and his thumb would be a dead giveaway, but at least he wasn't going to be recognized if they copied his face onto a wanted poster.

Stance deepening, David returned his gaze to the six-person mob that was now only ten paces away. He could feel the rough cotton of the bandana scraping against his lips and stubbly chin, breath misting and making his face feel hot and humid.

"That's him!" someone shouted, pointing at Ezra. Addressing David, they said, "This man's got a date with a noose. Step aside, or you'll hang with him."

David shook his head. He could explain that he was a peace officer, but they clearly didn't care about the law. They weren't going to let Ezra go to court, they wanted to dole out vigilante justice.

Fists tightening despite the pain, David thought, *They can try.*

CHAPTER 6

Long day. After two weeks with no sightings, captain finally decided that hunting coast side was a fool's errand. We're shipping out a ways tomorrow, going to see if the thulcuts are more active further out.

That means an unwatched amount of work to get the ships loaded. This won't be any day trip, we'll be spending two full days out to sea, and that means we have to pack in food, water, and add in hammocks for the crews so we've got somewhere to sleep. This is on top of the usual chores, but since captain's in a rush to get us atop our prey, we had to get it all done in a day.

My back aches and the crew's passing around the rum. I think I'll take my share before bed, I've certainly earned it.

• Journal entry, written by a sailor on a thulcut hunting ship

THE SIX PEOPLE SPREAD OUT, and David eyed the group, sizing them up as a whole. Four men, two women. Two torches, two steel pipes, a bat, and a crowbar. He labeled them in his head—*Torch and Sconce, Rod and Piper, Bat and*

Crowbar. Not the most original names, but he needed to track them as individuals in his head.

They didn't seem to take David seriously as a threat—they counted six versus one, they saw that he was tired, and determined that this wasn't going to be a hard fight.

David wasn't certain that their assessment was wrong. He could probably fight six people without magic, his spirit sense would help guide him, and he had practiced fighting groups before. The question was not if that was possible, but rather it was if he could beat them while tired, aching, and unarmed.

It wouldn't be viable if he let them make the first move. If they surrounded him and used their numbers to full advantage, he would be beaten all but immediately. His best bet was to strike first.

Leaping forward, he dove at the torch bearer furthest to the right of the group, but ducked away and instead juked towards the man with the crowbar, slipping between and behind the line of people. Two jabs to Crowbar's kidneys made him drop to the ground, though he kept his weapon in the fall and David couldn't retrieve it.

The punches made his hands burn with pain, and he pulled back, deciding to rely more on elbows and kicks. That was one foe down, at least until Crowbar could shrug off the hit and stand up.

Planting his feet, he backed up, trying to draw the five people remaining further away from Ezra. They had all turned to face David, at least, recognizing him as a threat now that one of their numbers was down.

Rod and Piper charged, and David did his best to react. He ducked under the high attack from Rod and stuck out his forearms to block the swing from Piper, accepting the bruises he'd accrue from that sort of block as a reasonable trade for the opportunity to strike back. Sweeping both arms down, he wrested the pipe from Piper's hands and came back with an elbow strike into their belly.

He would have liked to follow that up with a couple more strikes to disable Piper for longer, but had to abandon that, as Bat and Torch were moving in to attack him.

Ducking away, his back hit the far wall as he scrambled to dodge back from the two. This worked for a moment, but quickly left him surrounded by the four standing attackers as they moved into a semicircle around him, and he could see Piper was recovering her footing.

Torch and Sconce were the weaker links, their "weapons" were both short and stubby, and were almost as dangerous to the wielders as to anyone they'd try to attack. Pushing off the wall for momentum, David charged the gap between them, accepting a wild blow to his arm in exchange for breaking from being surrounded, and for the opportunity to take out Piper.

She wasn't ready for a follow up attack so quickly, and as David burst away from the other four, he rolled and grabbed her pipe from the ground, smashing the weapon into the back of her heel.

Piper cried out, and David rolled to his feet, spinning and swinging the pipe again so that it hit her other leg. He heard a satisfying 'Crack' and grinned. She wouldn't be walking soon, which meant he could consider her out for the count.

Four to go. Spinning the pipe in his hand, he stepped backwards and scooped low to grab for the crowbar without looking at it.

It was good to have a pair of weapons, even if they amounted to unbalanced metal sticks. The four remaining combatants—Torch, Sconce, Rod, and Bat—all eyed him warily as they spread out again.

"You're defending a bastard," Sconce said, her eyes glittering with fury. "You know what he did?"

David shook his head, holding his weapons out, crowbar in his left hand, pipe in his right, feeling his fingers ache and palms sting as he gripped them. He was panting into the bandana over his face, gulping in air to fuel his limbs.

"He killed a kid. Murdered her in her sleep," Sconce explained.

Hesitating, David glanced at Ezra, who was watching the fight with apprehension. "That's not true!"

He looked back at Sconce and raised an eyebrow, glad that he could catch his breath. Sconce shot Ezra a glare. "Why'd you go skulking around the docks that night, then?"

Ezra shook his head. "I didn't!"

David wasn't going to get a better opportunity to strike. The four were distracted, and he didn't want any more of the mob to come around and find them. He threw his crowbar at Rod and dove at Bat, who was to the farthest right of the line.

Bat raised his club to block David's pipe, but there was a moment where he lacked support from Rod, giving David time to drive a knee up into Bat's belly, making him double over and retch in pain.

Tossing the pipe to his left hand, David swung it to block a swing from Rod, feeling Bat rain clumsy blows on his back as he fended off Rod's attacks. The bandana was nearly ripped from David's face as Bat flailed with his arms. He drove another knee into Rod, shoved him away, and rolled backwards before Sconce or Torch could move in and attack.

He wasn't fast enough. Sconce managed to get in a solid

blow against his arm, and though his shirt didn't catch, the hot blow against his arm hurt like he'd been abandoned. David dropped the steel pipe, grunting in pain.

Staggering back further, he saw Bat on all fours, panting for breath to recover, while Sconce, Torch, and Rod closed in. He needed an ace in the hole, but he had no magic to throw, and no secret weapons up his sleeve. There was no chance he could talk them to a standstill, and no chance they were going to show mercy. He had to win this straight or he and Ezra would both be killed.

David shouted, wordless frustration and anger coming out in a roar. He was a wizard. This should have been trivial, but without power he wasn't even keeping up. He was going to lose this fight. Rather than charging, though, he stepped back, letting the three of them force him backward a couple steps at a time, edging away. They were too wary to make an all-out charge, which worked to his advantage, but they knew they had the upper hand as long as they were careful.

Sconce lunged out with an attack, which David couldn't parry. He had no weapons with which to do so, he could only duck and stumble backwards, relying on his sixth sense to ensure he didn't trip over anything.

David shouted a second time, slapping his hand against the wall to his right and feeling the pain in his hand from the action. He was angry. He wanted to scream curses, and he wanted to draw their attention.

Behind them, Bat began to stand, then a length of metal impacted his head with a loud 'crack!'

Standing above him, the grandpa held a crowbar he'd hefted from the ground. His frail arms were shaking, but he raised the iron bar a second time and smashed it down into Bat's head.

Bat sprawled out onto the ground, unmoving, and the

three standing fighters wavered, unsure how to react. David was the greater threat, sure, but they couldn't ignore the old man with the crowbar.

He wasn't the only one who'd entered the fray. Lala held up a pipe she'd scavenged from the ground, waving around the metal. David was worried she'd try and join the fight, but she just called out, "Hey, smelly!" and threw the pipe in his direction.

David caught the weapon in both hands, grinning at the three from behind his bandana.

Sconce finally caught up to the threat, shouting, "Take him!" as she spun to face the grandpa.

Still, it was clear that the dynamics of the fight had changed, and while Sconce charged her target, Torch and Rod only looked at each other, neither wanting to charge without their counterpart.

David leapt in at this confusion, striking his pipe against the back of Rod's hand. Rod cried out and dropped his own pipe, and David brought his weapon back towards Torch's head.

Torch had the wherewithal to block this strike, but the point was to keep the two of them distracted so that David could break through. Pushing the two of them aside, he ran towards Sconce, kicking at the back of her leg and yanking her down by the hair, sending her to the ground. Once she was down, Grandpa hit her with the crowbar a few times, ensuring she'd stay there.

Rod came in with a flying punch to try and take David by surprise, but David ducked and drove an elbow into his chest. Rod coughed, staggering back, and David spun to brandish his pipe at Torch.

Grandpa raised his crowbar to an unsteady guard, stepping up beside David. It was two-on-two, now, and the assailants apparently did the math and determined that they didn't like their odds.

They ran, dropping their weapons and sprinting down the alley.

"Yeah!" Lala shouted, whooping at their success. "Run!" She picked up a rock from the ground and tossed it after them, but it fell far short and kicked up dirt.

David watched, not lowering his guard until they were at the end of the alleyway and out of sight. Once the threat was gone, he dropped his pipe, staggered to the side, and slumped against the wall.

"They don't startle too easy," the grandpa said. "They'll be back soon, and in greater numbers."

David nodded, putting up a hand. He only needed a few moments to catch his breath, he was fine.

"What's that on your hand?" Lala asked, pointing. David realized he'd held out his left hand, showing off the brass thumb he wore there.

Closing his fist, David pulled his hand back. He didn't want her asking about the tattoos on his palm as well, assuming she could see them behind the torn skin.

Pushing himself off the wall, he stumbled a moment before straightening. The fight had been exhilarating. Fun, even, though it was more desperate than he preferred. Without adrenaline carrying him, though, the pains of his body began to catch up to him.

He realized that spirit was tingling in his necklace and cursed himself for a fool. He'd drawn power into the shield runes on instinct. That was a pointless waste of energy, a bad habit he needed to break until he got his voice back.

"I know a place we can hide," Ezra said, pushing himself up with his one leg. "Eh, if y'all help me get there, anyways."

Shuffling to his side, David grudgingly let Ezra put an

arm over his shoulder. He cringed at Ezra's touch, the weight and the tingle of spirit making him ache and itch and want to throw the injured man away, but he gritted his teeth and supported his weight.

Grandpa took Ezra's other side, instructing his granddaughter with a nod towards the end of the alleyway. "Go check and make sure nobody's waiting around down there."

They began a shuffling walk, in the opposite direction that Torch and Rod had run. The fight had been remarkably bloodless, but they still left four bodies lying in the dirt, two unconscious, two left immobile by pain or injury.

Lala reported that the street was clear of enemies, and so the three of them shuffled out, Ezra hopping in the middle on his good leg. "To the right," he said. "We're heading to Solden's shop, out on the docks."

David had no idea where "Solden's shop" was, but the grandpa seemed to know, and so they started limping in that direction. They drew many stares and whispers, but nobody tried to stop them as they moved down the edge of the street as fast as the three could go.

As they shuffled, the dirt roads shifted to wooden planks. The ocean came into view as they made it to the end of the city. An open air store was visible a block down, carts of fish and vegetables sitting out on ice for prospective customers to inspect. Few seemed to look too closely, walking past, or glancing at the prices, balking, and hurrying along.

Ezra nodded at the storefront. "That's it. See that door to the side?"

David nodded, feet scraping the dirt as they shuffled along. He wanted a place to sit, to rest, to sleep. Somewhere quiet, away from the bustle of the street.

"Hey!" someone shouted, far behind them. "Over here!"

Ezra swore, grunting, "Faster."

"Almost there," Grandpa muttered. "How close are they?"

Lala stood on her toes to try and see, but couldn't get a view over the heads of the adults. "I dunno."

"Stranger," Ezra said. "Go knock on the door. It'll take a second for them to answer."

David was more than happy to leave Ezra's side, free of the extra weight that came with supporting him. Jogging the last dozen steps to the door, he pounded the knocker three times, then turned to see who had shouted.

Torch and Sconce, it seemed, had found their greater numbers. A full dozen people followed behind them, and they were shoving aside pedestrians as they ran towards Ezra.

David raised his hand to knock again, bypassing the knocker by pounding his fist on the wood, pain jolting his fingers. He didn't stop knocking until he heard the door unlatch from the other side.

It swung open to reveal a young woman in slacks, a cotton shirt, and a lopsided top hat. David drank all that in, guessing that she was the shop owner labelling her as 'Solden' in his head.

"What?" she asked, looking around cautiously. "Who are you?"

David opened and closed his mouth wordlessly. He still had the bandana over his face, but even if he pulled it down, she wouldn't recognize him, and he couldn't easily explain his identity either.

"He's with me!" Ezra shouted from several paces away. "We need a place to hide out!"

Solden looked at Ezra and at the mob behind him, then

nodded and stood aside as a few things clicked into place. "Of course. Come in."

David stumbled in first, and a couple seconds later Ezra and Grandpa staggered in behind him. Lala was last in, then Solden slammed the door shut.

David looked around the room. They were in the back half of the storefront, and so wooden crates of fish and vegetables were stacked against the walls in piles.

Ezra slumped onto one of the fish crates that wasn't in a stack, relieved to have the weight off his leg. "Shane sends his regards. Mob of Divine out there, trying to kill me. I appreciate you taking us in, considering the danger."

"Can't they burn this place down too?" Lala asked, a question that had been on David's mind as well.

"Not here," her grandpa promised in an assuring tone. "Start a fire here, you could burn down half the docks. Too many peace officers around to break down the door, either, unless they're real quick about it."

"Unless the peace officers just turn a blind eye and let them in," Ezra pointed out. "Abandon me if there isn't at least one officer who turned a blind eye to that mob out there."

Solden shook her head. "I pay off a few of them to keep my paperwork in order as a business owner. They might turn a blind eye to you, but they won't turn one to me."

"Thanks, Solden," Ezra said, peeling up his pants leg to get a better look at his injury. "I owe you one."

"You owe me five or six at this point," Solden corrected, but she smiled genially and added, "But I'm not counting. We've got to watch out for each other, even the troublemakers."

"Especially the troublemakers," the grandpa added, ruffling Lala's hair, to her protest.

David slumped onto the floor, pulled the bandana away from his face, pressed his back against the wall, and shut his eyes. This place seemed safe, at least for a second he would take the opportunity to rest. Conversation continued for a minute or so, but he paid them no mind. Doors opened and shut, and he stopped hearing Grandpa or Lala's voices.

"... stranger? You awake?" Ezra asked, getting David's attention.

He opened his eyes, looking at Ezra. His neck felt bruised and stiff, and though David couldn't remember what had caused the injury, it hurt to nod. His fingers were tapping away automatically against his knee, and he realized his prosthetic thumb was open to view for anyone who cared to look.

"Thanks," Ezra said. "You saved my sorry hide back there."

David shrugged, closing a fist around his thumb to cover it up. He would have done the same for anyone.

"You're quiet," Ezra noted. "I like that. Terse. Only say what you gotta."

David shook his head, dug in one of his many belt pouches, and pulled out the notepad and pencil that he always carried. Flipping to a clean page, he wrote, 'I cannot speak.'

Ezra read the note, chewed on it for a moment and nodded. "Oh. Well, I appreciate what you did back there anyhow. Came in like a Watcher, you did, I thought we were done for."

David shook his head, making another note. 'If I were a Watcher, I wouldn't hurt nearly so much.'

Ezra laughed, and it was an honest, genuine laugh. "You're right on that. I know a guy who can patch you up, but—what're you writing now?"

He held up his next note for Ezra to read. 'Did you kill a child?'

Ezra's amusement died and his expression grew dark. "No."

David made another note. 'Why did they say you had?'

"That's a long story," Ezra said. "You're from out of town, I'm guessing."

Nodding, David flipped to a fresh page and wrote. 'We have time. You owe me the truth.'

Ezra sighed. "I do at that. Ever since the war, those Divine bastards have been coming in here, making life difficult for the rest of us. Said we were free to practice our 'pagan beliefs', but they keep harassing us, breaking up our meetings. If they could make it illegal to be Watched, they would, you mark my words."

David nodded, waving his hand for Ezra to continue.

"So about a week back, some people I knew were getting together for a little ceremony. One of their sons, see, had just turned twelve, they wanted to offer him up, see if he'd be granted the Watcher's blessings." His fists tightened as he spoke, and he said, "Someone called in a 'tip' to the 'peace officers', said they were planning to rob a pastor or somethin'.

"Before the dust settled, six of 'em were dead. Shot before they could answer the door. Never had a chance." Ezra took a deep breath. His face was pale, though if that was from his story or his blood loss, David could only guess.

'It was another false tip, then?' David wrote. 'They were looking to frame you, too.'

Ezra shook his head. "No false tip. I wanted a little payback. Thought to myself, if they were so scared of a pastor gettin' robbed, I might give them a reason to be worried. Took a pry bar, broke my way into his parsonage, started smashing stuff, y'know? Making him pay it back as much as I could for what they'd done. Didn't know his daughter was sick until the next day, when I found out she'd passed in the night. 'Course they blamed me, otherwise they'd have to admit that their gods couldn't heal her."

David sat in stunned silence for a moment, looking at Ezra. His story seemed a huge coincidence, but Ezra had given no reason not to be trusted. He'd helped save everyone today, and that earned him some benefit of the doubt.

Ezra sized him up. "You're not Divine, right?"

David shook his head and wrote, 'I'm Watched.'

"Figured," Ezra said. "You didn't strike me as pretentious. What were you doin' in that mob?"

'Following along to see what was happening,' David wrote. 'Once I saw the torch, I couldn't stand by any longer.'

Ezra nodded. "I appreciate that." He chewed on a thought for a moment. "I've got some people I'd like you to meet."

CHAPTER 7

The last of the gods to join himself in was Eatle. And so Tamel gave the bodies their form, and Amel their sustenance, and Falla their breath. Garesh gave them his strength, and Vod her knowledge, and then Ansire gave the bodies the spirit of life.

When asked what Eatle would be giving their people, however, Eatle said, "Hear me. Justice cannot be given to those who have committed no sin, and neither then can my nature be given. Only once these have crossed out of life can I share my nature with them, and it shall be given to each according to their own actions."

• The Tome of the Gods, Volume 6

"GO FOR A WALK. Look around the city. Don't wait around for me to get back." Adelyn wanted David to take her advice. It was obvious that he was cooping himself up, driving himself crazy with cabin fever as he waited for word from Harrington.

'I'll think about it,' David signed.

Adelyn took that for what it was: A deflection. She had

little doubt in her mind that David would consider going for a walk, decide not to, and finally settle in to sulk or do calisthenics while she was gone.

She had no real plan. David's recommendation of the docks was fine, but she felt like she could do better. As she pushed open the door, she looked around, hesitated, and struck out north. There was somewhere else she wanted to go.

The alleyways twisted off in random, seemingly bizarre directions, and she could barely see the sky for all the tall buildings around and the tangled mass of cables that ran from street poles to buildings like a spider's web. If she wasn't going on a well-trod route she'd never have found her way back to the boarding house without leaving marks on street corners to navigate by.

She passed a few street vendors, but the acrid smell of the snacks they had on offer only made her stomach turn, so she crossed to the far side of the road and passed them by. David had warned of people who would rob her in the street, so she kept her hands in her pockets, holding onto her coin purse and her boarding-house key to make sure nobody could rob her.

Arriving at her destination, she knocked on the door, waiting for Harrington to answer. She stood there with her hands in her pockets for half a minute, watching the slowly-spinning red and white pole set by the door, advertising his skills in medicine and surgery. The door was locked, but an 'Open' sign hung from a pin by the handle, so she knew Harrington was there.

The physician sorcerer opened the door halfway, making the bell jingle above the door frame.

When he saw Adelyn, Harrington blinked a few times

behind his half-moon spectacles and started to speak. "Adelyn, as I told you this morning—"

Adelyn pushed the door all the way open and walked in, not waiting for an invitation.

Harrington was a better sorcerer than she, if he wanted her to leave she wouldn't be able to stay, but that was not the point of the forced entry. She was making a declaration of intent.

"David's not here," Adelyn said, planting herself inside the open storefront and facing Harrington.

"I see that." He stared at her a moment, pointedly leaving the door open. "Why are *you* here?"

"Because you're full of it. You're not trying and failing to find a cure for David, you're just not trying." She'd grown suspicious the day before, when Harrington hadn't even made a pretense of explaining what he'd learned, and that morning he'd simply said there were no updates to speak of.

"These things take time" Harrington said, though he shut the door. "I can't learn how to restore a man's tongue overnight."

Adelyn pursed her lips and leaned against the wall, staring at him. "What have you learned?"

"I've been busy. Child, you can't expect me to work at your beck and call without warning and have me get to it right away." Harrington walked around his desk to put it between him and Adelyn, placing his hands on it and eying her.

"If you were too busy, you'd have said so," Adelyn pointed out. "You wouldn't say you'd 'found nothing'."

"Child!" Harrington scoffed, almost laughing. "I was being polite. I had assumed you would get the point."

"Oh, I got the point," Adelyn said. "What I don't get is whether you're sitting on your hands to drive up your fee, or if you have no plans to help and you're too chickenshit to say so."

Insulting him was risky, and foolish to boot, but Adelyn had no patience for bandying words and deflections.

Harrington watched her with a level look for some time. "I think you're out of your depth, child. How much do you know of David's history?"

Adelyn hesitated. She knew much of his background, at least the important parts, and Harrington presumably knew as well since he'd been the one to mention it. It hadn't been brought up explicitly, though, and she didn't want to out David by mistake, so she was at a loss for how to respond.

Seeing her hesitation, Harrington smiled.

He thinks he's beat me, Adelyn thought, immediately saying, "He's the Blue Flame. He fought with the Thirteen, and he killed more people than you can probably be bothered to count."

Harrington blinked, taken aback for only a moment. "Then you understand my hesitation. I'm not going to freely restore magic to a man who is familiar with such bloodshed."

"David's sworn off killing," Adelyn said. "The past is behind him."

Harrington shook his head. "People lie."

Adelyn stood up straight, planting herself. "He doesn't."

"People don't give up their nature in a heartbeat," Harrington said. "If he doesn't kill now, he will again."

"You were friends before the war, but that was a long time ago, he's—"

"We weren't friends," Harrington corrected quickly. "I knew him, but we were not friends. I don't make friends with people like him."

"You know why he lost his tongue?" Adelyn asked,

taking a step closer to the physician. "He was fighting for me, to save my family from an army of raiders who'd stolen them. He fought a wizard posing as the Blue Flame, and he would have won if he'd just killed the wizard. Instead, he left him alive, and because of that he lost his voice."

"What happened to him?" Harrington asked, turning up his chin.

Adelyn hesitated. "David? He—"

"The man who posed as the Blue Flame," Harrington explained. "How did you escape after he bested David? What happened to the wizard?"

"He's dead," Adelyn said. Harrington started to smirk, and so she added, "I killed him."

It wasn't strictly true—someone else had dealt the killing blow, as Adelyn was unconscious when he died. She'd won the fight, though, and would have finished him off if given the opportunity.

"And you want me to give you access to my library?" Harrington asked.

"I want you to tell David the truth," Adelyn said, taking another step forward. "That you're not going to heal him because you're too much a bastard to—"

Adelyn felt the spell before Harrington cast it. She assumed it was an attack against her and so started channeling energy into her shield runes, but before she could cast anything, Harrington barked out a short word and unleashed his own magic.

Rather than being hit with force, burned, thrown against a wall, anything Adelyn might have expected, she simply felt a sudden jolt at the soft tissue under her cheekbones, then her mouth and tongue went numb. She tried to speak, but her words were only vague groaning sounds without form or voice.

"I will not accept insults in my own place of business," Harrington said, firmly. "Especially not from a girl with little wisdom and littler sense."

Adelyn opened and closed her mouth, then tried to feel out the spell to sense what he had done.

"You are going to leave my shop, and you are never going to come back," Harrington said. "Tell David that he's barred from entry because of your stupidity, and that he's better off without his power."

It's not a sustained spell, Adelyn considered. She could feel no spirit in the air. If the spell had been going constantly, she would have been able to put a stop to it, to drain the power. This attack wasn't that.

The numbness was already wearing off, letting her shut her mouth to keep from staring agape for any longer than she had already done. For a flickering moment, the idea of striking back at Harrington crossed her mind—not to hurt him, but to get back for his own attack.

She settled for clenching her fist and tightening her jaw as much as possible given the lack of sensation. A fight with Harrington was not one she could win.

Shooting the physician one last glare, Adelyn stormed out of the shop, slamming the door behind her. After considering, she slapped his 'Open' sign to 'Closed', letting it swing as she stormed away.

As Adelyn walked down the street in no particular direction, she didn't have to navigate around anyone. People saw her walking with a temper and moved aside, clearing a path. It wasn't a wide berth, exactly, but it was still noticeable compared to her difficulty walking earlier.

I should stir up a tempest of rage more often, Adelyn mused, and that thought made her smirk. With that, her anger dispelled a little, and she almost ran into someone a few paces later coming the other direction.

Looking around, she realized she'd wandered off away from the path she knew. It hadn't been far, and she was able to remember what path she had taken, but it was still unsettling to consider how close she had come to getting herself well and truly lost.

Turning around, Adelyn walked back to the road with Harrington's shop and from there navigated her way back to the boarding house. She wasn't going to go inside just yet, though, feeling the need to blow off some steam before explaining to David that Harrington wasn't going to help them. A part of her wanted to go check on their horses, but it was a long walk back to the livery stable by the train station, and she didn't want to get lost.

With little else to do, she went to go look at the docks.

...

It was raining that evening. David didn't make it back to their boarding house until long after the sun had set, and the shady streets were positively inky. Dark clouds blocked out starlight, and there were no public streetlights, so the only light came from storefronts with their own lamps. In the deeper streets of the city, those lamps were few and far between, spaced out like lighthouses in a black sea.

Familiar as he was with the environment of the city, David still took some time to navigate his way back, making a couple wrong turns as he tried to navigate without much light.

When he finally made it back, he slumped in through the door, looking for a couch or chair and remembering that he'd stacked all the furniture in the kitchen. Rather than set something up, he dropped onto the floor, lying down on the wooden boards and staring at the glowing spirit light set into the ceiling.

"David?" Adelyn's voice came from her bedroom, and she stepped out a second later, eyes going wide as she saw him. "David! I was so worried, what happened?"

He looked up at her from his vantage point on the floor and made a sign in the air. 'I went for a walk.'

"You've been gone for eight hours!" Adelyn exclaimed. "Where did you even... is that blood?"

David sat up, making another sign. 'I'm fine, don't worry.'

Adelyn opened her mouth, then closed it. She didn't argue, for which David was thankful. Instead, she crossed to their kitchen, climbing over the couch so that she could get a pot and fill it with water.

"You're fine," she agreed. "Sure. Do you want coffee?"

David turned his gaze to make sure she could see his nod.

She put the water on to boil, then clambered back over the couch, sitting on the ground near David, sitting cross-legged facing him. "They've got laundry service here. You should get those bloody clothes soaking, so it doesn't stain."

David shook his head. He didn't much care about his clothes at the moment. 'I'll put them in the laundry chute later,' he signed.

"They're your clothes," Adelyn conceded. Unable to keep her curiosity at bay any longer, she asked, "What happened?"

His hands ached, but he pulled himself into a sitting position and recounted the broad strokes of that day's events. Adelyn listened patiently, only interrupting when something was unclear. He guided the story through the mob, the fire, the fight behind the building, and finally their flight and refuge.

As he told his story, Adelyn finished making the coffee, pouring two cups—black for herself, loaded with cream and sugar for him. That done, she poured the rest of the boiling water into a bowl and took a washrag from a drawer. She passed him his cup, and he held it in both hands, the warmth easing the ache in his fingers. It smelled nice, and tasted sweet at the back of his throat when he took a sip. He enjoyed the moment, then set down the mug to keep talking.

'It's fine,' he signed, as he finished his tale. 'Harrington can patch me up in the morning, then we'll go talk to these people that Ezra wants me to meet. Do you mind coming with me?'

Adelyn hesitated before responding. "I'm glad you're okay, and that you managed to help those people, but I'm not sure we should go to Harrington. Can I look at your hands?"

David frowned, signing, 'Why not?' before extending his palms. His leg hurt, his hands ached, he wanted all the medical attention he could get.

"He might ask how you got injured," Adelyn said, after a pause, taking the back of David's hand. His fingers twitched and he almost pulled away before letting her hold on. Dipping her wash rag in the water, Adelyn started to wash away the dirt and sweat. "And you don't want him going to the peace officers. You know they'd side against the Watched, they're looking for a chance to jump down your throat. That, and Ezra might think it odd if you show up without a scratch."

That was a fair point. He trusted Harrington, but explaining everything would be a lengthy, difficult process that he didn't particularly feel like participating in. He doubted it would lead to a conflict with peace officers, but it would be easier to stitch up his wounds and call it settled.

"Are you sure it's wise to go meet these people?" Adelyn asked, moving from one hand to the other, cleaning around his brass thumb before washing the rest of the hand. "You barely know Ezra."

David shook his head. He wasn't sure if it was wise. Signing, he pulled his hand away to explain, 'If it seems dangerous, we'll leave. I don't think he is planning anything tricky, though. You wanted me to get out and do things while we wait to hear from Harrington, this is something to look into.'

Adelyn chewed on her lip for a moment. "I..." She started, trailing off.

'You think it's a bad idea,' David finished.

There was a pause before Adelyn nodded in confirmation. "How do you know he's being honest with you? What if all those 'fake tips' and coincidences were real?"

'I don't think he's lying,' David said. 'He didn't have to protect me, and he didn't have to save the other people in that building.'

"Criminals can still protect their own," Adelyn pointed out. "You should take off your shirt, let me get a look at your other injuries."

Needing his hands to talk, David instead bit down on his lip to relieve some anxiety as he signed, 'I'm fine.'

"You're wincing every time you move," Adelyn said.

David heaved a sigh and winced, proving Adelyn right. Feeling resigned, he fumbled at his shirt buttons with swollen fingers, struggling to remove the shirt.

"Here, let me," Adelyn said, leaning forward to do it herself. "Did he say what the meeting was about?"

David shook his head as she undid the buttons quickly,

letting him shrug out of the shirt without stretching too much.

"Seems a bad idea to trust criminals," Adelyn said, grimacing as she looked him up and down.

'They are not criminals,' David signed, looking down at himself. Most of his left side was a mass of purple bruises, and the skin had split on his arm where he'd taken a blow from a torch. It was no wonder he ached so badly, he looked like he'd fallen down a substantial hill.

"Ezra is," Adelyn pursed her lips skeptically. "He smashed up that pastor's house, by his own admission."

'That is no reason to pass judgement on his friends.'

"I still think it's risky," Adelyn said. "Especially since you're injured. Can you wait a couple days to rest and recover before meeting them?"

'I made the plan for tomorrow, I'm going to stick to that,' David signed, before picking up his coffee for another drink. He wasn't chilly, but the warmth still felt good. Noting that Adelyn still wasn't at ease, he added, 'I can still run from danger easily, even with my leg.'

Adelyn hmm'ed, and asked, "What happened to your leg?"

Juggling his coffee to try and sign without setting it down, David found the task impossible and sighed, setting it on the floor so he could speak. 'I hurt it when I fell from the building. Will you still come with me tomorrow?'

"Of course," Adelyn said instantly. "Who else is going to make sure you don't get killed next time you go off saving lives?"

'Thanks,' David signed, before thinking to ask, 'What did you do while I was gone?'

Adelyn chewed her lip. "I went and saw the docks."

David waved his coffee mug in a gesture for her to continue.

"You didn't mention that the last two blocks of the city were built over the water," Adelyn said. "I'd imagined the edge of the water would be like a riverbank, but once you get to the coast it's a drop straight into black ocean. I knew of the ocean in theory, but I never realized it would be so huge, and…"

Smiling quietly to himself, David laid back down on the floorboards, listening to Adelyn's story of what she'd seen. He was glad his recommendation had been a good one, and her story, though banal, was a pleasant one to hear.

CHAPTER 8

Clear evidence shows that the WF Boundary exists across the entire realm of man, and at least partially beyond it. Though it's impossible to say with certainty whether the entirety of the realm was covered, all geological areas with identifiable stratification include this dark band of ash and minerals. This has caused some alarm, for if we assume that the other realms all include this band, then we must conclude that in the past some sixty to one hundred thousand years ago there was some kind of apocalyptic event which coated the entire world with ash.

Theories abound as to what could have caused this event, but the greatest concern is that it could happen again, and we would be unable to prepare for it. Some speculate that it could have been some sort of geological activity which released the ash from beneath the earth, but we know of no mechanism by which that ash could be released. If it came from the heavens, there's simply nothing that can be done about it.

Divine intervention is more plausible, though no less frightening. If a war between the gods was brought to the earth, it's entirely possible that the strength of their bouts could create a fire with enough intensity to create this level of ash fall, though the books of the Divine do not speak of such a battle. If this is true, though, then the war was likely caused by humanity's weakness or sin, and so we must be ever vigilant to never become so hedonistic as to trigger such an event again.

•Excerpt from paper discussing the Werthing-Fire Boundary, taken from the presidential archive in Triom

ADELYN WOKE up a couple hours later than she'd intended. Drinking coffee that late had kept her up into the wee hours, fretting over how to tell David what had happened, and once she finally got to bed she had slept like a stone. David hadn't woken her up, instead using the early hours of the morning to go out and buy a new pair of gloves and some bandages to wrap over his hands, both of which he had on by the time Adelyn came yawning out of her room.

The morning air was crisp and clean, and the smell of the city was—for the morning, at least—overcome with fresh salt air that Adelyn enjoyed. The walk was a lethargic one, owing to David's slow walking speed and slower navigation, but the sun was almost straight overhead, meaning that the alleys weren't so dim or dower as they were normally.

They arrived at the fish shop, and Adelyn rapped on the door. A pretty woman with a floppy hat came to the door, nodded at David, then eyed Adelyn cautiously.

"I'm with him," Adelyn said. "You are?"

Frowning, the woman eyed her, then finally gestured with her head. "I'm Solden. Come on in, then. You're letting the cold air out."

The room was chill as Adelyn walked in behind David, and she could see why. Cases of fish and produce were stacked around ice, to keep things fresh.

A scruffy looking man with a severely unshaved face was waiting inside, sitting on one of the crates, wearing clothes that looked ragged and dirty, smelling faintly of smoke. Ezra apparently hadn't left the safety of this refuge, staying all night to avoid those out hunting for him.

"David!" he declared, sitting up. His leg was wrapped in a cast, and he had a pair of crutches next to him. "I'd started thinkin' you weren't coming." His smile faltered as he saw Adelyn, and he asked, "Who's she?"

'A friend,' David signed to Adelyn.

"A friend," Adelyn repeated, adding, "And an interpreter. Unless you can sign?"

Ezra shook his head. "Afraid not."

"Then I'll be translating," Adelyn said. "Where's the people you wanted us to meet?"

"Eh, in back." Ezra frowned. As though she couldn't answer for herself, he leaned towards David and asked, "Is she Watched?"

David shook his head, and Adelyn took the opportunity to fill him in. "I'm Tarraganian. Don't worry, I've got nothing against you or your faith."

Ezra frowned. "Sure. I'll, uh, let 'em know you're here."

He walked to the back door of the storage room, and Adelyn shivered as he walked out.

'Are you ok?' David asked.

'I'm cold,' Adelyn replied, wanting to hide her unease with the situation. 'This room is full of ice.'

Holding the door open, Ezra called, "He's in here."

...

David could only see a glimpse of the room further back, which seemed to be lit by candles and stacked with further crates. A trio of people walked out, dressed as dockworkers, and David looked for distinguishing marks to tell them apart.

One stood a little taller than the other two, a young man in his early twenties, and as he walked in, the other two followed behind. Beside him, a young woman with a gaunt face was scanning the room, and a man about David's age with a scar on his cheek closed the door behind them. Their leader took point as they looked around, sized up David, and... froze.

Seeing them tense, David quickly sunk back into a combat stance by reflex. Once Adelyn saw that, she tried to do the same, tensing and looking from them to Solden, who picked up on the tension immediately and stepped back, eyes darting to the door.

David was in no state to fight, but Adelyn could back him up. She could raise a shield, get him out the door and to safety-

"This is him?" the leader asked Ezra, looking David up and down.

Ezra nodded, oblivious to the tension, the only person in the room who didn't seem ready to draw a weapon in a heartbeat. "Saved my life. Girl's his interpreter."

The taller one relaxed, and the two dock workers flanking him did the same. "Sorry. I wasn't expecting Ezra's friend to have someone with them."

David relaxed in tandem with the three of them, and Adelyn followed suit with what he did. Solden was still nervous, but excused herself to go check the shop front rather than raising a fuss.

David signed, and Adelyn translated. "What should we call you?"

"Shane. It means 'Light'. These are Brenden and Ansyr,"

he added, gesturing first to the man on his left, then the woman to his right.

"I'm Adelyn," Adelyn said, holding out her hand to shake, the bracelets on her wrist jingling. "You know David's name already."

Shane nodded, accepting her hand. "It's good to meet you, Adelyn."

David signed a question, and Adelyn repeated it with interest. "Are all your names in Sacrosanct?"

Shane responded with a nod. "Yes, mostly. We choose our own names, once the time comes. Many have started naming their children in the Watcher's tongue as well."

'What about Ezra?' David signed.

"What does 'Ezra' mean?" Adelyn translated, mistaking the question.

Shane tilted his head, but it was Ansyr that piped up and said, "Ezra's not picked a name yet."

Ezra cleared his throat, having to look up at everyone else from his sitting position. "So, about why I wanted y'all here. David, hoping you don't mind, I already told them you could fight like a Watcher."

David didn't respond to that. It was obvious that Ezra was interested in David primarily for his fighting ability, so he'd expected Ezra to spill the beans on that topic.

"Well," Ezra said, looking back at Shane. "I thought we might see if he wanted to come along, when..."

Brenden snorted, then put a hand to his mouth and pretended to cough.

Shane didn't even look at David before he said, "I appreciate your earnest attempts to find help, but he's a stranger to me."

"He's Watched," Ezra said. "He fought six people, while injured, and almost won alone." Leaning in to add an aside, he spoke in a furtive whisper that David could still here. "I think he may be blessed."

The two dock workers, Ansyr and Brenden, both straightened to attention. Shane looked at Ezra with something like surprise, though not as much alarm. "Are you sure?"

"Can't prove it," Ezra said. "And 's not like he can do much if he is, but it's a vouch for him a damned sight better'n I can offer."

"The Watchers will bless people regardless of faith," Shane pointed out. "But..."

Ezra grinned up at him, watching the wheels turn. There was a pause, broken by Solden returning to retrieve a crate and check in warily on her guests.

Adelyn coughed into her hand, then said, "Sorry, I'm a little out of the loop here. Blessed?"

"Is he a sorcerer?" Ansyr asked, her question refreshingly blunt.

Adelyn opened her mouth and started to say, "He's no—"

David put a hand on her shoulder, then nodded his head, signing to Adelyn. 'Tell Light I'm a wizard.' He had to use the sign 'Light' since he couldn't sign Shane's name without spelling it out, but Adelyn understood his meaning.

"He's a wizard," She said, glancing at David skeptically and signing, 'Are you sure it's smart to trust them?'

David nodded with confidence, and Adelyn looked back at him with equal skepticism.

"Do a spell, then, if—" Brenden started, yelping as Ansyr elbowed him in the side and whispered something to him.

Shane nodded. "David, if I show you something in confidence, can I trust you to keep it quiet?"

David nodded firmly, not needing to sign to answer that.

"Adelyn?" Shane asked.

"He's good for his word," Adelyn said. "And I'll keep my mouth shut so long as you're not hurting anyone."

Frowning to one side, Shane finally decided he could accept that. "It's a long walk, but we can get someone to look at those wounds once we get there," Shane said.

Pushing himself up onto his good foot, Ezra added, "I'll need a bit of a hand."

...

It was a long, circuitous route to their destination. Adelyn knew they couldn't be more than a mile as the crow flies from the fish shop, but they had walked at least twice that distance before they got where they were going, what with all the back alleys and roundabout turns that they took to navigate through the city.

Finally, Shane stopped in front of a tall building, even by the standards of its neighbors—six stories, which was excessive to the point of tempting fate by Adelyn's estimation. It had exterior stairs, and Shane took them up to the second floor before knocking on the door and waiting patiently. Ezra brought up the rear, struggling to climb stairs with one leg in a cast.

A call came through the door, a few muttered words she couldn't hear from the back of the group, and Shane said, "It's me. I've got some newcomers with me."

A pair of deadbolts clicked, and the door opened inward.

"Quickly," the occupant said, waving inside.

"There's nobody on the street," Shane replied, but he did as told, rushing into the building, waving for everyone to follow.

As Adelyn entered, she saw that the person at the door was around her own age, barely a woman. She wore similar clothes to Shane and his entourage, dock worker's clothes, but dyed all black to match her bushy black hair.

"Thanks, Efrin," Shane said, nodding to the girl who'd let them in. "Who's all downstairs?"

"Lotta people," She replied, counting on her fingers. "Lala and Den showed up a few hours ago, I think she's been 'entertaining' everyone with her stories for a while now. They might appreciate the break if you've got some real news."

Pausing, Adelyn looked at the girl. "Your parents named you 'Cold'?"

"I picked my name," Efrin said, giving Adelyn an appropriately icy stare. "Do you have a problem with that?"

Adelyn tried to walk back from the accidental insult. "Not at all." The names of these people seemed odd to her —strangely blunt to anyone who knew words in Sacrosanct, awkward to say otherwise.

"Thanks for keeping an eye out," Ansyr said, clapping Efrin on the shoulder as she walked past the young woman, strolling to the back of the room.

Adelyn couldn't tell where Ansyr was going, there was no visible back room or staircase. Shane had mentioned something about 'Downstairs', but Adelyn had assumed that he was talking about the floor below them, accessible by the staircase in front.

Walking to the small cot at the back of the room, Ansyr crouched, placed her hands at the base, and hefted to reveal what was beneath—a hole, and a ladder.

Brenden grinned at Adelyn's expression as he walked past her. "Not easy to find that, innit?" he asked.

Waving them all forward, Shane said, "We trust that you'll keep our hiding spot a secret."

"I couldn't find my way back here if I tried," Adelyn pointed out.

"Shane figured," Ezra added, as he reached the ladder and set down his crutches. "Anyone lookin' for a way to the basement'd search the first floor, so we put this up on the second. False wall downstairs, peace officers lookin' around gonna be none the wiser." He went down the ladder awkwardly, hopping on his good foot and sliding down the rails with both hands.

"I'll stay up here," Ansyr said, leaning in to Shane and giving him a kiss on the cheek. "Give Efrin a break from keeping watch."

"Are you sure?" Shane asked, adding, "Do you want me to bring you anything?"

"Hey, she already said it," Efrin pointed out, pushing past the two of them and hopping onto the ladder. "I'm taking a break."

"I'll be fine," Ansyr said. "Come see me in a couple hours?"

Shane returned her kiss, then nodded in answer and stepped towards the ladder.

David went down before Adelyn, awkwardly holding to the ladder's rungs with the sides of his hands, to keep from agitating the torn skin and blisters on his palms. She went down next, and Shane followed behind them.

The ladder went down further than Adelyn had expected, and when her feet touched floor, it was against wooden planks that didn't creak. She had to turn around to see the rest of the room, and when she did, she was again surprised by the scale.

"Welcome to our little home," Shane said, gesturing around. The basement was two or three times the size of the rooms above, with cloth dividers separating beds against one wall, a sparse cooking area and long dining table across from those, and no less than fifteen people occupying the space, not including those that had just arrived. More than half wore bandages or casts, and a couple more were in bed, seeming too weak to stand. Two were in heavy casts and bandages, practically immobile from all the dressing to their wounds.

A girl of around nine or ten was standing on the dining room table, waving her arms wildly and explaining a story to a captive audience composed of three people with heavy bandages and one content looking old man. When the girl saw Ezra, she abandoned her tale, leaping down with the clumsy energy of adolescence and running towards him.

"Ezra!" she exclaimed, grinning and leaping into a hug, making Ezra wince as he rocked back onto his bad leg to catch her.

"Lala," Ezra said back, rubbing his knuckles on the girl's forehead, then setting her down. "How's the realm's smallest dragon?"

The girl made a roaring noise and spun, waving her arms around dramatically.

"Is she the girl from the fire?" Adelyn asked, smiling at the child with more than a hint of nostalgia.

David nodded, adding, 'The old man is her grandfather.'

As distracted as Adelyn had been with the girl, she almost didn't notice when Ezra slipped away from the group, moving between the sick and injured, asking after their welfare or offering small words of encouragement.

Adelyn started to approach him, quietly watching as he spoke to an older man lying in one of the beds, but she felt a touch at her arm and saw Shane behind her.

"I should speak with you," he said, his face somber.

Looking at his expression, Adelyn asked, "Is this what you wanted us to see? The sick people?"

Shane nodded. "A couple people here are sick, but most of them aren't. We do what we can, but I don't know any healing, and medicine is expensive. We can barely keep this place stable as it is."

Adelyn nodded, looking around. One of the walls seemed to be seeping water in, mold collecting between planks. Shane followed her gaze, then swore.

"I've said a dozen times we need to pitch that wall so it'll stop leaking," he groaned, glancing back to Adelyn. "It sometimes seems like I'm the only one who can get anything done around here."

"I know the feeling." Her brow furrowed as she thought, and then she said, "How were they all injured?"

"A few, shot or stabbed in confrontations with peace officers," Shane said. "More don't live long enough to get here."

Trying to ask in a way that wouldn't come across as inflammatory, Adelyn asked, "Why do you get into so many confrontations?"

"Because they'll harass us for any damned thing," Shane explained, glowering. "They see someone they know is Watched, they assume we're up to something. Less than a decade ago, they came here as soldiers and enemies, now they're supposed to police us as equals."

"You fought in the war?" Adelyn asked.

Shane shrugged. "I played a signal drum. They wouldn't let me have a gun."

Adelyn nodded. "And now what do you do?"

"Mostly, this," Shane said. "I'm doing what I was supposed to. Helping people, where I can. Saving lives. Keeping my city from being abandoned to the Divine thieves who want to take it from us. There are people all over the city like Solden, willing to take in a soul in danger, and since we got this place set up we've been able to help those in need of more serious care."

Chewing her lip, Adelyn started to nod in appreciation, but she frowned mid-gesture as a thought struck her. She glanced back at David, who was listening to Lala chatter about something, Efrin and Brenden making up her new audience. Ezra had moved to get water for someone and start refreshing bandages. It was just her and Shane over in this corner of the room.

"Hold on a tick," Adelyn said. "Don't you want David to hear all this more than me? I'm just the tagalong, he's the one you invited here."

"David's a good man, I'm sure," Shane said, eying Adelyn. "But I knew he was on board to help people the moment I heard he ran into a burning building for Ezra's sake." Seeming to consider for a moment, he added, "Besides, I know a blessed woman when I sense one."

Adelyn paled for a moment as she realized what he'd said, but her panic quickly faded into confusion, then realization. He seemed not to have any sinister motives, at least not towards her welfare. Recovering, she sighed dramatically at the ceiling. "Lords abandon me where I stand if I'm not the *only damned* sorceress who can't sense the spirit in a horsefly a mile away. You're a sorcerer?"

Shane hesitated, but that was all the answer Adelyn needed, so it didn't surprise her when he nodded. She was still caught off guard a second later, though, when he added, "That's not how I knew."

"Then how?" Adelyn asked.

"You read the paper?" Shane said. "Great big front page story about a week ago, talked about a man who ran into fire to try and stop some bandits while a sorcerer girl saved the engine."

Adelyn felt the blood drain from her face as she considered the implications of what he'd said. "The whole town knows about me?"

"No, no," Shane corrected himself. "Didn't give your name, not even a description, but I can do the math. All that silver around your wrist was a good clue, once I knew I was looking."

Making a big gesture of shaking out the bracelets on her wrist, Adelyn held them up. "It's more convenient then walking around with a staff, if you ask me." Chewing her lip, she gestured around the room and asked, "You're a sorcerer, though. Is that how you've been able to get all this done?"

"It helps," Shane said. "It comes in handy when it's time to fend off peace officers or stopping fights, but mostly it lets me command respect and get people on my side. A Watcher's blessing is a pretty good character reference."

"Maybe I'll start running my own basement infirmary, then," Adelyn quipped. "Give you a little competition."

"You've got the blessing, but you're not Watched," Shane said. "Not sure that'd carry as much weight. You're welcome to try, though, and you'd get all my support in the effort. I don't suppose you're a decent physician?"

Adelyn shook her head. "I know 'Heyl'," she said. "That's about it. I'm still learning."

Shane's face fell. "I suppose that was too much to hope for. None of us know much in the way of medicine either."

"Surely there must be books on the subject," Adelyn said. "I haven't looked into it, but—"

"Any books on the subject are kept under lock and key in the library at the city vault," Shane said, cutting her off. "And even when texts on the subject crop up in the city, we aren't swimming in gold to be able to buy them at will, and they got bought up before we can scrape anything together."

Adelyn considered it for a while, then shook her head. "I'm sorry I can't help more."

Shane put up a finger. "That's not exactly true. We should get David over here, there's something else I want to talk to you about."

...

David watched with amusement as Lala, the little girl who'd threatened him with a kitchen knife the day before, pranced around and told the story of her and her grandfather's daring escapades. Her yarn included many asides and no doubt much hyperbole, but was a pleasant narrative despite the embellishment.

He was aware that Adelyn was quietly discussing something with Shane, but she seemed relaxed, unthreatened. They were in a basement, with the only way out being a slow climb up a tall ladder, so if it came to blows they would be in trouble. Adelyn could overpower half a dozen of these Watched, probably more, and David could lend a hand, but there were plenty of other people in the basement—fighting them all would be difficult

Apparently done with their conversation, Adelyn started walking back in his direction, and Shane followed behind her.

'Everything alright?' David signed, though he didn't see anything wrong.

Adelyn nodded subtly, then turned to the side to defer to Shane.

"In three days," Shane said, "The mayor is holding a town hall to discuss the hiring of more peace officers."

"That's bad!" Ezra added helpfully, sitting in a chair he'd pulled over.

Brenden rolled his eyes, but Shane nodded. "We know what they're going to say. The train robbery a few days ago, the troubles in the street, they'll make a case that the current law enforcement isn't well equipped enough to handle our city. The last thing we need is more peace officers coming in from Triom and kicking us around."

David frowned, then signed to Adelyn. 'I'm a peace officer. Can you mention that?'

"David's an officer," Adelyn translated helpfully. "I agree that most of the lot are useless, but not all of them are bad people."

"We know," Shane said, waving over Efrin. "And even if we had Constantine himself show up and argue our case, nothing's gonna stop them from getting more officers anyways."

David saw where they were going with this, pieces that he'd observed clicking together in his head. 'They want to get their own people hired instead,' he signed to Adelyn.

"We want to get locals on the force," Shane explained, confirming David's guess. "People we trust, who'll give a damn about the Watched who live here. That's our goal. If we can get a majority of Azah locals, preferably Watched locals, we can keep our streets safe and keep the president's people off our backs at the same time."

"You think they'll go for that?" Adelyn asked, raising an eyebrow. "If they think you're a bunch of criminals and troublemakers, that is."

"If we push hard enough," Shane said.

"Get the whole town behind us, show that we're a force to be reckoned with, they can't say no," Efrin added. "If they're scared of us fighting back, at least."

'Why do they need us?' David asked, waiting for Adelyn to repeat the question.

Brenden piped up with the answer to that one. "Because if we show up and we're not packing, we'll get thrown out on our asses."

"We need to be able to defend ourselves," Shane clarified, "Especially because we're taking Ezra."

Ezra blinked, looking up at Shane with bewilderment. "With my leg? I'd—"

"Because of your leg," Shane corrected. "And because of what happened to you yesterday. We can show everyone just how little our current officers care when its citizens are attacked and buildings are burned."

"You want David there so you can fight your way out again," Adelyn said.

Shane shook his head. "I want David to be there to show what our own people can do. He might not be a local, but he's Watched, and he was there when the peace officers weren't. Saved three lives, by my estimation."

"I'll be killed the moment they set eyes on me!" Ezra complained. "Leg or no leg, I'm not gonna win any sympathy points when they think I killed some kid."

"The mob was in a frenzy," Shane said. "They have no evidence, and the peace officers won't dare touch you for fear of starting a riot. Besides, that's why we're going with weapons and three blessed to keep you safe."

Three? David thought, looking around. There was himself, and Adelyn, but-

"Three?" Ezra asked, confused. "Isn't it four, with—ow!" He was silenced as Brenden thumped him on the back of the head.

"Dammit, Ezra," Efrin said. "Can't you keep that tongue from flapping for more than a minute?"

"What's he talking about?" Adelyn asked sharply.

Shane sighed, leaning on the table with his palms. "I'm

blessed. David, it's only fair that you knew. Adelyn is, too, which makes three." Giving Ezra a blunt look of annoyance, he added, "Besides that, there are two more blessed in the city and we've been *keeping it quiet,* because we don't want anyone to get wind of how many resources we've got access to, and because I don't want them getting hurt. You two, you're outsiders, so it's not tipping our hand to have you show up."

"That's a lot of danger you're throwing at us," Adelyn said. "While you're keeping your own people hidden."

"Not so much danger as you might think," Shane said. "We're going to be packing heat, and not only of the magical variety. We've got weapons, and we have a fair few people who are willing to put themselves in harm's way if it means making progress in the city."

David had heard everything he needed to. 'We're in,' he signed.

"David's in," Adelyn translated. "I still have questions."

"Ask them, then," Shane said. "We've got nothing to hide."

Adelyn chewed her lip for a long moment, clearly thinking over her question for a long time, as though she were afraid of the answer. Finally, she gestured towards the back of the room, towards a pair of beds. "What happened to those two people in casts over there? The ones who look like they broke just about everything that could break."

Shane pursed his lips, glancing between Brenden and Efrin, neither of whom seemed willing to answer the question for him. "Beaten by peace officers," he said. "For loitering in the wrong place at the wrong time."

"You're sure?" Adelyn asked, raising an eyebrow. David wasn't certain what she was getting at, but Adelyn seemed certain in whatever it was. She was no fool, and David knew she had a good reason for her suspicion, but he hadn't yet pieced together whatever she had.

"I'm sure," Shane said, returning her stare directly.

"I'm out, then." Adelyn ignored David as he sent a confused look in her direction. "Do what you want, but you're not getting my help."

CHAPTER 9

I asked mom what thulcuts eat, she told me that they eat naughty boys who get into trouble and ask too many questions.

That didn't sound right, so I asked dad, and he told me they eat sailors who drink too much.

That doesn't make sense either. If thulcuts eat people, then how come they barely ever get close enough to cities that I can see one? They mostly stay away, and the ones that do come close to eat sailors all get chopped up for meat.

I bet they eat mermaids.

•Diary entry from a coastal child, author's name unknown. (Note: Thulcuts predominantly small to mid-sized marine life, though they have been observed eating mammal flesh when it's available.)

THEY LEFT TOWARDS THE SEASIDE, guided by Brenden towards the coast so that they wouldn't get lost. Their trip had been a silent one. David preferred it that way.

He and Adelyn were going to argue, no doubt about it, but he wanted to wait until they were alone. Not for fear of being overheard, but simply so he could focus on the discussion without being distracted by the environment. They'd already put off the conversation for a while so David could be looked at by the Watched's physician and given some pills to help with the pain, but David was hoping they could wait to argue until they made it back to the boarding house.

"This is where we'll leave you," Brenden said, looking around. Shane and Ansyr had both stayed back at the safe house, as had Ezra for obvious reasons, leaving Brenden as their only guide. "You can find the way to your place from here?"

David nodded. The coast was abuzz with activity—sailors preparing to bring ships in once the tide changed, dock workers loading cargo from up the coast and sending it off to be sold or delivered, runners delivering messages up and down the docks at lightning speed, children no older than ten whose little feet barely touched the wooden boards that made up the coastline.

"We should be fine," Adelyn added. She received a long side-eye from Brenden, but didn't seem to mind.

"David, we'll expect you in three days," Brenden said, nodding to him.

David returned the gesture, eyes to the ground, trying to peer between the boards to get a glimpse of the water splashing against the real coastline. The beach was some ten feet below him, but it hadn't seen natural sunlight in decades, as the docks were built out and grew to cover the ocean. The wooden platform that they stood on was supported by heavy beams, little more than trees with their branches hewn off.

Adelyn demanded something of him in a questioning tone, and David had to pull himself away and repeat her words in his head to process what she had asked. "What on the earth's back are you doing?"

David looked at her, shoulders slumping slightly as he realized they were going to do this immediately. 'I'm helping them,' he said, stepping back a little bit so that a child with a creased envelope could sprint in front of him.

Adelyn took an impact from the runner, who had expected her to step out of the way. Her balance didn't even waver, of course, the child wasn't big enough to tackle Adelyn even if they'd been trying, so they bounced off her and kept running, shouting a curse at her in a heavy accent. "You're helping criminals," Adelyn said, watching the kid run away.

'They have no choice,' David said. 'If the peace officers are targeting them, they have to take refuge with whoever will take them.'

"Not that," Adelyn said, putting a hand to her forehead. She was clearly frustrated. David had missed something she deemed obvious. "They—"

David put up a hand and shook his head. 'People can hear us,' he signed. It was unlikely that anyone would be listening in to their conversation over the shouts and calls of working people, but he didn't want to risk it.

Adelyn's jaw visibly tightened, but she took the time to sign out what she had to say. Her hands and arms moved with violent intensity, adding emphasis to the words. 'David, they robbed the train.'

Blinking, David started to sign a question, but she'd anticipated what he was going to ask.

'The people who robbed the train were Watched. You fought a sorcerer with two accomplices. I threw two people off the train, and that shelter had two people in body casts.'

David took a deep breath, trying to shut out all the

outside stimulation that was making it difficult to focus. He started tapping his fingers out against his leg, but couldn't do that while responding, so he pulled his hand away and tried tapping his foot instead. It wasn't the same, but it had to do.

'How do you know they were Watched?' He signed, gaze darting around the path they were on. Seeing a cart coming their way, he added, 'We should move.'

"I'm fine right here," Adelyn said stubbornly. "We're not putting this off."

'The cart,' David explained, pointing. Adelyn turned and saw, then realized what he meant, stepping to the guardrail so that the heavy cart could pass.

'The peace officers said that Watched were responsible,' Adelyn signed, once they were clear.

'You trust them?' David asked, incredulous. 'Peace officers, who have been harassing and targeting Watched.'

"Yes!" Adelyn shouted, before reverting to signs. 'When everything else lines up, yes. Sorcerers aren't exactly a dime a dozen. Who else would it be?'

'Shane's not the only wizard in this city,' David said. 'The Watched are *not* responsible. You've got nothing except coincidence.' Adelyn had apparently decided not to give even the slightest benefit of the doubt to Shane or his companions, and was simply looking for reasons not to trust them.

The space was starting to clear, making a wide gap for ships to come in and make port. Runners continued to flit past them, but fewer carts were coming through, and most of the dock workers and sailors who weren't preparing to take in ships were backing away or moving elsewhere.

'If it wasn't Shane, or one of the other two he mentioned, who would it have been?' Adelyn signed, making fast, angry motions. 'Do you think it was Harrington who robbed the train? Or the other person in his book club?'

'No,' David admitted—he knew Harrington, the physician wouldn't do something like that.

'That doesn't leave anybody else,' Adelyn signed, staring at David, forcing him to look away or make eye contact. He looked away. 'Unless there's another sorcerer running around town that we don't know about. Either it was Shane, or it was one of his people.'

'There could be another sorcerer,' David signed. 'You don't know—'

"I do know!" Adelyn said, again reverting to a shout so she could interrupt David. "I know damned well, and you're just going along with them because you can't see the truth when it's an inch in front of your face!"

'I'm not a fool,' David signed. 'They may be keeping some things from us, but their intent is honest.'

"You don't know that!" Adelyn said, insistently. "David, for as good a liar as you are, you're the most gullible fool I know."

David's brow furrowed, and for a fleeting moment he met her eyes, signing, 'I am not—'

"Harrington isn't going to help you," Adelyn said, cutting him off again.

David staggered as though physically struck. He opened his mouth to respond, and only then realized he couldn't. Signing instead, he asked, 'What?'

"He's abandoned the both of us, because he doesn't like you," Adelyn said. "I went to confront him while you were out yesterday. He told me straight to my face that he wasn't going to lift a finger to try and help either of us."

'You,' David started to sign, confused and angry, his

hands shaking so much he could barely respond. 'You're lying, to—'

"I should have told you sooner, but I'm telling you now because you have to know," Adelyn said. "Do not trust these people. They're taking you in so you'll fight for them. Mark my words, they're going to take those weapons they're bringing and turn them against the first person who sneezes in their direction."

David found his fingers drumming against his leg on impulse, and he didn't pull them away. He had no response. Harrington wasn't going to help. He could send for Sarah, but she was all the way up in Triom, and she specialized in treating battlefield wounds. Maybe she could help, but even then, would she take him? It had been years, and-

He needed to find a post office, somewhere that he could send a letter. Or, better, somewhere with a telegraph. *Telegrams have come this far east, right?* Surely, a port city would have one. It'd be expensive, but that was fine, he had the money.

Turning, he started walking into the city. He had his notepad in a belt pouch, he could ask for directions if he needed to.

"David," Adelyn said, watching him go.

He kept walking, he could explain later, this was more urgent. She'd go back to the boarding house, and he'd meet her there.

"David!" Adelyn repeated. Boards shook from footsteps as she caught up with him, grabbing his arm.

David tensed and then jerked away, throwing off her grasp, wheeling on Adelyn. He'd drawn spirit into his necklace, but it just hung there impotently, unable to manifest into a spell without a wizard—a real wizard—to use it.

She paled upon seeing his expression, backing off. Turning away, David stormed off into the city.

...

Adelyn watched David stomp off into the mazelike streets of Azah. She wanted to run after him, but thought better of it. She'd give him space, for now.

It had been stupid to dump all that on him at once, but she hadn't seen another choice. He was going to throw in his lot with criminals and thugs, the people who'd killed that man on the train and tried to do a lot more.

Whether he pitched in with them or not, though, she had to do something more about the plans of these Watched. Even without David, they had a trio of wizards and many more armed thugs besides who would cause a lot of trouble whether David was there to help or not. No matter what they said, they were planning to cause trouble at the town hall, and if left unchecked they were going to get people killed.

As much as it pained her to admit it, she had to go to the peace officers.

Finding a peace officer station was easier than she'd anticipated. She had to ask for directions only twice, and it was easy to spot from a great distance. In a city of raw wooden buildings built in awkward stacks, a bright red building assembled of stone and mortar, nestled in an open courtyard, stuck out like a sore thumb. It wasn't just the peace officers station, it was also the city courthouse, but as far as she could tell it served the same purpose with a more pretentious name.

Adelyn wasn't sure if she should knock, or if she could walk inside. It was a public place, like a store or a saloon, but it was also more like a place of business.

Crossing her fingers, she pushed open the door and

strode inside, looking around. Benches sat against the back wall flanking the entrance, the only furniture in the waiting room—there were doors leading deeper inside, but they were heavy oak things that wouldn't be opened without a key. There was a peace officer visible, sitting at a desk, but they were only seen through a small window blocked by a steel grate.

"I need to speak to the sheriff," Adelyn said, walking up to the window.

The peace officer looked up from his work, raising an eyebrow. "The sheriff? Which one?"

"You've got more than one?" Adelyn asked.

The officer only gave her a blank look through the steel grate. "If you've had personal property stolen, you can file a report."

Adelyn tried to remember the sheriff's name. "Eh... I need to talk to Carol. No, sorry, Cara. Her name was Cara."

That at least got the officer's attention, though only slightly. "What about? She's currently occupied, but I'm sure someone can help—"

Adelyn interrupted him with a few words, which finally got the reaction she was hoping for. "I know who robbed the train."

Five minutes later, she was in a private office, sitting down across from Sheriff Cara Flintwood.

...

Finding a post office proved harder than David had anticipated. He didn't know the layout of the city well enough to find it on his own, and though he wrote a note asking for directions, the people who saw him trying to foist off a paper onto passersby took him for a drifter trying to sell something and gave him a wide berth. He did get a little help, but that amounted to vague gestures and pointing fingers that only got him more lost.

After two hours of fruitless searching, he was collapsed on a bench, feeling defeated. He'd have to go back to the boarding house and ask Adelyn's help in finding a post office, which meant he likely wouldn't get the letter sent until the evening or the next day.

Groaning up at the sky, he closed his eyes. This whole trip had been pointless. He could still help those Watched, but without magic, he was just another sword in a town that had plenty of those.

"Mind if I sit?"

David looked up to see a man not dissimilar to himself. Middle height, dark skin, a short shock of dark hair. That look was more common than not on the coast, though, so David thought nothing of it as he scooted slightly to the side to make room. He'd have preferred the whole bench to himself, but he couldn't justifiably take up a whole seat when it was meant for three.

"It's a lovely day," the stranger said. "I don't get to visit the coast often, but the weather's always so beautiful here."

Looking at the stranger skeptically, David considered his words. He looked like a local, but looks weren't always reliable. What was more odd was his comment about the weather, since tempests and rainstorms were common on the coast.

"I shouldn't really be here," the stranger continued. "Not that it's your business what I should and shouldn't be doing. I tend to chatter when given the opportunity. You like it here?"

David shook his head.

"No you don't like it here, or no you don't want to talk to me?" the stranger asked.

Sighing, David gestured at his mouth, then made a sign for 'I can't speak.' While the stranger wouldn't understand the sign, hopefully they'd get the—

'Sorry, friend,' the stranger signed back. 'Is this better?'

David blinked in surprise, then signed back. 'Yes.' Conversation with strangers was never something he cared much for, but the simple act of being able to carry on talking with this man overcame his usual misgivings. 'What do I call you?'

'That's not important,' the stranger replied, turning to face him. 'I'm a nobody. You seemed in a dower disposition, though, so I thought I'd try and share a little cheer with you.' His hands moved so quickly that it was almost a blur, and he used words David was hardly familiar with, making it difficult to keep up.

'I'm fine,' David signed back. 'Just lost.'

'Everyone feels lost, sometimes,' the stranger said. 'Keep up your faith, you'll find the right way through your tribulations.'

'No,' David signed, shaking his head. 'I am literally lost. Can you direct me to the post office?'

'Oh,' the stranger signed, nodding. 'Probably. But I don't think you're just looking for the post office. Can I give you some advice?'

'I'd rather have the directions, I really do need to find it,' David signed. Advice from strangers was less than useless, in his estimation, especially ones who were going on about faith.

'Hear me out, if you please,' the stranger insisted. 'I don't have much to say, and if you disagree, you're always perfectly free to ignore me.'

David decided to go along with the charade. If that was the price of directions, he'd pay it.

'Don't give up hope,' the stranger said. 'And don't discount the gods. Even when it seems like you've run out of places to turn, you can always seek help with a higher power, and you may find what you're looking for with them.'

Rolling his eyes, David looked away, throwing up his arms in resigned frustration. He didn't know the sign for 'Priest', so he signed, 'You're a religious leader? You're just preaching?'

'You could say that,' the man said, nodding.

'I don't want your help,' David signed, annoyed at the stranger wasting his time. 'I'm not Divine. Leave me be.'

'I didn't say anything about being Divine,' the stranger corrected. "You don't have to pray to any gods in specific to seek help from faith."

David rolled his eyes. 'And how do you suggest I pray without a voice?'

'Are your gods so weak that they must be shouted at to hear you?' the stranger asked.

David frowned. He didn't care for this stranger's pitch, but he didn't have a good answer to the question either. 'My gods stopped caring what I have to say a long time ago,' he said, though he hated to dodge the question.

'Did they?' the stranger asked. 'Or did you stop talking to them?'

David didn't even have an off topic response to that question, so he looked away and gave up responding. The stranger took that for what it was, the end of the conversation, and stood.

Before he walked away, though, the stranger said, "The post office is four blocks down, then a right, and another two blocks. The sign is easy to miss, but there's a fruit stand right in front."

He turned to leave, and David got up as well to go deliver his letter.

...

Adelyn sipped the coffee she'd been given, eying Cara as the sheriff mulled over what she'd been told. Adelyn had filled her in on the whole story, minus the parts including Harrington, and leaving off David's own magic, since neither seemed relevant.

"So you lied about him being Watched, then," The sheriff, Cara, commented, once the story was over.

"Do you blame me?" Adelyn asked. "He's still not done anything wrong."

"He didn't come to me to tell us what he found."

Adelyn shook her head. "He hadn't seen anything worth telling."

"Hiding out with criminals is worth telling, and Ezra's a wanted man. I don't suppose you can find your way back to that hideaway?"

"I could probably take you to the fish shop that we met them at."

It was Cara's turn to shake her head. "No good. We already know where that is, but we can't touch it without a damned good reason or certainty that they'll be there when we go to look."

"I don't want anyone to get hurt, when they show up. I'm going to try and talk David out of going to the town hall meeting, but I can't talk them all down."

"Do you know how many of the Watched are going to be at the town hall?" the sheriff asked, adjusting a notepad on the table to write down the answer.

"I don't," Adelyn said. "Maybe a dozen, but that's a wild guess."

Jotting that down, the sheriff added, "And they've got three wizards in total?"

"That's what Shane said." Adelyn flinched at the use of 'Wizard'. It was possible the Watched deserved to be called that, if they were going to rob trains and start fights, but it was still a harsh term that made her uncomfortable to hear.

"Any idea what kind of weapons?" Cara asked.

"No," Adelyn said. "They didn't fill me in on the details of their plan. I'd expect they have guns, they had a couple at the train, but I don't really know."

"Thank you," The sheriff said, sitting back. "This has been a huge help."

Adelyn felt some relief with the situation. "Will you be able to arrest them before they start a fight?"

"Of course we can," The sheriff assured her. "Not a soul should get hurt."

CHAPTER 10

Sheriff Flintwood: How are you doing today, Henry?

Subject: I'm not telling you anything.

Flintwood: You're looking at a long drop in a short noose. Someone got killed, and right now you're the only person we've got for it. I don't want to see you hanged, but there's only so much I can do. Give me something to work with here, Henry.

Subject: I don't turn on friends.

Flintwood: I don't need names, but give me something. What do you want the explosives for?

Subject: Nothing. We didn't want them.

Flintwood: You mean to say your accomplices stole them by accident?

Subject: No.

Flintwood: Then what?

Subject: We didn't want them, we just didn't want you to have them. I think the plan was to sell whatever we got. Probably already sent them up the coast for a sack of silver.

Flintwood: We've got people watching the black market. Nobody's been trying to push demolition explosives.

Subject: Then they're hanging on to them until they've got an opening.

Flintwood: Fine, then. Tell me about the town hall. What's the plan there?

•Excerpt from interrogation with prisoner. Note: After the question about the town hall, the prisoner refused to answer any questions and was silent for the remainder of the interrogation.

It was a tense three days. Adelyn barely spoke to David, and when she tried he would always push her away. She wanted to keep him from the town hall meeting, but no matter how many times she brought it up, he always rebuffed the offer.

That was when David was even around. He spent much of the day out of their boarding house, loitering around a post office, waiting for a response to a telegram he'd sent.

When pressed, David had tersely explained that he'd sent off to another healer who he knew from the war, and Adelyn presumed it was one of the Thirteen, but he wouldn't confirm that part.

More than once, Adelyn considered leaving. Her goal was to learn magic in the city, and as far as she could see that wasn't going to happen. She and David were barely on speaking terms, and there wasn't much else for her to do besides wander the city and risk getting lost for the sake of tourism.

She decided to wait, at least until after the town hall meeting. If David insisted on going, he'd get arrested, and would need someone to put in a good word for him from the outside. She owed David that much, at least. Once that was over, though, she was going to leave town and never look back.

The morning of the town hall started with a light drizzle, and Adelyn was greeted with wet socks when she got out of bed. There was water leaking in from the walls, and it was frigid. Adelyn didn't mind the wet socks too much, she could peel them off and change into dry clothes, but she'd hidden a bag with her money and David's journals beneath a loose floorboard, and she didn't want that to get wet.

A quick check determined that the bag was still dry, but she moved it a bit before putting the floorboard back to be safe, then got dressed into new socks.

David was already awake and pouring coffee when Adelyn left her room. He slid a mug across the kitchen counter towards her, but offered no greeting or comment besides.

"I still think you shouldn't go," Adelyn said, accepting the coffee. "It's dangerous. You might get hurt."

David ignored her, dumping a spoonful of sugar into his own mug and stirring it around, then walking past her to get to his room.

Adelyn knew at this point that he wasn't going to listen to her. She could push, plead, or beg, but none of that was going to matter. If she wanted him to stay away from the town hall meeting, she'd have to stop him directly.

Walking back to her bedroom, she took the silver bracelets from her dresser and clasped them around her wrist, mentally preparing herself for a confrontation. It wouldn't need to be a fight. She had magic, she could hold David back and make him see reason. It was still going to be the sort of tough friendship that he wasn't likely to appreciate.

Walking back out of her room, she crossed to the front door

and leaned against it, waiting for David to come out. He did, a couple minutes later, wearing his new gloves and heavy boots. He wasn't armed, except for a heavy knife on his belt that wouldn't serve as much of a weapon against a sword or a gun.

"I don't want you to go," Adelyn said, standing up straight.

David ignored the comment and started walking towards the door, towards Adelyn.

Adelyn put her palm on the door's handle, blocking access to it before David could force his way past. "David, I'm serious. Don't go."

'No,' David signed. 'I am going. There is nothing you might say to sway my mind.'

Swallowing on a dry throat, Adelyn said, "I know we've talked about this already, but I'm being serious now. Don't go. Please, trust me. If you go, bad things will happen to you."

'I don't trust you,' David signed, and Adelyn burned with shame when he said it, because she knew he was justified in his mistrust. 'Let me by.'

"I'm sorry," Adelyn said, drawing power into her bracelet so she could put up a shield and block David in. "But this is for your own—"

David's hand lashed out and seized her by the wrist before she could blink, and by the time her brain had caught up to the situation she was in midair and falling to the ground. Reactions kicking in, she tried to shout, *"Ansyr!"*, but the spell came out without effect, and Adelyn realized with alarm that David had pulled the spirit out of her bracelets in the same moment he'd grabbed her wrist.

There was a still second after she hit the ground, and David hesitated for a moment in uncertainty while Adelyn tried to suck in a breath and regain her bearings. He still had her by the wrist, but seemed almost surprised in that moment to be holding onto it, like he'd reacted on instinct and was only now deciding on a course of action.

His face finally shifted into determination, and before Adelyn could pull away, his hand slipped up her arm and twisted hard. She rolled with the move to keep it from breaking anything, but David had been the one to teach her that skill, and he anticipated the roll, lowering his weight and pulling so that she was flipped onto her side.

Once she was held this way, he delivered a kick to her belly, and the air was driven from Adelyn's lungs in a pained wheeze. David hesitated for a second time in indecision, and this time no more blows came raining down. Instead, he moved both hands to her bracelets, snapping them off one at a time and tossing them across the room.

"W-wait," Adelyn choked, trying to sit up as David turned to throw open the door. He didn't even look back before slamming it behind him and walking away with long, stiff strides.

...

Anger and adrenaline carried David for two blocks, then reality caught up with him and he sidestepped, leaning his weight against a nearby wall and releasing a breath he'd been unconsciously holding.

What did I just do?

He'd attacked a friend—perhaps his only true friend, the only one not forced associate with him by happenstance, the only one who he had more contact with in the past years than a few scattered letters. She'd been preparing to raise a shield, something to trap or immobilize him. Not an attack, not anything that would have hurt him. His response had been to take her down, to go for pain without consideration.

The only sound he heard was his heaving lungs, and the patter of his fingers against his leg. He wanted to go back, to apologize, but that was stupid. Adelyn wouldn't give him a second chance, and he'd be late to meet the Watched.

There was nothing for it. He could apologize to her later, if she'd listen.

Straightening, he started walking, forcing his legs to move. It was that or stay put and keep fuming, which wouldn't serve anyone. He'd keep working towards a concrete goal, focus his attention on something he knew he could accomplish.

The little fish market was as he remembered it—a little smelly, badly overpriced, lightly trafficked. Knocking on the door, he was greeted by Solden, her characteristic wariness no less sharp today than it had been last time he had seen her.

A long moment passed as she surveyed David, then opened the door and waved him in. "Another one of yours," she called, letting him in. "The foreigner!"

Despite the cases packed with ice, the small storage room was stifling and surprisingly warm. Eight people were there, not including Solden and David himself.

"Davey, my man!" Ezra said, grinning and waving. He'd gotten a change of clothes, and had a fresh cast over his leg, pants rolled up to make the injury plenty obvious. "How's life?"

Trying not to look shaken, David surveyed the rest of the group. Ezra, Shane, Brenden, and Ansyr. The girl who'd let them into the safe house. *Efrin, was it?* Three people besides, all in their early twenties, all looking fit and strong but not a one of them looking like veterans.

'Why're they all so young?' David signed, before realizing that nobody could understand him.

"What's that?" Ezra asked. "Sorry, I don't exactly know what you're saying there."

David shook his head. It didn't matter—these were the lot he'd be working with, it didn't matter why.

Shane stepped up to David, wearing a black rain slicker that went past his knees and a wide brimmed hat that cast much of his face in shadow, even with the spirit lighting of the storage room. "Is Adelyn coming?" David shook his head, to the disappointment of several. "Couldn't convince her, eh?"

Again, David shook his head, more emphatically than before. This wasn't a topic he much wanted to discuss, and he was sweltering in the crowded room besides. The sooner they left for the town hall, the better.

"Well," Brenden commented. "We might not have a full thirteen wizards, but they'll have to have some real sand to scoff what we've got to bear."

David started to sign in response, but this time he realized his mistake before even raising his hands all the way. He could go for his notepad, but it didn't seem worth the effort.

Adelyn's absence seemed almost palpable to David. To relax, he started up the drumbeat on his leg, tip-tapping out his usual rhythm. That made the claustrophobia easier to bear, and gave him a task to focus on besides thinking of what he'd say to Adelyn. The sound of idle conversation and comments between the eight people he didn't know was quietly reverberating through the room, but he drowned it out and ignored that as well.

"We should get ready," Shane said. To David, specifically, he added, "You don't need to partake in this ceremony if you don't care to, but it's something we do before we go out."

Stepping back, David watched as the five Watched in the room—excluding him and Shane, who stayed back, and Ezra, who remained seated—filed into a line, standing shoulder to shoulder. Each seemed to puff out their chest, standing at attention like soldiers eager to see combat, except lacking the discipline or training to know how to stand at attention properly.

Approaching the rightmost end of the line, Shane spoke to one of the Watched. "Embren, today—"

"It's 'Elben'," the Watched interrupted. "Not 'Embren'."

"Sorry," Shane said, eyes glancing up as he made a mental note. "Elben, today we fight to increase the order in the world, and to help the downtrodden. Will you act as a shield to protect those innocents, or a sword to cut down the wicked?"

"A sword, of course," the young Watched said, intoning the response as part of what was obviously a ritual.

Shane nodded, seeking in an inner pocket of his rain slicker and retrieving a long strip of red cloth with a small brass medallion hanging from the end. The Watched man in front of him bowed his head slightly, so that Shane could hang the medallion around his neck, saying, "May the Watchers bless you, then."

With the necklace in place, Shane also tied the cloth—a bandana, it seemed—over his face, concealing everything beneath his nose. With him equipped, then, Shane moved a step down the line, repeating his statement and his question again. He carried a medallion for each, and as far as David could tell, the question, 'A sword or a shield?', seemed only to determine what runes were cast in the medal.

When he got to the end of the line and reached Ezra,

Shane looked down at him. "You aren't going to be fighting today, and it'd defeat the point to conceal your identity."

"Give me something to hit them with anyways," Ezra said, reaching out a hand. "In case the Watchers bless me, I want something to toss around."

With a touch of reluctance, Shane passed him a medallion, placing it around his neck like all the others, then turned to David. "No medallions for us, we already have the Watcher's blessings," he said. "Would you like a bandana?"

David shook his head. He'd hidden his face while fighting for a cause once before, he wanted this to be different.

"Then we have only to pick our weapons," Shane said, stepping past David and stretching over an opened crate of fish, sitting on ice. He hefted the crate and set it aside with a grunt, then kicked the lid off the case below, revealing a hidden cache of swords, knives, and revolvers. The revolvers were in holsters, piled to one side, while the swords and knives were piled atop one another in a razor-sharp heap.

"What suits your fancy?" Shane asked. "You've got first choice."

David looked at the case, pausing for a moment as he considered. Shane proffered a revolver in his direction, but that was no good. Revolvers could be effective, but in the chaos of an uncontrolled fight, it'd be too easy to kill someone by accident.

Crouching to search through the crate, David moved aside a few of the loose swords, spotting what he wanted and seizing it by the hilt.

The hook was different from his old one. A long hook, bigger and heavier than his old dueling hook, it'd be more awkward but have superior reach. It wasn't royal steel, either, just plain forged steel, but it'd been polished to a mirror shine and as David held it in a gloved hand it felt right.

Holding the polished blade and testing its balance, David retreated from the case, only then noticing the looks of approval he was getting from the others.

"You know how to use a Watcher's hook?" Shane asked.

David pursed his lips. He didn't approve of the term 'Watcher's hook', since the Watchers did not carry weapons, but that was a difficult distinction to make clear without pulling out his notepad to write it out. Instead, he nodded.

"Sure you're not a Watcher yourself?" Ezra asked. "'Cause your timing seems *awful* convenient. If'n you need to decide who to bless—"

David raised a hand to silence him, then shook his head. He was no god, not by a longshot, and the comparison would be insulting to the gods.

"Everyone else, get armed," Shane said, looking around. "There are only four revolvers, Brenden and Ansyr each get one, we should give the other two to whomever is the best aim."

One at a time, the six Watched all picked their weapons. With the bandanas up, David couldn't tell a one of them apart—only Shane and Ezra were identifiable, both of them lacking anything to conceal their identity.

Taking out his notepad in the lull, David wrote a question. 'Is this everyone?'

Shane looked at the note, lips moving as he read, then said, "No, just everyone who'll be armed. We got the word out, as many people as we could talk to. Hopefully, the whole damned city will be showing up to pitch in with us. The locals of the city, anyways."

David wasn't sure how to feel about that. More people meant that their message was more likely to be heard, but it was also a big crowd of unarmed bystanders. If conflict did break out, there would be a lot of people who would need protection, and not many to protect them. David would have to pull up the extra slack.

Making another note, David said, 'If a fight starts and it looks like we're going to be split up, raise a magical shield that will follow me around. I can keep it charged and stable.'

Reading slowly, Shane sucked in a breath and seemed momentarily embarrassed. "How's that?"

David started to write, and Shane read over his shoulder as he scratched out the note. 'I lost my voice, but I can still control—'

"No, no," Shane said. "A shield that moves. I can raise one, but if I need it somewhere else, I've got to cast another spell."

Looking up in surprise, David watched Shane for a few long moments, then wrote, 'How much do you know about magic?'

"I'm self-taught," Shane said. "I know Sacrosanct, I know some runes, I figured out the rest on my own. It's not as though there's anyone to teach me."

Of course, David thought. He should have used the last three days showing Shane magic, but he'd assumed that Shane was trained, talented, that he knew what he was doing. It simply hadn't occurred to David that someone might have power for four years, but never manage to learn anything about how that power worked. Thinking back, he'd never seen Shane cast an actual spell. The young man might be a rank amateur, for all he knew.

'Raise a big shield before we're split up, then,' David wrote. 'With luck, this won't matter.'

"Let's hope so," Shane said, looking around the room. Their whole entourage was armed, now, holding swords and guns with postures that indicated inexperience. These people could handle themselves, sure, but they didn't have much practice with real weapons. Against unarmed opponents, it'd be an edge, but if they fought real, trained enemies, they'd be all but helpless.

David would have to protect them too, then. Shane as well, if Shane's control of magic was not up to scratch. Nobody else could be relied on. If a true battle broke out inside the city, David would defend the Watched, or nobody would.

CHAPTER 11

... Meanwhile, I've seen thulcuts get almost thirty feet of air after coming out of the water. No idea why they do it, but they can, and with those tentacles whipping everywhere and the barbs around their fins, I think it's safe to say they could do a lot of damage to even the toughest of scales.

So sure, maybe a dragon can fly around and run away, but that fire breath isn't going to do any good against the whole ocean, and if one gets close enough to do anything else the thulcut's just gonna grab it and drag it under.

• Transcript from an argument overheard at a bar, as to whether a dragon or a thulcut would win in a fight.

THE TOWN HALL MEETING WAS, appropriately, held in the town hall. Adelyn had no trouble finding it, asking for directions only once and navigating from there. It was built over the coast, standing entirely over the ocean, decorated with the presidential seal over the large doors leading inside.

Adelyn chewed on her lip, hesitant about going inside. She wasn't sure if she could face David. She hadn't meant to hurt him, only to hold him back until she could explain herself, but she'd still tried to ambush him with magic.

If she didn't pull him out soon enough, he'd get caught up with the Watched bandits. The peace officers might let him go, eventually, but she didn't want to put him through that if it could be helped. Sucking in a breath of sea air, she steeled herself and finally walked inside.

It was crowded, as was much of the city. The hall was at least a hundred feet across in every direction, a gratuitously large building by Adelyn's estimation. An aisle was kept free in the middle to walk through, but aside from that, people were pressed in with no clear delineation between various groups. There were no seats except on a raised stage at the end, and for good reason—the building was packed full, and seats would have only cluttered the place.

The room was heavy with people. Adelyn half expected the floor to break out from under them with every creak and every wave of movement that ran through the crowd, but it held easily. Despite the city's seemingly incoherent, overlapping layout, they built strong buildings.

Those on the right side of the room seemed to be composed more of locals—there were more individuals with dark skin, more wearing dock worker's uniforms, more with the shorter cut of hair popular to the coast. On the left, more formal clothes, more signs of foreign wealth.

She didn't see David, and so pushed her way into the crowd at the left side of the building, leaning against a back wall and watching for his arrival.

...

"Is everyone ready?" Shane asked, addressing the group as a whole, though he made sure to include David with a gesture. "Once we go in, there's no leaving. Abandon us now, if you are going to."

Nobody so much as hesitated. They were dedicated to this venture, they wouldn't be backing out.

Shane nodded, hand resting on the hilt of the sword he wore. It was cast bronze, not even steel, but he had refused to take any other weapon. "Then let's go. Remember—nobody speak. Nobody fight, unless someone attacks you. Nobody should so much as flinch. You're here to protect and defend. I'll make our case. It's not against the law to carry weapons, so if anyone gives you grief for it, just ignore them."

Throwing the double doors open with a flourish of his arms, Shane strode inside, his boots slamming against the floor loud enough to cut through the noise of the crowd. Two of the disguised Watched moved to hold open the doors, so that Ezra could hobble inside on his crutches. Behind that procession, the rest of them walked in, single file, lining up on the right side of the aisle. David stayed at the back of the line, hesitant to go inside.

The people in there were packed dense. He could never watch them all on his own. The buzz of that many people—their noise, their spirit, their body heat—was overwhelming to try and keep track of.

He would have to watch what he could. Taking a moment, he scouted out exits by glancing around. The main double doors were obvious, but there were also single doors placed near the front and back of the hall, matching pairs on the left and right side of the room. If something started, those would be the routes for civilian evacuation. There was no back door; the back wall of this building overlooked the sea, so any door would lead only to a steep, wet drop-off.

If combat began, things would be easier. Fighting had a flow to it. It was unpredictable, but things happened in rational ways, fighters and bystanders responding to fear or pressure or anger or pain.

As he took his place at the far back of the group, filling out the rear guard and ending up in final position by the doors, David had to remind himself that they didn't want any such combat to happen. The goal here was to end conflict, not to start it.

Even with that reminder, though, his ears twitched and his senses reported people and danger in every direction, and he was itching for a fight.

...

Adelyn observed the procession of Watched as they came in, making no attempt to hide the weapons carried on their belts. She spotted David, but he didn't seem to notice her in return, his gaze darting around the room nervously.

I should go over there, she thought. They came bearing pistols and swords. They were obviously ready to fight at the drop of a pin, and Adelyn doubted if they would wait until they were attacked. They would be looking for an excuse to brandish those weapons.

Ezra was visible at the front of the group, obvious without seeing his face because of the crutches he used to come in. He was a puppet, a character to hold up so that they could make their talking points seem more justified. It was possible he honestly was a criminal as well, someone deserving of justice as much as anyone else in that lot.

She looked around the building, trying to identify any peace officers hiding in the wings. Would they come in and arrest the group of Watched now, or wait until after the town hall was over? Looking around, she didn't spot anyone wearing a white uniform or sporting a silver badge, so she assumed they would come after the town hall. She would have time to get David out after all.

...

David was so busy watching for enemies, he almost didn't notice the friend come up in front of him.

"I want you to join us at the front of the group," Shane said. "You're an outsider who helped us. That makes our case stronger."

Hesitant, David glanced around. He wanted to stay at the back, where he could watch the main door and be the most useful, but there was no good way to make that clear. Besides, Shane had a point. They were there to make a case, fighting was a secondary consideration.

Following Shane, he walked up the aisle, taking a place next to Ezra.

"Ready to kick some Divine bastards into the ocean, Davey?" Ezra asked, voice pitched for friendly ears only.

"We're not here to fight," Shane said. "We're here to talk. Stand up straight."

"My leg's broke," Ezra complained.

"Your crutches seem unhurt," Shane hissed back. "We need to look presentable. Stand up straight."

David found himself automatically questioning his own posture, making sure his own back was straight and that his hands were at his side. He could hear muttering nearby from the left of the aisle, people whispering about the weapons and the masks, but he shut that out, concentrating on the task at hand.

At the front of the crowd, he saw a new danger. This many people, agitated and rowdy, could be more dangerous than any sword. If a riot broke out, the weapon-bearing Watched wouldn't be fighting their way out, they'd be press ganged into service as riot police, acting as a barrier between the two groups. They were a thin barrier, but hopefully they'd last long enough for the exits to be utilized, so that those who were there only to voice their opinion in a public forum would be able to escape.

A tall man in a tailored suit walked onto the stage.

"That's the mayor," Shane whispered, for David's benefit. "We didn't elect him, he was appointed here about six years ago, since we refused to surrender until the end of the war. Didn't trust us to pick our own leadership."

David nodded in appreciation for the explanation, watching as the mayor shouted for everyone to quiet down.

...

"Quiet down, quiet down!"

Adelyn watched a well-dressed man shout for the room to grow silent. From the back, she could only barely hear him, but as the chatter and murmurings of the room grew silent, she began to understand him better.

"You all know why we're here!" he called, voice still raised to carry. "To discuss the hiring of new peace officers. The proposition was posted a week ago, now we're going to hear what you all have to say. Those of you who want to speak, raise your hand, I'll pick you, you'll say your piece. But first, there are a few things I'd like to say."

Adelyn's attention faded as he dove into a speech about civic duties, something utterly pointless that he likely proclaimed before every such town hall. Her attention wandered around the room, and she noticed a couple things.

The doors on her side of the hall had been opened, letting in a cool breeze that helped combat the stifling heat of the crowd. However, the main double doors were shut, as were the others on the far side of the hall.

This wasn't much of an oddity, but it was enough to draw her attention. Straightening, she looked around, trying to determine the source of the discrepancy.

Maybe it's someone's job to open all the doors, and they haven't gotten around yet? But if that's it, why'd they shut the front door?

...

"Something's wrong," Shane whispered, leaning in towards David, low enough that even Ezra couldn't hear. David just barely picked it up, and then only because Shane's lips were mere inches from his ear. "There's never a speech before the people speak. He's stalling."

David frowned, piecing together the logic behind what Shane was implying. If the mayor was delaying, that meant he was waiting for something to happen.

Eyes darting around the room, David sought out the ambush. There had to be one, he just didn't know what it was yet.

Doors. The ones on the far end of the room were open, but the rest were shut. They were cutting off the exits. Those on the Watched side of the room were going to be fish in a barrel.

We have to go, David thought. They couldn't wait for this trap to spring. Frantic, he started to sign, but Shane quickly shook his head.

"I don't know what that means," he said.

Groaning in frustration, David's hands fumbled at the pouch on his belt that held his notepad, digging it out so that he could write the warning. Shane could see something was wrong, but he didn't know the extent of what was about to happen.

Fingers taking the pencil, David started to write, but before he could finish the note, the double doors of the main entrance were thrown open, and a peace officer shouted a word in command.

"Fire!"

...

Adelyn heard the shout, then watched in abject horror as a volley of rifle fire was released into the line of Watched.

The lead balls were aimed primarily at the long row of armed, masked Watched, but they took no special care with their aim, except to fire only to the right side of the meeting hall. Bullets ripped through the first four people in line, tearing ragged holes in their bodies and flying through into the crowd of locals who were gathered beyond.

From across the room, Adelyn felt a sudden burst of spirit. Not the focused power of a spell, just an untamed wave of energy that poured into the air, as much power as Adelyn could remember ever having felt in a single place.

Frozen, she stared on, barely hearing the screams of the people around her. People turned to flee, flooding out the two doors that were open.

Across the aisle, the people there turned to do the same, but found their doors blocked. Pressing against each other, the crowd swarmed into itself, finding no escape.

She watched and listened, frozen from action, as someone outside gave the order to fire again.

...

There was nothing anyone could do to stop the first wave of bullets that ripped into his companions, and there was nothing David could do without magic to stop the second round. He felt the energy lash out into the air as someone died to the volley, giving up their spirit in a way so tangible that it drowned out his sixth sense for a split second.

Shane was quicker on the draw. He drew that bronze sword of his, and the runes carved into it glinted and were suffused with power which only a sorcerer could feel as he pointed the blade and shouted, *"Ansyr!"*

Bullets fired, but bounced off the shield with little effect. David could feel the spell from all the way across the room, and knew it was a horrible waste of power—Shane lacked finesse, and had made up for it with raw strength. It was strong, but poorly made, and was hemorrhaging spirit with every second. That would work for now, but Shane would exhaust himself in pitched combat.

There were a small army of peace officers outside, though David couldn't count them past the throng of people and the doorway that blocked his vision. He felt another burst of immense spirit as someone else died, the power so tangible that David could have pulled it straight from the air if he'd wanted to.

"Slow them!" Shane shouted, not to David, but to all those under his command who were still standing. "I'll get the civilians out!"

Nobody had to be told twice. The magic shield Shane had raised in the doorway would last for another volley, maybe two, and that was enough for David to turn and charge. Building speed, David unclipped the hook from around his belt, running straight into the next volley, trusting Shane's shield to protect him.

He didn't count how many of the Watched were with him. Stopping to check on his allies would mean letting the shield expire, and giving up the charge.

Feeling himself reach the shield, David lashed out with his free hand, pulling the energy out of the air and depositing it in the necklace he wore, simply lacking anywhere else to put it. The firing line of what he now saw were fifteen peace officers, in the middle of chambering another round in their repeating rifles, were not ready for him.

He'd sworn never to take a life, but that didn't mean he

had to hold back in this fight. He trusted that his weapons were not inherently lethal, and that he wasn't going to have a chance to get in a powerful blow even if he intended to.

The first peace officer in the line got struck across the face with David's hook without even trying to dodge, and his expression showed more surprise than pain as he got knocked to the ground. Nobody expected a lone man to charge fifteen, and that's why David was able to breach their firing line at all.

They were trained riflemen, but clumsy fighters in hand to hand, and David exploited that for all it was worth. His spirit sense let him feel every attack as it came in, and subtle body movements were enough to dodge most of the punches and kicks thrown his way. A few would be trying to draw a bead with their rifles, but as surrounded as he was by officers, they'd shoot their friends before striking him.

Normally, he would have strung them out in a line, fighting a few at a time, using their numbers against them. Right now, he didn't care. They'd just fired into a crowd of civilians, and David needed to buy those civilians time to escape. He allowed himself to be surrounded, driving fierce kicks into any exposed flesh he could find, using his long hook as defense.

He missed his own weapon. A shorter hook would have come in much handier in the close throng he immediately found himself in, but the long hook he'd acquired was too awkward, too clunky. Better than nothing, but not ideal.

It was a process of seconds to go from a brutal charge to being fully surrounded, fighting desperately to ward off blows from peace officers who'd finally drawn mauls and clubs to strike back, but that was fine by David. He knew he would never win this fight.

He only had to draw their attention long enough for the other Watched to come support him.

By charging like a madman and fighting with the fury of an army, he'd scattered their ranks, broken their firing line, and distracted more than half the officers in one fell swoop. The band of Watched had mismatched weapons and little battle discipline, but they didn't need discipline to charge in after him, swords and knives swinging, revolvers barking in harmony as they shot into the officers.

The tide of the fight quickly changed. Though still outnumbered three to one, the Watched had momentum, and they had swords and revolvers against cudgels and rifles that were too long to be of use in close quarters.

David extricated himself with a few quick turns, letting the melee play out for a moment as he ran back inside to see what was going on.

Shane had blown a hole in the wall. He looked positively exhausted, but he'd used a spell to break out a chunk of the wall eight feet high and half again as wide. David could see now that heavy crates had been stacked up against the true doors, blocking them, but that no longer mattered—the people were able to flow out the new makeshift exit in a rush, scrambling to flee the scene of the fight.

For his part, Shane was kneeling by the injured, blood on his hands as he held one of them. Two people with masks had been killed, one more was lying on the ground and spluttering. More civilians were on the ground, whether dead or alive David wasn't certain. He felt a burst of spirit outside and knew that someone had been killed, but there was no way of telling which side they were on.

Ezra was looking around in confusion, uncertain what to do. He was unarmed, he couldn't run or fight with his injured leg, but he was unwilling to abandon Shane and run with the other civilians.

"Cowards!" Shane shouted, though his voice carried more despair than anger, and David wasn't certain if he was yelling about the people fleeing when they could help, or the peace officers who'd ambushed them. His hand was gripping the survivor's tightly, as though by holding on he could ensure that they wouldn't slip away into death.

David had no inspiring speeches to give. The momentum outside wouldn't carry for long, and in order to win this, they'd need a sorcerer. Grabbing Shane by the arm, David heaved him to his feet and pointed forcefully at the door.

Shane got the point. Exhausted though he was, he pulled the spirit from the blood on his hands, loaded it into his sword, and charged out to join the fray.

David ran after him, planning to rejoin the melee, but as he ran outside he felt something new that changed the math of the fight.

Power, in mass quantities, being readied for a spell. It wasn't coming from Shane, though, it was coming from—

Shouting out in warning, David spun to face the peace officer's witch who had just arrived on scene.

CHAPTER 12

When you're fighting a magic user, traditional theory says to get in close. Even a novice can raise a shield that will block bullets or arrows, but blocking three pounds of sharpened steel is another matter entirely.

Unfortunately, this traditional theory has its own gaps. Modern combat magi have learned to use their sixth sense to enhance their combat reflexes, and craft magic into solid weapons, creating a melee threat far more dangerous than they already were at range. In times like these, the best practice seems to be to run, and live to fight another day.

•Essay on combat magic and defense, taken from the Presidential Archives in Triom

DAVID HAD NEVER MET the witch before, but he could sense the danger from her on sight. Her head was shaved beneath a wide brimmed hat, and she wore a long leather jacket decorated with runes, armored strike plates on her chest.

Her weapons were traditional magic tools, a lengthy staff

in one hand, a trio of wands held between the fingers of the other hand like claws. From her grip, and her posture, she knew exactly what she was doing with those wands.

Heart sinking, David took his hook in both hands and raised it in a defensive posture against her. He couldn't count on backup. Even with Shane's power, the Watched would be lucky to handle the peace officers alone, much less a trained witch.

It was up to him.

Roaring a wordless battle cry, he charged at her from twenty paces away. He could feel the spirit radiating from her staff, so bright to his senses that it drowned out all else. Whatever she was preparing, he wanted to close with her and cut it off before she could cast the spell.

The witch bared her teeth in a grin as she saw him coming. David knew the reflex. In the war, he'd had dozens of heroic fools who thought they could charge in and kill the Blue Flame before he could respond. She seemed to think that David was just another one of those fools.

If she blasted him with the big spell she was preparing, there was little David could do. But if she took him for harmless, and tried to go for something more conservative...

The witch flicked out the hand holding her wands and hissed a brief chant. Energy coalesced into matter, and something dark and gelatinous flew towards David like a thrown projectile, wobbling slightly in the air as though it were barely contained, trying to burst out of its skin.

Perfect.

Twisting his hook, David positioned it, readying for the dark matter to splash against the steel, trusting that the metal would sap the strength from the magic and weaken it enough for him to get by.

As the blob of energy neared the blade, the witch

twisted her hand up and called another word, and the spell's form split, passing by David's hook without ever touching the metal. A hint of energy was wicked away in the process, but not nearly what David had been hoping for.

Whoever this witch was, she was good. Her magic splashed out in four directions, striking David at the wrists and ankles, and as soon as it touched his skin, it gained weight and mass. He dropped to the ground, the weight of small boulders suddenly pulling his limbs down, making wood splinter as he fell. His hook went flying. Where the dark energy hit the boards of the street, they stuck and held fast, clinging in place to further impede any chance of escape.

If she'd meant to kill him, he would have been dead. Sparing him was a mistake on her part. David couldn't cast a counterspell, but this magic was being fueled by raw spirit. He could feel the power buzzing, giving form to the heavy blobs of dark energy, and if he could feel it, he could use it.

Sapping the power from the spell, David rolled to the side and drew the side knife from his belt, throwing it at the witch to distract her a moment.

She'd been ready to cast the spell from her staff, but upon seeing David break free, she swore in confusion and returned her attention to him.

"How?" the witch shouted, as she batted his knife from the air with a word. Her tone was confused, but not as angry or upset as David had wanted—he was still five paces away, and needed her off her guard long enough to come to grips.

She wasn't going to give him that chance. No longer content to simply restrain him with a spell from her wand, the witch spun her staff, shouting a mouthful of words as quick as she could to release her spell into the world.

Ten black needles as long as a man's arm burst into

sudden reality, and David's reflexes, already honed by years of training, seemed to stop time for a second as he watched his doom play out.

He was about to die. It was unclear how those needles would kill him, but it was perfectly obvious that they would get the job done. Diverting one needle might be possible, maybe even two, but she'd apparently decided that it was better to take out the primary threat first and deal with the others later, so the black points turned and sped forward like a whole quiver of arrows towards David's head.

Shane was too far away, too distracted, too inexperienced to help. Even if he knew that David needed a shield, he wouldn't be able to raise something in time.

David didn't even bother raising his sword to block the bolts. It didn't matter. Even if he could block two, or three bolts, that left seven to skewer him like a kebab.

He turned to dodge to the side, rolling out of the way, but the bolts were so fast, and they turned to follow, barely caring as he juked out of the way. He'd sucked energy into the shield necklace he wore, but that was as useless as the roll without a voice to cast spells. They were feet away, and all that was left to do was throw his hands in front of his face in a stupid, desperate gesture that was worth less than nothing.

Energy suffused him, a wash of spirit that surrounded him like an eggshell. Powerful defensive magic, layered on itself so that if the first shield was punched through, a second barrier was there to take the impact, and a third, and a fourth.

That was beyond Shane's ability. In fact, it was a trick David had once used, before he was confident enough in his defensive magic to block attacks off individually and forgo broad spectrum shields entirely.

The lances of dark power splashed against the barrier and splashed into smoke, breaking like water against a beach. They were incredibly precise magic, but each carried fairly little force on its own, and the shield was made of a bulwark of spirit strong enough to withstand the attack ten times over.

David heaved a sigh of incredible relief as he looked for the source of that shield, but he already knew who'd cast it. Adelyn had entered the fray.

...

Adelyn felt lightheaded for a moment as she recovered from the shield she'd thrown up. She had no idea how strong the magic spears were that had been launched against David, so she'd gone with the strongest barrier she knew how to put up. That meant forgoing energy or even blood, and using her memories to fuel the shield.

It wasn't as dramatic as it sounded, because she'd memorized passages from a Divine holy book for this very purpose, but it was still a one-trick pony. She wouldn't have the strength to use that spell again until she memorized more holy passages, but it had done its job.

Coming out of the double doors, she looked between the two fights. The Watched looked like they were struggling against the peace officers, but as far as Adelyn was concerned, David came first.

The witch looked confused, which was perfect. It gave Adelyn the chance to run over, scooping up David's hook off the ground and tossing it to him. "Getting yourself killed again?" she called.

David's expression flickered for a moment, but settled on a grin. Maybe it was only because she'd saved his life, but at least he was happy to see her.

"Hey, witch!" Adelyn shouted, facing the woman who'd

tried to kill David. "It's two on one now! Sure you don't want to back off?"

In response, the witch sank into a low stance, jammed her three wands into slots on her belt, and raised her staff. Sharp black energy coalesced around the staff, black mist growing and then hardening into a razor's edge, turning the length of wood into a functional greatsword longer than the witch was tall.

Adelyn swallowed. That was new.

...

David held out his hook, watching the witch arm herself with magic, his own weapon no longer feeling particularly long in comparison.

He'd seen this technique before, using magic to create weapons. It was not something David favored using himself. If he wanted a sword, he'd bring a sword and save himself the spirit it took to manifest a weapon. Still, it had its advantages—you could create weapons of impossible size without having to worry about weight, and you could punch through shields far more easily than with plain blasts of force.

Pulling the silver chain from around his neck, he held it out to Adelyn, never taking his eyes off the witch. She didn't need the tool to defend herself, she had her bracelets, but he'd channelled spirit into the necklace on reflex, and she'd be able to use it.

As Adelyn accepted the chain, the witch charged, sweeping her sword like a bat, coat swirling around her. Fighting against a sword almost seven feet long wasn't a common martial style, and David had to improvise to defend it. He swung his hook to meet the blade, praying that it had physical form, and was pleased when steel met spirit with a 'clang'.

Twisting, he hoped to wrench the greatsword away, but

instead the steel of his weapon simply broke off the tip of the greatsword, shattering the end of the blade like glass. The witch pulled back, muttered a word, and her greatsword reformed into its full length with a puff of black smoke. Meanwhile, his own sword had managed to stay in one piece, but there was a large melted chunk just below the hooked end of the blade. Even steel wasn't a perfect defense, and if he kept whacking his blade against hers, he'd end up without a weapon before too long.

No disarming her, then.

Leaping to the side, David tried to flank her. Surrounding a witch wasn't as useful as a normal soldier, she'd be able to sense his motions and feel his movements no matter where he stood, but she couldn't attack in every direction.

Adelyn took his lead, moving in the opposite direction, her hands raised, ready to cast a shield should the witch attack again. She threw in an attack of force, trying to hit the witch while her back was turned, but the witch whipped back around and threw up a shield of her own, protecting against the clumsy magic projectile.

Realizing what they were doing, the witch responded immediately, stabbing out in David's direction so that he had to parry and back off, then swinging around her magic sword with tremendous speed. There was no weight to the blade, so she was able to whip it around in a full half circle in the span of an eyeblink.

Adelyn yelped and shouted the word for a shield. The sword hit and was slowed enough for Adelyn to duck out of the way, but as David tried to charge in, the witch had already regained control and spun it around wildly, not even aiming, slapping him on the arm with the flat of the blade.

The attack carried him off his feet and sent David flying, kicking up dust and splinters where he landed.

David could feel the buzz of spirit in the air, explaining the half of the fight he couldn't see. Adelyn was trying her best to pitch in, launching spells of force and heat, trying to land a solid blow. The witch was responding in kind with invisible shields, not even facing Adelyn as she shut down the attacks. Without his sixth sense, it'd have looked as though Adelyn was simply waving her arms uselessly while David did all the combat, but in truth, the witch was fighting off attacks from two opponents, and she was winning easily.

The long hook was still gripped in his left hand—his prosthetic thumb locked in place over it, and wouldn't come loose simply because he had his senses knocked out of him for a moment. He came up swinging, roaring out a battle cry and throwing his hook into a powerful attack that was aimed for the witch's head.

Sensing his attack coming in, she ducked back and swung her magic blade in a low attack meant to take off his ankles. He leapt at her, sword arm off to the side, but his free hand ready and available to punch her right in the jaw. Her sword struck the dock underneath him and barely slowed as it cut through the boards.

He realized his mistake too late. The diving tackle was fast and powerful, but he couldn't control his momentum in the air. There was nothing to push off of. His hook was off to one side, still held loosely in his hand, too far away to be much use in defending his face.

There was nothing he could do when, less than a foot from slamming into the witch, she shouted, *"Shtap!"* and swatted him down like a fly.

Her attack was clumsy compared to the sharp bolts of

energy, no doubt thrown out on reflex, but it did its job. Force hit him in the small of his back, and David dropped to the ground, slamming into floorboards. His chin hit, and a tooth cracked as he bit down hard from the impact.

...

Adelyn tried throwing another bolt of force at the witch, but it was blocked with little more effect than any of the others had. The limitation of her magic tools was becoming plain—she had nothing to attack with that couldn't be blocked by the most basic of shields. Heat, force, these things would win a usual fight, but they were easy to block with a barrier made of spirit.

She could wear the witch down, maybe, force her to go toe-to-toe and match spell for spell. That could tire her out, but only if the witch played fair and didn't try to stop Adelyn from going for the most obvious ploy in the book. The witch didn't seem like she was going to comply, whipping around that massive sword of hers and forcing Adelyn to dodge back.

David was dazed on the ground. There was no help coming there, not right away. Adelyn had to win this on her own terms.

Raising her hand, she changed tactics, channeling power into the air bracelet and whipping up a windstorm. The witch could block force and fire, but maybe—

No luck. The witch barely had to even respond, adjusting her shield ever so slightly and killing the wind in a heartbeat.

The witch started to move in for another attack, raising her magic sword for a wide sweep, but before Adelyn had to figure out how to respond, the witched stopped and spun.

The peace officers were done for. The boards of the road

were slick with blood and bodies. They hadn't gone down without a struggle. More than one of the Watched was on the ground, too, but once Shane had pitched in, the tides had turned. Only a tiny pocket of resistance still stood, two peace officers standing back to back, fighting off six Watched on their own.

Adelyn swore, trying to throw another attack at the witch, but the witch ignored her and stalked towards the more important fray.

"Run!" Adelyn called to the Watched, stopping to check on David. He was dazed, but not dead, so she took his hook and left him.

Shane saw the witch stalking towards them at a comfortable pace, but called back to Adelyn, "I'm not leaving the injured!"

"There's no choice!" Adelyn shouted back, running towards him.

The witch, holding her sword out in one hand, drew a wand and flicked it back towards Adelyn with an arrogant lack of care. Gelatinous energy flew towards her and, before Adelyn could dodge, struck her on the chest, sticking in place and growing tremendously in weight.

Adelyn frantically tried to pull the sticky energy away as the weight of it drug her to her knees, before realizing the simpler solution and simply draining the spell of power. It slowed her down, though, and before she could catch up, the witch had reached the fight.

Shane tried to turn her away, but his magic sword was bronze, not steel, and when the witch flicked out her massive blade in a swipe, his weapon was thrown from his hands, skittering to a stop by the town hall's open doors.

Adelyn caught up, trying to drive in at the witch with David's hook, but the witch spun and parried that attack away before twisting back towards the Watched, warping the damaged weapon even further. Her black blade went past Shane, hitting one of the others who were still busy fighting the police.

The blade cut halfway through its victim's side, sticking firmly in place and eliciting a scream of pain and horror. If it had been a true sword, it might have been stuck there, but the witch twisted, letting the end of the weapon shatter off and turn to smoke, then pulled her arm away and rebuilt the blade to its full length.

Adelyn tightened her grip on the hook, trying not to look at all the blood. "I'll distract her! Get out of here!" she shouted, swinging the hook at the witch a second time. With this attack, though, the witch didn't even bother blocking, she simply stepped forward out of Adelyn's reach.

Shane looked like he wanted to argue, but he conceded the point and repeated her suggestion. "Run!"

The four standing Watched needed only the permission. They turned and fled, leaving the last peace officer holding a club against nobody.

The witch sent a few simple spells after them, more blobs of gelatinous power, but Adelyn was at least able to block those attacks and let the few standing Watched escape. She was getting tired, the magic making her exhausted, but the blood on the ground provided all the spirit she could need for the time being.

"You run too!" Adelyn shouted to Shane. She had her misgivings about him, but this trap had been her fault, and she wasn't going to let him die because of it.

Shane shook his head, but before he could shout a response he was forced to dive to the ground to avoid another sweep of that massive black sword.

Adelyn came in again, throwing energy through her

bracelet so that the witch would have to defend against both magic and the hook at the same time. Adelyn couldn't hit the witch, but she could be enough of a nuisance that the witch couldn't completely ignore her.

She has to be getting tired, Adelyn thought, sweeping her hook down in a wide arc that would shatter the magic blade, leaving the witch defenseless for the half second it took to reform.

The witch dismissed the magic holding the blade together, leaving only a short staff in her hand. Adelyn's attack hit nothing but air, swinging down with far too much momentum to stop easily, slamming the hook into the ground where the warped metal finally snapped, leaving Adelyn with only half a sword. Seeing the opening, the witch dove in with a stabbing motion, throwing magic at Adelyn's chest from an inch away.

Black force hit her and she stumbled back, her lungs on fire. She couldn't breathe. It felt as though her lungs had been filled with cement, forcing out all the air to make room for quickly hardening rock.

She tried to gasp, but couldn't inhale. She could feel the spirit crackling in her chest, and sapped away the energy in a panic, but even as the rock in her lungs vanished, the breath she could bring in was short and weak, and it ached to try.

Coughing, she tasted blood in her mouth, and though the witch had turned back to face Shane, Adelyn threw up a shield with a slurred word and stumbled away.

The last peace officer, at least, had seen fit to flee to a safe distance rather than continue fighting, so it was only the witch left, standing over all the dead and injured bodies with her massive sword.

Three magic users had fought the witch, but none of them could do more than slow her down. David was back on his feet but moving slowly, Adelyn could hardly breathe for the pain in her chest, and though Shane was uninjured, he had no weapons left and was dodging away from the witch's sword with no way to fight back.

Ezra threw one of his crutches at the witch. It was a stupid, clumsy attack that didn't even hit, but it got her attention for a second.

"Hey, you, Divine hyp-oh-crite piece of ass!" he shouted, from the open doors of the town hall, standing on his other crutch and his one good leg, his hand raised with fingers twisted into a symbol that Adelyn would have recognized long before she learned to sign. "Aren't you supposed to hate magic?"

That got the witch's attention a little better, though she kept her sword pointed towards Shane.

For the first time since the fight had started, the witch shouted back. "I'm not Divine! I'm Tarraganian."

Adelyn swallowed guiltily, and didn't miss the sidelong glance that Shane gave her.

"The hell are you helpin' them for, then?" Ezra crouched to pick up Shane's sword, waving it at the witch wildly, as though to stave her off.

"I'm fighting for the country, not the Divine," the witch shouted back.

"Can I tell you somethin'?" Ezra asked. It was ridiculous, and everyone there knew it. This was a distraction, a desperate attempt to delay the witch long enough for everyone else to catch their breath.

The witch didn't respond. She was, it seemed, done with questions. She moved towards Shane, swinging her blade in a killing blow. Once he was dead, then it would be quick work to kill Adelyn, and then David, and then probably Ezra and the other Watched as well.

Ezra grinned stupidly, pointing the sword at the witch, and shouting, "*Shtap!*"

CHAPTER 13

Honestly, we've got no idea. Best guesses place the number at around eight hundred, but those are loose at best. It's hard to take per-capita measurements, because some places just have a lot more magic in them than others, so to speak. High estimates are just above a thousand, with the low end coming in at around five hundred, but it all depends on how you measure and what time frame you're looking at. Interesting thing is, though, best as we can tell the number of sorcerers isn't relative to population. Reports from a century, even two centuries ago show that the estimates were about the same as they are today, and there's never been a record of more than a thousand or so sorcerers coexisting at the same time.

• From lecture on the nature of magic, responding to the question, "How many sorcerers are there?"

THE SPELL WHIPPED out of the sword with enthusiastic force. It wasn't refined or elegant. In fact, it was one of the most brutish, crude pieces of magic David had witnessed in a long time, but it was also an unwatched terror of raw power.

It struck the witch, it struck the ground around her, it struck a half dozen downed peace officers and a few of the Watched besides. The witch shielded herself from the worst of it, staggering only a little from the blow, but as her attention was swayed, Shane snatched one of the necklaces off of a bleeding companion and threw a quick blast of force at her. It was weaker than Ezra's by far, but it forced the witch to raise a second shield.

David staggered closer, head still ringing, and watched Adelyn pitch in another attack. It was also easily blocked, but the trio of spells coming in and the energy cost were clearly taking their toll.

Ezra shouted another spell, weaker than the last but no less brutish, and the deck of the street shook. "Had enough yet?"

The witch narrowed her gaze, whipping around her staff, reforming the sword to lash out at Adelyn, but Adelyn danced back and parried away with the hook she'd taken up. The defense clearly pained her, and she was sent into a coughing fit, but before the witch could follow up, blasts of scattered force came at her from behind and to her side, and she had to shield herself against them.

Shaking his head clear, David made it to Adelyn's side, taking his hook from her and sinking into a defensive pose.

Looking between the four of them, the witch seemed to think it out. No matter who she went after, there would be attacks coming from all sides. Her blasts of magic could be shut down, and it seemed she wasn't efficient enough to trade spell for spell against three people while fighting a fourth in hand to hand.

The witch ran.

Ezra started hobbling after her as boots pounded on the street, but Shane held up a hand. "Don't. We need to leave before more peace officers can arrive. Just get to Solden's shop, for now."

Ezra nodded, but still shouted after the witch, "You'd better run!"

"Congratulations on the blessing, by the way," Shane added, kneeling to check on the wounded, pausing long enough to look around at the Watched who were still standing. "Ansyr?"

In response, Ansyr pulled off her bandana, showing her face. "I'm fine."

Breathing a sigh of relief, Shane stood, announcing loudly and to nobody in particular. "If you can move under your own power, get ready to move out. If you need help, ask for it now."

"Your leg," Adelyn commented to Ezra, noting that he had abandoned his crutches but was still limping along.

"It's not so bad as it looked," Ezra explained. "We were playin' it up a bit. I can walk well enough."

The street was deserted. The sounds of gunfire and combat and screaming had apparently delivered a clear message to the people of the city, and so they'd abandoned the area for now.

Scavengers looking for scraps to steal would show up soon, and then peace officers who were called in as backup when the first wave obviously failed, and then life would return to normal. In hours, this fight would be remembered only by the bloody stain on the floorboards and the repair crew working to fix the town hall.

David felt tired and his body ached, but he had two good arms and two good legs, so after getting a thumbs up from Adelyn to show she didn't need his immediate help, he went inside to check on the wounded there.

He found five bodies inside, three of whom were dead.

The fourth was Efrin, and it was clear from the holes in her chest and side that she wasn't going to make it. She gave him a pleading look, but when she tried to ask for help all that came out was a bloody cough.

David stared at her for a moment, caught in indecision. He couldn't move her, and it was painfully obvious that no amount of medical attention would help given all the blood she'd lost already. There was nothing he could do to help, and so he regretfully tore his gaze away from her and checked on the lone survivor who was still inside.

This survivor was a middle aged man. He'd only taken a lead shot through his thigh, and it had missed any major arteries. He couldn't walk, but David retrieved Ezra's second crutch, and with that the man was able to hobble under his own power.

"Any of ours?" Shane asked, looking up at David as he helped the man out onto the road. David shook his head somberly, and Shane swore. "Bastards. They knew we were going to be here, they didn't give us a chance."

David did the counting in his head. Four dead inside. Another three Watched dead out here, plus it looked like at least half a dozen peace officers—several more of the officers had fled, and a good number were on the ground, clearly playing dead, or bad enough injured that they couldn't care anymore. They were ignored, for now, since they posed no threat. Thirteen dead in total.

He'd seen much worse violence, but the killing made him clench his fists in anger. He'd come here to protect these people, and failed miserably. Thirteen dead was thirteen too many. If he was this useless without magic, it would have been better for him to stand in the way of the bullets as a human shield.

Brenden was still alive, though his arm was broken and

he'd been clubbed over the head hard enough to knock him out for most of a minute. When asked where he was, he gave a nonsense answer, but he was able to stand and walk, so Ezra left him and helped the other surviving Watched, who'd been shot through the belly.

"Just us, then," Shane said. "You know where we're going. No time to lose."

...

Adelyn followed along in their bloody parade, gaze lingering on the bodies they were leaving behind. There were so many dead. Not all of them had even been train robbers.

She'd called this in. She'd told the peace officers to show up. This was all because of her.

Trudging after the others, taking shallow breaths because it hurt to do anything else, she tried to excuse what she'd done.

I didn't know they'd show up with guns. They were supposed to stop the fighting, not start it. I didn't—

She didn't believe it.

This wasn't her first time witnessing death. In point of fact, she'd most likely killed someone when they were rescuing her town from those raiders in the Beor Keep, but that had been more bloodless than this, and it had gone by too fast for anything to stick with her. She'd had nightmares about that night for a while, but those were nightmares of being trapped in dark halls, or being burned alive in endless fire.

This was different. Seeing those people—innocents, bystanders, helpless victims—gunned down, left to bleed out or try and crawl away, wasn't the same by a long shot.

And it had been her fault.

...

It was slow going by normal standards, but quick considering the damage they'd all sustained. Shane was the only one among them still relatively whole and unhurt. They brought the injured man who was borrowing Ezra's crutch, which made seven of them in total that showed up at the fish market looking for refuge.

Solden was working at her shop, but when she saw the party, she paled. "I heard the gunfire. Are you okay?"

"We need shelter," Shane said, looking up and down the docks to see if anyone was coming after them. "Quickly."

Solden chewed her lip. "Peace officers won't care much about the money I give them, not with all this."

"We won't be here for long," Shane said quickly. "We'll slip out the back. If they give you trouble over it, I'll pay you back the extra cost."

She mulled it over, chewing on her cheek, then spat on the ground and said, "You know I wouldn't turn you out. Get in here."

Shane nodded gratefully, and Solden opened the door to let them in.

The usual thrill and euphoria that followed a good fight was nowhere to be found. David was sad and angry and tired. There'd been nothing good about that brawl, from its origins to its ending, and now he wanted to find a quiet place where he could curl up in a ball and sleep.

Adelyn came in behind him, though, and coughed blood into her hand, which told him that such a peaceful thought wouldn't be possible.

'You're hurt,' he signed to her, as the door was shut.

"It's noth—" Adelyn coughed again, grimacing in pain, then chose to sign rather than to speak. 'It's nothing.'

'You're coughing up blood,' David pointed out. 'Ask Shane if he knows of a doctor who can help.'

'Almost everyone here needs a doctor,' Adelyn signed back quickly. 'I don't need help as badly as some.'

David gritted his teeth, feeling a space where one of his incisors had chipped, then pulled out his notepad and wrote a message for Shane. 'Adelyn is coughing up blood and needs medical attention.'

Shane read the note, then looked at her. "I know a couple people," he said. "But I don't know how much they can help. I am going to call for them anyways, but it has to wait until we can make it to the safe house."

'Anything is good,' David wrote. 'How long will that take?'

"We're all no doubt wanted, now," Shane explained. "I can't say. It won't be quick."

David would have drug Adelyn straight over to Harrington's medical center and damn the man if he refused to help, but it was probable that the known places of medicine were being watched. He nodded, then turned back to Adelyn. 'We're getting you help.'

Adelyn nodded absently, taking light breaths. "Is... is there a bathroom here?"

Shane glanced at Solden, who stepped in to give directions. "To the right in the back office. Don't mess with anything in there."

Adelyn nodded, quickly picking her way through the room and exiting in that direction.

"Ezra," Shane said, as she left. "I don't suppose your blessing came with any stunning insight on how to heal people with magic?"

"Sorry, Shane," Ezra said, shaking his head. "Only insight that came to me was that I should probably teach that witch outside a lesson."

Shane nodded. "We're going to need bandages, then.

Our supplies are all back in the safe house, but..." He paused, head bobbing from side to side as he thought it over, then turned to David. "There are towels in the bathroom."

David nodded, turning to obey.

...

Adelyn wiped at her face and eyes, sobbing in great, painful chokes. It hurt to cry, but she couldn't keep it in any longer. Her sleeve came away from her face, smeared with blood, snot, and tears.

She'd held it together long enough to get to safety, and then a little longer to find somewhere private, but that was all she had in her. This was too much. It wasn't what she'd wanted, she just—

A knock came at the bathroom door. Two quick raps, then two long ones.

David had insisted on working out a couple knocks in case he needed to tell her something but couldn't sign. That knock was simply, "I need in, it's urgent".

Sniffling, she heaved a painful breath, climbing to her feet. She tried to clean her face a little, but that was a hopeless task. "C-come in," she stammered, her voice cracking.

The door swung open. David stood there, staring at Adelyn's face a moment, taking in the tears.

He didn't say anything. Instead, he stepped around her, opening the cupboard below the sink. Nestled between a few pipes were a large stack of wash towels, which he picked up and carried away, leaving Adelyn standing in the bathroom door.

A few moments passed, and she could feel more sobs building deep in her chest. Before they could manifest, David walked back in, shutting first the office door, then crossing into the small bathroom door and shutting that as well.

They stood like that, facing each other for a long moment. David opened his arms, holding them out, letting Adelyn choose whether or not she'd return the embrace.

She seized him and pulled into a tight hug. David wrapped his arms around her as the sobs began anew, splashing tears that soaked through his cotton shirt.

They stood there, Adelyn's face buried in his shoulder, her vision dark and blurry, her arms gripping him so tight it was probably painful. David shared in the hug for as long as she did, a comforting center for her to hold onto.

His shirt collar was a mess when she pulled away, and in the bathroom mirror she could see that the wrinkled cloth had left imprints on her forehead and cheeks. Her chest still hurt and her mouth tasted of iron, but that was nothing by the pain she felt in her heart.

"I... it's my fault," she said, looking down at the floor. David would avoid her eye contact anyways, but she couldn't look him in the face.

In her peripheral, she saw him shake his head in reassurance, but she cut him off with a raised hand. Her voice was barely a whisper, nothing that would carry, as she said, "I c-called in the peace officers. I told them the train r-robbers would..." She couldn't finish the sentence. She'd managed to get out the important thing.

David stared at her, eyes studying her face, trying to determine something, maybe to come up with words of comfort that'd make her feel better.

"Go on, tell me I'm wrong. Tell me it's not my fault." Adelyn said, not wanting the comfort. She wanted David to get mad, to kick her to the floor and then throw her into the street. She didn't deserve his comfort. "You can't. You can't, because that'd be a li—"

'It is your fault,' David signed, simply, but without anger. 'I am so, so sorry.'

Wiping at her nose, Adelyn stared at him in confusion. Their eyes met for half a second before he looked away, staring instead at the smeared blood on her cheeks. "W-what?"

David hesitated before responding, considering his signs. 'You made a terrible mistake trying to do the right thing. You were stupid and naive, and people died because of it. I know exactly what you are feeling. I know how it hurts.'

She blinked. The ache she felt in her chest was still there, but it had abated for a moment. "It's not the same."

'It doesn't have to be,' David signed simply, his expression sad but firm. 'I'm here for you.'

Adelyn wiped at her face again, trying to wipe away the watery mucus trickling from her nose. Her lungs didn't ache so badly anymore, so long as she didn't try to take long breaths. "How do I make it right?"

David shook his head. 'You can't make it right. But you can make things better.'

She slumped against the wall, tired numbness overtaking her. "What do we do now?"

'A doctor is coming to look you over,' David signed. 'We send a runner to get our things from the boarding house, and lay low with the Watched until it's safe to leave the city.'

"I mean with the Watched," Adelyn explained. "The peace officers. I want to help, to..." *To make up for what I did.*

Nodding as he understood her question, David signed, 'I don't know. I don't know how we can help, beyond hiding.'

Clenching her jaw, Adelyn considered possibilities for a while longer, then straightened. "I think I do."

...

David couldn't get Adelyn to explain what she was thinking. She told him to go wait with the other Watched, and he obeyed. Shane asked after Adelyn's welfare, and Ezra asked why he had blood on his shirt, but David didn't bother to answer either question.

A couple minutes passed. When Adelyn came out to the group, her face and hands were washed clean, and though her jacket couldn't be cleansed from every speck of blood and dirt, she'd wiped it off as best she could.

"You said you have two more sorcerers," Adelyn said to Shane, stepping into the room and glancing around furtively. "Can they fight?"

"It's about all they can do," Shane said. "We're all self-taught. We can't go in like that witch, though."

"I need to meet them," Adelyn said. "And we're going to need a lot more weapons. David knows how to fight with magic better than anyone. He can train you some, at least give pointers."

All eyes were on her in a moment, and Shane chewed on her words for a half second before he answered her. "You're not one of us, Adelyn."

"Hear me out, first," Adelyn said, coughing into her arm. "I think I have a plan that'll make sure you never get hit like this again."

"And how're you gonna do that?" Ezra asked. Shane shot him a glare, but the question already hung in the air.

"You've got four people who can do magic, now," Adelyn said, her confidence building a little as she gained momentum. "That's two thirds of the city's sorcerers, by my count.

Six, if you count me and David. And we got our asses handed to us by a single cocky witch."

Shane's visage darkened notably. "I just had friends die by my side. Don't belittle what happened today."

"I'm not belittling it," Adelyn said, shaking her head. "I know what today's cost was. I'm making a point. You can't use your own power. You're toting around War Machines and using them to throw rocks."

"So David'll teach us how to fight?" Ezra asked. "What's the big deal about that?"

Adelyn shook her head, a flicker of a smile crossing her face. She was clearly building up to a reveal, though David couldn't fathom what it was. "I'm going to give you more than combat. I'm going to give you all the magic known to man."

"And how do you plan on doing that?" Shane asked.

Adelyn shrugged, her casual air slightly undercut when she winced and put a hand to her chest. "We're going to rob a library."

CHAPTER 14

EXTRA: TOWN HALL LEADS TO FATALITIES
Peace Officers Quell Riot at Town Hall, Thirteen Dead
The town hall meeting to discuss the hiring of new peace officers ended in violence today. A group of Watched militants interrupted the discussion, instigating violence which quickly spilled out of control. Peace officers on the scene were able to respond quickly due to a tip-off they'd received from an anonymous citizen, which was corroborated by threats they'd received in the mail. By using magic, the militants were able to escape after killing several peace officers and civilians.

If you have any knowledge of where the Watched militants are hiding, please report tips to Sheriff Cara Flintwood at the city courthouse. If you see any of the pictured individuals, do not approach. All are considered to be armed and extremely dangerous.

•Extra printing, Azah Gazette. Note: Included were sketches and descriptions of Ezra Fisher, Adelyn Mayweather, Shane Farren, and David Undertow

. . .

Adelyn's statement got exactly the reaction she'd been hoping for. Surprise, a hint of confusion, then realization as, one by one, the others in the room figured out what she was talking about.

"The magic books they keep at the city vault," Shane said.

"It's full of more books on magic then we could carry away," Adelyn said, though she didn't know how extensive it was. "Harrington wants to hoard all that knowledge, but we need it more than him. Anything you need to know—healing, fighting, illusions, you name it."

"You're not the first person to think about robbing the city vault," Shane said. "It's too risky."

"Last time we talked about it, we didn't have six blessed," Ezra pointed out.

"We'll talk about it later," Shane said.

"But—" Adelyn started.

"Not now," Shane said curtly. "We need to get out of here first. Until then, we drop it. Our first goal is to get back to the safe house."

"That's not gonna be easy," Ansyr said, piping up. "Whole city's watching for us to make a move."

"The peace officers know that you hide here, too," Adelyn commented, thinking it out loud. "They're probably gonna be here soon. They might even be setting up an ambush outside, waiting for us to try and leave."

"How do you figure?" Shane asked.

Adelyn paused, realizing too late that she had given away something she'd learned straight from the sheriff. "Just a guess, but someone had to have seen us come inside here and reported it."

To her relief, Shane shook his head and said, "I got that part, yeah. But why do you assume ambush?"

"What else would they be doing?" Adelyn asked, a little confused. "They had no qualms about shooting before."

"It'd make more sense to tail us back," Ezra pointed out. "Find out where we've been hidin'."

Shane tilted his head towards Ezra, acknowledging his explanation. "If we're too overt we might run into an ambush, but chances are good we won't ever see them coming until they're tossing torches down into our basement."

"So what do we do?" Adelyn asked.

Ezra grinned a toothy smile at her. "We find some rope."

...

David was paying idle attention to the conversation, but his mind was elsewhere.

He didn't know what to do about Adelyn. Her heart had been in the right place, but she'd lied to him twice on this trip and caused irreparable harm to those back at the town hall who'd never be getting back up.

Watchers knew, he'd made his own terrible mistakes when he was young, far worse than anything she'd done. Even acknowledging that it was hypocritical, though, he couldn't fight down all of the judgement he felt.

She'd lied to him, again. First going to Harrington without him, then going to the peace officers. Noble goals aside, she was willfully making decisions that affected his life without first saying what she was intent on doing.

Ezra came over and clapped him on the shoulder, jolting David out of his contemplation. "We're gonna get moving, Davey, Are you all ready to go?"

David rubbed at his shoulder, catching Adelyn's eye so he could sign to her, 'Where are we going?'

"The safe house," Adelyn said. "I don't know how we're getting there, though."

"It's simple," Ezra said, swinging open the door to the back office. "We're going to walk."

Shane shrugged, flashing a half smile as he walked into the office. "Help me move this desk?"

David frowned, then understanding came over him. They were far enough out to coast that they weren't standing over real ground, but instead on the platform that had been built to accommodate more growth. There was beach beneath them.

He thought about the implications of that for a moment, long enough that Shane relaxed in his place by a corner of the desk and said, "Eh... gonna help me with this or not?"

Blinking, David quickly moved to assist, hefting his end and sliding the big wooden desk a few feet to the side, revealing a trap door.

"The peace officers know that smugglers like to travel under the decks," Shane commented, as he threw open the trap door, revealing murky blackness below. "But hopefully they won't think to look for us down there."

Whispering his own name, he produced a werelight that floated down and exposed the eight foot drop to a rocky beach, splashed with knee high tides that were flowing in and out.

Ezra brought over a hank of rope and started lowering it, tying off the length with a sailor's knot onto part of the trap door built for that purpose. "Who's goin' down first?"

"I will," Shane said. "Adelyn, David, I want you two to bring up the rear. Once we're all down, I'm killing the light so we don't look too obvious to passersby. If we get caught in an ambush before you get down the rope, leave us. We can't fight down here, and most of us are too injured anyways."

"I'm not going to do that," Adelyn said, a sentiment that

David shared. He wasn't about to abandon these people, even if the odds were stacked that badly against them.

As it turned out, the determination wasn't necessary. Though it took some effort to get everyone down the rope, they encountered little conflict on the way down. David's boots filled with water as they touched ground, but he did his best not to shiver as he started trudging forward into the dark.

...

Adelyn worked her way down the rope, moving slow and trying not to strain herself or do anything that would require deep, and therefore painful, breaths. Shane's light was appropriately quite good—it kept the whole area visible, a bright expanse that showed off the splashing water and the rocky beach below effectively.

She hit land and let go of the rope, so that one of the gangsters could pull it back up, then turned to Shane. "That's everyone."

"Okay then," Shane said, pointing to his side. Dim light was visible far to their left, coming in from the end of the docks. "Use the coast to navigate. There won't be enough light to see by, so watch your step, and keep that light to your left. Don't try to go too fast, don't wander off. If you hear something, say something. When we get where we're going, I'll call out and draw a new light. Everyone understand?"

The ragtag group of them shared a series of nods. Adelyn could do that easily. The cold water was not to her liking, but she'd waded through creeks before, this was little different.

Shane killed the light, and Adelyn sucked in a sudden, painful breath.

The light to the left wasn't half so bright as she'd

thought. Under the docks, it was the next best thing to pitch black, with no sound except for the sloshing of water and her own heartbeat in her ears.

Adelyn was not afraid of the dark, but this wasn't just dark, it was pitch black. She'd only been somewhere this dark in her life once, a few months before, on the night she'd almost died.

She stood there, frozen for a moment as she tried to keep from panicking. Pain built in her lungs as her breath ran away into hyperventilation. She could hear the people sneaking up on her, she could almost feel the spirit in the air as hidden assassins crept around her, seconds away from striking.

No. There's nobody down here but us.

It was a meaningless act, but she shut her eyes to try and focus. Her vision barely changed between open eyelids and closed, but when the blackness was her own decision, it wasn't so claustrophobic.

There were no assassins, no bandits sneaking up to try and stab her in the back. The only dangerous thing down here was the risk of hypothermia.

Keeping her eyes firmly shut, she started trudging her way forward. She opened them a couple times to quickly ensure she was still walking the right way, but besides that, she kept them shut, slowly moving one foot forward at a time, bracing herself against the current when it pulled at her calves.

She could do this. It wasn't so bad. Just keep moving, just keep shuffling forward, try not to trip on a rock or bump into anyone.

No trouble at all.

...

It was dark out by the time they reached the safe house

—not simply shady or dim, as the city was in that state for most of the day every day, but truly dark, with the sun below the horizon.

Once close to the hideout, Shane had checked that the coast was clear, then guided them all up a ladder onto the dock and in through the city.

David's toes were numb. It was to be expected, wading through the icy water, but that didn't make it any less uncomfortable. Worse, as was pointed out once they got into the safe house, there was no way to light a fire. The spirit-powered stove gave off enough heat to keep the room from being truly unbearable, but there wasn't much space to crowd around it, and David deferred the heat to the members of their party that were more seriously injured.

Pulling off his boots and socks, David rolled up the hem of his pant legs so that the wet material wouldn't be slapping against his ankles. It would actually slow the drying process, but he cared less about that and more about immediate relief from the cold.

Shane came down the ladder much later than the rest of the group, commenting to Ezra once he was on the ground floor. "The others are on their way. We'll talk about this plan once they arrive."

"I don't see what's there to talk about," Ezra said. "It's two choices. Doin' something, or sittin' on our hands waiting for the Watchers to do all the work for us. I'm not one for sittin' on my hands."

Instead of responding to the jibe, Shane walked over and put a hand to David's arm. "Do you have something to write with, Davey?"

David nodded, stepping away so that Shane had to release his arm. Everything above his knees had stayed dry, so his notepad and pencil were still fine.

Lowering his tone slightly, Shane asked, "Can you do it? Show us all how to fight like real blessed?"

David considered the question for a long moment, then produced his notepad so he could write the response. 'Fighting isn't what makes a sorcerer.'

Shane bobbed his head as he read that, repeating the question in different terms. "Sure, but like how that witch fought."

'I can,' David wrote. Whether or not he would, that was another question, but not one he had to bring up right away.

"Can you do it in a hurry?" Shane asked. "I'm not on board with this heist, but if you can really teach us it'd still be useful."

David shook his head. That wasn't remotely plausible. It'd take him five or six days just to cover the basic groundwork of magical combat. From how he'd seen Shane fight, even that was going to be necessary. He had a knack for throwing around power, but his fundamentals were flimsy at best.

And he still fared better against the witch then I did.

Even with such a weak grasp of his power, Shane was still stronger than David. For that matter, Ezra was still stronger than David. A spiteful part of him wanted to refuse to teach them, so that his relative usefulness in combat wouldn't shrink any more, but that was selfish and stupid.

He needed to get his voice back, and for that, he needed Sarah.

'Can you send someone for me,' he started to write, wanting to know if his message had been received yet.

Footsteps were heard faintly above, and Shane looked up. "Someone's here." Seeing David's startled expression, he quickly added, "Not an enemy. Let me see who it is."

Shane strolled to the ladder and quickly scaled up,

leaving David alone in the crowded basement. Without anyone to read it, David abandoned the note he was writing, setting aside his pad.

Ezra walked up behind him, putting a hand on David's shoulder.

Why can't these people just say hello? David thought, quickly growing tired of the familial contact that was used to start a conversation among these Watched. He jerked away from Ezra's grip, but tried not to show annoyance as he turned to face him.

"I'm gonna try somethin' once we start talking about the robbery," he said. "You want to do it, right?"

David shrugged. He thought its goals were noble, but he hadn't heard enough about it to decide if it was a good idea or not.

Ezra frowned, but persisted. "You at least want to see it talked about, maybe draw up a plan?"

David nodded at that. He'd at least like to see it discussed.

"Then get ready to follow my lead," Ezra said. "I'm not sure I'll need you, but just in case."

...

Adelyn sat on the edge of a bed, staring at the ceiling as the doctor put his ear to her chest, listening carefully. She'd insisted upon his taking care of everyone else first, but now that the others had all been bandaged and looked after, she was the only one left in need of his care.

"And you say you can breathe just fine, but it hurts when you take deep breaths?" he asked, standing up and looking at her. He didn't look anything like Harrington—young, dark skin, with crooked wire framed glasses that were tied to his head with string since a chunk of his right ear was missing. He'd introduced himself, but Adelyn had missed the name.

"That's right," Adelyn confirmed.

"I need Shane's help," the physician said. "Let me go find him."

"I thought he didn't know any healing spells?" Adelyn asked.

"I don't need spells, I need him to feel around for some spirit," the doctor explained. "See if you've got blood pooling in your lungs."

"I'm a sorceress," Adelyn pointed out.

The doctor hesitated. "Oh, eh... well then. Can you feel any blood pooling in your lungs, then?"

Shutting her eyes in concentration, Adelyn tried to feel out the tingle of spirit that she associated with blood. It was difficult to distinguish from the general feeling of life that accompanied her body, or any body, but it seemed like there was an abnormally high concentration in her mid-chest.

"I think so," she said. "It feels like it, but I can't be certain."

"You've got a contusion, then," the doctor explained. "Pretty bad one. If I didn't know better, I'd assume you got kicked in the chest by somethin' big and mean."

"I pretty much did," Adelyn commented dryly. "Only it wasn't a kick. What's that mean for me?"

"Gonna be a damned bad week for you," he said, sitting back on his stool. "Don't stress yourself too much, get lots of rest. It shouldn't kill you, unless you're running around, getting in dangerous situations a whole lot."

"A week?" Adelyn asked. That was frustratingly long to be bedridden, but as she raised her tone to ask the exasperated question, the shooting pain in her lungs reared up and sent her into a coughing fit.

"At least a week," the doctor amended. "I'd say two, but I don't know how realistic that is for you."

"Thanks," Adelyn said, chewing on her lip as she thought it over. She pushed herself to her feet, and walked over to Shane who'd just come in from upstairs. "We should make plans for a week from now."

"Lower your sails, there," Shane said, tucking a roll of paper into his belt, his jaw tight in frustration as he dismissed her. "I haven't even agreed to your idea yet. You're not the first person to think of robbing that library, but they've got it guarded better than the president's vaults. We can't shoot our way in."

"You've never outnumbered them before," Adelyn pointed out. "Six of us, only two of them—Harrington and that witch."

Shane shook his head. "Five of us, not six. And we've got a collective seven years or so of experience as a group. They've got an order of magnitude more than that, and all the books and studying besides."

"So we have to be careful," Adelyn said. "And clever. But if you don't do anything, you're going to be just as vulnerable every time the peace officers show up."

"They weren't s'posed to show up in the first place," Ezra commented from a few paces away. "That's what's been stuck in my craw. How'd they know we were gonna be there?"

"That's a damned good question," Shane said, drawing the rolled up paper from his belt. "And I think we've got an answer."

Slapping it down on the table, he let the paper unroll for everyone to read. Adelyn recognized it as a newspaper, and quickly skimmed the headline to see what he was talking about.

"Peace officers quell riot at—what? That's not what happened!" she said. "The bastards started the fight!"

"Keep reading," Shane said, pointing his thumb to a line lower on in the article.

"Peace officers on the scene were able to respond quickly due to a tip-off they'd received from an anonymous citizen, which was corroborated by threats they'd received in the mail...." Adelyn felt her throat go dry as the article identified her.

"It's bullshit," Ezra said, leaning over her to read it. "They're making up crap to justify their attack after the fact."

"You said it yourself," Shane said, shaking his head. "How'd they know we were going to be there? The article even identifies that we've got three people who can do magic. How'd they know that?"

Ansyr was the first to say it. "We've got a rat somewhere."

"Exactly," Shane said. "And we're not going to do anything stupid while we've got someone snitching out our actions to those Divine murderers. We lay low, we wait, we get stronger. The Watched have been blessing us more and more, lately. Four of our number blessed in as many years. We keep our heads down until we've gathered more strength and this has all blown over."

Adelyn started to argue, but Ezra went to bat for her before she could start. "And what happens when the snitch tells 'em where this hideout is, boss?"

"Ezra," Shane said. "I appreciate your fervor, but—"

"Not Ezra," Ezra corrected. "I'm blessed now. I've earned my name, more than most anyone in this room. You can't deny me that."

Shane rocked back, surprised at the insolence, but he

either couldn't or didn't want to argue the point. "Fine. What do you pick for your name?"

"Rahk," Ezra said. "And I don't feel like waiting around for another hundred officers 'n another couple witches to roll into town and start burning us out before we strike back."

"I don't want to see more of our people hurt, Rahk," Shane said, putting emphasis on the new name.

Ezra—or rather, Rahk—threw up his arms, then tottered slightly and had to put a hand against a shelving unit to keep his balance. "Neither do I, which is why we need to be strong enough to defend them. We need those books."

"Talk of this doesn't leave this shelter until we know who we can trust," Shane said. "I've sent for our other blessed. Until then, lips are sealed. Got it?"

"I don't take orders from you," Rahk said, stepping forward.

"Then do it as a favor to me," Shane said, rubbing the bridge of his nose in frustration. "Okay?"

Rahk nodded, turning his back to Shane and walking away.

CHAPTER 15

We first grew suspicious of black market weaponry being traded out of the apartment after getting a tip from a street informant. After watching the street for a week, we confirmed that there were gatherings of Watched who met semi regularly at the address, often late at night.

We prepared to strike the apartment at the next gathering to catch them red handed and seize any weapons they had available. Due to the nature of the sting, we requisitioned two sets of spirit armor, which were carved with runes to protect against bullets.

After observing three individuals enter the apartment, we moved in, taking up a position by both front windows and the door. There was no response when we knocked, so an officer breached the door and entered. After an altercation, four of the adults inside were killed, and one was taken prisoner. We do not know the location of their two children. We believed them to be inside at the time of the sting, but the only exit was a back window five stories up, and they did not have time to climb down before we would have apprehended them.

- Peace officer report, archived in the Azah City Courthouse. Note: File serial number linked to a pair of kitchen knives taken from the scene, kept in impound as evidence.

Adelyn felt the fool for lying in bed, fully awake, with no intention to sleep, but that had been the doctor's instructions. Rest, don't be too active, let her lungs heal. If she didn't have something to do, she should be in bed, avoiding physical activity.

She still felt useless.

Sleep was an option, she was tired enough for it, but she wanted to be there when the other sorcerers showed up. Sleep could wait until after she'd met them.

As she saw Shane come back down the ladder she sat up, propping her back up on a couple pillows so that she could watch while still meeting the technical requirements of bedrest. He led the way for two people, who Adelyn assumed would be the so-called 'Blessed' he'd made coy references to.

They were so... young. It was a bit of an unfair judgement for Adelyn to make, she was barely sixteen, and they were probably of an age with her, but she'd been expecting people a bit older, or at least as old as Shane or Ezra.

By the looks of them, Adelyn guessed they could have been brother and sister. The boy was a little taller, a little more slender, with hair buzzed close to his scalp, standing behind the girl, whose hair was combed into a pair of neat braids.

The arrival of these newcomers was surely a good enough excuse for her to get out of bed, orders to rest be damned. She swung her legs out and stood, putting a hand to her chest for a moment before walking over to the newcomers.

"I'm Adelyn," She said, sticking out her hand in greeting towards the girl.

The girl looked at Adelyn's hand for a moment, then back up at her, staring into her eyes. "It's nice to meet you, Adelyn. We heard about you on the way over."

Adelyn chewed on her lip, then glanced over at the boy. "Eh... and you are?"

"Atof," The boy said. "Eh, Topher, though, you can call me Topher, and this is my sister, Mina." He pronounced the O in his real name with a long 'Ah' sound, the correct pronunciation for Sacrosanct words, but the nickname as 'Oh'.

Thinking back, Adelyn tried to translate those names in her head. Atof, that meant 'Water', but Mina...

She glanced at David, quickly signing, 'What does her name mean?'

'Salt,' David signed back, tapping two fingers over one in a shaking motion.

Adelyn smirked, addressing Topher. "Saltwater. I guess you picked your name first?"

His expression conveyed chagrin as he replied. "Yeah."

Mina added, "Together, we're the ocean."

"We're the youngest people in the city to pick our own names," Topher added, beaming and sticking out his chest in pride.

"I'm the youngest," Mina corrected. "You're older than me."

Topher rolled his eyes, though Mina couldn't see the gesture. Adelyn got the sense that this exchange had been had before, more than once.

"That's because you're sorcerers, right?" Adelyn asked. "You both got, eh... Blessed?"

Nodding, Topher said, "At the same time, near as we can tell."

"The night our parents died," Mina added, her tone remarkably flat for what she'd just said.

Adelyn stared at Mina, who returned the stare without blinking. "I... I'm sorry," she said.

"Don't be." Mina said. "Their textiles and clothing are much more popular now."

Adelyn's staring only intensified, until Topher stepped in. "Dyed. She's joking."

Adelyn was momentarily confused, until she realized what they were getting at. Mina had been telling a joke. "So your parents aren't dead?"

"Oh, they are," Mina clarified. "Peace officers murdered them."

"I—" Adelyn looked at Topher for confirmation, and he nodded solemnly. Unsure what else to say to the strange girl, Adelyn turned her focus and addressed Shane. "We should talk about the heist."

Shane nodded, pointing to the table. "Let's sit down, though."

They collectively made their way to the table. Adelyn lingered slightly, watching the siblings as they walked. Mina gave David a wary look and took a chair at the far side of the table from where David sat, but Topher happily sat down right next to him, taking the spot Adelyn had been planning on going for, so she had to sit down next to Topher instead.

Shane took his place at the head of the table, implicitly making himself the leader of the conversation. That didn't surprise Adelyn, since he seemed to be the leader of this group as a whole, but what did surprise her was Rahk, limping over to sit at the far side of the table, straight across from Shane.

Ansyr briefly hesitated by Shane, though she didn't sit down. They shared a quiet discussion, then Ansyr walked away, heading towards the stove.

"We've never had a formal meeting like this before," Shane said, mostly addressing the siblings. "There's four of us now that've joined our official ranks, so I think it's time we set up a couple ground rules."

"I agree," Rahk said. "First rule: Whatever we decide here, everyone's got to go along with."

Shane sighed, putting a hand to his forehead and rubbing at his temple. "That's ridiculous, Ezra. You—"

"Rahk," He corrected. "I've picked my name already. In the eyes of the Watchers, I'm the same as you, don't you go denying me that."

Shane's jaw tightened, but he said, "Fine, Rahk. You can't make people go along with something if they don't want to."

Rahk threw up his hands. "Then why even vote? It'll take all of us to rob the place. You can kick out your feet and go fishin' if you don't want us to go. If we decide to go forward, you gotta promise not to back out and abandon us. In honesty, this'll matter to everyone, so we should get everyone 'round this table and—"

"*Fine,*" Shane said again, cutting him off. "If everyone else goes along with this plan, I won't back out. Adelyn and David can back out at any time, though, we can't force them to join us if they don't want to."

"Majority," Rahk countered. "If the majority goes along, everyone has to pitch in."

"It's the same thing, Rahk," Shane said with another exasperated sigh. "There's four of us, David and Adelyn are only guests. We don't move forward on a tie."

"Majority," Rahk repeated, though he finally dropped the issue. "And a second rule. What we talk about here don't leave this table. We can't tell no one else about what we're going to do."

"I was going to suggest the same thing," Shane said. "We can't have another letter get sent to the peace officers telling them exactly what we're planning. We'll keep Ansyr in the group, and Brenden, in case we need manpower. I trust them. Not a word to anyone else."

"So we agree?" Rahk said, looking surprised that he hadn't needed to argue.

"What if the rat's one of us?" Mina asked, pointing to David, then to Adelyn. "It's awfully convenient that the peace officers found us just after these two showed up."

Adelyn swallowed and started to open her mouth to defend herself, but Rahk beat her to it. "I think the paper was telling stories to justify the attack. And besides, if they were going to send us out to sea without a harpoon, they wouldn't have saved our backsides once the peace officers showed up."

Topher nodded at that, and Mina was mollified enough that she didn't push the objection any further.

Turning to Adelyn, Rahk said, "If nobody else has anything else to add, Adelyn, you want to tell them what you're thinking?"

"You all need to learn better magic," Adelyn said, picking up the thread immediately. She didn't want to get involved in their internal politics, but she did need to help this group, and as best she could see, that meant going forward with this heist. "There's a whole library of magic books in this city, sitting around, waiting for someone to come take them. If David teaches you all how to fight, and we make a plan, we can steal those books.

You'll never have to worry about being outmatched again."

"What's the plan?" Mina asked. Even though she looked to be about as old as Adelyn, Adelyn couldn't help but think of her as a child.

"I don't have one, yet," Adelyn said. "That's part of why we're here. To work out a plan."

"We don't need a plan," Shane argued. "Because it's too risky no matter what the plan is. Even if David could show us how to fight in a week, which he already told me he *can't do*, we'd be going up against way too much security, not to mention that witch who kicked our asses today, and whatever Harrington might be able to do to stop us. There's no plan that will beat out that math—if we fight them, we lose."

"Don't gotta fight them," Rahk pointed out. "They gotta sleep, sometime, and we can be sneaky."

"I'm not scared of any witch," Topher said. "We're blessed, same as her."

"No, you're not," Shane said. "None of us are the same as her."

Adelyn glanced at Topher and gave him a half shrug. "He's right. Fighting her should be a last ditch effort. We chased her off today because she wasn't expecting us all, but it was close. If we have to fight her, it'll take all of us working together if we want to be sure of winning."

"So we fight her all at once," Topher said. "No problem."

"How are we getting into the vault?" Mina asked. "Whether we can fight her or not, we've got to make it into that vault."

"That's on you, Adelyn," Shane said, turning his body to face her. "It's your idea, so what's your plan?"

She felt the eyes all turn on her, and didn't know what to

say. Her idea was still in its infancy. Adelyn had never organized a harvest festival before, much less a heist.

"I don't have one," Adelyn said, feeling stupid. "I know the books are at the city vault, that's about it."

David nudged her, signing a question that she translated immediately. "You say you've talked about robbing the place before. That means you must know about their security, right?"

"I do," Shane said. "Like I said, it's impossible."

Adelyn sighed. "Care to fill me in? I can't make a plan if I don't know what the problems are."

Shane frowned to one side, then nodded. "Fine. The city vault has a constant guard of at least eight people. It's staggered, so even during shift changes, there's four people who stay on watch while four more come in. Alarms are all over the place, so if anyone sees something suspicious, they just have to ring a bell and the whole town will be over us."

"Eight people doesn't sound too bad," Adelyn said. "Six of us, with magic, we can take them out before they can raise a call."

"That's just the start," Shane said. "They've got a few coin exchanges for people to trade in currency and making small withdrawals, but all the valuables are stored in a steel vault. Eight inches of steel on every facing, so there's no way we can blast our way in with magic. It's so heavy that they had to drive piles into the ground to keep it from sinking. Inside that, they've got a second layer of reinforced bronze security vaults. One's got the money in it, another has the library."

"Why bronze?" Adelyn asked. "Why not more steel?"

"I don't know," Shane said. "But even if that means we could blast our way through the second layer—which we can't—it would wreck the interior of the library and make enough racket to alarm the peace officers."

"So we get the keys," Adelyn said.

"How?" Topher asked, skeptically.

Chewing her lip, Adelyn said, "I'm still working on that part. But this doesn't sound impossible. We need to get through two doors and eight guards. Easy."

"That's only the security we know about," Shane said. "And we have to get in and out without any alarms going off, or we're dead. If we screw up, or if there's something we didn't know about in advance, we've got to face the witch and the rest of the city. It's too much of a risk."

Mina cleared her throat, then asked, "Wouldn't Harrington have the key to his own vault?"

"That's right!" Adelyn said, seizing on that. "He has a couple books in a locked box at his shop, I saw him use a big ring of keys to open it. We can pretend to hire his services, distract him, and steal the keys while he's not looking."

"Do you have the coin to hire him?" Shane asked. "Because we've barely got the money for bandages and saltwater."

"You don't pay us," Mina mentioned, giggling at her own pun.

"I don't—" Shane blinked, then shook his head. "Adelyn, you're investing money we don't have into a plan that'll get us killed."

David leaned in, signing a quick message which Adelyn translated. "We have the money, at the boarding house we're staying in." As an aside, she added, "It's enough silver to keep Harrington on retainer for half a year."

There was a little muttering, and not just from around the table—that sort of extravagant wealth apparently wasn't seen as a blessing, or perhaps they felt it unfair that Adelyn and David had so much while they were barely scraping by.

"So we get the silver from your boarding house," Rahk said, "Go steal the first key. That seems simple enough. We've already got two thirds of the plan, assuming we can beat eight guards."

"There's still a couple of wizards you're not considering," Shane said. "And we have no idea what sort of magical defenses they've got protecting their books."

Again, David chipped in his commentary, this time a bit of magical knowledge. Again, Adelyn translated as close to word-for-word as she could manage. "Magical traps won't be a threat... He says that anything truly dangerous would take an unreasonable amount of spirit and concentration to keep going, and we'd feel it long before we stumble into the trap." She waited for him to continue, then finished, "What we have to watch out for are alarms and early warning systems, those can run for much longer with almost no spirit."

"Well, do you think you can suss those out, so we don't wander into 'em?" Rahk asked, glancing at David.

David nodded once, his expression confident, even brazen.

"Then what's the issue?" Rahk asked, looking back to Shane. "We've got the money, we've got the numbers, we've got the magic. I think that's a plenty solid groundwork."

"Hardly," Shane said. "But if you're done, we can vote."

"We don't have the whole plan put together yet," Adelyn said. "Give us some more time to work out the details."

"Details don't matter," Shane said. "I don't care about the details. You're putting all of us at risk, and you're going to bring down the whole city on our heads for a few books. Are your details going to change that?"

Adelyn sighed, but didn't have an option except to shake her head.

"Then we're not doing it," Shane said. "I'm voting for the option that won't get any of us killed."

"And I'm votin' for the option that'll get us someplace," Rahk shot back.

All eyes turned to the siblings. Topher exchanged a brief look with his sister, then glanced at Adelyn. "You sure this plan will work?"

"If it doesn't, I'm dead with the rest of you," Adelyn said, adding under her breath, "Please."

"Then I'm in," Topher said.

"That's two votes for yes," Rahk said, looking at the girl who hadn't yet decided. "Mina, 'sup to you."

"Don't be an idiot," Shane added. "This is too risky."

Mina looked between the two of them, then shrugged. "I like the plan."

Rahk sat back, grinning. "Then that settles—"

"I said," Mina interrupted him. "I like the plan. I didn't say yes."

"That's a no, then," Shane said, starting to stand. "We're not—"

Mina cleared her throat, giving him a pointed look. "Would you let me finish?"

Looking at Topher, Shane sighed and sat back down.

"What I want to know is," Mina said. "Can we trust these people who came out of nowhere? We don't know their background, we don't even know if this guy's half the sorcerer he says he is."

"You haven't seen him fight," Rahk said. "He's amazing."

"I don't care if he can fight, I want to know why," Mina said. "You see a sorcerer come out of nowhere without a tongue and willing to pitch in to any cause you throw at him, you see a hero. I see a lot of questions."

"He fought in the war," Adelyn said. "Have you heard of the stone warriors?"

"We're not stupid," Rahk said. "Course we have. Almost won us the war. He's one of them?"

Adelyn nodded. It was a comfortable lie, one she'd believed for a while before learning the truth. She needed the Watched to go along with her plan, and if they believed David was a war hero, that'd get them on her side. "And I'm a farmer, I got my power about a year ago. David was there to help when some raiders attacked my town, he's taught me everything I know about magic."

Mina looked past Adelyn, to David. "Is all that true?"

Adelyn glanced at David, biting down on her lip. All he had to do was nod, and it'd be settled, but she knew him well enough that it wasn't going to be that simple.

David was tapping his fingers on the desktop, and the gears turning in his head were almost audible. It was enough of a reason to be skeptical, but maybe he could pull out the deception with a clever twist of words, or—

He shook his head.

Mina sat back in her chair, and Adelyn heard Rahk swear under his breath. Topher looked suddenly uncomfortable with his seating choice, but didn't get up and move just yet.

"Okay then," Mina said. "No. We're not—"

David put up a hand to stop her, buying himself time to fish out his notepad from a belt pocket. Adelyn realized what he was doing, but couldn't think of how to stop him short of grabbing the notepad away.

"David, don't," Adelyn said. "You don't have to—"

Setting down the notepad and holding out the pen, he

paused just long enough to give Adelyn a steady look and shake his head before jotting down a note and passing it to Mina.

"What's it say?" Topher asked, leaning over to try and see what had been written, squinting with difficulty to make out the letters.

Mina scanned the note, lips moving as she read the words, and her face paled a bit as she finished reading it. "David served on the president's army in the war," she said, looking around the table. "He was the Blue Flame."

CHAPTER 16

Ira: Tell me about Azah.

Robert: Large coastal city, fairly major trade center. It's on the west side of the peninsula, not the most vital target, but it's still a bit of a sticking point.

Ira: Because of the church, right?

Robert: More or less. Nobody wants to be the general who burned down the great Church of the Divine.

Ira: Is the Blue Flame still recusing himself?

Robert: The White Death talked him down, but he's still pulling hard to take their campaign north.

Ira: Is there anyone in my army that isn't refusing to attack on moral grounds?

Robert: The auxiliary division.

Ira: They'll take point on the assault?

Robert: No, ma'am. They are refusing to attack on practical grounds. Spirit plate rusts out with all that salt air, it'd triple their maintenance costs.

Ira: Fine. Keep razing the coastline, but put Azah to siege. We'll have to starve them out since I've got a whole army of conscientious objectors.

Robert: Yes, ma'am.

•Classified transcript of conversation between Commanding General Ira Johnson and General Adjutant Robert Carson, discussing the siege of Azah.

Silence pervaded the room to the beat of confusion, lasting perhaps half a second before anyone could process and understand the full meaning of what she'd just said. David watched, uncertain if his gamble had been a good one, unsure if his trust had been misplaced.

"Watchers abandon me," Shane whispered, scooting back in his seat slightly.

David focused on everyone who was in earshot, watching for threats. Topher was trying to decide if he should move to a different seat, there was no threat there, but Shane had reached for a bronze amulet he kept in his pocket and a few paces away, by the stove, Ansyr had put her hand on a knife.

Rahk was the last to react, looking confused for a heartbeat before he shoved himself away from the table in a start, almost falling backwards in his chair. "Shit!"

All this was expected. Concern, surprise, those things were fine. What David was hoping for was that the concern would not give way to fear, that the surprise would not give way to anger or aggression.

'Aside from being a Stone Warrior, everything we've told you is true,' he signed, and Adelyn translated faithfully.

"That's a huge thing to leave out!" Topher started. "You —watchers, you—"

"He's the same man you were talking to a minute ago," Adelyn said, more eloquent in her defense of David than

David thought he could have been. "The same man who saved Ezra's life, and who fought for you this morning."

"He's the reason we're under the president's thumb," Shane said. "He won battles for the same people we're fighting against to this day."

David nodded. That was all true. 'For what it's worth, I objected and refused to participate in the attacks on the coast.'

Adelyn translated that, but it seemed not to carry the reassurance that David had wanted.

"It might have been better if you had," Shane pointed out. "At least then it would have been quick. They destroyed our ships and left us to starve. We couldn't surrender, because they'd not accept the surrender until our queen gave in."

"Until we killed 'er and surrendered in 'er place," Rahk pointed out.

The table started to rattle a bit, floorboards vibrating as David tapped his heel against the floor in rapid succession so he could sign to Adelyn, which she translated directly as he spoke. "After the war, he swore to never take another life, tell a lie, or break a promise made in good faith. He's not the same man he once was."

"Then why are you telling us all this?" Shane asked.

David didn't sugarcoat. 'Mina wanted to know the truth.'

Adelyn translated what he said. The table fell silent for a moment.

Mina broke the silence. "He's got a point, even if he's not exactly a... *Cultt* of personality."

That took Adelyn a second, translating 'Cultt' to 'Blue' in her head. The joke made her groan once she got it, but it helped deflate some of the tension in the room.

Topher groaned. "Can you go five minutes without a joke, please?"

Nodding her head, Mina said, "Sure, I can, but why try?"

"You know the truth, now," Adelyn said. "Are you still willing to work with us?"

"He's a mass murderer," Shane said.

"He's a *Watched* mass murderer," Rahk pointed out. "And he wants to help us."

"He works for the president," Shane added.

David shook his head at that one, objecting to the comment. 'Not since the war ended,' he explained.

"I'm in," Mina said. "I asked for the truth, he told it. That's enough for me."

Shane didn't respond. He was busy staring at David, trying to make up his mind on something. David looked away, avoiding eye contact, until Shane shoved himself away from the table and stood. "I'm not going to have any part in planning this. I'll help when asked, that's it."

Spinning in place, he stomped towards the exit and clambered up the ladder noisily, Ansyr following after him to try and calm him down.

"Well," Mina commented, once he was gone. "Something's got him feeling blue."

Topher stood and walked off as well, though his arms waved in an exaggerated motion that implied his reaction was to his sister's comment, and not to anything involving David. He made it as far as the stove and then stopped to fix some coffee, calling over to see if anyone else wanted some.

"It's terrible," Mina commented about the coffee, before anyone could say yes. "We buy the stale leftover grounds from a street vendor."

"Do you have sugar?" Adelyn asked, calling over to Topher.

"Not a grain," Topher called back. "I could make it a bit harder if you wanted, though. We've got some under-the-shelf stuff that'll cover up the taste of the coffee."

"No thanks," Adelyn said.

David signed to ask for some, and Adelyn repeated the request. What he really wanted was a bed and some privacy to rest, but while their hideout had plenty of cots, the only privacy was the curtained off corner where a toilet had been installed, and David didn't particularly feel like taking any time to relax and decompress over there, so coffee would have to do.

"You sure?" Topher asked, once Adelyn translated. "Oh, but I guess you don't care about the taste."

David chewed his lip a moment before responding. 'I can still taste it, I'm only missing the front of my tongue.'

"Oh," Topher started, then he blushed and turned back to the stove, mumbling something under his breath.

Still set on discussing the heist, Rahk tried to bring the conversation back in line. "It'll be us responsible for planning this shindig. Better get started hashing out the details if we're going in a week."

Nodding, David began to sign. He'd been thinking about this while they were talking, and had tried to think of all the major problems they'd face. 'There will be six hurdles to be overcome. The first is money—we need to get our silver, which means going back to a boarding house.'

Translating for him, Adelyn panted for a moment, then added, "However we get the money, we'll have to be subtle. If they figure out we're up to something, we're dead in the water. They know where we were staying, but I hid the money so it's probably still there even if they searched the place."

David nodded at that. 'Once we have the money, we'll

need to get into Harrington's medical center, which means we need someone injured enough to need his help, and it means someone who looks like they could afford it. If we show up looking ragged and threadbare, he'll be too suspicious.'

"Who do we injure?" Mina asked. "I'd like to volunteer Topher, if you don't have a better suggestion."

"Hey!" Topher called, in the middle of scooping out coffee grounds. "I resent that."

"We can probably find someone else who isn't wanted," Adelyn said. "I'd volunteer myself, but that's a bad idea for a couple reasons."

"No, no, I'll do it," Topher said. "I don't mind the pain, but I would've preferred to volunteer my own neck instead of being put up to it."

"Please, your neck will be fine. We'll just break your legs or something," Mina replied with a cavalier grin.

'With that out of the way, we have to figure out how to get past security, and how to get inside,' David signed, wanting to continue with his planned set of six problems. 'I can show you how to knock people out from a distance, or to otherwise disable them.'

"Why not kill 'em?" Rahk asked. "So they can't identify us."

David looked at him flatly, and signed, 'I am not going to show you how to kill them. The guards aren't the ones we are fighting against.'

Once Adelyn translated that, Rahk said, "They're workin' for the same people we're fighting against, though. And while we're at it, we should see about getting into the main vault—half the money in that bank should be ours anyways."

"How's that?" Adelyn asked.

"You know how we said they burned our ships in the war?" Rahk said. "Well, that means merchant ships, too. Just so happens, a bunch of rich assholes who'd never done a real day of work in their lives had some merchant ships ready to go the second we surrendered. Azah's one of the biggest port cities this side of the peninsula, and just about every ship is owned by someone from the capitol. You ask me, anyone who helps them funnel money away from this city deserves a bullet in the back."

Adelyn took that in, shaking her head in his general direction. "That's awful, but we're not killing them. We're stealing books so we can protect and heal ourselves, not to get revenge."

Rahk looked skeptical, but didn't argue.

Topher returned to the table with two mugs of coffee, one for himself, one for David. It was clear from the color that Topher's coffee had been diluted, though David was too far away to smell if that dilution had been done with water or something stronger.

'Thank you,' David signed, before continuing. 'We will need the peace officers off our backs. This is not a situation where we can run to Solden's place and wait out the storm. Once we do this, they'll be coming after us hard. We need a clean getaway.'

"That's four problems," Mina said. "Is the fifth that we're all a bunch of sloppy incompetents?"

David hesitated, and Adelyn smirked as she translated for him. "David wouldn't put it in those exact words, but you do need training. He says we might have to fight that witch again, and we have to be able to win that fight without an excessive amount of collateral damage."

"And what's six?" Topher asked, grimacing as he sipped his coffee.

David looked at Topher, then signed to Adelyn. This time, she did rephrase his words on purpose, to soften the blow a bit before she addressed Rahk. "We need to get Shane on board. He may have agreed to help, but if he's not putting any effort into this we'll have to work twice as hard to pick up the slack.

"Abandon him," Rahk said, but he nodded. "But I'll try to talk to him. And y'all better get started on showing us to fight. We've got a lot of work to do in a week."

...

David kept the three Watched busy for the rest of the evening, between discussions of magical theory and further discussions of plans for the heist. Adelyn pitched in where she could, translating for a while and contributing her thoughts, but she ultimately had to call it a night well before anyone else, the pain in her chest growing too insistent for her to keep talking all night.

She retired to bed, and David resorted to using a pen and paper, scratching out notes and instructions that quickly began to fill up his notepad.

Shane didn't return. It was likely he was just up the ladder, sulking two stories above, but Adelyn wasn't going to make the effort to go and check at the moment. Climbing that ladder sounded like work, and Adelyn needed to rest more than anything else.

For his part, David seemed to be enjoying himself, at least as far as she could tell. He finally had a rapt audience to teach magic and swordplay, one less troublesome and easily bored than Adelyn had been these past weeks. He could dazzle Rahk, Mina, and Topher with the wonders of his knowledge, the intricacies and beauty of magic, even small anecdotes about his time in the war.

It was less a class and more a dumping of information

onto minds eager to listen, but that was fine. All that David had said while Adelyn translated was useful, and she doubted it changed once she stepped away and let his notepad fill in as intermediary, even if Topher seemed to be a bit of a slow reader.

Despite his fervor to learn, Rahk was the next to tap out, though that only made sense since neither of the siblings had participated in that morning's fight. He pulled a glass jar full of clear liquid from a cupboard by the stove, took two tin mugs, and then limped over to the bed next to Adelyn with one crutch under his arm and plopped down, propping his cast leg up on the bedside table.

"Care for a drink?" He asked, sloshing the liquid into both mugs before she could say whether she wanted some.

Adelyn picked up her mug anyways, sniffing it to see if it seemed palatable.

She almost dropped the mug, recoiling from the acrid odor of alcohol and burnt hair. "What is that?"

"Paint thinner, I think," Rahk said, smirking as he sipped from his own tin mug. "I'll drink it, if'n you don't want any."

"I'll rip out my sinuses and save it the trouble," Adelyn said. "Help yourself."

Rahk poured her mug into his, then set hers upside down atop the glass jar so that it was resting over the lid. "So how'd you get mixed up with one of the Thirteen?"

Thinking on the best way to put it, Adelyn said, "He was working as a bounty hunter, sort of. Raiders had attacked my town, kidnapped my family, I needed someone to help get them back. He came through for me."

"He have magic back then?" Rahk asked.

"Yeah, though he didn't tell me straight off," Adelyn said. "He keeps his cards close to his chest, which I am fine with considering the lengths he went to help me when I needed it."

Rahk nodded, looking over at the magic study session still going on a little ways away. "I like that. Bren's a man of action. A little fidgety and shy, but I suppose that can't be blamed considering." He used David's 'name' in Sacrosanct, rather than just calling him David, which took Adelyn a moment to parse.

"He was fidgety and shy before he lost his voice," Adelyn mentioned. "But I like him too."

Rahk took a long drink from his mug, grimaced, and bent to set it down by his foot. "People around here, it's all talk, talk, talk, no action. I've been sayin' for years, what we need is action, but you ain't got no authority unless you're blessed, and nobody'll even hear you out without a name. Now *I'm* blessed, though, and I'm gonna see here that things start to get done."

"Taking the safe course isn't inaction," Adelyn said. "Shane set up this place, didn't he?"

"Set up a place to hide," Rahk said, chewing on the inside of his cheek as he thought. "Mina's well enough, a little silly. Eager to get to fightin', get back for what they did to her parents. Brother's a bit skittish, but I can tell he's wantin' to get to it, too."

"Why haven't they?" Adelyn asked, sitting up a little. "Why weren't they at the town hall?"

Rahk glowered as he spoke, staring at the training session. "Shane don't want them getting in fights. Wants to keep 'em secret, so nobody knows what we've got in our back pocket."

Adelyn nodded. "That's reasonable. He's just being cautious."

"That caution's got a body count," Rahk said, leaning in

and snatching up his cup once again. After draining it, he said, "What, seven dead? I don't care he couldn't've known, he's still responsible, and I ain't forgivin' for that."

"Thirteen dead," Adelyn said. "If you count the peace officers."

"Peace officers can get thrown in with thulcut chum," Rahk said, gesturing towards David. "Damn 'em all, 'cept Bren over there. If we'd killed 'em all, today would almost have been worth it."

Chewing her lip, Adelyn pointed at the jar. "I'll have a little of that, if you don't mind."

Rahk grinned at her, then flipped the spare tin onto the table, dropped his down next to it, and filled both with a sloppy pour.

It tasted about as well as it smelled, burning on its way down, and Adelyn started coughing painfully. Rahk almost looked concerned, but she waved a hand at him, steadying herself and swallowing down the moonshine. Once down, it felt warm and comfortable, tingling in her throat like a gentle fire that helped fight away the basement's cold chill.

"Careful, careful!" Rahk exclaimed, though he was grinning. "Take it slow if it's your first time. She kicks hard and burns like a grease fire."

The coughing fit caught David's attention, who signed in her direction, asking if she was okay. She signed back the letters 'OK', nodding as well to emphasize the point, and David returned to his teaching.

Watching the exchange, Rahk asked, "How do you remember all that?"

"What, the signs?" Adelyn asked, looking back at him. "It's just the same as remembering words."

"Yeah?" Rahk asked, sipping his moonshine. "How do you say my name?"

Adelyn chewed her lip, thinking about the question. "That's actually tricky. We don't have signs in Sacrosanct. You could spell it out," She signed out the letters with hand motions, making an 'R-A-H-K' in the air, "Or you could use the regular word instead of the Sacrosanct one." She put out a hand flat and waved it inward, colliding with her other hand and dividing her fingers, the sign for 'Break'.

Rahk watched that, remarkably thoughtful considering his boozy demeanor. "Like this?" he asked, mimicking the motion, but his hand landed between the wrong fingers.

Shaking her head, Adelyn showed him the correct way a second time, explaining the details. He repeated the gesture, getting it right.

"That's not too hard," Rahk commented, waving his arms through the gesture a couple more times to get the hang of it.

"If you know how to sign the alphabet, you can say whatever you want," Adelyn commented. "The rest of it just speeds up conversation, makes it less of a headache to get out a sentence or two."

"Sure," Rahk said, raising his mug. "What do we toast to?"

Adelyn chewed her lip and thought about it, then said, "How about to your, eh, blessing?"

Rahk grinned, and they clinked the metal tins together with a slosh and a click. "To my blessing. Always thought I'd get picked someday."

Adelyn took a more tentative sip this time, choking down the burning liquid with a grimace. "Yeah? Never any doubt?"

"A bit of doubt," Rahk said, grimacing at his own drink. "What burns me up though is I don't know who my Watcher was."

"How's that?" Adelyn asked.

"Watcher had to be there for me to get blessed," Rahk said. "But the crowd was such a mess I couldn't say who it was. I know my calling, at least, so that's something."

"Calling?" Adelyn said. She felt out of her depth with Rahk's religious talk, but it was interesting enough to keep her attention.

"Y'know," Rahk said. "My purpose. Reason I got picked. David's calling was to win the war. Guessing yours was to save your town, from what you told me. Shane had to get this place set up, lay the groundwork. Now it's my job to bring his work up a level and take back our city."

Pausing, Adelyn set down her cup. "You think you can do that?"

"With the Watchers on my side?" Rahk asked, throwing back the rest of his drink. "Definitely."

CHAPTER 17

A merchant and a fisherman were arguing about the old legends.

"It's simply impossible that Barius could have killed ten wizards in a single fight," The fisherman said.

The merchant replied, "When I am feasting in the god's halls for eternity, I'll ask him how he did it."

"And what if Barius is cast out with the heretics and liars?" the fisherman asked.

"Well, in that case," The merchant said, "You can ask him."

•Taken from a collection of jokes written in a private collection.

"It's windy up here," Mina commented.

"We're on a roof," Shane said, squinting a bit as he looked around. "It's always windy this high up."

Mina nodded, wiping the water from her face. "Wet, too."

Shane gave an exasperated sigh. "That's because it's raining."

David had no comment. He'd brought along his

notepad, of course, and showed them some basic signs in case they needed to communicate, but this was idle chatter. He did not like idle chatter.

The three of them had scaled a building two blocks away from the boarding house. It hadn't been hard to find someone sympathetic to their cause who had a top-story apartment in the city, and despite the peace officers trawling the streets for any sign of the people who'd been at the town hall, David and Shane had been able to get this far without being noticed by judiciously keeping their heads down and using a handful of covert lookouts to look for any checkpoints that might stop them.

It was perhaps a bit overcautious, and climbing up two city blocks from their destination was certainly more than was necessary, but that was as close as David was comfortable. A bit of basic scouting had reported no less than three plain clothes peace officers keeping an eye on the boarding house, loitering in places that had a view of the entrance without any clear purpose or reason to be there.

Adelyn had been skeptical of this report, saying that there was no way to be certain how many officers were there if they were not in uniform, but the point remained that officers were watching the entrance to the building. Or, at least, somebody was.

On account of that, they were going in through the roof.

"We should get moving," Shane said. "The longer we're up here, the more likely we'll be noticed."

That was sentiment David could agree with. Ensuring that the rope wrapped around his waist was still cinched tight, he rested his hands on the straps of his backpack and started walking in the direction of the boarding house.

The city's architecture played to their advantage. Most buildings were attached, or near enough for it not to make a difference, so when they reached the end of one building it was a simple matter to simply climb up or down the difference to the next. Their route had been planned out to avoid any buildings that were vastly higher or shorter than their neighbors, so no heavy climbing was involved at this stage.

They kept their footsteps soft as they moved around, not wanting to alert the people in the buildings below to their presence. The rain was both a blessing and a curse. It camouflaged their footsteps and kept people from looking up at the sky, but it would make the magic all the harder when it came time.

Shane had forgone his rain slicker and hat, though it would have been perfectly reasonable considering the mild showers that were coming down on them in a pitter patter. It would have been too recognizable after the town hall. David, for his part, had a new hat of his own, a brown jacket over his cotton shirt, and had swapped his black gloves for brown horsehide instead. Anything to distance themselves from how they'd looked two days prior.

They reached the end of the first block of buildings, which meant it was time for magic.

The next street over was too far to jump. With a running leap, David could possibly have grabbed onto the next ledge, but only with a significant amount of luck. Missing that would mean falling four stories onto hard brick road. Expecting all three of them to make it across without injury wasn't remotely reasonable.

David slung the pack from off his back and got to work on setting up the spell. It would be possible to use brute force to create a bridge of pure spirit, but that would have left one of them too exhausted to be of much use if conflict arose.

Untying the string that held the backpack tight, David

pulled out a set of three large jars, a funnel, and a short stick. Each jar was filled with sand made from crushed up quartz that had been tinted with pigments to create a trio of colors.

He emptied the entire jar of untinted quartz, creating a large circle on the roof that would serve as a base for the spell. There were three more identical jars still in the bag, two for planned spells, one as a backup.

Rain started pitting the circle of powdered quartz almost as soon as he made it. This plan had been made assuming dry weather conditions and unlimited time to prepare the runes—now, he was going to have to work fast.

Opening the bag of red sand, he raised it to the funnel and quickly began pouring it out, stenciling the necessary runes as quickly as possible without sacrificing precision.

Mina said something sarcastic and Shane responded with a pithy word, but David ignored them.

Feeling adrenaline start to buzz as he unscrewed the black sand, David began pouring it out in small rings, using the wooden stick to make marks and indentations in the sand. Shane would be the one casting the spell, so it had to be impossible to screw up, precise, perfect. Adelyn would have done it better, but she had to rest and heal, so Shane was their next best sorcerer.

The soft rain continued to muddle the runes even as he placed the last one, stepping away and sealing the jars of quartz to be packed away back in the bag.

He signed to Shane, one of the basic words they'd taught him. 'Go.'

Shane knelt, placed a hand on the circle of quartz, and began to focus. He'd practiced this spell half a dozen times the day before, today was no different except for the rain, muddling the runes and eating away at spirit like hot water poured over a sugar cube. Mina sat down next to him, and he placed a hand on Mina's chest, readying the spell.

The chant was short, but precise, and Shane intoned it perfectly. His will was made manifest through David's runes and in a moment Mina became flush with power, glowing to David's sixth sense. The magic suffused her with strength and power. It wouldn't make her more resilient against the fall, but it would hit like a jolt of pure adrenaline and fire being poured directly into her veins.

Mina took a breath, stumbling back as Shane cast the spell, then clambered to her feet and grinned. "Is the coast clear?"

David crept to the side of the building and looked. A few people around, but not many, and nobody was looking up. There was a spider's web of power lines running across the street just below where they were placed, providing a minimal amount of cover, but hopefully it'd be enough. He gave her a thumbs up and a nod, backing away.

"How can you know if the coast is clear?" Mina asked. "We're a half mile away from the ocean."

While David stood there, puzzling out the joke, she turned towards the edge of the building and started to run.

The leap carried her over the gap, through the air, and another ten feet besides. She landed with a thud, but there was nothing to be done about that, they had to hope that anyone beneath her wouldn't think enough of it to investigate.

Shane repeated the spell twice more, though each casting was less solid than the last. Applying it to himself, David could feel that the glow of spirit was less vibrant, and by the time he got around to casting it on David, the runes were half blurred and Shane was visibly tired.

The magic entered David less like a blazing fire in his

blood and more like a warm ember. He could reinforce the spell with more spirit, but that wouldn't help—the issue was one of precision, not strength. The spell was too diffuse, but without stopping to recreate a second set of runes, there was no solution. It would have to do.

Shane made the leap, landing on a soft cushion of air that Mina had prepared for them to soften the sound of landing after her own. Coming up in a roll, he waved for David to follow.

Feeling strong, but still taking all the precaution he could, David backed up to the edge of the roof before building up into a run. His boots pounded on the roof below, building a full head of steam, so that when he reached the edge of the roof and kicked off—

He soared through the air, feet waving over nothing. For a second there was nothing but him, the wind, the water dripping down over his hat and into his face.

Feet hit the roof, though instead of a hard impact it came as a soft tumble, like landing on a stack of hay. He rolled through the cushion of air, arms splayed out to catch himself before he slammed into anything hard enough to break a bone.

Sitting up dizzy, David tried to get his senses back and mostly managed to. Mina and Shane were already up, and though Shane offered him a hand, David chose to pick himself up instead.

"Halfway there," Shane said, dusting himself off. "Do you think anyone saw us?"

David shook his head. He couldn't hear anything down at street level that seemed to arouse suspicion.

Shane started walking, and they resumed their careful pace, edging towards the boarding house. David's hair felt wet, and waving a hand over his head, he realized he'd lost his hat.

Well, nothing to be done about it.

His hair quickly soaked through as they walked, dripping down his forehead and into his eyes. Wiping his brow, he was able to clear away the water for a moment, but it quickly returned.

Stopping, David tried to think of anything he had to help with the rain, but he'd not brought a bandana or anything else he could use to cover his head.

Blinking away the water, he resigned himself to putting up with it. Shane hadn't worn a hat either, and he was dealing with the water fine.

"That last spell felt a mite fuzzy at the end there," Shane commented quietly as they clambered down to the next roof. "This rain gonna be a problem?"

David nodded. It had been a problem already, and the next spell wasn't going to be any easier, though it'd only need to be cast once.

"Should we call it off, then?" Shane asked. "It's not too late to back out."

"I think it'll be fine," Mina said. "If we can't go with the plan, we'll punch through the ceiling the old fashioned way."

"That'll draw more attention than a town crier," Shane said. "If we can't do the spell, we pull out."

David knew he could do the spell, that wasn't the problem. The question was whether Shane could pull it off. He kept walking.

Seizing the top of the next roof, he heaved himself up, walking up and over to come into view of the boarding house.

Its roof was all but flooded. Water had pooled across the

top, deepest near the clogged drain at the front end of the building, and rather than flowing into the drainage ditch, it was spilling over the roof's lip. Even at the shallowest, it was enough to come up to David's toes as he hopped down into the puddle.

Shane looked around, then jumped down to David's side. "Can you work in this?"

David pursed his lips, considering. If they unclogged the drain, all this water would go pouring down to the street. That would help, but it would also flood the street below with a torrent of sudden rainwater, which would draw a lot of attention. He was skeptical, but nodded anyways. It would be worth it to try.

The first thing to do was to locate their point of entry. It would be somewhere near the back of the building, but they needed to get it precisely right, or risk exposing themselves and leaving an obvious trail.

Crouching, David unlaced his shoes and socks, stuffing the socks into a pouch on his belt and tying the shoelaces into knots so they could hang around his neck. They were soaked anyways, and he wanted his feet to be directly touching the roof's boards. Cold rainwater sloshed around his heels as he waded forward, concentrating to try and feel the signature aura of iron beneath the water and pitch-sealed wood.

He shut his eyes to keep the water out and began tapping his fingers against his leg to shut out unwanted distractions. Shuffling back and forth in a grid-like pattern, he moved up and down the edge of the roof, searching out with his sixth sense, waiting, until he could feel—

Iron. He'd found it. Stopping in place and opening his eyes, David knelt onto the board off the roof, soaking his pants with cold water. Once in place, he removed the silver necklace he wore, channelled energy into it, and dropped it onto the floorboards.

Exactly as he'd wanted to happen, the spirit started flowing out of the silver and into the water, and from there, dissipating in all directions. Like a light in a dark room, it showed him the precise outlines of everything around, highlighted in his mind by how it responded to the power.

He'd intended to mark out the outlines of the laundry chute with chalk, then work out the spell from there, but that wasn't going to be possible. Instead, he took the boots from where they hung on his neck and placed them at the close corners of the chute, marking it off in a simple but effective way.

"How're you going to handle this rain?" Shane asked, watching. "It's just going to muddle the sand before you can make any runes."

David shook his head. It wasn't sand, it was crushed quartz, but that wouldn't keep it from being washed away. There was a different plan for that.

They couldn't sweep away the water with magic. Water took a lot of power to move, for one, and the spirit used to keep the rain at bay would muck up the important spell anyways. If he moved quickly enough, it might be possible to work through it, but that would put an extra burden on Shane to cast the spell precisely and quietly.

For that matter, they couldn't just let the water flood down the chute. That'd be sure to draw attention, and it would be liable to wreck the boarding house's basement. David could anonymously pay for the damages with the silver once it was recovered, but only if they recovered the silver.

David shook his head to try and get some of the water out of his eyes as he pulled off his backpack and started removing jars. It was going to take all of their supplies to do this. There'd be nothing for the spell to cross the street back the other way, and no backup if he failed.

Before he opened the jars and exposed the quartz to rain, though, he shrugged off his jacket, handed it to Mina, then started uncoiling the rope from around his waist. Once that was done, he passed the rope to Mina as well, then started unbuttoning his shirt.

"What are you doing?" Shane asked.

"Shh," Mina said, staring at David as he handed her his shirt. "He's busy."

David felt exposed and cold. Rainwater that had started soaking his collar was now dripping down his back and over his chest as he knelt over his work surface. The tattoos on his arm were visible, over eight thousand black dots that rippled as he began unscrewing the first of the jars. He could put the jacket back on, but they were in a hurry and he was already thoroughly soaked.

Popping open the first of two of the uncolored jars of crushed quartz, he began pouring them out in lines that outlined the laundry chute below. The rainwater quickly began pulling it away, but not as fast as he could pour it out. In moments, he had short walls of quartz, a couple inches high on all sides, creating a weak moat.

Extending a hand towards Mina, he accepted his shirt, wringing it out and then using the cotton to soak up the water that was pooled inside the moat. He had to sop it up a couple times, but managed to get the interior mostly dry. Water droplets continued to collect, and the quartz moat would only last for another minute or so, but that was fine.

Breathing deep so that his hands wouldn't tremble, David got the last three jars open—one each of clear, black, and red. This part was already in the plan. Assemble the rune, let Shane do the spell.

In under a minute. With water in my eyes and filling up my gloves.

The base was the same, or near enough. He poured out a square of white quartz, using a hand to make the edges a bit sharper and more precise, then began spelling out the runes. It was a spell with a lot of elements—force, heat, a protective barrier to keep in sound.

So many runes were required that the grammar verged on convoluted, and as David neared finishing the magic, he began rushing himself to finish before the moat failed.

He clapped his hands as he finished, stepping back and looking down at the sandy pile of runes. It was terrible craftsmanship, and growing worse by the second as raindrops pitted the markings he'd made, but that would have to do.

Shane pursed his lips, then knelt in David's place, put his hands on the pile of quartz, and readied the magic.

It is not going to work, David thought, observing. *He is going to mess it up. It will make a lot of noise, and the peace officers will come, and I just used all our quartz, so—*

Invoking the magic, Shane brought his will into reality. The wood beneath the quartz cracked audibly, but not as audibly as it should have, and then a perfect square of wooden boards broke out from the rest of the roof, a couple feet wide. It fell inward a couple inches, hitting an invisible barrier.

Quickly snatching away the square of wood, Shane let the quartz fall off the top of it, sprinkling down into a long metal chute below. The magic had worked as intended—they now had a way into the laundry chute.

"Looks like I'm up," Mina said, leaning in to look down

the narrow metal tunnel. She was the smallest member of their group, so she'd been volunteered for this part of the plan. "The money is underneath the floorboards in the second bedroom, yes?"

David nodded. Unless the peace officers had found Adelyn's paranoid hiding spot, that's where their coins had been kept.

Mina shoved David's clothes into Shane's hands. Then, taking the rope she still held, wrapped it around her own arms and shoulders and fashioned a quick harness. It seemed that proficiency with knots simply came with the territory, as she was quickly able to secure the rope over herself so she could be lowered.

"Try not to drop me?" she asked, passing the rope to David.

David nodded as he accepted the other end, holding it slack as Mina stepped over the quartz moat that was already starting to leak. She placed her palms on the edge of the roof, swung her legs down into the narrow gap, lowered herself, then let go.

The rope went taut in David's hands, and he started letting it go slowly, feeding Mina down the chute at a comfortable pace. He could see her slowly slipping further away into the cramped, dark chute. If something dangerous came up, she would be on her own.

She weighed fairly little, even for her size, so David didn't have too much trouble letting her down. It was three stories to the appropriate room, where she would have to jimmy open the chute from the inside and slip into the boarding house's room. From there, she would be on her own, David couldn't even see her.

The chute rattled as Mina slapped it once—that meant 'Stop'. She'd made it down. David held the rope in place, waiting, trying to squint down the chute to see how she was doing.

Barely visible, Mina wriggled, working at something David couldn't make out, and then slipped forward through an opening. Gone, for the moment. The rope went slack as she touched ground and started supporting her own weight, removing the harness so she could move about freely.

Nothing to do except wait. If Mina got caught, she'd try and fight her way out. If that failed, she'd send up a warning. Otherwise... they'd wait.

Shane made an idle comment, but David ignored it, waiting to feel the rope go taut, watching his moat as he waited.

It had come half apart, with heavy rivulets of water flowing through and down the laundry chute. That wouldn't do. David had extra of both black and red quartz, so he popped open those jars and used that to fortify the barrier, standing against the water for a little longer. Once Mina got out, they could stick the chunk of roof back in place and keep out most leaks, but for the moment it was all he could do to keep from flooding the boarding house's basement.

"Do those tattoos mean anything?" Shane asked a second time, examining the many black dots ringing his arm. "Come on, I'm just trying to make conversation while we wait."

One for every person I killed, David thought. He hated the black dots arranged along his arm, but they were his reminder to never take up death as a weapon again. To Shane, he only shook his head. That was a conversation he never wished to have, and especially not with Shane.

Shane nodded, looking around the rooftop for a while longer as David formed the sand moat with his hands, keeping it together.

"You've got more scars than I'd have expected," Shane commented, finally. "Didn't think the Thirteen ever really got hurt. There stories behind those?"

David sighed. Shane was insistent about bringing up things he didn't want to talk about. Every scar on his body did have a story behind it, but almost all were unpleasant. Most ended with David killing the person who gave him the scar.

Snatching his jacket from Shane's arms, David pulled it on, covering his arms and chest so that the scars and tattoos would no longer be visible.

"Sorry, touchy subject," Shane said as he glanced down the hole they'd made in the roof. "She's been gone a while. Think she's okay?"

David's jaw tightened, and he bit down on his lip to focus and think. Shane wasn't being intentionally aggravating. He was stressed and concerned about Mina, and about all his people. He had been extremely clear about not wanting to go forward with the robbery at all, but here he was anyways.

As frustrating as it was to put up with Shane's questioning, David couldn't begrudge him for being anxious. There wasn't much David could do to calm Shane's concerns, but even so, David wouldn't be mad about them either.

The rope went taught, and a second later, David heard three slaps against the inside of the laundry chute. Pulling hard, he drug up the rope, peering down the chute to ensure that it was Mina, and not some peace officer who'd taken Mina's place as part of a trap.

She was down there, sure enough, and she was grinning. That seemed a good sign, so David kept pulling, dragging Mina up the three stories back to the roof. She wasn't any heavier, but going up was harder than going down, and by the time she was up, his arms had started to ache.

Grabbing the lip of the roof, Mina pulled herself up the last few feet, holding a large, familiar coin pouch in her grip as she did so. As her head poked out from above the chute, struggling to pull herself the last couple feet out, she beamed up at Shane.

"So, we've got the coins now," she said. "I don't suppose that this will *change* your mind?"

Shane stared at her a moment, then looked over at David. "You can drop her, if you want."

CHAPTER 18

Inspection report: Boys who installed this didn't know tacks from tassels. Safe door's big enough, I suppose, but the whole interior's just a big box. It's not so much a safe as it is a big oyster. Anyone with brains will crack the thing open and take whatever they want. Might as well be guarding a box of tinfoil, except at least the tinfoil would make a lot of noise rustling if someone cracked it open.

My recommendation's to gut the whole thing, install some actual security and an extra layer of defense. You'll lose some space, but space isn't running at a premium next to security. Put in some real alarm systems, too, so you can get backup even while your guards are busy or distracted. I've got quotes below, but even if you don't hire me you seriously need to get someone, otherwise you're gonna get cleaned out and you'll lose more money than you'd save.

• Excerpt from remodelling proposal for Azah Bank and Trust, penned by Miranda Graves.

ADELYN GLANCED AROUND NERVOUSLY, wishing they could do

this somewhere more private. The alley they were loitering in was empty and hidden from any main thoroughfare, but anyone could come wandering in at any point, and then they'd be stuck with a few things to explain.

The pile of garbage they were crouched behind provided a modest amount of protection against on-looking eyes, but also meant that the alleyway reeked of rotting fish and refuse.

Topher had been insistent that they stop here. This alleyway was only a block and a half away from Harrington's medical center. The safe house, meanwhile, was half a mile as the dragon flies and twice that on foot. He was the one having his leg broken, after all, nobody was going to argue the point.

"Get changed, quick," Rahk said, shoving the bag of clothes into Topher's arms.

Topher started to disrobe, then looked at Adelyn and blushed. "Can you, uh, check for peace officers or something?"

Adelyn smirked but nodded, turning to look at the street and give Topher a bit of privacy. "You know I've seen bare legs before," she commented. "It's hardly the height of immodesty."

"Sure, but it's the principle of the thing," Topher said, tossing his work pants to the ground. "Why are you two here again? I could have done this all by myself."

It was a rhetorical question. Everyone had agreed it was better to send backup, in case Topher needed to make a quick getaway before Harrington could fix his leg. Adelyn and Rahk both had to keep their heads down, but nobody else was less conspicuous, so it had come down to whoever volunteered. Mina could have come along without risking exposure, but she was the least experienced combatant out of all of them and Shane wanted to keep her safe.

"Not gonna throw you out there like Divine chum," Rahk said. "Besides, you're not gonna break your own leg, are ya'?"

"I'm sure it'll be fine to just break a toe," Topher said. A second later, he added, "How do I look?"

Adelyn turned, inspecting Topher's outfit. The clothes they'd purchased weren't gauche or extravagant, but they had still cost more than Adelyn's good church clothes, and that wasn't taking into account the extra silver they'd had to spend to get the Beor silver exchanged for regular coinage. Topher was posing as the son of a wealthy merchant, who'd fallen while climbing. It was a ridiculous way to spend their money when the Watched were in need of much more important supplies, but there wasn't any way around it if they wanted Topher to serve as their distraction.

Still, as she looked him up and down, Adelyn had to admit that the clothes looked good. Unlike his loose, faded work clothes, the new outfit was tailored to Topher's body perfectly. It made him look taller, and outlined his figure to make it readily apparent that, while not a musclebound brute, Topher was not lacking for fitness.

Reaching in the pocket of his bright new vest, Topher retrieved a pair of glasses, brushing the hair away from his ears as he put them on and adjusted the way the set.

After blinking a couple times, Topher turned to look at Adelyn, blue eyes more obvious behind the frame. "Well?" he asked, gesturing to his outfit. "How do I look?"

"You look good," Adelyn commented, looking him up and down. For once, she didn't have trouble seeing him as her peer, instead of as a child they were dragging along.

Topher beamed. "You bet I do. But how're the clothes?"

Adelyn rolled her eyes. "Run a couple fingers through your hair, muss it up a bit. You did just fall half a story, after all."

Nodding, Topher ruffled his hair a bit, making it stick up at odd ends, then looking between Adelyn and Rahk, sticking out a leg. "Well? Which of you wants to do the honors?"

Chewing her lip, Adelyn glanced at Rahk. "I could, if—"

"Let me handle it," Rahk said, sifting through the garbage for a moment, looking for something. "Topher, sit down and stick out the leg you don't like as much."

Grimacing, Topher nodded. As he obeyed, though, he asked, "And we're sure that Harrington can fix—" He screamed as Rahk suddenly brought down a broken chunk of brick in an overhand attack, fulfilling his namesake and smashing the improvised bludgeon into Topher's leg.

The bone cracked audibly, though Adelyn could still barely hear it beneath Topher's shriek of pain. Rahk crouched and slapped a hand over Topher's mouth to shut him up, but he continued trying to call out, eyes bugging out as he shouted a cry of pain into Rahk's hand.

"Shh, shh," Rahk said, putting a hand on Topher's shoulder. "Hurts like Watcher's spite, huh? Just keep it in for a little bit, you'll be okay. Okay?"

Topher stared him in the eye, shaking his head a bit, fingers still clapped over his lips to keep him from making noise.

"*Okay?*" Rahk repeated. "You're a tough man. You want to kick those Divine bastards out of our city?"

This time, Topher's head twitched in a tiny nod.

"Then you'll have to put up with pain a damn sight worse'n this," Rahk said. "Feel it. It hurts, but you're stronger than your leg. Got it?"

Topher nodded again.

"Got it?" Rahk repeated insistently.

This time Topher's nod came emphatically, his eyes no longer so wide.

"I'm takin' my hand away," Rahk said. "You're gonna keep your mouth shut all the way to Harrington's, then you've got to focus. Don't take painkillers, they'll dull your nerves. Understood?"

When Topher twitched his head in agreement yet again, Rahk pulled his hand away. "Don't look at the leg unless you're wantin' to puke. Need a hand up?"

Topher's bobbing head briefly changed to a shake, refusing the help. He seized the garbage bin by his side, heaving himself up, wobbling unsteadily. His expression was locked in a tight grimace of pain, lips trembling, but he kept his mouth clamped shut. Adelyn couldn't be sure, but she imagined that if he dared open his mouth for a moment, he'd start screaming again.

Using the wall as a crutch, Topher hopped out of the alley, off-balance. He couldn't use his leg, obviously, and it would have seemed strange had he shown up with a crutch.

Adelyn quietly crept behind him, keeping a safe distance, but staying within line of sight. This was where she and Rahk came in—Topher had to make it a block and a half down the street with that leg, carrying ten silver daggers sewn into a vest pocket. A wealthy lad like him, clearly injured, was half guaranteed to attract unwanted attention from street thieves looking to make a quick bit of coin.

If someone attacked him, they'd have to call off the plan and think of something else after they rescued him. That wouldn't do anyone any good, though, so their first goal was to keep the attack from happening in the first place.

Trying to seem casual, Adelyn leaned against the wall at the corner of the alley, eyeing Topher as he limped away.

"You're lookin' more like a thief than anyone on that street," Rahk mentioned, plopping down on the wall next to her and roughly rolling up a cigarette.

"You smoke?" Adelyn asked, still staring at Topher to make sure he was safe.

"Nah," Rahk replied casually. "But it's less suspicious to be standin' around with a cigarette than without. Quit starin'."

Adelyn broke off her gaze. "How am I supposed to know he's in trouble if I don't watch him?"

"Don't watch the target," Rahk explained quietly, gesturing with the rolled tobacco as he fished out a matchbook. "Watch the people watchin' 'im. See who's curious, and who's hungry."

Following his gesture, Adelyn looked around. Topher was drawing a lot of eyes—most of the eyes on the street, in fact, those who weren't busy working or bustling along to get somewhere fast.

Some of the older people on the street looked on with concern for the hurt boy. Others, younger, carried more curiosity. A few even wore expressions of derision on their faces, thinking that the rich boy deserved to get hurt.

"Looks fine to me," Rahk said, casually scanning the street. "If someone were gonna make a move, they'd have started towards him already. He'll be fine, besides."

"You sound pretty confident," Adelyn said. "You know something about Topher that I don't?"

"I know he's been laying low since he got blessed," Rahk said. "Watchers don't pick chumps for their blessing. He's still got a job to do."

"So, what?" Adelyn asked. "You think sorcerers are immortal?"

"Not immortal," Rahk said. "But the Watcher's aren't stupid neither. They won't pick someone who can't do what they need done. After that, it's up to the sorcerer in question to watch their own hide. You ready to go?"

"I'll be ready once it's been five minutes," Adelyn said. "We need to give Topher time to move to the back room."

"He'll be there soon," Rahk said, nodding. After a half second's consideration, he added, "While we're here. Something I've been meanin' to ask you."

Adelyn froze, glancing over her shoulder at Rahk. "Yeah?"

Rahk started rolling another cigarette, deftly wrapping up the tobacco he had no intention of smoking. "Why the about face? You weren't gonna help us 'till the town hall, then you showed up 'n saved our asses. What convinced you?"

Chewing her lip, Adelyn shrugged. "I wasn't planning to help you, I wanted to keep an eye on David, but once the fighting started I saw people who needed help and couldn't stand by."

Nodding, Rahk lit up the loosely rolled cigarette, holding it between his fingers. "You didn't believe us, huh? Thought we were full of it when we said the peace officers were a bunch of killers?"

Adelyn shook her head. "I was wrong."

Rahk looked at the glowing tip of his cigarette, watching it burn down. Minutes passed, and he said, "You should probably scamper on over there, it's been long enough."

"Are you sure?" Adelyn asked, glancing around. "Has it been five minutes?"

"Roundabouts," Rahk said. "Get a move on. Be careful."

"Make sure nobody comes in after me," Adelyn reminded, taking as deep a breath as she could manage without too much pain. Walking forward, she approached the medical center, trying to look as casual as possible. She was keenly aware that her stride was stiff and awkward, and she wanted to run to the door to get off of the street as quick as possible, but she forced herself to keep a walking pace.

She didn't see anyone approaching her. Reaching the door, she tried the handle, found it unlocked, and slowly pushed it in.

The hinges didn't creak. It was a boon that Harrington took time and care to keep his shop maintained, since a loud, squeaky set of hinges would have given Adelyn away in an instant.

As the door was opened a few inches, Adelyn shot her hand up to grab the bell above the door, holding it in place so that the hammer couldn't ring and announce her presence. Pushing the bell up, she opened the door the rest of the way, slipped inside, shut the door, and finally lowered the bell back into place.

As she'd hoped, Harrington and Topher had already moved to the back room, and were having a loud conversation.

"Ow! Azahim protect me, old man, be careful!" It was clearly Topher, but he had pitched his voice high and nasally to sound more obnoxious than usual.

"I need to get these pants out of the way, son."

"Well be careful! It hurts!"

Adelyn crept into the room, trying to decide where to look for the keys first.

The far wall was a stack of shelves and drawers from floor to ceiling, with a ladder to get things from up high. A glass display cabinet was against the left wall with various specimens and knickknacks displayed, which Adelyn could safely write off. More low shelves populated the front wall, though they only came up to knee height to keep from obstructing the windows.

Harrington's desk took up the right wall, next to the door that led into the exam room in the back. The desktop was populated with scattered papers and notes, a small spirit powered coffee pot nestled to the side. His coat was thrown over the desk chair, and there was half a sandwich wrapped in wax paper sitting atop a loose pile of receipts.

She tried a first drawer at random, sliding it out carefully, finding a neat collection of rolled bandages. No luck. Shutting it, she moved to the next drawer, but she already knew that this wasn't going to work. There were dozens of possible drawers, and only one of them would have what she was looking for. Brute forcing the problem wasn't going to be fast enough.

"Hold on, now, let me get a look at this." Harrington's voice came from the other room, his tone calm and soothing, exactly the same as it'd been when he was examining David's wounds.

Adelyn checked the next drawer and, not finding the keys, moved on to the next. Still not finding any keys, she stood back, looking around, trying to think it out.

He wouldn't keep his keys in a random drawer, they'd be somewhere specific.

From the other room, she heard Harrington's voice carry, his tone no longer so calm. "Son, I've seen a lot of broken bones in my day, and I know what a fall looks like. Why don't you tell me what really happened?"

Topher's voice cracked as he responded. "I-I fell. I was climbing, and—"

"Okay, let's try this again. You can tell me what

happened to your leg, or you can march right out of my shop."

Adelyn's breath caught, and she turned to the door. If Harrington came out now, she wouldn't be able to get out quietly. She would have to run for it, and pray that Harrington didn't question why his door bell was ringing.

"Wait!" Topher exclaimed. "I-I got in a fight."

"That's more like it. Who started it?"

"Eh... they did."

Given a reprieve on time, Adelyn spun around the room, looking around for the keys. Harrington's desk sat in the corner of the room, and Adelyn walked over to that, checking the drawers.

Nothing. She found papers, some receipts, even a drawer full of glittering silver and bronze coins. No keys.

"So how'd your leg get hurt, then?"

"I was walking down in the south side of town—you know, where all the Watched live. My dad told me not to go over there, but I didn't listen. Some kid came up, started pushing me around, saying I had to get out of 'their part of town', I told them to shove off. Next thing I know, I was flat on the ground, and he had a brick, and—"

"Does your dad know you're here?"

"Well... not exactly. I don't want him to know I was over there... I know you can do magic to heal stuff, I figured he didn't have to know. I have money!"

"You should tell your father what happened. I'm loathe to take money from a child. Go, get your father, have him come in with you and then we'll take care of that leg."

"Please? It's my money, fair and square. I really don't want him to know."

Topher was doing his best to stall, but it seemed like Harrington wasn't going to concede the point. Adelyn had checked every drawer in the desk with no luck, and she was out of time. Unless she went back to checking random drawers on the wall, hoping to get lucky, there was no certain way she could find those keys.

"Get your father. I'm sorry, but I won't fix your leg any other way." Footsteps started tapping towards the front room, Harrington approaching so that he could escort Topher out. Adelyn froze, ducking behind the desk for a tiny bit of cover, hoping she wouldn't be seen.

"Wait!" Topher yelped, his voice cracking into a panicked squeak. "I-I started the fight. That's why I can't tell my dad."

Harrington's footsteps faltered and stopped. Adelyn took a breath and renewed her scan of the room, looking for what she could have missed.

"And why should I help you stay out of trouble when you're going around starting fights, young man?"

"They deserved it. There's this guy, Ezra, from the east end. He made a pass at my sister, gave her a hard time when she told him to shove off."

There was a long pause, while Adelyn tried to think. *I work in this shop day in and day out. I'm a jerk. Where do I keep my keys?*

Harrington's voice echoed through the door. "You've lied to me twice now. I think you're lying to me a third time with this story about your sister."

Topher's voice didn't betray a hint of deception as he said, "Mister, I don't play around when it comes to protecting my sister."

Adelyn looked around the room one last time, then almost slapped herself as she realized where to look. Turning, she started fishing through the pockets of Harrington's coat. The first pocket contained only a small coin purse, and the second was empty, but on the third she struck gold.

It was an effort of self-control not to cheer in triumph as Adelyn fished out the ring of keys, holding them carefully so that they wouldn't jingle. The vault key was instantly recognizable by the serial number and the "Presidential Bank and Trust of Azah" emblem stamped onto the bow. It took a little dexterity to slip the key off the ring without making the keys jangle against each other, but Adelyn managed it, slipping the rest of the keys back into place. With luck, Harrington wouldn't notice that it was missing for a couple days.

"Sit up on the table there, son. It looks like a clean break, I should be able to get you patched up in no time."

CHAPTER 19

Flintwood: Your 'friends' have abandoned you.

Subject: Bullshit.

Flintwood: It's been almost two weeks, Henry. Nobody's come for you.

Subject: I know you're lying.

Flintwood: Henry, Henry. Normally we get at least a 'Husband' or 'Sister' show up, concerned and asking after their relative's welfare. Can never post bail, of course, and the moment we start pressing for details they run off, but you didn't even get a fake cousin looking after you.

Subject: My friends won't abandon me.

Flintwood: Well, they'd better remember you soon. I've got you about another week before the judge sets a date for your execution. I wish there was more I could do to help, but I can't justify cutting you a deal for nothing, Henry.

Subject: Nert.

Flintwood: I'm sorry?

Subject: My name. It's not Henry, it's Nert.

• Excerpt from interrogation with prisoner.

. . .

Adelyn sat to one side of the long table, mulling over some plans for the heist and turning the key over in her hand. Topher had walked back to their safe house a couple hours before, his leg fully healed and his expensive clothes discarded in a dumpster somewhere.

The chair next to her scraped against the floor as Topher slid into the seat, placing down two steaming cups of coffee, one watery, one black and thick. "You like it strong, right?" he asked.

Adelyn shook her head. "I like it to taste decent, but beggars can't exactly be choosers."

Flashing his teeth in a grin, Topher stood back up and hurried over to the cupboard, returning with a little container of sugar and scooping two spoonfuls into Adelyn's coffee. "I may have taken a couple extra pins out of the fund when I was getting those clothes fitted. Don't tell Shane."

Adelyn considered scolding him for the waste of money, but there'd been plenty left over to buy medicine and bandages even after his outfit, so it wasn't like he'd hurt them any by splurging. "Thanks," she said, sipping the coffee. It was still sludge, but the sugar helped mask the bitterness. "Good thinking back there, by the way, keeping him distracted."

"Oh, that?" Topher grinned and waved a hand dismissively. "Bigoted old ass, I could wrap him around my finger without even trying."

"Still, good thinking," Adelyn repeated. "I thought our goose was cooked back there, but you got him to heal you anyways."

"Speaking of the healing, I got a question for you," Topher said, sitting back down next to her and adjusting his glasses. "It's about magic."

Glancing his way, Adelyn asked, "You're keeping the glasses?"

"They make it easier to read," Topher said, blushing. "Couldn't justify buying a pair before, but now that I've got them, no need to throw 'em out."

"Okay," Adelyn said. "Magic question, then. Why not ask David?"

"'Cause he'll give me a big speech and a dozen asides about technique, and I'm only curious for trivia's sake," Topher said.

"Okay, sure," Adelyn said. "What's the question?"

"Right, so we've just been goin' over the basics, and I get that the stuff the doc did is way beyond me right now, and it'll take some practice and all," Topher said, stuttering a bit over his words. "But when the doc patched up my leg, he didn't cast the spell and then let it run, he kept on chanting and goin' on through the whole thing."

"Okay," Adelyn said. "I'm following that so far. He kept the spell going. What's the question?"

"Well I thought once you cast a spell, it was cast," Topher explained, slurping his coffee as he talked. "And I know you can reinforce it with more energy to keep it running after the fact, but that's not exactly the same thing, you know?"

Adelyn nodded, taking a drink of her coffee. "Okay, I think I've got it. He wasn't just casting one spell, he was casting a bunch of little spells that worked on top of each other. I've seen it in combat, too, if you know what you're doing you can modify a spell that's already been cast so it does different stuff."

That caught Topher's attention. "How's that? David said precision magic weren't much use in a duel."

"I don't think it has to be precise," Adelyn said, though

she was treading into unfamiliar territory. "A lot of what I saw wasn't fine surgery, they were making fireballs move off course or changing a shield to protect against different things.

"That's nifty," Topher said. "Seems a fair sight more useful than blunt barriers and what not."

"Sure," Adelyn said. "If you can pull it off. If I've got someone throwing a fireball at me, I don't want to rely on my terrible aim to get that attack out of the way, I want to be totally protected against it." Chewing her lip, she looked at his cocky expression and added, "Don't try it, if that's what you're planning. If we go up against that witch and you try something fancy that you haven't practiced, you're going to get yourself killed."

"Who, me?" Topher grinned. "I'm impervious, you don't gotta worry about me getting hurt."

Adelyn raised an eyebrow at Topher, then glanced down significantly at his leg, which had been broken only a few hours earlier.

"Oh, well, sure, but that was on purpose," Topher explained. "I'm impervious in a real fight, you know? Nobody's gonna get me down without me getting them down first."

While Adelyn had noticed Mina walking up behind her brother, she was still caught by surprise when Topher's sister grabbed the back of his chair and jerked back, sending her brother crashing to the ground in a clatter.

Half the heads in the room spun to look at the source of the noise, and several hands reached for weapons until they saw Topher swearing on the ground, his sister standing over him with a smarmy grin.

"What? I was just testing his theory," Mina said, looking

around at all the faces watching her, then down at her brother. "Still feeling impervious?"

"That was cheap," Topher groaned, pushing himself up out of the chair. "You know my leg got broke today?"

"You're fine," Mina said, rolling her eyes, picking up the chair she'd just knocked down and sitting in it. "Are we going to start this meeting, or what?"

...

'What did you do to practice magic before I came here?'

David had written out the note earlier, and now passed it to Mina. He was curious if they'd even bothered to train before they had a teacher.

"Under normal circumstances?" Mina asked, curious. In her hands, she was smoothing down a six foot holly staff with a bit of sandpaper, smoothing off the bumps and rough edges so that it would be ready for carving. "We didn't. Took about a year to get this place built, that took most of our time, and we didn't have anything to learn from."

David followed her gesture around the room, then wrote out another question. 'How did you afford to build this place?' It wasn't exactly a palace, but since they'd dug it out and furnished it from scratch, it was still impressive.

Tilting her head and staring at the ceiling for a moment, Mina shrugged, running the grit of the paper down the length of the staff in a long motion, then holding up the staff to look for any imperfections. It was taller than she was, but she held it steadily, her expression not betraying any reaction to the weight of the stick. "Mostly busking. Little performances around the city, plus we'll sell crap to tourists. Lots of people pass through the city for a day or two, and all of 'em seem to want something to remember this place by."

That didn't seem to fit David's memory of his childhood. There'd been plenty of street cons and performers, sure, but there hadn't been any tourists. Nobody particularly wanted to go on a trip to a coastal town that was built entirely out of mud, timber, and colorful vulgarity, and Azah didn't seem that much different than his hometown of Westbrig.

Mina saw his expression and laughed. "What, not expecting tourists would want to come to a craphole like Azah?" David nodded sheepishly, and Mina bobbed her head in agreement. "City's not so bad if you have money. The Church of the Divine's one of the biggest in the realm, too. Lot of Divine pilgrims come here to pay special sacrifice or whatnot, and they usually come with money. Normally we'd be out making bank right now, Eatle's Day is coming up and that brings in all the travelers wanting to pay homage."

David thought about it, then wrote, 'That church is probably what saved your city.'

Mina raised an eyebrow as she read it. "How's that?"

'Most coastal cities were burned, but you were put to siege,' David wrote. 'They probably didn't want to destroy a monument like that.'

"Oh, right," Mina said. "Kind of wish they had torched the place, even if there were less tourists, we'd also have less Divine in the city in general. Still—" She paused, holding up a hand and looking over to where her brother and Adelyn were having a conversation. "You hear that?"

David frowned and shook his head, unsure what she was talking about.

"My brother's about to make a fool of himself," Mina said, passing the staff she'd been working on to David. "Hold this?"

David accepted the rough staff, watching as Mina got up from her seat and walked over. Now that he was paying attention, he could hear that Topher was bragging about his invulnerability, right until Mina grabbed the back of his chair.

...

Shane sat down at one end of the table, and Rahk positioned himself on the far end, creating a tension that even David noticed.

Mina was still in the chair she'd taken from her brother, and Topher had thus gotten seated on the other side of the table, keeping a watchful eye on her. Adelyn and David were across from each other as well, the six of them forming the entire heist team, plus or minus a few others they might need to recruit.

"We have one key," Rahk said, cutting straight to the chase. "Now all we need is a way into the secure area where they keep the vaults and a way past the guards."

"Which is still impossible," Shane said. "All you've done is inconvenience a physician a bit and waste David's money."

"I did some skulking around the bank while you were out and about getting your leg broken, and those guards aren't playing around," Mina said. "They're armed to the teeth, but they don't have much in the way of magic protection. I could only peek inside the vault area, so I can't say what kind of security they've got in there, but I can't imagine it's a pushover either."

"We can figure out the guards later. We just need to get another key to get through that door, right?" Adelyn asked. "Could we steal it?"

Shane shook his head. "It's a key and a combination lock to get into the vault room. Not to mention, the keys are kept in places a lot more secure than an old man's coat pocket."

David had an idea, and nudged Adelyn to have her

translate. 'Could we sign up for an account? That'd get us in.'

"No can do," Shane said, shaking his head. "Even if we could get a lock box in their vault, access is prohibited to daytime hours, and you have to be let in by a government employee. We'd never be able to so much as peek into the library, let alone carry away its contents."

"Let's blow up the vault door, then," Rahk said, nonchalant. "How tough can it be?"

"It's steel, right?" Adelyn asked.

Mina nodded. "Big door, too. One of those big handles that looks like a ship's wheel, lock's about as big as my fist."

"That's not gonna be quiet to punch through," Adelyn said. "And we can't use a spell to quickly break the lock or do something subtle."

"I'm not talking about magic," Rahk said. "Why not—"

"*No,*" Shane cut in. "We're not talking about that. Blowing down the door is gonna make too much noise and alert the peace officers, it's not an option. We can't force our way through that door."

"Anyone else think it's ironic," Mina commented, "That they are keeping out thieves with a steel door?" When that didn't get a response, she added, "A steal door. Steel? Steal? Anyone?"

Rahk picked up the conversation before it could be permanently derailed. "Don't suppose you know how to crack a lock, eh, Bren?"

David almost ignored the comment, before realizing it was directed at him and shaking his head. While he might have been able to pull off a spell that would work in spite of all the steel, he couldn't teach that level of precision in a day or two.

"Is the whole place made of steel?" Rahk asked. "Why not go around back and burn our way in?"

"I think so," Mina said. "The majority of the building is wood, same as the rest of the city, but the vault walls are all steel, lined with bronze on the inside."

"Then we've got no plan," Shane said. "We can't get the key and the combination, and we can't blow down the door silently."

'Something is bothering me here,' David said, getting Adelyn's attention so she could translate. 'We know it's lined with bronze so that they can have spells working inside, but does anyone know what the spell is.'

"Could it be a whammy?" Topher asked, once Adelyn had relayed David's words. "A blow to the head that will blast anyone who tries to get in outside of business hours."

'That is not likely,' David signed, letting Adelyn convey his words. 'It would take too much power, and would be useless if more than a single person tried to break in.'

"Here's a question," Mina asked, stepping in. "If it's a spell, it can't be switched on and off by just anyone. They'd need a sorceress to come in and reset it every night during closing hours. I don't think Harrington is the type to do grunt work like that, is he?"

"So we take out the witch," Rahk suggested. "Put her underground, so nobody is around to reset their magic at night."

David shook his head immediately, and Adelyn picked up his objection without needing clarification. "We're not killing her to pull this off," she said.

Rahk sat forward in his chair. "Why not? That witch deserves it, you've got to agree there."

He had a point, but David didn't object to the killing, and he explained. 'Killing her before the heist draws too much attention to us. Even if they do not piece together what we are doing, we will bring down heat from the government that we cannot deal with.'

"Government's already lookin' for us," Rahk objected.

"They can look harder," Shane said. "If we kill their witch, without provocation, they'll call in the whole army to come find us."

After a few seconds of silent contemplation, Mina piped in. "This is a stupid question, but what if it's not a spell?"

"How do you mean?" Shane asked, leaning in.

Mina sat forward, looking at the ceiling and waving her hand to gesture for more time. "Give me a moment here… I'm thinking on it. I don't think they bring in the witch every night, though, that'd be foolhardy and she'd never get a break." After a brief pause, she said, "It could be a machine. Could they have something that can tell if someone's in the room?"

That got Adelyn's attention. "That's definitely possible. A seismograph can sense spirit, I've seen those before. David?"

'The steel walls pose a problem,' David signed. 'They could set up a seismograph, sure, but if the walls are solid steel, it could not carry a warning anywhere.'

"Okay, another stupid question," Mina said. "Why can't they run a copper wire into the vault?"

'Because,' David started, but he stopped before signing anything else. He was going to say 'Because the walls are solid steel', but that wasn't confirmed. It would be trivial to put in a small hole somewhere, insulate it, and run a wire through. Without blueprints, it would be impossible to confirm, but it was possible. 'They could.'

"Would that work?" Shane asked.

'They'd need to run two wires,' David explained, after considering it. 'One to carry power in, to keep the seismograph running, one to send a signal out, but yes that would work.'

Rahk grinned. "So we can cut off the power going into the vault room, that'll stop any spell they've got waiting for us."

"How do you plan on figuring out the right cable?" Shane asked, frowning in one corner of his mouth. "There's about thirty power lines on that street. We can't cut out power to the whole street, that'd attract too much attention."

Adelyn cut in. "We don't have to."

"You got a plan?" Rahk asked.

Nodding enthusiastically as the wheels turned in her head, Adelyn said, "We don't have to cut off power going in the vaults, we just have to cut off power going out. That'll be easy to find—it won't be carrying much spirit, so we'll be able to tell it apart from all the other cables. All we have to do is wait until it's raining."

"How's that gonna help?" Topher asked.

Mina had perked up—she apparently knew something David couldn't decipher, because she said, "Won't that attract too much attention anyways?"

Chewing her lip for a second, Adelyn shook her head. "No, because they won't realize it's an emergency."

"Back up a tick," Topher said. "What're you on about?"

"The warning spell," Adelyn said. "If we go in there and mess it up, that will let them know that we're in the vault, and they'll get together a posse of peace officers to come kill us. But if we wait until a night when it's raining, and then cut off the outgoing power from the spell..."

It finally clicked in David's head, a second before Mina finished the thought. "They'll think that it's leaking, and they'll have to come unlock the door to figure out the problem."

"Wouldn't they realize that the power was cut?" Shane asked.

"No," Adelyn said. "If water seeped into the cable, it would look exactly like a power outage, unless there's something I don't know about how they set it up."

David held up a hand, offering a correction. 'If we cut the wire, it will be too sharp, but I can pull the spirit out slowly and make it look genuine.'

Rahk interrupted her, saying, "And if they think that the library's floodin', they'll send someone packing to get that fixed. We just gotta wait for them to unlock the door and get in to where the vaults are, then bushwhack 'em."

"And what if we're wrong?" Shane asked. "What if, instead of a maintenance worker, they think it's an emergency and send a whole platoon?"

'I will not cut the line, my plan is to take out the spirit,' David signed. 'If more than one person shows up, you leave, I restore power, and nobody will be the wiser. They'll be confused as to why the spell failed, but that is it.'

"No harm, no foul," Rahk added. "We can do this. All that's left is getting past the guards. Eight guards, six sorcerers, that's easy even if we are knocking them out."

Shane sat back in his chair, crossing his arms and considering it. "Next time it rains, then. Shouldn't take long."

CHAPTER 20

WANTED
>Alive
>Adelyn Mayweather
>Disturbance of the Peace, Assault of a peace officer, Aiding and Abetting Fugitives
>Reward: Three Silver Swords
>Armed and extremely dangerous, believed to be a witch

WANTED
>Dead or Alive
>David Undertow
>Murder, Disturbance of the Peace, Assault of a peace officer, Conspiracy Against the State
>Reward: One Silver Sword
>Armed and extremely dangerous
>•Posters distributed in Azah. Sketches were included of the fugitives.

. . .

It didn't take long.

The next rain was two evenings later—a day before the medic had told Adelyn she would be okay to resume physical activity, technically, but she wasn't too concerned about one day. The pains in her chest had been reduced to a minor twinge and her breathing no longer seemed to be impaired, so she assumed it was fine.

Shane lined up everyone who was participating in the heist. Eight people in total. Adelyn, David, Rahk, Mina, Topher, Brenden, Ansyr, and of course Shane himself. Six people of a magical persuasion, and two without, but Brenden and Ansyr would be serving only as lookouts, away from any of the action.

"Gather 'round," Shane said, kneeling by a solid wooden chest that he kept in the corner of the safe room. "If we're doing this, it'll be with the Watcher's grace. Adelyn, handle your own prayers however you want."

Adelyn nodded in appreciation. Shane clearly didn't approve of her beliefs, but he wouldn't give her any flak for them, and she was thankful for that even if she got a couple dirty looks from Rahk and Brenden at the mention. She'd already made her prayers upstairs, cleaning a corner of the apartment and beseeching the Lords for protection, so all she had to do now was wait for the Watched to finish their own ceremony from a few paces away.

The five Watched lined up in front of Shane, along with David, standing with his chest out and head held high. Shane started with him, saying a few words, then tying a bandana over David's face and mouth, placing a wide brimmed hat over his head. The apparel was practical, they needed it to keep their identities hidden from the peace officers, but Shane still treated the disguises with the same reverence he might apply to a set of holy relics.

Returning to his storage chest and then moving down the line, Shane gave the same treatment to the young siblings. Once he got to Ansyr, though, his performance changed slightly. He altered his speech, asking her a question, then offering a necklace to go with the disguise. Brenden got the same treatment, receiving his own necklace in turn.

Finally, Shane reached the last person in line. "Rahk," he said. "This'll be the first time you've run with us since your blessing. Are you ready?"

"I am," Rahk said. They stared at each other for a long moment, and Shane didn't move to progress the ritual.

Dropping to one knee, Rahk raised his head so that he was looking up at Shane. None of the other Watched had done this—they had all been presented their disguises as equals, even the two who had not a lick of magical talent. Still, Rahk lowered himself, waiting for his turn.

Shane hesitated, then repeated his words. "Today, we work to increase the order in the world, and to help the downtrodden. You, who bear the mantle of the Watchers, will join us in this holy endeavor. Rise, and take your place with the rest of us."

Rahk rose, all but his eyes obscured by his new mask. Rather than simply stand in line, though, he pushed past Shane, crouched by the wooden chest, and withdrew the last matching set of hat and bandana.

Turning to face Shane, Rahk said, "Your turn."

"I can do it myself," Shane said, extending a hand to take the bandana from Rahk.

"Sure," Rahk said. "But that's true for any of us, 's not the point. You don't want the blessin', that's fine too."

Adelyn watched Shane's chest slowly rise and fall as he took in a long breath and looked at the other Watched in line, and then the leader of their group nodded. "I'll accept the blessing," he said, finally, sticking out his chin.

Rahk nodded, then glanced at David. "Bren Cultt, would you do the honors?"

Shane stiffened. "Now wait a minute, I—"

"You want the blessin' from the oldest and most experienced of us, right?" Rahk asked. "That's the whole reason you get t'do the honors normally, right? 'Cause you're the most senior here?"

"Well, yes," Shane said. "But David—"

"Bren's as much a one of us as anyone," Rahk said. "And he's been blessed longer'n any of us. Did ya' think I was gonna do it?"

Adelyn took her attention away from the argument for a moment to glance at David, curious what he thought of this. She couldn't see his expression, nor anyone else's, but his fingers were drumming quietly against the side of his leg and his tense posture conveyed uncertainty. To Adelyn's best guess, he would go along with the ritual if Shane consented, but if it was refused, David wouldn't complain.

"David can't say the words," Shane was arguing, as Adelyn turned her attention back to the conversation.

Rahk laughed in Shane's face, then said, "Do you think that the Watchers can't speak in signs? They're immortal, I'm sure they've found the time to learn a few languages."

"Fine," Shane said, finally looking over to David. "Do you want to do this?"

Stepping forward tentatively, David nodded, and a second later he was handed the bandana and hat by Rahk.

He signed the words as faithfully as possible, to Adelyn's reading, while Shane stood like a statue and waited for him to be done. Tying the bandana proved a trick, David's fingers were not so deft as those of a dock worker, and beneath thick leather gloves he had to fumble with the knot for a while before getting it tight. The hat was easier, going on Shane's head without issue.

"We're set, then," Shane said, voice muffled slightly by the bandana covering his face. "Rain's not gonna get any heavier. Are you all ready to go?"

"One more thing," Rahk said, crouching by the storage chest and digging out a spare hat of a different style and a strip of cloth that was a different color and shape than any of the bandanas.

He tossed the spare disguise to Adelyn, who caught them out of the air. "No ritual for me?" she asked, her tone conveying the joke.

"Don't want you gettin' an extra double set of wanted posters," Rahk said. "Though if you want a ritual, suppose we could get someone to dress up as a dragon and dance around for a while."

"Has this been washed since last time it was worn?" Adelyn asked, holding up the stained fabric.

"Think so," Rahk said. "'S just old."

Adelyn nodded, tying the cloth over her face. "Good enough for me."

...

The streets were shadowy and dim during the day, but at night they were black.

Storefronts were occasionally fitted with torches or lamps, but those were only bright enough to illuminate little patches, not the whole street. On another night, the starlight and moonlight might have been enough to provide a little visibility, but the dark rain clouds blocked out that source of illumination. The only other usual source of light on the street—people, walking about with torches—was absent, as nobody wanted to be walking around in the heavy rain.

As such, David had an easy time sticking to the shadows as he crept through the city. An occasional strike of lightning would thunder above, lighting the streets for a few moments, but that would pass in the time it took for his heart to skip a beat.

Brenden and Ansyr had gone ahead, scouting the street. They had lamps with charged spirit batteries stuck to the bottom, which they'd light if they noticed any kind of threat. The batteries wouldn't last long, especially in the rain—perhaps an hour, if they were lucky—but it was enough to give ample warning for their purposes.

Everyone else was holding back by five minutes. There was no point in rushing forward, then being forced to loiter in the street and the rain while they waited for David to do his work.

Rubbing a hand at his face, David tried to navigate the street while effectively blind. He'd considered taking off the bandana for this part. If someone saw him wearing a mask while he was walking down the street, they might find it suspicious. Ultimately, though, he'd kept it on, because his mere presence skulking around the city at night was going to be nearly as suspicious, and it'd be hard to even see that he was wearing the disguise in the darkness.

He'd memorized the route. Three blocks forward, a left, two blocks, a right, two more blocks and then left at the wide fork, then one more left for the final block. Not hard, unless he missed an intersection, in which case he'd never find his way there until the sun came up.

Unfortunately, his sixth sense was almost useless here. Water would wick away and diffuse spirit, and the rain effectively blinded his ability to detect his surroundings. All he could feel was what was on his own person. The new hook on his belt, the silver chain around his neck. Blinded by darkness, unable to hear anything except the patter of rain and roar of thunder, magic senses cut off by rain, David was reduced to feeling his way down the street, using the rare lantern or streetlight as waypoints to navigate, using his hands to keep from walking into obstacles.

He made it to the last left, then looked around for any lamps. He didn't see Brenden or Ansyr shining a lamp, so the coast was clear.

Stumbling forward, David counted his steps, walking close to the building to his left so that he could sense it despite the rain. The front of the Bank and Trust building would be well lit, but around back, the squat wooden building was as dark as the rest of the city.

He trailed one hand against the wall and kept the other raised into the air, feeling for a street pole that would serve as his ladder to the roof.

Hand touching wood, David stopped.

Found it.

Grinning beneath his bandana, David grabbed the tall wooden pole, heaved himself up, and began the task of shimmying to the top. Once he was eight feet up, metal spikes were driven into the sides to serve as handholds, and David was able to climb the rest of the way up the pole with no trouble.

There was a spider's web of tangled wires mounted at the top of the pole, power coursing through them with an unmistakable tingle, lines running off in every direction. Almost half the cables, though, were pointed in a single direction, running towards the bank and trust.

Here, David's sixth sense finally came in handy. The rain blurred what he could feel, but the power running in the lines was so acute and sharp that he could still follow it clearly. Water ran into his eyes, so he shut them tight. He wouldn't need to see for this part.

His grip was eroded a bit as water ran around his gloves, but he held on tight as his feet found purchase on the spike handholds, clinging tightly with one arm so that he could not fall.

Squinting in the rain, he tried to work out his next step by sight, but the rain and the dark blurred his vision past the point of usefulness. Lightning flashed, burning a microsecond image of the knotted wires into his vision. He was now close enough to the spirit lines that he could reach up and touch them, leather gloves dragging against the rubber coating all the cables.

There were more than a dozen individual cables running, supplying power to all the buildings on the street, and—if their theory was correct—delivering signals out of the vaults. David couldn't feel the currents of power running through the individual cables, but the buzz of power that hung in the air was unmistakable.

Shimmying a step higher, he sought out a solid grip with his left hand. He could feel a water spout off to his side, water sluicing from the top of the pole all the way down to below the street, where drains would direct the runoff into the ocean. Grabbing the topmost handhold, he clamped down his brass thumb over it and flexed his fingers, holding onto the steel spike tightly so that he would be anchored down and could use his right hand freely.

Reaching beneath his bandana, David bit down on the tip of his right glove and pulled it off with a jerk of his head. Once his fingertips were free, he extended his reach up towards the buzz of power running through the spirit lines. Wet fingers touched the narrow rubber lines, and he closed his hand around the first, feeling out the power in the cable.

Spirit tingled, and for just a moment, David's senses ceased to note the cold water running down his face and back, the itchy band of the wide hat that he'd been given, the slowly building tension in his limbs as he hung off the side of the pole. For that moment, there was nothing but him and the spirit in the cable.

Power was coursing beneath his fingers, strong as almost anything he'd ever felt. Memories flickered through his mind, days spent on the practice ground learning to use power without waste, to cast spells with ruthless efficiency and precision. Later times, on the battlefield, killing his first soldier, racking up a body count as he fought to win the president's war.

He couldn't remember every kill, the faces bleeding together from dozens of conflicts, and he had to trust his past self that the count he'd made was accurate. His left arm bore a single black dot for each person he'd killed, if that count made in the heat of battle could be trusted to accuracy.

He *could* remember every spell. Or, at least, it seemed that he could. Thousands, tens of thousands, maybe hundreds of thousands of times, he'd harnessed this power and brought it to life, turning his desire into reality as he manipulated the forces of life granted to him by the Watchers.

All that was gone now.

Has Sarah responded? Maybe-

Lightning flashed, and David snapped out of his reflection, regaining his focus on the task at hand. There was too much power in this cable. Anyone who had set up a warning spell that sent out this much spirit was a rank amateur.

David shifted his grip, moving to the next cable and

feeling it out. Still too much—this cable was thicker, and carried even more power than the last.

There were ten more lines, but David only had to check three before he found his target. The tingle of spirit could still be felt, it wasn't a dead line, but the power flow was minimal, almost imperceptible with all the rain coursing around it.

He checked the remaining cables to be certain, but they all carried a significant current. There was only one cable sending such a minimal charge. This was it, then. Once David cut the signal, a bank employee was supposed to come running.

So, David cut the signal.

That done, he prayed that the bank employee would stick to their half of the script.

It was simple enough to pull the spirit out of the copper wire, even with the rubber coat. The coating was designed to keep the power from fading naturally, it couldn't protect against deliberate sabotage.

Once he started pulling out the power, David couldn't stop until someone showed up. If he allowed the signal from the spell to resume, it would be an obvious sign that something was amiss. In order to sell the deception, to make the bank think that the spell had been damaged by rain leakage or flooding, the spell had to be cut out until a maintenance worker arrived to unlock the door.

Clinging tightly to his perch, David waited.

...

"How long do you suppose it'll be?" Adelyn asked, tugging at the straps around her wrists and forearms. They'd made new tools just for fighting the witch, and though Adelyn agreed it was a necessary precaution, the wooden rods fastened to her arms made them feel stiff and awkward to move.

She and Rahk were waiting in an alley where they could see the entrance, tucked off to one side while they watched for a repairman to arrive. Shane, Mina, and Topher would be in a far alley, to watch from the other side. Security would all be inside, so for now they were all in hiding.

"Shh," Ezra said, hissing out a whisper. Though he was only a couple feet away, Adelyn could barely see him, and the voice seemed to come from nowhere. "The dark will keep us hidden, but keep your mouth shut. The night won't break his ears."

"Sorry," Adelyn whispered back. "I—"

Ezra nudged Adelyn to silence her a second time. "Shh. Someone's coming."

Looking up, she saw a lamp moving past, but it wasn't headed towards the entrance of the bank. It was headed around back.

...

The lamplight was noticeable even behind David's shut eyelids. It wasn't incredibly bright, but amidst the pitch-black night, it still stood out.

Still, there wasn't anything he could do in response except try—and fail—to keep his heartbeat from accelerating. If it wasn't the maintenance worker, then they would pass by without conflict. If it was, well, David couldn't do anything to hide—he had to stay where he was, and pray to the Watchers that he wouldn't be seen. His only option was to continue clinging to the pole, and wait until the situation changed.

The rain continued to pour, and David couldn't easily turn his head to watch the lamplight's approach. He thought the light was getting brighter, but that could have been his imagination. His hand tightened on the water spout, and he felt the metal bend slightly under his grip.

Nobody would look up, not in a downpour like this. They will keep their head down, get inside, and be none the wiser.

Finally, the person carrying the lamp got close enough that David could hear their voice. They were talking to themself, grumbling about the weather and the failure of their alarm.

"... going to strangle that damned contractor if I have to reset a single rune. He promised it'd be completely waterproof." The voice was low, gravelly, and feminine.

Whoever it was, she stopped directly below David and started fishing with a ring of keys. If she'd seen David, she hadn't betrayed any sign of that, but he could hear her, and he could see the subtle glow of her lamp. As high up as he was, David would be cast in heavy shadow, but he wasn't invisible.

Lightning flashed, bathing the street in bright light for a fraction of a second, making David visible for the span of a heartbeat.

...

From the alleyway, Adelyn watched the maintenance worker move out of sight behind the back of the building. "They weren't supposed to do that," Adelyn whispered.

"Front door's probably too much an inconvenience," Rahk whispered back. "Go get the others, have them swing around back. I'm going to follow, make sure Bren's not in trouble."

And with that, before Adelyn could protest, Rahk ran off into the night.

CHAPTER 21

Dear Sally, I have something that I need to say to you,
And though this will be hard to read I hope you see it through,
Though once I said I'd never lie and I'd always be true,
I simply cannot stand that foul coffee that you brew.
• Folk song, "Dear Sally", Verse 1

DAVID FROZE, clinging to the pole and doing his best to look invisible. The woman below likely hadn't been looking up when the lightning had flashed, but if the light had cast his shadow somewhere that she was looking at, she'd be able to raise her light and turn to see him pretty easily.

A moment passed, then two. David couldn't look down at her without moving, and moving would have made more noise than he was willing to risk. He waited, listening, to see if she would react to his presence.

If she saw him, she made no sound and gave no response that David could notice. He couldn't make out her grumbling over the patter of rain, but the sound of squeaking hinges was obvious enough, as well as the sound of the door slamming behind her.

Sliding down the pole, David dropped two handholds at a time until he was low enough to jump down. He made a splash as he landed, muddy water splattering his pants, but it was necessary to get down quickly and inform the others. If they hadn't seen the woman coming around back, they could be waiting endlessly out front for a person who'd never come.

Before he could start running, though, he heard a short, low whistle. He spun to look, but now that the woman's lamp was gone, the alley was as dark as ever. Pinching his lower lip, David sucked in air in two quick bursts, creating a pair of loud, sharp whistles in response.

"Shane." A dim light appeared in the darkness, revealing Rahk a few paces away. He held a steel long hook out, handle first, and said, "Others are comin' round this way in a moment. They go in?"

David nodded, accepting the hook from Rahk.

Grinning, Rahk said, "Let's head inside, then."

Balking, David moved to keep the door shut, wanting to get the others in place before they moved in. Their plan had been made with the assumption that everyone would come in through the front door, where the layout was fairly open and the path to the vaults obvious. They didn't know how the back of the bank was arranged, and he didn't want to go in blind and get surrounded.

Rahk caught the brass handle before David could stop him. There was a couple second's pause where he jiggled the handle to no effect. David thought it might be locked, but there was no such luck. Twisting the knob just right, Rahk swung the door open, slipping quietly inside. David wasn't about to let him go in alone, so he sighed, buckled the hook onto his belt, and followed Rahk in.

The back hallway that they came into was remarkably plain. White walls, a single dim bulb giving off light, a couple doors on each side. David could see a T intersection twenty feet up, but Rahk had stopped after only two paces and held up a hand for David to do the same.

It wasn't hard to see why. The second door on the left was open. Light and conversation were both spilling out of it.

"Miranda! What are you doing here this time of night?" the guard, or whoever was speaking, sounded surprised but not upset. If anything, David would guess they were excited for the intrusion, it gave him something to do on an otherwise boring night.

"Beats the crap out of me," the woman's voice was jovial, if still a bit grumpy. "I was all settled in for the night with a good book and a glass of brandy when the buzzer started going off. Runes in the vaults are acting up."

"Ain't no intrusion. I was there not five minutes ago, thing's still locked up tighter than a Watcher's hatband."

"Naw, I wouldn't figure there had been. Probably a leak somewhere, got in and shorted out the wires. If I'm lucky I'll just have to patch the leak and mop up, but it could take me awhile. Is that coffee fresh?"

"I put on the pot an hour ago."

"May I?"

"Help yourself."

They continued chatting, but David's attention was pulled away. Rahk had tried the two closer doors and found one to be unlocked, showing the way into a small broom closet. David quietly stepped inside and Rahk followed behind, closing the door most of the way, leaving it open enough that they could see what was going on in the hall.

They waited.

...

Adelyn's boots made loud splashes as she ran to where Shane and the siblings were waiting. They had a whistling code they'd worked out, but she simply rounded the corner and whispered in their direction.

"Someone showed up, but they went around back!"

"What?" Shane hissed back, stepping partway out of the alley. "Do you know it was the right person?"

"No, but they looked pretty urgent," Adelyn said. "Rahk went to go follow them and check on David."

"If it's the wrong person, and we don't see the real guy coming because we're chasing strangers out back, the whole heist is scrubbed and we'll have to abandon it," Shane said.

"I know," Adelyn said. "At least one of us should wait here, just in case."

Topher raised a hand. "I'll do it. You three go, I'll keep an eye out."

Looking at Shane expectantly, Adelyn said, "Good enough for you?"

Shane nodded, then commented over his head, "Mina, you coming, or are you gonna stay with your brother?"

"I see no reason to play it *that* safe," Mina said, with a frown. "That is, the safe I want to play for is... never mind. I'll come with you."

They glanced up and down the street before running out of the alley, skirting the edge of the large bank building and making their way towards the back.

The alley was barren as they turned into it. Adelyn dug in her pocket and pulled out a short, thick wooden rod, no bigger than her thumb and inscribed with runes of light, holding it out with stiff arms. Whispering a word, she held up the now-glowing rod and looked down the alley. She could see the street pole that had power lines running from it, but David was nowhere to be seen.

"There," Mina said, pointing. "A door, by the pole."

"Suppose they went in?" Adelyn asked.

"Where else would they be?" Shane replied. Hefting his staff, he started walking towards it.

...

David peeked out through the tiny slit left in the doorway, watching for the repair woman. He could faintly hear conversation, but he couldn't tell if it was winding down or getting started.

A new noise entered his range of hearing, a metallic click-clack. It took him a second to recognize the sound of the back door handle, jiggling as someone tried to open the door. As it had done before, the handle stuck, but that wouldn't hold for long. If everyone came bursting in, the game would be over. The vault door was still locked. Exposure wasn't an option.

Rahk swung the closet door open and pushed past David, extending the stubby wand in his hand and hissing his own name. *"Rahk."* The handle crumpled in on itself like a metal can being crushed by a stone. It stopped jiggling.

"Did you hear something just now?" Miranda's voice came from the next room over, wary but not nervous.

"Naw. What'd it sound like?"

"I'm not sure..." She trailed off, and David pressed himself against the wall of the closet so that Rahk could get back in and close the door with all possible speed.

David heard footsteps in the hall, but with the closet door shut there was no way to see what was going on.

A long three-count passed, then Miranda called, "It must just be the storm!"

...

"Handle's locked," Mina announced, stepping back from the door. "If David or Rahk had gone in through there, they wouldn't have locked it."

"Then where are they?" Adelyn asked.

"I don't know," Mina said. "Slipped around front?"

Shane rubbed his forehead, stepping back. "Dammit. We need to get back into position out front."

"What about David?" Adelyn glanced down the alleyway in hopes that she might see him, but no luck.

Shaking his head, Shane said, "We can't go off looking for them. He and Rahk can take care of themselves, and if they're caught we can't do anything about it. Let's move."

...

David held his breath as he listened to footsteps strolling away. If Adelyn was on the other side of that door, and she thought it was being held shut, she might simply blow it down with a spell. He put a hand on his hook sword, but if someone blew their way inside, it wouldn't be down to a fight. They would have to run.

Breathing deeply, David waited, ear pressed against the door of the closet.

No sounds of destruction. Miranda was saying something to the guard, then she was walking away, and finally David allowed himself to relax.

"We have a problem," Rahk whispered, his head only a foot or two from David's ear.

David wanted to ask, 'What?', but there was no light in the closet to sign or write. Fortunately, Rahk seemed ready to explain.

"Our plan was to knock out the guards in an even fight.

Six on six. But we don't know if or when the others are gonna come in, and I can't hold back. I'm not sure I can knock 'em all out safely. Might have to kill a few."

Pressing his lips into a line, David tried to think of how to answer that. Rahk was right—knocking out an opponent with magic took longer, required more precision, and was generally harder than killing them. The guards would be armed with real weapons, too, not pipes and sticks.

Rahk wouldn't let him call off the heist and go home. If it came to it, David was certain that he would go on alone rather than back down.

Anyways, David couldn't respond as long as they were in the closet. Grabbing the handle, he pushed the door open and stepped out into the dim light of the hall.

"I know you're not happy with this," Rahk whispered, his voice barely audible over the patter of rain hitting the roof.

David nodded stiffly.

Rahk shrugged. "If you have a better plan, I'm all ears."

Thinking, David gestured to himself, then down the hall, trying to convey what he was thinking to someone who couldn't sign.

Rahk quickly stopped him, whispering, "Adelyn showed me the letters, you can spell it out for me."

Oh. That made things simpler. One letter at a time, David signed out, 'I fight. You shield me.'

Sucking in a breath, Rahk hissed, "You sure? That sounds liable to get you killed."

Better me than anyone else. David thought, but he only nodded.

"Okay," Rahk said. "But if it looks like you're in too much trouble, I ain't gonna hold back."

Inclining his head a fraction of an inch, David allowed it.

Rahk wouldn't hold back if David were killed, so he might as well step in before that, if it came up.

Before it came to a real fight, though, it would be prudent to take things from a six-on-two to a five-on-two. Moving forward, sliding his feet across the floor to keep from making any footsteps, David crept towards the open door where Miranda had spoken to a guard.

The smell of hot coffee and burnt tobacco drifted faintly out of the room, and David settled in to wait outside the door frame.

...

"What now?" Adelyn asked, as she ducked back into the alley where the others were hiding. "Rahk wasn't over there. He's gone."

"That's two people missing," Shane said. "Maybe they went running off after that pedestrian, maybe they got caught by peace officers. We've got no idea where they are. I think we need to call this off and go find our people."

Thunder rumbled, and Adelyn vehemently shook her head. "David can take care of himself, so can Rahk. We've made it this far. We have to hold out a little longer, the plan can still work."

Topher cleared his throat. "No, it can't. If David's not pulling power out of the cables, then they won't need to send anyone to fix the system."

"Maybe they're already on their way," Adelyn said, though she was grasping at straws. "If someone is already walking here, they wouldn't know that the signal is working again."

"Do you think that's likely?" Shane asked.

"It's possible," Adelyn argued, eyeing Mina. "We should wait a little longer."

Mina stepped in, pledging her agreement. "Give it a little time. There's not much harm in waiting."

"Five minutes," Shane said. "Then we go find our people."

...

David was starting to worry that the guard would stay on break all night, when he heard wood scraping against wood and felt a shift in the spirit coming out of the room. For a second, there was a creak of metal and the sound of running water that blended with the sound of rain, then the metal creaked again and the guard started walking to leave.

Rahk, a few paces to David's right, held his breath and pressed himself against the wall a little tighter, not wanting to give up their presence until the last moment.

The guard stepped through the doorway, lips moving to whistle some sort of tune as he returned to work. Before the sound could echo out into the bank, David slipped behind him, one arm wrapping around the guard's neck, the other covering his mouth and nose. At the same time, David's feet shifted, moving his legs so that he could usurp the guard's standing position, pulling him back and off balance.

To his credit, the guard didn't fall into a complete panic. His arms flailed for a moment, but once he realized what was happening, the guard shifted his weight and started driving elbows into David's side, shouting a muffled call for help into David's fingers.

The blows hurt, but David gritted his teeth and gripped tighter, cutting off blood flow into the guard's neck. A couple seconds passed, and the guard's elbows lost their strength. A few more seconds, and the guard went limp.

Dropping the guard gently to the ground, David flipped him onto his stomach, pressing a knee into the small of his back.

Rahk stepped in then, taking over control of the guard. The chokehold was effective, but wouldn't keep him out for long. David could have choked him for longer, but not without inflicting serious brain damage or worse. Instead of that, he let Rahk move in with rope and cloth, gagging the guard and quickly binding his hands and arms.

It was only then that David was able to get a good look at the guard and his apparel. His uniform—a black jacket with silver buttons and a black pair of slacks—was formal but loose, to offer free motion in combat. A whistle hung about his neck, and a small ID was in his breast pocket. Rahk relieved him of the revolver that was held in a belt holster on his right side, but left the sword sheathed on his left.

The whole process took about thirty seconds, plus another ten to drag the guard to the closet, dump him inside, and crush the handle with another spell.

"That's one. Other five aren't gonna be that easy." Looking down the hall, Rahk added, "How long do you suppose it'll take before she gets the vault open?"

David shrugged, pointing. *We might as well go look.*

"Fair enough," Rahk said. "I've got your back."

CHAPTER 22

Day one out to sea.

That's weird to write. I haven't spent more than a day out to sea since the war.

Anyways, we spent the first six hours sailing straight out away from the city. Rest of the time got spent going in circles, looking for prey. Even with a three ship party and all these supplies, captain doesn't want to risk going any further out. Bless that man.

Didn't find anything, but we've got tomorrow to keep looking. Chum'll run out before the evening, so one way or the other we'll be back home by sunset on day three.

Day three. Watchers, I'm getting old.

Can't help but hope we don't find anything. Extra pay'd be nice, but after last time I feel a little guilty. Getting sentimental in my old age.

•Journal entry, written by a sailor on a thulcut hunting ship.

DAVID WALKED FORWARD with his eyes closed and his hands

out, navigating by his sixth sense. It slowed him down, but it let him feel what was coming around the corner, which was critical. If they were about to walk into a guard making his rounds, they needed to have all the warning that they could get.

The bank layout wasn't complicated. The T intersection past the break room split out towards two rows of rooms arranged against the back of the building. Some were likely storage, or offices for those employees who didn't need to interact with the public, but David didn't particularly care about their purpose.

From there, the hallways turned in, pointing towards the front of the bank. Offices lined the outside edge of this hall. Once at the front of the bank, there was a line of booths for tellers during operating hours, and in front of those, a large foyer where customers would come in.

All this was built to surround the centerpiece of the bank, the vault. Though wooden walls were built over it, David could still feel the massive bulwark of steel to his left as he progressed counterclockwise through the bank's halls, at a speed that would hopefully put them on the far side of the guard doing rotation through those same halls.

They reached the end of the hall, where it opened towards the teller booths and, more critically, the vault door. David could feel five people, not including himself and Rahk. Two figures flanking the exposed steel of the vault door, a third standing right in front of the door's handle, and the last two out in front of the teller booths, watching the entrance.

Four guards, plus the maintenance woman. The last guard was no doubt on the far side of the vaults, making his rounds.

Raising a hand, David signalled for them to wait as he

opened his eyes. Miranda hadn't opened the vault door yet. If they started the fight now, their plans would all be worthless.

Rahk crept forward to peek around the corner, looking to see the guards for himself.

"They're packing heat in those holsters," he whispered, stepping back. "Looks like big revolvers. Six shooters. Ones by the door have rifles, the two by the vault had swords, too. Steel should be easy to watch out for, it'll be harder to shield against."

David bobbed his head slightly. As long as Rahk could keep the bullets off of him, the swords wouldn't be a problem. That was an uncertain 'if', but he would have to trust the inexperienced sorcerer that far.

"You boys staying dry?" Miranda asked, her voice echoing through the empty bank, her speech a bit stilted as though she were asking the question while looking for something.

"Don't gotta go outside unless we seen something suspicious," One of the guards cajoled. "A night like this, we just do our best not to see anything."

Miranda laughed, the sound bubbling up with infectious mirth. "Tell me about it! If it were comin' down any harder when that alarm went off, I'd have put in some earplugs and gone back to bed. Had to do something, though, the chime would keep Sam up all night and that's just not a situation I'm willing to deal with."

"How's he doing, anyway?"

"Just lost his first tooth," Miranda said, her tone proud, though also distracted. After a second longer, she added, "Bayd abandon me, I think I left my notebook back at my apartment. I don't suppose one of you remembers the code for the door?"

One of the guards tutted. "You know we're not supposed to tell no one. You could be an imposter, come to rob us!"

"Reuben, I was at your wedding."

"A really dedicated imposter. I got the code, don't you worry."

"Thanks."

David turned his head slightly, frowning as he listened. Closing his eyes for a moment to focus on his other senses, he felt around, then snapped open his eyes and pointed down the hall behind them. The other guard was approaching, having finished his coming around the rest of the bank.

Rahk's eyes widened, spinning and raising his stubby wand, ready to cast a spell.

Too soon. The door isn't open yet.

He risked a glance around the corner, looking for a fraction of a second. A guard was standing at the vault door with Miranda, manipulating something together.

The footsteps got louder and closer, nearly at the corner. "What do we do?" Rahk hissed.

David gave him a blank look. There wasn't anything they could do, besides hope and pray.

Tapping his fingers against the side of his leg, David looked up at the ceiling and focused for a moment. *Watchers, please—*

The guard came around the corner and froze, staring at a pair of Watched sorcerers that were not where they were supposed to be.

Rahk put out his hand in a placating gesture, one finger rising to his lips, silently pleading with the guard to keep quiet. His other hand was raised out, palm down, his wand held loosely between his middle and index finger as though it were a pencil.

From the bank lobby, David heard the heavy shifting

sound of massive oiled hinges as they started to move, then Miranda's voice as she asked, "It's dry. What the—"

The guard jammed his whistle into his mouth and blew, producing a shrill wail of sound as he reached for his gun.

"*Shtap!*" Rahk shouted, hitting the guard with a powerful blast of force that threw him against the back wall. The guard's head slammed into the wall, eliciting a meaty cracking sound as skull met plywood and won, leaving a large dent in the wall at eye level.

David pressed himself against the hallway wall with barely enough time to avoid the steel jacketed ball that whizzed in front of him a heartbeat later.

A quick glance at the guard to his right showed that he wasn't moving. David hadn't yet felt the eruption of spirit that accompanied death, but the guard was out for the count.

Four left.

Rahk spun the wand in a circle between his fingers and called out, *"Ansyr gild!"* The grammar was clumsy, but it created a reasonably durable shield against projectiles out in front of the hallway that would keep bullets off of them for a moment.

David stepped out to examine the scene. Already, the guards had taken up positions of cover. The pair who had been by the door were now crouched behind teller booths, and the two by the vault door had split up, one ducking into the open vault and the other crouching behind a desk.

As soon as David came into view, one of the riflemen started firing, bullets piercing the shield with their force greatly diminished. One bullet struck David over the shoulder, and it felt as though he had been pelted by a stone, bruising him but not piercing his cotton shirt.

David dodged to the side against the next bullet, not

wanting to receive another welting blow as he sized up the situation. Only one guard was firing, hand moving smoothly on his repeating rifle so that a bullet rang out every couple seconds in a rhythm so steady it could have been put to music.

Raising a hand, David felt Rahk's shield, then poured energy into it so that it'd block the bullets for a while longer. Another bullet came through, but in breaking through the reinforced barrier it shed nearly all of its speed, hitting with so little force that David barely noticed.

The shield couldn't move, Rahk wasn't yet experienced enough to create a mobile barrier. If they wanted to progress, they would have to raise a second shield.

"What are you doing?" Rahk asked in exasperation, pressed against the wall as he watched David. "Waiting for them to run out of ammo?"

Giving his head a little shake, David tried to plan. Eight shots had been fired in the course of twenty seconds, and as smoothly as the first guard stopped, the second picked up the beat, smoothly aiming and firing bullets that patterned against David's chest as the first guard began to reload. It was obvious that the bullets were doing nothing to threaten him, and for a second he wondered what the point was.

Understanding clicked into place. They weren't trying to win, they were trying to stall until reinforcements could arrive. With four people shooting, they could fire constantly until out of ammo, and by then, a whole brigade of peace officers would be breaking down the doors.

That told David a few things of note. The guards were experienced enough to be wary, but well trained enough that they could keep a level head with almost mechanical precision. Even the guard who'd found them in the hall had kept his cool long enough to blow his whistle and sound the alarm rather than panicking. They wouldn't be chumps in a fight, and they wouldn't be easy to outmaneuver.

Ducking against the wall so that he wouldn't have to keep maintaining the shield, David heard the gunfire ring out one final time then stop. He looked to Rahk, gesturing with his head and one hand, then fishing in his pocket for a particularly potent tool that he'd brought along.

Rahk nodded, understanding at once what David had in mind. They'd practiced this a couple times at the safe house, and though it had seemed like it'd only be needed in a last resort scenario, now the time had come for them to use it.

The chalk that they had brought along wasn't anything special, a lump of soft limestone that had been cut into a rough pencil shape. The runes that it inscribed onto the wall, though, were clean and sharp and as accurate as David could make in a moment's notice.

David hadn't bothered to memorize any jokes since losing his tongue, anything that would create a safe pool of memories he could convert into spirit. For power, then, he had to pull the pen knife from a pouch on his belt and use it to cut a slice along the palm of his hand, letting the blood pool up and sapping out the spirit so that he could charge up the runes that he'd just marked down.

Just because David couldn't cast spells, that didn't mean he was no longer a wizard.

Once the runes were sufficiently charged, blood dripping down the wall where he'd marked it, David nodded and stepped out of the way. Rahk spun in, slapped his hands against the wall, and called out, *"GILD!"*

Without a modifier to create a gust of wind or wave of heat, the thunderclap of power that roared into the bank was composed of pure spirit, rippling out in all directions and slamming into everything that got in the way.

If any of the guards hadn't been behind cover, they might have been thrown across the room. As it was, the energy crashed into their improvised barricades, knocking cash registers to the ground and throwing papers into the air in a tempest. What force remained then staggered the guards, knocking them to the ground and disrupting their otherwise steady aim. The only guard to keep his feet was the one ducking into the bank vault.

On the heels of the magical tempest came David, his long hook drawn and ready for battle. It was eight running strides to the centered desk, and a running leap carried David over the counter and across, sliding off the desk and onto the ground behind one of the guards.

He could feel the steel of the man's revolver with almost perfect clarity, an echo of the spirit that had crashed into the room a second prior, and that made it easy to dodge to the side and avoid his aim without looking.

The guard fired twice, then put a hand on the hilt of his sword and went to draw. Before he could get his blade unsheathed, David brought his hook down with bone breaking force against the guard's leg.

He screamed and went down, and David kicked away his revolver before turning to run towards the teller booths.

A revolver cracked behind him, but the shot was intercepted by a magic shield, raised in the space of a heartbeat as Rahk came out to join the fighting. Feeling the invisible barrier with his sixth sense, David ignored the guard and his revolver, focusing solely on the two guards in front of him.

He could feel the two rifles being pointed his way. Rahk's shield was only covering his back, and though David was fast on his feet, he wasn't fast enough to close the distance before those guards could pull the trigger.

Hesitating, David dropped to the ground and turned himself sideways, rolling as though he were on fire. Two bullets shot out in the same heartbeat, but the aim could not track his sudden drop, and so the shots missed.

Even with a repeating rifle, it took a second or so to pull the lever, and another moment to cock the hammer back and fire. An experienced rifleman could fire eight shots in ten seconds, which was impressive, but still gave David time to come out of his roll and jump over the desk before a new round could be chambered.

David did so, gladly, driving a kick towards the nearer guard, expecting him to be too busy with his gun to block a kick.

His expectations were wrong. The guard had, apparently, done the math and figured out he wouldn't have time to fire again, and so instead had taken his gun on the stock and barrel in a two-handed grip and swept it up like a staff to block David's attack.

The barrel of the gun impacted against the back of his heel, sending David flipping tail over teakettle into the ground. He managed to take the landing on his arms and come out in a roll, but it left his back exposed, and while the one guard had been preparing to engage in close quarters combat, the other had decided to continue chambering a bullet in his gun.

A steel ball punched a hole just below his right shoulder, spraying blood onto the floor and staggering David forward. He'd been lucky, the shot hadn't hit anywhere vital. Still, it hurt enough to be distracting, and when he spun to face his attackers, his right arm felt unusually weak and heavy.

Gritting his teeth, David switched to a two-handed grip on his hook and charged.

...

Adelyn leaned against the wall of the alleyway, watching and listening. Nobody had approached the front door of the bank, and their time was almost up.

"That's five minutes," Shane said, a second later. "We're leaving."

"Hold on a second longer," Adelyn said, putting up her arm and raising a finger as she tried to listen. "Did you hear that?"

"Hear what?" Topher asked, stepping up next to her.

Adelyn frowned, brow furrowing as she tried to figure out what she'd heard. "It sounded like a whistle."

"I didn't hear anything," Shane said. "Over this storm, I'm not sure we could hear a ten piece band."

"Just a second," Adelyn said. The whistling had stopped, but now she could hear a rhythm of sharp cracks. "Is that gunfire?"

Mina cocked her head. "Gunfire that keeps a tempo?"

"What else would it be?" Adelyn asked. "It's not the storm, the storm wouldn't keep a beat like that!"

"I'm not certain," Shane said. "And we're not kicking down the bank doors until I am pretty *damned* certain."

"At least wait a second longer," Adelyn insisted. "It's something new, at least."

Shane pressed his lips into a line, but settled back into the alleyway.

A moment later, the thunderclaps stopped.

"Whatever it is, it's over now," Shane said. "Our people aren't going to show up by coincidence. We need to go find them."

"A little more time." They were so close, Adelyn wasn't going to let them leave without an argument.

"You've had your time," Shane shook his head. "We're sticking to the plan. You can stay behind if you want."

Chewing her lip, Adelyn tried and failed to think of a good reason to wait longer. When nothing presented itself, she slumped her shoulders and nodded in resignation.

Hefting his staff, Shane nodded, leading them out into the street.

They hadn't taken five steps when a powerful surge of energy washed out from the bank. Even over all the rain, the power of the spirit was unmistakable, and all four of them noticed it.

"It's—" Adelyn started.

"I know," Shane said, already turning to run towards the bank's front door.

CHAPTER 23

One method I've found particularly successful is to temper the truth with the native's beliefs, melding their fiction with our fact. If the world is a great single organism, for example, then perhaps their 'Watchers' are like the immune system of the world, fighting sickness and impurities. (Note that, for this metaphor to work, you might have to explain what an immune system is. Virology is not a popular science amongst these coastal cities.)

The example above is utter nonsense, of course, but it serves the purpose of explaining the truth with a metaphor that they can understand. Once your subject is comfortable with the idea of the Lords, then you can begin to explore the idea that perhaps their old beliefs were false.

•Notes from a Tarraganian minister on converting peoples of other faith.

DAVID'S EYES were barely focused as he watched the two guards, concentrating more on what he could feel than what he could see. Two long barrels of steel, two short, stubby revolvers that were still in holsters. His own hooked sword, held in both hands and ready to strike.

The guards didn't fire straight away, instead moving sideways and parallel to one another in a practiced motion, spreading out. Against a normal foe, that would force someone to turn their gaze to one guard or the other and lose sight of whoever they weren't watching.

David wasn't at such a disadvantage, but he didn't want them to know that. Feigning that he couldn't track all their motions, he cautiously stepped back, then turned to face one of the guards, his injured back to the other.

They aimed and fired, but David had time to feel their motion and easily dodge out of the way. David could keep dodging their aim as long as it was only one person, which was fine, but his hope was that they would charge him, and then—

The guard behind him ran forward at the same time as the one in front, and David spun the long hooked sword in his hands so that the curved end was pointed behind him. Stepping back, he held the hook firm, bracing it as the guard, unable to stop their momentum in time, ran into the end of his weapon.

Swinging around to confront the guard in front of him, David fished the man's ankle and twisted, sending him to the ground, buying time so that he could turn to face the standing guard and drive a kick into his sternum.

A flash of steel behind him served as a split second warning that the downed guard was going for his revolver. David turned back and drove the heel of his boot down on the guard's hand, breaking a few fingers before he could aim the gun he'd drawn.

The fight wasn't won, but it was going well for him.

Before he could finish disabling either guard, though, he felt a heavy load of spirit building just outside the bank doors.

The witch. Peace officers had arrived faster than he'd expected. Driving one last kick at the standing guard, he ran and jumped back over the teller counter, trying to decide if he should fight or simply flee.

...

Raising his sword, Shane poured spirit into a spell, hesitated for half a second, then blew down the bank doors.

Adelyn ran inside the moment the way was open, immediately spotting two bank security guards who were looking towards the back of the bank with confused expressions. One was sitting up off the ground, the other was standing in a hunched position.

Neither stood a chance. In the second it took them to reel and face the destroyed entrance to the bank, two sorcerers and two sorceresses had each drawn up some kind of spell and called up magic in an off key harmony. Fire, air, and raw force all whipped around the guards, sending them both backwards and onto the ground.

It was a flurry of confused energy, but it carried enough power to do the job. One guard slammed into the teller booths, another was thrown far to the side and had his shirt catch fire.

"That was easy," Mina said, watching as the dust settled. "Why didn't we do this in the first place?"

...

David landed behind the booth, foot slipping on a loose pile of papers that had been scattered onto the ground. He grabbed the counter and kept from sprawling, and the sudden jolt on his arm sent a shock of pain through his shoulder as his momentum ceased.

Run, or fight?

He couldn't leave Rahk behind, but a quick survey showed that Rahk was doing just fine for himself. The guard whose leg David had broken earlier looked to be out cold, and the last one standing was pinned on the ground, her face contorted in pain as Rahk twisted her arm back.

If it is just the witch, we can—

Four spells ripped out from the doorway in unison, ranging in degrees of clumsiness. Even a master couldn't throw out that many spells in such unison, but the spirit in the air was disparate and clumsy, as though thrown by a quartet of relative amateurs.

Oh.

David stood, wincing as he turned to face the four figures in the doorway, right about at the same moment that the lead figure was, based on her tone, saying something sarcastic.

He couldn't tell the figures apart easily; only Adelyn was obvious due to her mask being of a different color and style, and by the carved wooden bands strapped to her forearms. It took a second for him to distinguish Shane, who was a bit taller and was armed with his bronze sword, and a second longer still to keep the siblings distinct in his head.

Once he'd confirmed with a visual scan that they were all unharmed and okay, David turned and walked over to Rahk's side, crouching to assist in grappling the guard, choking her out in a handful of seconds.

"Well, that got them sorted," Rahk said, wearing a broad grin on his face, his thick wand held tightly in his hand.

David recognized the grin, having felt that same rush of successful combat a thousand times. Despite the wound in his shoulder, he shared in the endorphin rush and nodded. They were still on high alert, but for a brief moment while the two of them watched their companions approach from across the bank, they reveled in the thrill of battle.

He didn't recognize the figure coming up behind them until it was too late.

Part of it was the steel vault, throwing off his senses to what was behind them. In his mind, though, he had been distracted and off his guard, not paying attention closely enough to stop what would happen.

The figure was only a couple paces behind them, and in their hand, they held an eight-inch length of steel. David tensed as he noticed, crouching his shoulders and starting to spin so that he could defend himself as he parsed out what exactly he sensed.

Rahk's eyes widened as he saw David's motion and felt the same presence a heartbeat later. Energy coursed into his wand as he, too, spun around, his reflexes kicking into a desperate grab at warding off the new attacker.

David realized from his senses what his eyes would confirm half a heartbeat later, but he had no time to react.

Miranda's eyes widened, and her voice broke halfway through the words she'd started to form. "Wait—"

"Rahk!"

Spirit lashed out from the wand, an attacked focused by single-minded desperation and the clarity of panic. Miranda wasn't thrown across the room or slammed dramatically into the floor, her head just snapped back with a sick 'crack', and a moment later, a surge of energy pulsed into the room, the overwhelming burst of spirit that followed the end of a life.

David saw what she looked like for the first time. She was on the older side, with silver streaking her shoulder-length hair and deep smile lines in her face. The tool belt she wore was worn and old but well maintained, new leather replacing straps that had worn out, and she had callused hands that, with the tool belt, belied a long, experienced career.

A crescent wrench that was resting forgotten in her hand slipped out of her fingers and clattered loudly onto bronze tiles. The rest of her fell a moment later.

David's brain caught up halfway with the situation, and he tried to shout "No!" several seconds too late. His wordless cry carried about the same meaning, and equally little effect.

Rahk stared for a moment, his mouth agape. Then, he spun, saying, "She snuck up on me! You all saw it!"

Nobody said anything. Everyone had felt the burst of spirit, of course, but the others were still halfway across the bank and wouldn't have had a good view of what had happened.

Adelyn snapped out of it first, running to cross the remaining steps to the vault. "What happened?"

David quickly signed, 'Panic fire.'

"You killed her?" Adelyn asked, wheeling to face Rahk.

"She shouldn't have snuck up on me," Rahk said, cheeks flushing as his tone took on an angry note. "It's not my fault!"

"What happened?" Shane asked, walking up to them.

"She came up behind me with a wrench," Rahk said, jumping in before Adelyn could try and explain. "I hit her on reflex. Wasn't my fault."

Shane glanced to David, raising an eyebrow. When David didn't respond, Shane turned more directly and asked, "Is that what happened?"

David nodded, though his confirmation didn't quiet Rahk's rising anger.

"My word's not good enough?" he demanded, stepping towards Shane. "I—"

"Shut up!"

Everyone stopped, glancing towards Mina, caught off guard by her outburst.

Clearing her throat, Mina said, "The library is about ten paces away, and I'm pretty sure that peace officers are on their way."

There was a few seconds of pause, then Rahk nodded. "Shane, you've got the key."

Shane clenched his jaw, but stuck a hand in his pocket and shoved something towards Rahk. Rahk took the key, turned, and walked into the vault.

It looked about how David had expected. Bronze tiles and plating covered the walls, to allow spirit to function inside. Wooden cabinets were lined up to the left and right, and three heavy bronze-plated doors were set against the far wall—miniature, bronze versions of the heavy vault door that they'd come in through.

Rahk approached the leftmost door, fished the key into the lock, twisted it, and spun the handle. With a gentle pull, the door swung open.

...

Adelyn stared at the body on the ground for twenty seconds, only pulling her attention away when Topher touched her arm.

"We can't do anything for her now." His hand lingering for a moment before he pulled it back, looking away from the body.

"I know," Adelyn said, glancing up at him. "But... are we going to leave her like this?"

"They'll bury her proper," Topher said.

Adelyn felt her eyes starting to get wet, but bit down on

her lip hard and pushed away the thoughts that were forming. Still, she stayed by the woman, finding it difficult to pull herself away.

"Hey," Topher said. "It's not your fault. We all agreed to this, knowing someone might get hurt."

Adelyn pulled her eyes away from the body, looking at Topher instead. "It was my idea."

"But you didn't vote for it," Topher argued. "Come on, we should go get what we came here for before the peace officers arrive."

Adelyn took a deep breath and nodded, walking with him through the steel doorway and towards the open inner vault.

She sucked in a breath when she saw it. Hundreds of books, maybe even thousands, sat on row upon rows of shelves. It wasn't a huge space, perhaps six feet wide and eight feet deep, but the walls were neatly lined with volumes, each of which contained a vast trove of magical knowledge.

Shane had doffed his backpack, which was little more than a large canvas bag with shoulder loops made of rope, and produced from it five more identical packs which he distributed out. "Six books each, no more."

Rahk was looking up and down the shelves with searching eyes, scrutinizing the titles of the books with more care than Adelyn would have expected. He took the pack, but didn't immediately start stuffing it with books, instead taking his time, selecting one title and stowing it before returning to his careful search.

Adelyn wasn't so thorough. She scanned the shelves until she saw what looked like medical texts, grabbed two at a time, and started shoving them into her pack. Despite

Shane's warning, she took almost a dozen books, shouldering the pack and testing the weight.

Mina and Topher had both followed a similar procedure, and Shane was only a little more careful. Soon, it was only David carefully pulling books off the shelves, and Rahk apparently scanning the books for something he wasn't easily finding.

"Hurry up," Shane said. "They'll be here soon."

David nodded, putting two more books in his bag and slipping the straps over his shoulders. He gave a thumbs up, pushing past them and out into the wider vault area.

"Come on, Rahk," Shane said, waving an arm to leave.

"Go on ahead," Rahk waved a hand at him, still scanning the titles. "I'm right behind you."

Shane gave his head a terse shake, then glanced over his shoulder towards the exit. "We're not leaving anyone behind. Come on."

"Go check the street, then, make sure we're still safe," Rahk said, dismissively. "Thirty seconds."

Shane's jaw tightened, but he complied, gesturing for everyone else to follow. Adelyn did so, jogging lightly towards the front doors.

Adelyn noticed that the guard by the vault door was starting to stir, but a quick glance around revealed that she didn't have any weapons on her, and the nearest thing she could possibly use was a revolver some twenty feet away on the ground.

Still, she pointed this out. "One of the guards is awake."

"Leave them," Shane said. "If they stand up, we can knock them back down."

Topher gave the stirring guard a wide berth, but Mina stepped right over her as though the guard were just a sack of potatoes that was in the way, and they kept moving. David was a couple paces behind everyone else, glancing around towards the two hallways behind them, but no threats were making themselves visible and he seemed content to keep moving.

Shane peered out the door as they reached it, though the gesture was mostly a token. "I can't see a thing."

Topher tried to assist, but quickly came to the same conclusion. "If anyone's out there, we won't know until they're within spitting distance."

"I think that's an exaggeration," Mina said, peeking over his shoulder. "You can spit pretty far."

Adelyn spotted David tense out of the corner of her eye and looked around, confused until she heard Rahk shout a spell from the vault door.

"Bren!"

Her immediate thought was that they were under attack, as a gout of fire burst out around the entrance to the vault, but a quick glance around the room revealed no new attackers, and the spell was too broad and unfocused to be an attack unless Rahk had simply failed to aim with any sort of precision.

He's burning down the bank.

A thousand thoughts crowded towards the forefront of Adelyn's mind, but after a flicker of eye contact with David, she knew what had to take precedent. "The guards!"

She started running, getting her feet moving even faster than David. Everyone else stood agape in confusion, but there was no time to explain, one of the guards was only a few feet away from the vault entrance and Rahk probably hadn't bothered to shield them from his broad attack.

Pouring spirit into her bracelet, she shouted, *"Gildfell!"*

Wind sprang into existence, a massive gust that pushed back the spreading flames and created a temporary path for her to run through. Putting out the fire would've been ideal, but she didn't know a spell for that, so she would have to settle for keeping the flames at bay for a little while.

"I'm fine!" Rahk shouted over the crackle of flames, mistaking the reason for her approach.

"I know!" Adelyn yelled back, crossing to the guard by the vault door.

Her eyes were open, and she'd rolled onto her side, but the guard had otherwise made no move to try and flee. After looking and deciding that the woman's legs were intact, Adelyn knelt and put an arm under her shoulder, helping the guard up.

Rahk looked almost puzzled for a second, then angry. "They're peace officers!" he shouted, stepping in front of Adelyn to block the way to the exit. The fire was spreading out from their position, and Adelyn could see that David was occupied with helping a guard whose leg had been broken.

"They're people!" Adelyn pulled the woman to her feet. The guard seemed bleary, but held most of her own weight and didn't wobble once they were upright. "Get out of my way!"

She watched his expression, indecision plain as emotions flickered across Rahk's face at high speed. Annoyance, anger, and frustration, but also uncertainty. He didn't want to fight her on this, but Adelyn couldn't tell if it was because he was indifferent, or if he thought he'd lose.

"Now!" Adelyn shouted, putting as much force into the words as she could.

Rahk stuck out his chest for a moment, looking like he was going to argue, then deflated and spun, sulking towards the door.

Giving a rueful smile, Adelyn said, "Come on," taking as

much of the woman's weight as she could. It was hard for Adelyn to take the guard's weight gently with the implements strapped to her arms, but Adelyn was less worried with being gentle and more with saving her life, and the guard seemed to share her sentiment. They shuffled through the closing gap in the fire, taking the long way around the teller booths.

She was annoyed to see that the others were still standing hesitantly by the door. Two guards were still lying out cold on the wooden floor, and there were an additional two that she hadn't yet accounted for, though David would hopefully know where to get them.

"Give me a hand!" she shouted at the three of them. Topher, with uncertainty, stepped forward to take the dazed guard, but that was all.

Abandon you, Adelyn thought. Maybe they wouldn't kill the guards themselves, but the Watched group would apparently let the guards die without much hesitation.

As she ran to help one of the unconscious guards, though, she realized that her assessment was wrong. They weren't uncertain how to respond to the fire. Shane, at least, wasn't sadistic, he'd help if it didn't put his own people in harm's way.

They were worried about something else, and there was only one thing that Adelyn could think of for them to be worried about.

"Peace officers?" she called.

David's head snapped in her direction, distracting him for a moment from setting down the guard with the broken leg. The guard slipped from his arms and yelped in pain as they landed on the ground with a mild 'Thud'.

"Lining up outside!" Shane called. "Can't tell how many!"

Adelyn got an idea. "Get these guards to the door!"

"We don't have time!" Mina said. "We need to—"

"Get them to the door, then we'll run out the back way!" Adelyn shouted. "They won't leave the guards to die!"

Or, at least, Adelyn *hoped* they wouldn't leave the guards to die. If the peace officers were busy pulling the guards to safety and possibly even giving them medical attention, it would buy them time to run in the other direction.

Shane realized what her idea was and ran over to help, getting the fourth unconscious guard and hefting him in a firefighter's carry. Rahk was standing by the door, visibly annoyed but unwilling to protest.

As they got the fourth guard to the entrance, Adelyn pushed the door open a crack and peeked outside.

It was still dark, but now a half dozen points of light lit up the street, and she could see shapes—a lot of shapes— moving in the street. She shut the door before anyone could fire on her, then nodded towards Shane.

"That's a lot of them alright. Who knows the best way to get to the back?"

David stepped up and pointed towards the hallway to the left of the vault. The fire had spread out in the way, so Adelyn started gathering power for another burst of wind to get through.

Stepping forward, Shane beat her to the spell, waving his staff to one side and calling, *"Bren jet,"* his words coming a little slow as though he were piecing together the spell as he cast it.

The flames obeyed the call, moving to the side, though unlike the windstorm Adelyn had been planning, it did nothing to clear the smoke that was building. The masks over everyone's faces, soaked in rainwater, provided a cheap filter that helped against the smoke, but Adelyn still found herself coughing as they moved through the opening in single file.

Rahk took up the rear, spinning and adding an extra burst of flame as they made it to the hallway.

Shane shouted something at him in annoyance, but Adelyn was distracted by the guard slumped against the far end of the hall, and the visible dent in the wall above him.

"I'll get him," she said to David, running to the man that was left. He was small for one of the guards, which meant he still weighed almost two hundred pounds, but Adelyn had regularly hauled around eighty pound bags of corn on her family's farm, and while lifting him was a chore, she was able to drag him towards the exit faster than the fire was approaching.

As they reached another turn and approached the backdoor, David stopped to open a maintenance closet, pulling out a guard who was fully conscious, but trussed up like a holiday turkey.

"There's a fire," Adelyn said, dropping the unconscious guard to the ground and reaching for her knife. "Get your friend out of here. He hit his head pretty hard, so be careful with him." David pointed out where to cut, and she freed the guard in a few moments.

"We don't have time for this!" Rahk shouted angrily. "The peace officers are right outside!"

"You set the fire," Adelyn pointed out, helping the freed guard pick up his coworker. The guard, it seemed, didn't have the fight in him to try and take on six people under those circumstances.

Topher checked the back door, trying the handle and finding it stuck. "The door's broken," he said.

With a quick spell, Mina blew the door off its hinges,

flopping it down into the mud outside as she commented, "It opens just fine for me."

Shane drew a light and walked outside, looking around. "It's clear!" he said. "Everyone keep your heads down, we may get out of this without a fight yet."

David pushed through the door first, looking up and down the street and pointing to the left. Adelyn couldn't guess why he had decided on that direction, but she trusted his call and so followed him down the alley.

CHAPTER 24

Given the influx of between five and eight thousand pilgrims every year for the Eatle's Day celebration, Azah wavers between being the first and second most populous coastal city west of the peninsula. When compared to the cities on the peninsula, as well, there are similar results—though this is mainly due to the largest peninsula cities being razed during their conquest.
 • Report on the surviving postwar coastal cities.

DAVID NEEDED SOMEWHERE quiet so he could think.

Rahk lied to me.

Someone he trusted had made a promise not to try and kill people unless it was necessary, then he'd set a fire with reckless abandon. David couldn't decide how to process that, and until he had a chance to sit down and think it over, David knew he wouldn't be able to put it out of his mind.

Rain was still pattering down on his hat, and he knew in his head that there were peace officers only a couple seconds away, gathered around the corner, but that concern was at the back of his mind.

Had he always been planning that?

He tried to replay the evening in his head, to reconsider what Rahk had said and done, trying to put it all into context. The white noise of the rain and cracks of thunder drowned out any attempt to focus.

A good fight would have helped him clear his mind, but he didn't want his mind clear, he wanted it free of distractions so that he could focus on something. Instead, rain splashed down in front of his face and soaked into his boots, and the neat hole in his shoulder pulsed with a dull ache that demanded his attention even as the cold rain numbed the worst of the pain.

Someone shouted something, but he couldn't tell what it had been over the rain and his own thoughts. They were probably asking something about directions, so he pointed forward to explain that he intended to keep moving forward. They were pointed towards the coast at the moment. In the dark, he wouldn't be able to find the way towards the safe house, but if they made it to the coast, it would be much easier for them to orient themselves.

Did he mean to kill Miranda?

They came to the end of the road they were on, and had to decide which way to fork. David couldn't see far enough down in either direction to know which way was better, and stood there paralyzed by indecision.

He looked to the right, then to the left. Both were equally dark and unclear.

Did he block out the others on purpose?

That seemed unlikely. Rahk was clever, but he wasn't prescient. Besides that, it wouldn't have benefited him any, and—

Someone bumped David on the arm, knocking him out

of the chain of thought. They yelled something at him, then started running off to the right.

Blinking and wiping water off his chin, David followed the figure, unable to tell in the darkness which of his companions it was.

David followed passively as the new leader navigated the rest of the way. A quick check ensured that everyone was still together, and there was nobody apparently following them, so David stopped caring and let himself lag back and follow along.

The heavy rain had dwindled to a light shower by the time that they reached the safe house. After raising a light and looking around carefully to make sure nobody was watching them, Shane led them up to the second story and waved them all inside.

David pulled off his mask the second they were indoors, and his hat came off a second later. He felt soaked to the bone and wanted out of his wet clothes as fast as possible.

Someone said something, which he missed. They touched his arm, and he looked over to see that it was Shane. David pulled away from his touch, but listened this time.

"Can you go down a ladder with your injury?" Shane asked.

With my injury... David looked at his shoulder, then back up at Shane, nodding in affirmation.

Giving a quick gesture with his arm, Shane said, "Then get downstairs. I'll help bandage that wound in a minute."

David complied, wandering over to the cot that hid the trapdoor going downstairs. He was able to lift it with one arm and start his descent down, climbing slowly and holding onto the rungs with only one hand, avoiding his injured side.

Once downstairs, he shrugged off the backpack full of books, dumping it by the entrance and making a beeline towards an empty bed at the back of the basement hideout. The room was lit, and he could finally see that a pink stain had soaked the right side of his shirt, blood mixed with rainwater.

He peeled off the shirt, self-consciousness about his tattoos outdone by the desire to be free of the sopping wet clothes. From there, he unbuckled his belt, letting it fall with his long hook to the ground. His boots came off next, and his socks, and after a moment of consideration he stripped off his pants and gloves, leaving him wearing only a pair of boxers that had managed to stay mostly dry, and the silver necklace that he preferred to never be without.

He could hear everyone else downstairs, arguing about something, but before he entered that discussion he needed to parse things out for himself and decide what he thought. Lying down on the bed, he pulled its thin blanket over himself, rolled onto his back, and finally took the time to think.

...

Adelyn slid down to the basement, coming in on the heels of David, dropping her books down and making a beeline towards the stovetop so she could make a pot of coffee. It would be bitter sludge, but she wanted something hot and bracing to calm the trembling in her limbs that she couldn't shake.

Shane came in behind her, looking around. "Are Ansyr or Brenden back yet?" he called immediately, looking around.

Glancing over her shoulder, Adelyn checked, but saw no sign of them. There was the standard collection of sick and injured, the surgeon they'd asked to show up early in case his services were needed, and a few other Watched who were hiding out from peace officers. No sign of Brenden or Ansyr.

"I don't see them," Adelyn said, using a match to start a fire in the stove. "But they said they might end up taking shelter somewhere else, if it looked like making it back here would be too difficult. They're probably fine."

Shane nodded, turning to face the ladder as Rahk came down into the basement. Without preamble, he shouted, "What were you thinking?"

"Abandon 'em. None of our people got hurt, so who cares?" Rahk said simply, walking past Shane and setting his own bag down on the long dining table.

Shane sputtered, turning to shout something else at Rahk, but he was clearly grasping for straws in regards to what he could say. "But why?"

Rahk looked over at Shane like he thought Shane was stupid. "They're a bunch of presidential bastards. I want to make 'em hurt. If I could've burned down the whole vault, I would have."

Adelyn thought about that, and got a sinking feeling in her stomach as she set the water on to boil. Turning to face Rahk, she asked, "Did you burn the library?"

"You're damned right I did," Rahk said, his expression proud as he set out a couple books on the table in front of him.

"Those were irreplaceable," Adelyn said. "The information in them—"

"Wasn't no good to us," Rahk said. "Anything we couldn't carry away was worthless."

Adelyn blanched, then tried to think how much of the library they'd been able to carry away. Maybe forty books, out of a collection of at least a thousand. Nobody was printing new magical texts, and old ones were increasingly hard to come by, and Rahk had just casually destroyed all that knowledge like he was taking out the trash.

"Lords..." Adelyn mumbled.

Mina strolled in, dumping her bag in the pile by the ladder. "How much did we get away with?" she called out, a question to nobody in particular.

"Plenty," Rahk called back. "More than plenty. We've got the largest set of information in the city."

Mina whistled, then her stride caught as she realized the implications of what he'd said.

Topher was the last one in. He didn't spot the pile of bags, and so set his own backpack down by one of the beds, sitting down to start unlacing his boots.

One of the Watched who'd been taking shelter in the hideout—Adelyn couldn't remember his name—walked over to the dining table. "What happened?"

"We pulled it off," Rahk said, gesturing towards where David had apparently gone to sleep. "A couple hitches. Me and Bren had to fight the guards all on our lonesome, but we took care of 'em. Bren got hit, but nobody else got hurt. Burned down the whole bank while we were at it, too."

The unnamed Watched grinned. "Well done. What's the plan now?"

"Now we take the fight to them," Rahk said, returning the grin.

"Hold it," Shane said, stalking over to the table. "That's not the plan. We got these books so we can heal one another and protect ourselves better. We're not taking the fight anywhere, we don't want a fight."

Rahk glared back at him. "We'll see what happens."

The water had finished boiling, and Adelyn poured in

the coffee grounds. "Someone did get hurt," She said. "You killed the mechanic woman."

"That was an accident, and she wasn't one of ours anyways," Rahk said casually, noting that Adelyn was fixing coffee. "Pour me a cup of that once it's done?"

"Sure," Adelyn said automatically, though a part of her wanted to say no just to spite him. He hadn't gotten anyone killed with his fire, but that wasn't for lack of trying.

"Thanks," Rahk said, selecting one of his books, standing, and walking away.

...

David stared at the ceiling, half expecting it to start dripping water like a leaky roof. He could faintly hear the pitter-patter of rain coming from outside, but it was no longer the deafening roar that clouded his thoughts.

He arranged everything he knew about Rahk in his head, puzzling it out one piece at a time. Rahk had been chosen by the Watchers to be given power, which implied that he wasn't a complete idiot, but that didn't mean he was a good man.

The Watchers, at least as far as David believed, were stewards who would select individuals to be given power, but stewards weren't perfect, and their criteria for choosing was not always clear. If the Watchers only gave power to good people, David doubted he'd ever have been selected. It was entirely possible that Rahk had only been given power by a panicked Watcher who had been watching the events of the town hall meeting and needed a hasty way to turn the tides of the fight.

Maybe the Watchers don't exist.

David ignored that particular line of thinking for the moment, as it raised too many questions and not enough solutions. The Watchers could be put aside for now, the real question was Rahk.

He claimed he had set fire to the bank to cause financial pain to the peace officers and the government, which was probably true. However, that couldn't be it, if he simply wanted to cause property damage he could do that at any time without significant risk. Rahk had set the fire deliberately after the heist. He wanted to hurt the guards, then.

The question was 'why'. The guards, though technically peace officers, weren't actively contributing to the harassment of the Watched in the city. Rahk didn't have a vendetta against them, so he wanted them dead for another reason.

After a long moment of consideration, David could only think of one reason to set the fire and try to kill the guards. Rahk must have wanted to trigger a reaction from the peace officers. If he wanted to start a fight, that would be the best way to do it: Get the peace officers mad enough to draw them into a confrontation, then get ready with a proverbial loaded gun to fire as soon as the officers kicked down the door.

Before he could get any further with that line of thinking, Rahk appeared and sat down on the cot next to David, saying something in a tone that implied greeting.

David sat up slightly, the blanket sliding down to his waist as he stared at Rahk. He put both his hands face up in front of his body, which was the sign for 'what', but conveniently also looked like a gesture of confusion.

"Just saying that I picked you up a book," Rahk said, waving the book he held in the air.

A book... David mused. That seemed an odd thing, since everyone had grabbed a lot of books, and David hadn't been looking for anything in particular. He tilted his head, trying to read the title, but it was written with runes and was too far away for David to read clearly.

"Adelyn told me you can't sign any of our names," Rahk said, "Because you don't have signs for Sacrosanct. Turns out, there are." He passed the book over, and David was able to look clearly at the runes on the cover.

It took him a second to read, switching gears in his brain to read runic grammar and syntax. Roughly, it translated to, *Sacrosanct Words as Verbal Signs.* Turning the book on its side, David saw that the spine was written in plain letters and confirmed his translation. *Sacrosanct Sign Language Dictionary.*

"Now you can say my name without spellin' it out," Rahk said. "I still don't know hardly more than letters, but if you're gonna be around a while, it only seems fittin' that we be able to talk to each other."

David stared at the book for almost a minute. He was confused as to why his vision was starting to blur, until he wiped at his eyes and his hand came away more wet than it should have been.

Why am I tearing up?

He set down the book and looked back up at Rahk, signing a couple words.

"I don't know what those mean," Rahk said, his expression open. "But I'm going to take a guess at 'thank you'?"

David nodded. He still couldn't quite put to words why the book meant so much, but it had clearly struck close to home.

"Well, don't just sit there!" Rahk exclaimed, smiling. "Come on, I want to know my name."

David nodded, then wiped his eyes again and carefully opened the book, scanning the table of contents. 'Rahk' was traditionally spelled with an R, but some older dialects had different phonetic spelling, so he had to check to make sure before flipping to the Rs and looking up his friend's name.

There were well-drawn illustrations accompanying appropriate runes and descriptions, and David followed them carefully, closing a fist around his thumb and moving it from in front of his chest out, like he was hitting the air in front of him with a backfist.

"That's me?" Rahk asked, mimicking the motion.

David nodded. It was possible he was reading the instructions wrong, but the sign simply *felt* right, and he knew it was correct from that.

"Nice," Rahk said. "Once you've got more of 'em worked out, will you show me?"

Again, David started to nod, then on impulse he signed 'Yes' instead.

Rahk flashed his charming grin. "Thanks. I'll let you get some rest, you looked pretty out of it, but I wanted to get that to you first. Don't forget to get your shoulder patched up before you fall asleep."

David signed 'thank you' for a second time and laid back down, pulling the blankets up and holding them over his chest. He kept his right hand over the top of his left to conceal his thumb, still feeling a little embarrassed about the prosthetic, but for once he didn't much mind having his tattoos exposed.

He didn't get back to his train of thought for several minutes, wondering if and why Rahk would try to provoke a fight.

A moment later, his heart dropped into his stomach as all the pieces fell into place.

...

Adelyn finished pouring the coffee into a trio of mugs—one for herself, one for Rahk, and one for Topher, who had requested a mug. It was difficult to carry all three without spilling, but she was able to keep them balanced to where Topher was sitting.

There, she snagged one of the book bags, picked up the two remaining mugs, and then walked over and set Rahk's cup in front of him, finally sitting down herself to sip coffee and look more closely at the books she'd gathered.

Rahk sat down across from her, reading one of his own volumes. A quick glance showed that he had skipped their objective of getting books on healing magic, and instead chosen volumes on combat and violence.

Adelyn rolled her eyes and returned to her reading. Before she could get through the index of the first book she'd picked up, Shane sat down next to her, staring hard at Rahk.

"We need to talk," he said.

"I agree," Rahk said. "This was a great success. Where are we going to hit them next?"

"*No*," Shane said forcefully, gritting his teeth and putting his hands on the table. "We need to talk about your cowboy move back there. We're a team. We're supposed to work together, not pull stunts liable to get everyone else killed."

"We weren't ever in danger on account o' me," Rahk said. "Only real danger came from y'all trying to get the guards out of harm's way, even that was barely a threat."

"If you say so," Shane said, "But you should have told us about it first so we were ready."

"What, so you could hold a vote?" Rahk asked. "It was a spur of the moment idea, we didn't have time to get into an argument."

"Then why'd you tell us to go ahead while you stayed behind?" Shane asked.

"'Cause I was looking for a book for Bren over there," Rahk said, gesturing to David.

Looking in the direction that Rahk had gestured, Adelyn saw that David was getting to his feet and walking wearily over towards them, looking like he was ready to throw up.

"Are you okay?" Adelyn asked, watching him scoot out a chair and sit down, staring straight at Rahk. His head twitched in a shake, and she could see that his muscles were all tense, like he was getting ready to throw a punch or perhaps get out of the way of something.

'I need my notepad,' he signed to her, his right arm moving a bit stiffly.

Raising an eyebrow, Adelyn said, "I can speak for you, it's fine."

David's jaw tightened even further and he twitched his head again, signing emphatically. 'I need my notepad.'

"Eh... give me a minute, I'll find it," Adelyn said, standing up and running over to the small chest where David's belongings were kept, those that weren't in a soggy pile by his bed. A bit of searching found his notepad and a reasonably sharp pencil, which she brought back and handed to him.

David gave her a thankful expression and took the pencil in tight fingers, writing a note with heavy impressions that left dark black letters on the paper.

He picked up the notepad, ripped out the note, and slid it across the table to Rahk, his palm over the note so that neither Shane nor anyone else could see it.

It didn't matter to Adelyn. She'd been watching him write it out, and saw the note plain as day.

'Did you send the town hall threats?'

CHAPTER 25

Flintwood: What do you know about our local bank and trust?
Nert: Not much. What's this got to do with the train?
Flintwood: Your 'friends' just murdered a city employee and cleared out the vault.
Nert: What?
Flintwood: You didn't know about that?
Nert: No. It was always too much of a risk.
Flintwood: Apparently not. That bank vault was probably the most secure place in the city. Maybe even more secure than our courthouse. Funny that they decided it was worth the risk to get some gold while you're sitting here a few days away from a death sentence.
Nert: You're lying.
Flintwood: Do you want to see the body of the woman they murdered? It's a gruesome sight, with all the burns, but—
Nert: No, but... they wouldn't abandon me.
Flintwood: They already have. Face it, Nert, I'm the last friend you've got. You want to skip a date with a hangman, you've got to give me something to work with.
Nert: What do you want?

Flintwood: Where are they hiding? We know you've got a little hole somewhere that you go to ground in.

Nert: I won't give you that.

Flintwood: Then tell us where you go for a break, then. Anywhere they might duck into for an hour or an afternoon until the smoke clears.

Nert: And if I give you that, you'll let me go?

Flintwood: We'll let you live. Anything else depends on how useful your information ends up being.

•Excerpt from interrogation with prisoner.

DAVID WATCHED CAREFULLY as Rahk read the note, his brow furrowing for a moment as he looked up at David, laughing uncertainly. "Come on, you know me better than that," he said, crumpling up the paper in his hand.

He's evading the question.

David clenched his pencil so hard he worried he might snap it as he wrote out his question again. He already knew the truth, but he needed to hear it from Rahk's lips. 'Did you send in the town hall threats?'

"Bullshit," Rahk said, crumpling the second note as well, stuffing both papers into his pocket. "You know that was a bunch of crap they wrote up to justify it after the fact. You think there was a concerned citizen, too?"

David simply nodded. He knew for a fact that a concerned citizen had expressed worry about the town hall, if Adelyn could be called a 'citizen'. He wrote out a new question, passing it to Rahk as well. 'Did you kill that child?'

"What's he saying?" Shane asked, looking between Rahk and David. "What are you talking about?"

Rahk's brow furrowed deeply, face contorted in furious thought. "Why would you—" His eyebrows shot up, eyes wide as he looked at Adelyn. "You told the peace officers we were going to be there! You're the concerned citizen!"

Adelyn blanched, and her expression gave away the truth before she could try to lie. "I—"

"Is that true?" Shane asked, his gaze snapping to Adelyn.

David noticed that they were drawing the attention of others now, several Watched sitting up and looking over towards the table. A few of the people confined to bed rest while they healed had been injured at the town hall, and mentioning the massacre got their attention immediately.

"I—" Adelyn stammered, her eyes wide, looking to David for some kind of reassurance that he didn't know how to give. "I knew you robbed the train, and I didn't realize—"

Trying to soften the blow, David wrote down, 'Rahk sent in the threats', and handed his notepad to Shane.

Rahk saw the note first, and snatched it away. "That's crap," he said, showing it to Shane but providing his own commentary. "He knows I didn't, but he's trying to protect the girl. You know he's been on her side since they showed up, he'd say anything to protect her."

"David doesn't lie," Adelyn said. "Not ever."

"And we're supposed to trust you on that?" Mina asked, piping up. "Not saying I wouldn't believe him, but you're hardly trustworthy yourself if he's lying to protect you."

"It's her fault," Rahk said, standing and pulling the stubby wand from his belt. "You know how many of our people she got killed? I *said* we shouldn't trust any Divine assholes."

"I'm not Divine," Adelyn spluttered, standing and stepping back. "I'm t-Tarraganian."

"So's the *other* witch working for the peace officers," Rahk said.

David unfocused his eyes, trying to feel out the entire

room. It was an enclosed space with a lot of people in it and fairly little iron to fuzz the spirit in the air, so he was able to quickly and accurately map the whole room in his head.

The picture it painted wasn't pretty. They weren't going to be able to get to the ladder and out without fighting four sorcerers and half a dozen other Watched who were healthy enough to fight, and that fight was not one that David would have wanted to take even when he had his powers.

Rahk was channelling power into his wand, getting a spell ready. He knew the odds as well as David, and clearly was willing to risk the fight.

"Wait," Shane said, putting an arm on Rahk's shoulder.

"Can't keep her locked up, we don't exactly have a prison," Rahk said, pitching his voice loud so that the whole room could hear. "You want to let her run around, knowing she got our people killed, knowing she'd do it again in a heartbeat?"

"I wouldn't—" Adelyn started. "That's why I wanted to rob the vault, to make up—"

David stood up sharply, thinking things over, drawing perhaps half the eyes in the room. Maybe, *maybe* if Adelyn raised a strong enough shield, she could buy a couple seconds, and David could start a brawl that would slow down the Watched long enough for Adelyn to get out. They wouldn't risk chasing her down through the streets, not when there would be peace officers crawling through the city looking for them, so she would be safe.

There was no way to communicate that plan to Adelyn, though, and David suspected that she'd refuse to run and leave David to die.

Only one option, then. David stepped in front of Adelyn, raising his hands out to his side.

"Bren, move," Rahk said, trying to stare David right in

the eyes. David avoided his gaze, looking past him and trying to ensure nobody was sneaking behind Adelyn with a gun. "I like you. We'll talk about this later. She has to go now."

David didn't budge. Rahk would have to go through him if he wanted to kill Adelyn, and David didn't think that Rahk would do that.

Pouring even more power into his wand, Rahk raised it, mouth opening.

"Stop!" Shane said, reaching forward and grabbing Rahk's hand. The spirit in the wand vanished in a second, dispersing into the air as Shane grounded out the energy. "We'll just take their weapons."

Rahk looked angry, but he clenched his jaw and nodded. David could tell that Rahk had used a lot of energy in trying to gather the spirit for whatever attack he was planning, and all that on the heels of a night of action had probably left Rahk more winded than he'd be willing to admit.

Shane gave David a curt nod and he stepped to the side, the silver chain around his neck shifting against naked skin. Adelyn's hands were trembling as she unclasped her bracelets and dropped them, the silver clinking loudly as they hit the wooden tabletop.

"Does someone have a gun?" Shane asked, looking around.

One of the Watched by near the back nodded, stepping forward and retrieving a pepperbox from a box by his bed.

"Watch them," Shane said. "If they do anything fishy, shoot them."

...

Adelyn wasn't sure how long she'd been awake for, but she also knew that she wouldn't be able to sleep until she knew there wasn't someone sitting a few feet away with a gun pointed at her.

The surgeon had wrapped up David's shoulder with a bandage, though in Adelyn's opinion, he'd been less than gentle with David's wound. She watched David snore away on his bed, blanket pulled up to his neck, seemingly unconcerned by their captivity.

She envied that, wishing she could get herself to sleep that easily. Her eyes wanted to close, but her brain wouldn't stop worrying.

"We're not going to try and escape," Adelyn said to the man, looking more at his pistol than his face.

"Sure you aren't," he said, showing his teeth in a sarcastic grin.

"David promised he wouldn't try to run as long as you didn't try to hurt us," Adelyn said, yawning and rubbing at her eyes. "And I'm not going anywhere without him. You can take his word for it."

"I'm not takin' nobody's word," he said. The man looked almost as tired as Adelyn felt, but he was the one holding the pistol. "I'm keeping an eye on you 'till someone else comes over to do the same."

Adelyn sighed, lying back onto her bed and fuming. She wished that David had talked to her before confronting Rahk, but she couldn't be mad at him. This was her fault, not his, she'd been the one to tip off the peace officers. Even if Rahk had been the one to send in the threats, Adelyn had gotten into this hot water by herself.

Shane was still awake too, pacing on the far side of the basement shelter, but Adelyn didn't have the opportunity to go talk to him. If she even stood up from her bed, the man watching her would get twitchy with his trigger finger, and Shane hadn't seen fit to walk over to Adelyn.

As far as she could tell, nobody else was awake.

Forcing her eyes shut, Adelyn tried to get to sleep. It had to come soon, she knew, though how soon she couldn't tell.

Just as her thoughts were starting to swirl and her brain was fogging into a dream, she heard boots land on the floor by the ladder. After a long pause of hesitation, she sat up and looked to see who it was.

Brenden. He'd finally shown up, and going by the deep circles under his eyes, he hadn't slept either.

"Where's Ansyr?" Shane asked loudly, looking up the ladder.

"I don't know," Brenden said, panting. "Solden is dead."

Adelyn sat straight up. She wasn't tired anymore.

"What?" Shane asked, his voice carrying across the empty room.

"I was hiding out in her fish shop," Brenden said. "Same as after the town hall, figured I'd be safe for a while to rest, then I could go out the back way. Peace officers kicked down the door. Solden tried to stall so I could get out the back way, but when she stepped in their way, she got shot. I only just escaped."

Shane's expression darkened so obviously that Adelyn could tell from all the way across the room. "Abandon me—how did they know you were hiding there?"

"I don't know," Brenden said. "I wasn't followed, and I'm damned sure nobody saw me go in."

Shane thought for a moment, then his face went pale. "Oh... oh no."

Brenden didn't piece things together as quickly. "What is it?"

"Everyone up!" Shane shouted, ignoring the question. He all but sprinted to the nearest bed, shaking awake Topher, shouting for the others to get out of bed. "Now!"

It took him half a minute to get all the able bodied people in the room awake, save for David, who was still sleeping like a log.

"Listen up!" Shane shouted, leaping on top of a table. "We need to get the word out to Kin, Vota, Jet; anyone who's ever sheltered us, anyone who's paid off the peace officers to give them a bit of slack. They need to go to ground. Get them out of the city if they have to, but get them somewhere safe."

"What's going on?" someone shouted at him.

Shane swallowed, Adam's apple taut against his throat. "They've declared war."

Rahk stepped forward and clambered up onto the table next to Shane. "Shane, you should lead them through the city. I'll stay here and try to keep track of everywhere we've been."

Shane paused, glancing over and making eye contact with Adelyn for a second. "Okay," he said, looking around into the crowd. "Topher, you stay here too, start hitting those healing books. We're going to need some magic in a hurry. And someone find out where Ansyr is, make sure she's safe."

"Good thinking," Rahk said, but Adelyn thought she saw a flash of annoyance in his expression that was gone in the time it took her to blink.

It took less than a minute for the people in the room to get their shoes on and to gather any weapons that they might have on hand. Rahk came over to where Adelyn was watching everything, but only to talk to the man holding her at gunpoint and explain that he should join the rescue party. David was still asleep through all of this, and Rahk was sure that he and Topher could handle Adelyn if she started to act up.

Within two minutes, the basement shelter was empty,

save for four figures. Topher had put on his glasses and was poring over the new magic books, and Rahk was busy for the moment preparing notes on who and where the peace officers were likely to go after.

Adelyn desperately wanted to stay awake to follow the action. But she was also desperately tired, and the gun pointed at her head had been, for the moment, taken away. Exhausted, she closed her eyes, fell back against her pillow, and was asleep in seconds.

...

David didn't move when he woke up. He was experienced at being held captive, and knew to take any minute advantage he could against his captors whenever possible. If they thought he was still asleep, for example, he could analyze the situation and decide how to proceed instead of letting them do it for him.

He could hear shouting and the sounds of many people moving quickly, and after a second's concentration he gathered a mental picture of the room. By the sound and feel of it, Shane was standing on the table, calling to the whole room to try and rouse anyone still sleeping. Something had happened, something bad enough that it was kicking Shane into action. A few moments later, David gathered that the peace officers had started an offensive against Watched hideouts.

Rahk is getting what he wanted, then.

The thought was troubling, though David couldn't think of anything he could do about it. His usual plan when captive would be to prepare a magic weapon of some kind using whatever tools were on hand. As long as he had a bit of blood and a scrap of cloth, there was rarely anything that could stop him from fashioning a tool to escape with.

That wouldn't be necessary, even if he'd been able to use

it. They hadn't taken his silver necklace, so he was armed with a shield, but he was as impotent as it had been for months.

As he moved a little bit to get more comfortable, he felt a lump beneath his pillow and remembered the book Rahk had given him. That book was practically an encyclopedia of magic runes and tools. An arsenal, certainly, but one that was no more useful than the necklace unless...

David started working on a plan. If the safe house was sufficiently cleared out, with as little a guard as possible, he could give Adelyn the book and his necklace, and they could fight their way out. Escaping the city would prove difficult if there were peace officers everywhere, but it was possible they'd be able to slip out of the city in the confusion.

If they were taken captive, he could explain his identity, and if he was lucky, that'd buy him immunity from his crimes, but Adelyn would be left in the lurch. Besides which, it sounded like the peace officers weren't interested in taking prisoners in for questioning.

Once he heard that Rahk and Topher were going to be left behind, David abandoned his plans of escape. He was proud of how strong Adelyn had become in less than a year, but she still wouldn't be able to fight off two sorcerers with only a book and a necklace.

People started filing out of the basement, following Shane's lead up the ladder. A moment later, it was only the four of them. A moment after that, David heard Adelyn's light snoring and knew she was asleep.

From here, he had a lot of options. After considering them all, David rolled out of bed, sitting up and reaching to put on his clothes. They were still lying in a heap on the floor, though they'd at least dried out since last night—a small mercy.

"David!" Rahk shouted from across the room, noticing the movement right away. "What do you think you're doing?"

David looked up at Rahk, holding one boot in his hand. *What do I think I am doing...* It had to be a rhetorical question, so David ignored it and resumed the task he was working on. With his pants and boots on, he started gingerly putting on his shirt, careful around his shoulder.

Rahk began stalking towards him, and David noticed that he had one of Adelyn's silver bracelets around his wrist. "David, you're not supposed to get up. Sit right back down on that bed, so I don't have to make you."

Looking back at Rahk's face, David stared at him, looking at the point between Rahk's eyes. He couldn't be certain if the threat was legitimate or not. Certainly, Rahk had the power to knock him off his feet, but it was a toss-up whether or not he would.

Pulling on his gloves, which were still damp around the fingertips, David flexed his hands and channeled a whisper of power into his prosthetic thumb, feeling the brass cogs and servo shift stiffly. Water had apparently gotten into the prosthetic, and he'd have to take it apart and oil it at some point to keep it from seizing up entirely.

He knew only one way to be sure if Rahk would attack him. Standing, David walked over to the stove.

Rahk grabbed his shirt by the back collar and yanked hard, meaning to throw David to the ground. It was a clumsy mistake—had Rahk simply blasted David with magic, there would have been no contest, but in a grappling situation, David had the clear edge. He ducked and shifted his weight, turning to grab Rahk's arm and throwing the young man to the ground.

There was a heavy crash as Rahk hit. He was clearly

unprepared for David to strike back, and took the landing poorly, sprawling out on the ground.

David took a deep breath, looking down at Rahk, making eye contact with the bewildered wizard for a moment before turning and continuing his walk towards the stove.

They'd caught Topher's attention, and he was watching the situation warily from behind a medicine book, but apparently decided not to get involved just yet.

David kept his sixth sense focused on Rahk, watching for an attack, but nothing came of it. Grabbing the kettle, he filled it with water from the pump, set it on the stove, and let it come to a boil.

Rahk started walking over, his bootsteps heavy and deliberate, but instead of addressing him directly, David scanned the table for his notepad and pencil, sitting down and grabbing the writing tools.

Seeing that David wasn't looking for a fight, Rahk hesitantly stood over him, visibly angry, but just as visibly unsure of what to do. Scratching his pencil against the notepad, David passed him a simple statement.

'Please, sit down. I would like to talk.'

CHAPTER 26

I'm a fool.

Writing from the brig, and I'm lucky they even allowed me a couple creature comforts in here. Watchers know I don't deserve it.

Whistle got blown for a sighting, and we all went to work. We're experienced, we know what we're doing, should've been easy, but this was a big son of a gun. Suckers as big as my head, fins at least eighty feet long. Teeth like you wouldn't believe.

The beast set into our ship with a rage, too. All thrashing bits and writhing, knocking about the men. Took down our mast, but we had the thing dead to rights. One of the other ships had nets out, got it all tangled, and the thing was clinging to us, perfectly still. Everyone'd been knocked about, but I was right starboard, and I could see the thing's face. Its little eyes were both scarred over, blind, and I had a perfect shot to its main eye. Harpoon in my hand, everything, the beast was dead in the water, I just had to throw.

But abandon me to the ocean if I could do it. It looked right at me, stared me in the face, and I just couldn't kill the thing. Before anyone else could get a shot, then, it ripped out our mast, threw off the nets, and swam off, diving too deep for us to get to it.

We're floating adrift until we can get the mast back up. Plenty of rations to get us through the night and back to the coast tomorrow, but I'm not so sure I'll survive the trip. Chances are good I've got a date with the ocean tonight.

Anyone's reading this, tell my mom I love her, and that I've got three tacks hid in my old room beneath the dresser.

•Journal entry, written by a sailor on a thulcut hunting ship.

Rahk tentatively sat down across from David, staring at the note for a long moment before passing it back. "What do you want to talk about?"

David looked over to where Topher was sitting at the far end of the table, buried in his books with a panicked expression on his face, trying to cram the information from dozens of tomes into his head with an hour of reading.

'You should let Adelyn help with the healing magic,' David wrote.

"You think we'd trust her with that?" Rahk exclaimed. "She sold us out to the ocean without a harpoon, we're not about to hand her a bunch of weapons and trust her to play nice."

David bit down hard on his lip, rattling his fingers against the table for a moment while he considered Rahk's words and his own response. 'You do not need to hide it now. I know you sent in those threats. You are equally responsible for what happened as her.'

Rahk's face went red as he read the note, and after glancing at Topher, he leaned in to whisper his response. "She did it because she wanted to get us killed, I did it because I wanted to get the peace officers killed. *That's* the difference."

David had to chew on that for a while as he thought it over. Finally, he wrote, 'Adelyn was stupid, but she is not sadistic. If you do not let her help with the healing, more of your friends will die than have to.'

Glowering, Rahk looked up from the note. "I'll make you a counter offer. Stop protecting the treacherous witch, I'll back you up and say all is forgiven. She's the one who betrayed us, we can't blame you too much for protecting your friend."

David's first instinct was to immediately say no, but he suppressed that for long enough to ask a question. 'And if I stop protecting her, what happens?'

"You're forgiven," Rahk said immediately upon reading the note.

'But what happens to Adelyn?'

"Oh," Rahk said, looking at the note. "We can't let her loose, she'd lead the peace officers right here. Only choice is to give her a lead ball and a short burial."

'Abandon that,' David wrote immediately.

"I can't protect you forever," Rahk said. "Eventually, you'll have to give her up, or you'll have to share her fate. Hardly a fair end for a man like you."

A man like me. David thought about that for a while. He didn't understand why Rahk venerated his military service so much, considering that David had been fighting for the wrong side, and he regretted much of what he'd done besides.

The water had reached a boil, and David walked away from the conversation for a moment so he could start fixing coffee. He didn't want any for himself, but if refugees and survivors were about to start pouring in, it seemed like they'd have a powerful thirst for something hot and bracing.

What David didn't understand was Rahk's endgame. He was stirring up trouble, starting fights and putting his enemies in harm's way, sure, but to what end? The government had a nearly limitless supply of peace officers and soldiers, and wouldn't let such an important port city fall into anarchy.

He decided to ask as much, writing out his question. 'There is no chance that you will be able to control this city. What is your plan?'

"Abandon control," Rahk said. "I want to make the Divine bastards bleed."

'But you'll get your own people killed,' David wrote.

"You know how many Watched live on the coast?" Rahk asked. When David shook his head, he continued. "Neither do I, but it's a damned lot, and with the Watchers on our side, we can't lose."

'The army beat you once,' David pointed out.

Rahk crushed that note in his hand. "Bren Cultt, I like you, but your time is long gone. The Watchers chose you for a task, you completed that task. Abandon you, you can't even use your blessing anymore. It's *my* turn to do *my* job, and if you're not going to help, the least you could do is get out of my way." Without giving David the chance to respond, he pushed up to his feet. "I've got more important things to be working on right now. Think about whose side you're on, and whether it's worth it to die for that girl."

Walking away, Rahk left David at the table to think.

A moment later, David stood up as well, walking back to his bed and pulling the book of signs out from under the pillow, flipping through it and looking for useful runes that Adelyn would be able to use in combat.

Half an hour went by in silence. Topher got up to pour himself a cup of coffee, but David paid him no mind. David was about to give up his task and get some more sleep, when he heard footsteps above, and then coming down the ladder.

"Clear a bed!" someone was shouting. "She's been shot!"

David sat up, trying to look and see who it was that had been injured.

Five people in total came down the ladder, two of them working to help down a third. Some woman he didn't know had a large bloodstain smearing most of her shirt, looking like it'd come from a belly shot. Topher sprang into action, bringing one of his books with him and running over to her side, frantically flipping between pages to try and find a spell that would work.

Rahk took point on his own job, asking where the five of them had come from, determining who was going to be most effective at finding other Watched in need of help and ultimately sending two of the Watched back up the ladder.

Topher managed to stop the external bleeding, though it was unclear if that would be enough to save the woman's life. He couldn't heal her internal bleeding, and it would all come down to how much damage the bullet had inflicted. Once he was sure there was nothing else to be done, Topher washed off his hands, refilled his coffee, and went back to reading.

This time, he only got a five minute reprieve before more people came pouring down the ladder. Nobody had injuries as serious as the woman, but Topher still had to take stock and ensure everyone was okay, and Rahk was busy working out where and who would still need rescue or warning.

David worried that all this extra traffic into the safe house would draw the attention of peace officers, but after a third cluster of people arrived, Rahk started directing clusters of Watched to go out and start trouble in other parts of the city, anywhere that would draw attention away from the safe house. It was a token effort, but hopefully enough to keep them safe for a while.

The shelter started to fill up pretty quickly, even with Rahk sending back half the people who came in. The coffee that David had prepared was gone within an hour, and when someone else made a fresh pot, it was gone in half that time.

Pretty soon, David found that the space up to his bed was getting crowded, and soon after that, he was leaning against the wall, his book of signs tucked underneath the bed where hopefully nobody would think twice about it, avoiding dirty looks from the Watched who'd heard about the events of last night.

...

Adelyn felt someone shake her arm. She groaned. It had been impossible to sleep for the past hour or so, once the shelter had started to fill up, but she'd stuck her head under a pillow and tried to rest for a while longer anyways. Now, though, it didn't seem like that was going to be an option.

"We need this bed," Someone was saying. They shook her arm again. Adelyn sighed, sitting up and rubbing the sleep from her eyes, looking around to see how full the room had become.

To her surprise, there were at least eighty people crammed into the shelter, and it didn't seem like the inflow was going to stop any time. Slipping on her shoes and tying the laces, she tried to make her way towards the coffee she could smell in the air, but upon reaching the stove she found that the pot was empty and they were out of grounds.

Grumbling, she looked around the crowd for David, ultimately spotting him by the wall. It seemed possible that they might be able to slip out in the confusion, but she noticed as she made her way through the room that more than a couple of the Watched were giving her suspicious or even contemptuous looks, and a glance over her shoulder confirmed that Rahk was only a couple paces away from the door. Slipping out while nobody was watching wouldn't be possible.

Reaching David's side, she asked, "Are you okay?"

David shrugged, giving her a blank look. It appeared as though he was trying to watch everyone in the basement shelter all at once, and struggling to keep up with the vast number of people that were down there.

"I think I have a plan," Adelyn said, though it was a lie. "I'm still working on it, but we might have a way out of here."

In reality, she saw no way out, but she wanted to be reassuring. David still didn't say anything in response, but he gave a small nod of his head, which Adelyn saw as an improvement.

Mina got back a little while later, and Topher immediately roped her into helping with his healing magic. Adelyn couldn't see much of Topher, but he was clearly running himself ragged fueling all the healing spells, even using the victim's blood wherever he could as a source of spirit. Adelyn moved to go help him, but David reached out and stopped her with a gesture, shaking his head and explaining with terse signs that she wouldn't be allowed.

By the time Shane had returned, there were more than a hundred people crammed into the basement. The space, normally cool and comfortable, was hot and stank from the sweat and dirt of far too many people in far too little space. Nobody had more than a couple feet of room around them, and anyone who was hurt but not critically injured was being forced to share a bed with other patients.

Rahk climbed up onto the table, having to squeeze between a couple people to get up, and once he was up he had to shout a couple times to get the crowd's attention.

"Everyone, listen up!" he shouted, his voice carrying just enough to be heard over the shuffle and murmur of the tightly packed crowd. "I've got some numbers here, and I think it's important that y'all listen to 'em."

He held up a piece of paper and read from it. "I've run the numbers and figured from what everyone's told me as they came in. By my figures, at least forty of us have been killed by peace officers this morning. There are another thirty or so people unaccounted for, and only Watchers know how many people got hit that weren't even a part of all this, just 'cause they're Watched."

He waited for a long beat to let all that sink in, then cleared his throat and continued. "Obviously, we don't got enough food for all of you. We can hide everyone for a night or two at most, but we're gonna get pretty hungry, and it's gonna start to stink. Way I see it, we've only got one thing we can do."

It was obvious that he was setting up a call and response, and someone in the crowd was happy to oblige him. "What's that?"

"We take the fight to them. City of a hundred thousand people, there's only a couple thousand peace officers, and only one of 'ems a witch. We play our cards right, we can give 'em something a little more important to focus on than killing bystanders who can't defend themselves."

Shane finally managed to push his way to the front of the crowd, and though Adelyn could see that he was annoyed with Rahk for taking center stage, he still played right into Rahk's prepared speech. "What exactly do you propose we do?"

Rahk allowed himself a smile, looking out at the crowd. His expression flickered when he saw Adelyn watching him, and he pointed right at her. "Get them out of here, first. Haven't decided what we're doing with the traitors yet, but I don't want them to hear this all the same."

About half the heads in the basement turned to face Adelyn, and she looked around warily. For a moment, it seemed like someone might take the initiative to shoot her right then and there, but Topher piped in with the rescue.

"I'll keep an eye on them!" Topher shouted from the other side of the room, raising his hand and pushing himself up on his toes to be seen from across the crowd. "Upstairs, where they can't hear. I need the break, anyways."

"Thanks," Rahk said to him, waiting while the crowd parted and allowed David and Adelyn a route to the ladder. Topher went up first, taking the pistol from the other guard and grabbing his staff from by the exit so he'd be well armed, and Adelyn went up after him a few seconds later.

David was slow coming up the ladder, and Topher had to keep the cot propped up for a while so that he could clamber out and get clear.

Adelyn eyed Topher, trying to think if she could take him out before he could cast a spell. He was holding the quarterstaff in one hand, and she knew it was designed to throw around raw force—if she could grab it, maybe she could overpower him or even cast a spell back his way, then run before anyone else could come up the ladder after them.

"You two can run if you want," Topher said, setting down his staff on the cot and sitting down, propping the pepperbox pistol between his knees. "I won't stop you."

"I—" Adelyn started, a hot retort coming to her lips before he had finished speaking. "Wait, what?"

Topher dug into a pocket and pulled out David's notebook, holding it out. "I read what you said, David. I always knew I didn't like Rahk, but this confirms it."

"Help us, then," Adelyn said. "Confront him about it."

Topher leaned back over the pistol and began fiddling with the hammer. "He'll deny it. You see how popular he was down there? I'd get thrown into your lot, and that's not a place I want to be in. Just punch me someplace where it won't leave a permanent mark and run for it, I'll make up a good story."

"What are you doing?" Adelyn asked, gesturing to the gun.

"These things are more trouble than a thulcut," Topher explained, adjusting the firing pins. "If you don't load it careful, the whole thing will blow up in your face when you try to fire it."

David signed something, and after a quizzical look from Topher, Adelyn translated. "He says we can't leave."

"Why not?" Topher asked. "Sure, peace officers are everywhere, but we've had a whole host of people who managed to get here alright."

Shaking his head, David insistently signed, 'We can't leave. Rahk isn't going to fight the peace officers.'

"Why's that a problem?" Topher asked, once Adelyn finished relaying the message. "And you heard him down there, right? He was pretty clear on what he wanted to do."

David shook his head and started to explain. 'He isn't going to fight the peace officers, it's not what he does. He's—'

Adelyn realized what David was getting at. "He's going to go after bystanders. He doesn't want a fight, he wants chaos."

Pressing his lips into a line, David nodded.

Topher considered that for a moment, swallowing. "Well... damn. Tomorrow is Eatle's Day."

Adelyn tried to remember what that was. She knew that it was some sort of Divine holiday, but she couldn't remember the specifics. "Why's that a problem?"

"Because," Topher said. "The Divine church by the coast is going to be packed full, and the entire thing's made of wood. It seats at least a couple thousand, more if the extras don't mind standing around. Rahk wouldn't even need help if he wanted to kill some folks there. Fire department would show up pretty quick, but that'd kill a few dozen people at least, maybe even a hundred if he gets help barring the doors."

David swallowed and tensed, and after a second of consideration, Adelyn realized why. "Answer a question for me," she said. "Did you really rob that train?"

Topher's brow furrowed as he followed along with what she was getting at. Whoever robbed the train, they'd taken a few cases of military explosives.

Forget killing a hundred people or more, Rahk was going to take down the whole church.

They sat on the ground by the cot, silently thinking about what they could do.

"What if we blew up the church before them?" Topher asked. "So people don't get packed in for the holiday."

"There's always going to be a few people inside," Adelyn said. "Praying, or whatever. Whatever plan we come up with, it has to be something that won't get anyone killed. Besides, Rahk can just target someplace else. I'm sure he'd be happy blowing up a random street corner."

"Right," Topher said.

So far, they had been devoid of any good plans. A direct

confrontation was a bad idea, unless they could convince Mina to join them. Going to the peace officers was even worse—either the peace officers wouldn't believe them, and they'd be arrested, or the peace officers *would* believe them and it would kick off a massacre of Watched.

"And we know for certain that he's going to go for the church?" Adelyn asked. "What if we're wrong?"

"I can't think of a better target, if we're right that he's going to go for civilian death," Topher said. "Blow up the supports, the whole thing will fall into the ocean, crushing anyone inside. What if we got Harrington to help?"

"He wouldn't help us," Adelyn said, shaking her head. "He's a cowardly ass who'd call the peace officers on us the moment we showed our faces."

David got up and walked to the door, peering out the window for a moment before returning and signing to Adelyn. 'We need to wait and find out what Rahk is planning exactly. He's got a small army at his disposal, and probably plans on using them.'

"You're assuming that the Watched will go along with whatever he tells them to do," Adelyn said, after relaying his signs to Topher. "What if they're not willing to go along with mass murder?"

"He might not tell everyone everything," Topher said. "He didn't tell us he was going to burn the bank, after all. Might lie to them all. And if we call him on it and ask what his real plan is, he can always just deny it."

"So call him on it," Adelyn said, thinking about it for a moment. "Make him deny it in front of them, then he won't be able to go along with his plan without losing face."

"That... might work," Topher said, chewing on the idea. "But I can think of a few ways it might go wrong. Maybe everyone really will be okay with mass murder, or maybe he'll deny it then blow up the church anyways and blame it on me, since I'd be the one who mentioned the idea to everyone."

'We need Mina,' David signed, letting Adelyn translate. 'Without her, we're outnumbered on real spellcasters.'

"Want me to go get her?" Topher asked. "We can try to talk her over."

David glanced at Adelyn, and she shrugged in response. She didn't have any better ideas. "Go get her," she said, adding, "Be subtle about it."

Topher nodded, then shooed her and David away from the cot they were leaning on so he could lift it up and climb down the ladder.

Glancing around the empty room, Adelyn commented, "It's our last chance to make a run for it, if we wanted to."

David didn't have to say anything to that. They both knew that there would be no running away from this, not when so many people needed their help. Even if Adelyn felt a twinge of doubt that they'd be able to stop Rahk or the other Watched, she was certain that David would try to stop them all on his own if he had to, and Adelyn wasn't going to leave him to the wolves.

A moment later, the cot behind them bumped, then got pushed up from inside and Topher came climbing back out, this time followed by his sister. Adelyn noticed that Mina was also wearing one of her silver bracelets, and wondered if Shane had taken the third.

"You're too trusting," Mina said to her brother, once she saw that David and Adelyn hadn't run away. "And you two are stupid. Why didn't you run?"

Adelyn chewed on her lip for a moment, trying to frame her response in a way that'd be convincing. "We think that

Rahk is going to do something bad, and we want to stop him," she said.

Mina glanced at Topher. "And you're with them on this?"

Topher nodded. "Rahk actually did send in threats before the town hall meeting, hoping to start a fight. We're worried he's going to do something similar, and that it'll put a lot more Watched lives in danger."

"What do you think he's going to do?" Mina asked.

"Blow up the Church of the Divine," Adelyn said. "If he wants to kill a lot of people, that'd be the best way to do it."

"Sounds like a blast to me," Mina said, though it seemed like her joke was more on reflex than anything else. "Could you hear the meeting going on down there?"

Adelyn shook her head. None of them had even been trying to hear what was being said. "What was he saying?"

"Pretty much the same thing you're saying," Mina said. "'Cept he's trying to sell it off as a good idea. Come on, they're about done, let's go down and talk to them."

Topher frowned. "Are you sure that's a good idea? We don't want to draw attention to ourselves and get caught before we have a way to stop him."

"Shane's literally foaming at the mouth," Mina said.

"Literally?" Topher asked.

Mina grinned. "I mixed soap in with his coffee." A moment passed, and she lost the cheesy smile. "Seriously, though, he's pissed off and ready to abandon Rahk to the ocean. We get Shane on our side, it'll be all of us versus Rahk, and there's no way he'll take those odds even if everyone else in the shelter is gung ho about blowing up the church."

David looked around hesitantly, then nodded.

"You three go down first, I'm going to make sure the street's clear, then I'll be right behind you," Mina said, cracking her knuckles. "Topher, for now just play like they're still captives."

Smirking, Topher looked to Adelyn and David and said, "Head on down, captives."

Adelyn nodded, lifting up the cot and sliding down the ladder. David came down slowly, as expected, and Topher went down after them.

Turning around at the bottom of the ladder, Adelyn saw that a good chunk of the room had turned to look. Rahk was still standing on top of the table and was staring at her too, looking annoyed.

"What's going on up there?" Rahk called, as David made it to the bottom of the ladder.

"Uh," Adelyn said, biting her lip in hesitation. "Mina said you were done..."

Topher dropped the last couple rungs, bending his knees to soften his harsh landing. Noticing all the staring faces, he asked, "Eh... sorry, are we interrupting something? My sister said you had finished up."

"We haven't," Rahk said. "Atof, can you please get them out of here so I can finish?"

Topher looked like he was caught off guard by Rahk's forgoing his nickname, and stammered for a moment. Before he had a response, they heard the cot moving upstairs, and Adelyn glanced up to see that Mina was coming down the ladder.

"We'll leave," Adelyn said, to fill the awkward silence. "Once the ladder's clear."

Mina dropped the last few rungs in the same way her brother had, looking around.

"You said they were almost done," Topher said, raising an eyebrow.

"Sorry, Toph," Mina replied. "Had to get you down here somehow."

David was moving before Mina finished the word 'Down', leaping towards the ladder in a last-ditch effort to get away, but Adelyn didn't feel the spirit growing in Mina's bracelet until Mina had twisted and barked out a simple spell.

A gust of hurricane force winds struck David, spinning him away from the ladder and sending him to the ground. Topher looked at her in surprise, but he'd left his staff upstairs and didn't have another weapon—when Mina cast a second blast of wind, it took Topher off his feet.

Adelyn didn't bother getting hit with the attack; she put up her hands and dropped heavily to her knees in surrender.

Rahk reacted with confusion and anger, his voice raising as he shouted, "Mina, what the—?"

Mina cut him off. "Topher was gonna stick a knife in your back. He was siding with these two." More quietly, she added, "Sorry, brother."

"I was not!" Topher shouted, startled, still prone on the ground. "I wanted to talk!"

"They were cooking up a plan to protect the peace officers!" Mina shouted, crouching by her brother and taking the pepperbox pistol from his belt. "We're gonna need to keep an eye on all three of them."

Adelyn glared at Mina, but the rage burning in Adelyn's eyes apparently had no effect on the girl. "You said you were going to—"

"I lied," Mina explained simply.

Eyes going wide, Topher said, "You're going along with this?"

Mina looked at her brother, the usual humor gone from

her eyes. "The Divine killed our parents. Rahk's right. Abandon them, and anyone who wants to protect them." Raising her voice again, she shouted over to Rahk, "By the way, it doesn't take three crates of those explosives to wreck up a train. What if we took the extra and blew up the church, too?"

Adelyn felt her throat tighten. "You weren't going for the church?"

"You know how the city was bringing in new peace officers?" Mina asked. Adelyn nodded. "Their train comes in tomorrow. We were gonna take out the bridge. Your idea with the church will just be gravy."

...

David sat silently, fuming to himself. He felt like an idiot. He'd blindly trusted Mina, and now they were worse off than they'd been before Topher had tried to help them.

No less than four guns were being used to hold the three of them captive—in addition to the first guard, a few more of the Watched had taken it upon themselves to assist in guarding the captives, and David could hardly adjust his sitting position without someone cocking a pistol in his direction.

"This was my fault," Adelyn said. She was sitting cross legged next to him, and looked about as miserable as David felt. "All of this. I'm sorry. We're all gonna be killed, and it's because I was an idiot."

"I probably won't get killed," Topher said. "So don't keep me on your conscience."

"Thanks," Adelyn said dryly.

The room was still hot and humid, but to David's relief, the chatter had died down as many of the Watched had found a place to sleep, either sharing a bed or lying down on the floor. A few people were still awake, guards included, but enough of them were asleep that the shelter was no longer a buzz of activity.

Tomorrow, the Watched would disperse through the city, plant the stolen explosives, and thousands of people would die.

CHAPTER 27

The issue persists that the president, though successful in his conquest, is still proving to be unprepared for the leadership he's won. It's been eight years since the final peace treaties were signed, and yet postwar conflict still burns as hot as ever. The country is not being treated like a unified nation, but instead like an occupied territory. Promises made before the war of unity and equal treatment haven't been broken, per se, but they've been mostly ignored as the reconstruction period drags on longer and longer with no sign of fixing itself. If this sort of political apathy continues, the problems across the country could metastasize and spark a second great war as our citizens forget the hardships of old and try to return the realm of humanity back to its old, primitive state.

•Excerpt from a letter between two legislators in Triom, discussing the state of the nation.

AS BEFORE, Adelyn couldn't get any sleep while a gun was trained on her head. She tried, shutting her eyes and thinking thoughts of dreamland, but her body would not cooperate. By the time morning had come around, she could feel a restless buzz in her fingertips that told her she was running on fumes.

The Watched had started up early. Getting the crates of explosives up the ladder and out of the shelter took a few people working in unison with lots of rope and shouting, and from there they had to quietly disperse into the city without drawing attention. Emptying a building of more than a hundred people quietly was going to take time and care, and so the earliest parties started clearing out before the first rays of sun would even be peeking into the city.

Adelyn wasn't clear on the specifics of the plan, but she'd managed to gather the general idea. Watched would spread out through the city, gathering any allies who hadn't already been in the shelter. A couple teams, led by Rahk and Shane, would deliver the explosives—one group going to the edge of the city to destroy the bridge outside of town, the other sneaking under the docks to bomb the Church of the Divine.

That evening, the explosives would go off at the same time, and that'd be the cue to Watched across the city to start causing chaos—starting fires, blocking streets, doing anything to harass the peace officers and slow down emergency services.

And she couldn't do a damned thing to stop it.

Even if there wasn't a barbershop quartet of guards keeping her held at gunpoint, the three of them were simply not enough. It was a losing prospect on every step of the way.

As the safe house started to clear out, Shane walked over to them and sat down.

"You four take a break," he said to the guards. "We're out of coffee, but get some water and take a leak, I'll keep an eye on them."

"Sure you can handle all three?" one of the guards asked in a wry tone.

"I've got a blessing on my side, they're unarmed," Shane said, dismissing the concern. "Nobody's gonna be around to relieve you later on. Take the break."

After a little hem-hawing, the four guards agreed, standing and walking away to get some water or stretch their legs.

"You're going along with this, huh?" Adelyn asked, glowering at Shane as the guards left.

"I'm sorry," Shane said, nodding. "But it's this or turn my back on everything I've fought to build for the past eight years. I can't walk away from my people."

"Your people? They're going to get killed!" Adelyn exclaimed, sitting up a little straighter. "Rahk wants to start a war, and there's no chance that your side is going to come out the other end alive!"

Shane lowered his face a bit, clenching a fist and shaking out the silver bracelet he wore; Adelyn's third one. "Don't you tell me about war, girl. You've never been in a war."

"Maybe not," Adelyn said, trying to project confidence. "But I've been in a battle. Can you say the same?"

Staring into Adelyn's eyes, Shane thought for a while before he said, "If I try to stop them, I'll be fighting my own friends. I won't do that. Rahk's plan is horrible, but it's what we're doing and I can't change that."

Adelyn stared right back at him. "You're a coward."

"I care about my people," Shane said. "I'm loyal."

Clenching her jaw, Adelyn fought down the urge to keep

insulting Shane. He wasn't being outright hostile at the moment, and pissing him off wouldn't help her any.

"Maybe if you had guts," Adelyn said, ignoring her better judgement. "Rahk wouldn't have stolen your work out from under you."

Anger flashed in Shane's eyes, but he didn't move to strike her. "You're right. Maybe. But if he's the one calling the shots now, then that means he gets to decide what we're doing with you. I wouldn't be too hopeful about my odds if I were in your shoes."

Adelyn's anger was doused, and she realized that he was right. Topher had lost any say, and as long as Rahk could keep Mina on his side, Shane wouldn't have any authority.

Shane stood and backed up a few paces, waiting for the guards to return before he walked away.

Looking at Topher, Adelyn saw that he was asleep where he sat, a thin line of drool dripping from his open mouth. She frowned, then looked over to David, who had his eyes shut but didn't seem to be asleep.

"David," she said, trying to get his attention. "Are you awake?"

David opened his eyes, glancing over to her and signing, 'What is it?'

"I want to talk," Adelyn said, signing, 'We need to figure out how to escape.'

"Hey!" one of the Watched said, gesturing with his pistol. "What're you saying?"

"Nothing," Adelyn said. "We're just talking."

"Well talk so we can hear ya'," The guard said. "Don't want you saying nothin' fishy."

"He's not got a tongue," Adelyn said, quickly signing, 'I'll pretend to talk about something.' "What do you recommend he does?"

"I don't care what he does," the guard said. "But you use your words, else I'll decide to shoot you."

"Fine," Adelyn said, putting up her hands. "Anyways, David, what do you think?"

Pursing his lips, David said, 'This is a stupid way to communicate.'

"I agree," Adelyn said. "Coming to the city was a bad idea."

'They are going to figure out we're up to something,' David added.

"That's probably true. We couldn't have known," Adelyn agreed.

'I've got my silver necklace,' David said. 'If I can get it to you, can you raise a shield?'

Adelyn nodded. Trying to make up both sides of the conversation in her head was proving a nuisance, and she didn't know if she could keep it up for long without it being painfully obvious that she was trying to dupe the guards.

'Once we get out, I have no idea how we can save both the church and the train,' David signed. 'One by itself would be hard enough.'

"I think you're going to have to pick," Adelyn said, trying to think of something she could say to follow that up. "If you want to get out of this alive, you may have to give me up."

David shook his head. 'We're not going to pick. We'll save them both.'

"That's not possible," Adelyn said. "Just—we can't do both."

Shutting his eyes, David waited for a moment then signed out his reasoning, beginning with a word that Adelyn didn't recognize. '*Something* wants to start a war. It's not about saving the people today. If we only save one, or the other, that war is going to happen, and the death toll from today will seem like nothing once it's all said and done.'

"What was that?" Adelyn asked.

'The goal isn't to kill people,' David started to explain. 'It's to elicit a reaction from the peace officers. If—'

"No, I understood that," Adelyn said. "But what was that first word you said?" David repeated the sign once, and Adelyn knew for certain that she hadn't seen it before. "Yeah, that."

'It means *Rahk*,' David said, signing out the letters. 'In Sacrosanct. He found a book of Sacrosanct signs for me.'

"Oh," Adelyn said. "Do you still have it?"

David gestured with his head, and Adelyn waited a couple seconds before casually looking around and spotting the book on the floor beneath a nearby cot. That was their ticket out of there. If she could use the runes inside, she'd have a weapon.

"So you're not going to pick," Adelyn said. "In that case, I'll decide for you. Abandon me to my own devices."

"What're you on about?" one of the men watching her asked. "Abandon you?"

Adelyn glanced at the guard. "Rahk promised to go light on David, if David stops defending me. I'm not going to get a friend of mine killed, so I'm trying to convince him to be a little less stubborn."

The guard blinked at that, but accepted the answer.

'We have to go to the peace officers,' David signed.

"That's what got us into this mess in the first place!" Adelyn protested.

David shrugged. 'We don't have the manpower to do this on our own. They've got a witch, and a lot of people working for them.'

"Won't that still kick off a fight?" Adelyn asked, trying to phrase her question as ambiguously as possible."

'Maybe. But it won't be the same. The peace officers won't have the same public support. It's the only way to get the manpower we need.'

"What's going on here?" Rahk asked. He'd come up out of nowhere, or at least Adelyn hadn't noticed him.

"They're having a little chat," one of the guards explained.

Frowning, Rahk said, "And none of us know what he's really saying. We're leaving in thirty minutes. Bombs are gonna go off in three hours, and we can't have any interference or cooking up a plan to stop us. Tie his hands."

...

David sat back against the wall, twisting his arms against the ropes. It wasn't that slipping out of them would do much good, what with the gun still trained on his head, but the position was making his shoulder ache and he wanted to get more comfortable.

"Hold it," one of the men said, cocking his revolver. David could almost see down the barrel, and doubted that it would be possible to miss at this short range. "Stop squirming."

Clenching his jaw, David nodded stiffly and agreed with the demand. It wouldn't do him any good to be shot.

It was two hours and six minutes before the bombs would go off, if David's count was accurate.

The room was almost empty, save for the four Watched still guarding them. There had been some debate on how many people to leave, but it had been decided that they wouldn't be a threat as long as Adelyn and Topher were watched carefully. More than four guards would be unnecessary.

"Adelyn," Topher said, looking around. David didn't have to look at him to tell that he was anxious, he could tell from the smell of sweat and the sound of his breathing. "If we don't both survive this, I want you to know—"

"Forget about that," Adelyn said. "If it doesn't help us escape, I don't want to hear it right now."

"You're not escapin' nothing," the guard with the revolver said, waving the barrel of his gun towards her. "You're not even talkin' about escaping."

"Sorry," Adelyn said. "Not talking about escaping."

David could see the book they needed, only a few paces away, that'd give Adelyn or Topher all the weapons they would need to escape. Even his own necklace would probably be enough, at least in Adelyn's hands, to shield them from gunfire.

All he needed was a half second where a gun wasn't pointed at his head, but that wasn't looking like it was going to happen anytime soon.

Topher cleared his throat.

...

Adelyn turned her head to look at Topher as he said, "I have to pee."

"Bullshit," the leftmost guard said. His head was shaven and the wrinkles on his face seemed to only grow deeper as he scowled.

"Come on," Topher said. "You've had us at gunpoint for hours, and I'd been keeping busy the whole day before that. I'm about ready to carve a second grand river through the city."

The scowling guard exchanged a glance with one of his peers, then sighed. "Get up. Slow."

"Thanks," Topher said, pushing himself to his feet at a comically lethargic pace, holding his hands out to his side as he started walking to the curtained area in the corner.

Grumbling, the guard led him across the room, his revolver never wavering from Topher's back as they walked.

Adelyn watched, waiting for the moment that Topher would spring his trap and turn on the guard, but it never came. He crossed the room, pulled aside the curtain, and Adelyn finally realized that he wasn't pulling the wool over the guard's eyes.

As she turned her attention away from Topher, she felt something tingling against her senses. The build of spirit was slow, but not particularly subtle, and she realized after a second that it was coming from David. Even if the distraction Topher'd created wasn't an intentional trap, it had distracted one of the guards for a moment, and that was the best opening they were going to get.

Adelyn watched the three remaining guards carefully. One had a rifle, one a revolver, and the third still had his little pepperbox pistol. The revolver was the most dangerous here, so she'd focus on him the most while trying to shield everywhere as much as possible.

The man with the rifle looked over when he heard water start flushing, and Adelyn took her moment. Lunging to her side, she grabbed the chain around David's neck and shouted, '*Ansyr!*'

In the instant that she formed the shield, Adelyn threw it forward on impulse, so that instead of being wrapped around her and David, it was built just inches in front of the guards. David had charged his silver necklace as full as it would go with power, and though it was more a precision tool than a blunt instrument, that was enough for Adelyn to make an incredibly strong barrier.

The revolver fired, bullet hitting the shield and ricocheting wildly. To his side, the guard with the rifle tried to aim and fire, but the barrel of his gun dragged against the shield, its steel barrel moving through the barrier of spirit like a hot iron bar pushed through ice. It left big holes in the shield as he forced the gun towards Adelyn, but there was enough delay that it didn't matter.

David was up before her, managing to dodge to the side and get around the shield even with his hands tied behind his back, driving his shoulder into their original guard before the pepperbox pistol could even be fired. This left Adelyn without any magical tools, since the silver necklace was still on David's person, but she didn't need one for the moment.

Getting to her feet, she leapt forward and sucked the spirit out of the air in one motion, barrier vanishing as she moved to tackle the middle guard, grabbing his arm so that he couldn't use his revolver. It fired anyways, echoing like thunder from such a short range, but the bullet hit the floor and the only injury it caused were minor scratches as splinters got thrown into the air.

They struggled for the gun, grappling awkwardly and trying to wrench the revolver free. The guard had a better handhold, but Adelyn was stronger, and neither was able to make any headway until David drove a heavy kick into the guard's knee, bending it sideways and eliciting a scream which Adelyn ignored, finally tearing the pistol free and turning to aim it at the guard with the rifle.

She was too slow on the draw, and could see the rifle pointed at her chest while she was still fumbling to find the trigger on her own weapon. She had no time to react or dodge, but before the guard could plant a lead ball in her chest, a foot swept out Adelyn's legs from under her and she dropped to the floor, hitting the ground with a thud as a bullet whizzed over her head.

Head ringing, Adelyn saw David jump in a flying kick towards the guard, knocking the weapon out of his hands and sending them both to the ground. Without arms, David couldn't traditionally pin the guard, but he rolled and drove a the heel of his bare foot into the guard's stomach, then into his groin, disabling the man with pain and buying David time to roll over and get to his feet.

Adelyn took the revolver in her hand and looked at it for a moment, finally getting her finger onto the trigger as she aimed it at the guard she'd taken it from. She heard a gunshot from across the room which drew her attention, and upon turning to look she saw that Topher was on the fourth guard's back, one arm wrapped around the guard's neck as he tried to keep the guard from shooting him with his other arm.

Raising her revolver, Adelyn squeezed the trigger and shot the guard. A second passed while his eyes bulged, then his legs gave out and he fell to the floor, Topher still clinging to his back all the while.

"Stop!"

Spinning, Adelyn saw the guard with the pepperbox pistol standing five paces away, holding his gun towards her with a steady grip. He looked scared, but he wasn't letting that fear effect his aim.

"Anyone move so much as an inch, I'll blow their head off," he said, though given his gun he seemed more likely to only put a small hole in her head. Either way she'd be just as dead. David was a couple steps to her right, no closer to the guard, and with his hands still behind his back, he couldn't stop the guard from firing any better than she could.

"Don't!" Topher shouted, getting to his feet and kicking away the revolver by his foot in spite of the guard's orders. "If you pull that trigger, you'll blow up your own hand."

Eyes narrowing, the guard wiped at his mouth with his free hand and gave Topher a level look. "You don't got the magic to do that."

"I don't need it," Topher said, taking a step forward. "I had that gun while I was upstairs, and I futzed with the firing pins."

The guard squinted at him, then pulled back the hammer on the pistol dramatically. "I don't believe you."

"Then shoot," Topher said, taking another step forward. "I don't want to hurt you, I want to stop Rahk from bombing my city, but if you want to lose your hand that's your choice. Otherwise, drop the gun and surrender."

Adelyn looked between the guard and Topher, taking shallow breaths and waiting to see what would happen.

"Bah," the guard said, dropping his gun to the ground and stepping back. "Rahk's gonna kill you anyways."

"He'll try," Topher said. "Hands behind your back."

For extra insurance, Adelyn pointed her revolver at the guard to keep him in place while Topher untied David's hands, then walked over to use the same rope to tie up the guard.

"Good planning," Adelyn said. "Did you know we were going to get betrayed, or was it just a guess?"

"A bluff, more like," Topher said, picking up the pepperbox pistol and handing it to Adelyn. "This gun should shoot just fine. Abandon me, I don't think there's enough powder to blow off your hand even if it did misfire."

"Dammit!" the guard shouted, jerking against the rope around his wrists. "I knew it!"

"No, you didn't," Adelyn said. "Or you wouldn't have dropped the gun."

Topher smirked, then nodded towards the exit. "Grab any weapons we might need, then let's get out of here."

Looking across the room, Adelyn asked, "Do you think we'll come across the witch?"

CHAPTER 28

I was perhaps too excited as I traveled north to examine the specimen. Could the rumors be true? Had these farmers and backwoods ruffians really uncovered the body of a god?

Early reports sounded promising. A skull bigger across than a man's arm span, found partly buried and preserved in a barren stretch of desert near the edge of our realm. A doctor had apparently examined it and been unable to find any signs of forgery or fakery, and a sample sent to my lab showed that it was real, fossilized bone material.

I took it upon myself to make the three month round trip to look at the specimen in person. It wouldn't take so long if they had any sort of modern transportation in this part of the world, but without any rail system for most of the way and without even a road for the last eighty miles, the travel was excruciatingly long.

Still, I did not mind on the way up. What could it be? If not the skull of a god, perhaps an ancient race of giants, long since lost to memory and time? Perhaps a being from some realm well beyond human knowledge?

I'll spare you my waiting. It was a thulcut skull. A bit warped by time and age, but still obviously a thulcut skull. Gods know how it got there, but I can now confidently say that the trip was not worth my time.

- Report on the identification of an unknown fossil found in the northern desert.

As they emerged from the second floor apartment, David was already cooking up his plan. It wouldn't take all of them to talk to the peace officers. If anything, he would be a hindrance in that situation. Adelyn and Topher could go. He had to get to the stables, get his horse, and get across the bridge in time to stop the train.

'You two together,' he explained, feet barely touching the stairs as he ran down to street level, facing halfway backwards so he could walk and talk at the same time. 'I'm going on my own.'

"You can't fight a sorcerer by yourself," Adelyn said, pulling a pair of straps tight on her arm. "All you've got is a hook, and we don't even know who or how many you'll be up against."

'I don't have to fight, I have to stop the train,' David pointed out. 'Go.'

Adelyn bit down on her lip for a moment, clearly weighing the odds in her head.

Topher grabbed her arm before she could announce her decision based on the circumstances. "We don't have time. Come on."

David started running. He briefly considered going for subtlety, to avoid being stopped by peace officers or Watched who might be keeping an eye out for him.

Subtlety is too slow. If they want to stop me, they will have to catch me first.

It wasn't raining, but the puddles on the ground had yet

to dry up from showers earlier in the day. David splattered himself with mud as he stomped through them, going at full speed towards the edge of town.

...

"We don't have time," Topher was saying. "Come on."

Adelyn looked at David one last time. She didn't want him to get killed on a suicide mission, but they were out of time and options.

She shook her head and followed Topher down the stairs. "You know how to get there?"

"I have a few shortcuts," Topher confirmed, flashing her a grin. "Try and keep up!"

He spun on his heels and started running through the streets. Adelyn jumped, then started off after him, making loud splashes in the mud as she tried to catch up.

Despite Topher's warning, he did seem to slow a bit as he rounded a corner, giving Adelyn the chance to catch up. She was taller than him, her legs carried her further with every step, so once she was by his side she gave into temptation and put on a little extra speed, getting a couple paces ahead of him. She had to give up this extra speed and let Topher catch up before too long—he had to lead the way, after all—but she let herself stay ahead for just long enough to show off. Her chest throbbed mildly as she took in deep breaths, but it was so minor that she barely noticed the pain.

Topher waved a hand off to the side, then ran off into a narrow alleyway that Adelyn had barely seen. The passage was just wide enough for her to fit through it, and even then she had to slow down to duck under a pair of spirit lines that had been run between the two buildings.

Adelyn had to grab the wall beside her to slow down as Topher put up a hand and stopped suddenly in front of her, peeking out the end of the alleyway and checking that the coast was clear before he walked out onto the street.

"Keep your head down," he whispered back to her as he stepped out, staring at his shoes as he shuffled down the street.

It didn't take Adelyn long to figure out why. A little ways down the street, someone had overturned a fruit stand, and a crowd had gathered on either side of the scattered mess of fruit and boards. A couple figures were shouting from both sides, and though it looked like neither group had come to blows yet, it didn't seem like it would take much to set off a brawl.

Crossing her arms and tucking them against her chest, Adelyn shuffled on the far side of the street past the rabble. The wooden rods and leather straps on her forearms were still visible, but she wasn't about to discard her only real tool for fighting the witch. The meager disguise would have to be enough. If push came to shove she also had the pepperbox pistol in a pocket, but neither the pistol nor her arm guards would be much good against an angry mob.

Don't recognize me. Don't recognize me.

She repeated the thoughts in her head like a ritual prayer, speeding her pace as soon as they were past the crowd, only barely resisting the urge to break into a jog.

"This way," Topher said, gesturing and guiding them down another alleyway. He had both of the revolvers tucked under his jacket, where they were better concealed, and he was holding his carved staff as though it were just a walking stick. They'd left behind the rifle, for visibility concerns. Once they were in the shady cover of the alley, he added, "It's a lot faster to go down the main thoroughfare, but I don't think that'll be the only trouble we'll encounter out there."

"Is it still faster if we're slowing down to get past the crowds?" Adelyn asked, and Topher immediately nodded. She chewed on her lip for a second, then shook her head. "Faster is faster. Let's risk the main street."

"You sure?" Topher asked, glancing out of the alley.

"We don't have time to waste," Adelyn said. "If someone spots us, we'll shield the road and run for it."

Topher sucked in a breath. "I don't know how much energy I have for big magic like that, but I'll do what I can."

Adelyn almost conceded to taking the long way around, but she steeled herself before she could agree to taking the easy way out.

Stepping back onto the street, she said, "Let's go."

...

David wished he'd taken more time to learn the layout of the city. He could have bought a map and studied it, or taken the time to wander the streets and learn his way around, but he hadn't and now he was paying for that carelessness.

He knew the direction of the train station, and from there it would be an easy shot straight out to the bridge. As the crow flies, it was just a little over a mile.

The issue was, the streets in the city didn't run as the crow flew. They twisted and turned, hitting random dead ends and cul-de-sacs and bending at odd angles that left him without any bearing as to which way he was facing. The sun was high enough in the air that he was mostly running through well-lit streets, but while that made it easier to move down a given path, it did nothing to help him navigate the labyrinthine city. Making his way towards the coast was easy; the roads all pointed in that direction. Making his way away from the coast, though, was proving an immense chore.

By the third time he was forced to backtrack away from a path he'd chosen, David was starting to get frustrated. He didn't have time to stop and buy a map, but he also didn't have time to keep running down dead end paths. Asking for directions, too, seemed like a poor idea, since he'd first have to stop and write out his request, then find someone willing to read it, and all the while hope that nobody recognized him either from wanted posters or from the Watched safe house.

With the right spell and enough spirit, he could have made himself weightless, leapt over the buildings and cut a line straight to where he was going, but that was well beyond him. He had no voice, no runes save for his silver necklace, he hadn't bothered to memorize any old jokes to use as power.

I'm useless without magic.

He knew it was true without having to be told. All he had to do was get to the train and hail them to stop, and he couldn't even do that.

David's feet were still pumping beneath him, carrying him down a new route, but at this thought he slowed to a stop and took a moment to look at his surroundings. He'd been running hard for fifteen minutes, and had almost no idea where in the city he was. Closer to the train station, probably, but beyond that he was clueless.

The street he was on was wide and empty. The Watched, he knew, would be causing trouble closer to the coast, ready to slow down emergency services once the church blew up.

Still, the road seemed surprisingly empty. There were pedestrians a block away, but no market shoppers, not even a food stand set up nearby.

Fingers drumming against his leg, David shut his eyes and tried to think.

The train runs through the city to carry cargo. How does the cargo get to the trains?

It wouldn't make sense to run transport carts through the mazy back streets of the city. There had to be some kind of main route from the coast to the train station. A thoroughfare, or—

A river.

David felt stupid upon realizing it, for not having considered it sooner. The drawbridge wasn't a decorative part of the train's route—it ran right above a wide river, and was the perfect place to bring cargo in from the ocean without even having to unload ships first.

He didn't have to navigate all the way through the city to get to the train station. All he had to do was find the river, and run along its edge all the way to the bridge.

Doing a little math in his head, David worked out how long that would take. He'd have to backtrack towards the coast, and it'd be almost two and a half miles of running when it was all said and done.

That'd take half an hour, maybe forty minutes given the road conditions, and if he had to sneak past any Watched. He'd been running for twenty minutes, and had started with two hours of time.

He would be left with an hour to stop the train.

Plenty.

Turning, he started running towards the southwest, heading towards the river.

...

"I've been thinking," Topher said, staring at his shoes as he trudged around a small mob that had gathered in front of Harrington's medical theater. Adelyn couldn't see Harrington anywhere, but the crowd was apparently struggling to get in through the front door, so she suspected he was inside and keeping it shut one way or another.

"What about?" Adelyn asked, resisting the urge to stare or to try and figure out what was going on more precisely.

"How we're both probably going to die before this is all said and done," Topher said. "Or locked up in jail for a hundred years. Even if the peace officers work with us, we're still wanted."

Adelyn spared a glance down at Topher. "You're not backing out on me, are you?"

"No," Topher said quickly, "I—far from it. I just don't want to die without getting some things off my chest."

"Oh," Adelyn said, blinking once. They were almost past the crowd, now, and she started to pick up her pace again to a brisk walk. "You've got regrets?"

"Don't you?" Topher asked.

"I've been on the coast for three weeks and I never got to see a thulcut," Adelyn said, avoiding the topic. "I'm disappointed about that."

"They're not all they're cracked up to be," Topher said. "Big fleshy things with tentacles. Once you've seen a couple, they all start to look the same. Anything else? We're up against certain doom here, if there's anything you want to say..."

"My sins are between me and the Lords," Adelyn said, hardening her words with annoyance. "What are you doing? Fishing for an apology?"

"What?" Topher said. "No!"

"Are you sure?" Adelyn said. "Because we both know it's my fault we're in this mess to begin with. If I hadn't come to town, you wouldn't be in this mess."

"Yeah," Topher said. "Because half the people I know

would be dead. Adelyn, you saved our butts at the town hall."

"I caused that," Adelyn corrected, adding, "Well, Rahk did too, but I pushed it over the edge."

"Adelyn, you might be new to this, but that sort of thing is how life is here," Topher said, avoiding eye contact with her. "The peace officers at the town hall were barely a step up from usual. I've been blessed for a year, and I've spent that time hiding out, waiting until it seemed safe to use my power. You didn't do that, you stepped up and did what was necessary, and then you decided to put together the whole heist on top of that. You're awesome."

"Your point?" Adelyn asked, uncertain where he was going with this. "I'm not as great as you think."

"You are. You don't sit around and wait for the moment to be perfect, you just act, and it's great, and—" Topher said, stopping mid-sentence. At first, Adelyn thought he had seen some sort of danger, but when she looked at him she saw that his cheeks were flushed pink and he was staring at his toes. Forcing himself to continue, Topher added, "And, if we both survive today, I'd-I'd really like to kiss you."

Adelyn blinked, losing her stride for a moment and having to walk quickly to catch up to Topher. "That's what this is about?"

"I—yeah," Topher admitted, finally meeting her eyes, though his blush was as pronounced as ever.

"And you couldn't think of a better time than now to bring that up?" Adelyn asked, trying to keep from raising her voice. "We're kind of in the shit here."

"I guess not," Topher said, falling silent. Ten seconds passed, then he raised his gaze to meet hers. "Or... actually, no. Now is exactly the time, because we're always in the shit here. If I wait until you and I are both safe and at peace and don't have people counting on us, I'll never get to say anything, and I'm tired of sitting back and waiting for something to happen when I can be like you and do something about it."

Adelyn didn't respond. The road had a slight bend in it, and she peered around to see if there were any more mobs or crowds in the way. Her fears were confirmed, and so she ran her fingers through her hair to brush it in front of her face, stuck her hands in her pockets, and slowed down a bit. It was a larger crowd than she'd seen so far, and they were arranged in front of the courthouse in a loose mob.

She was planning on going in through the side entrance, which hopefully wouldn't be mobbed in the same way. They only had to get through to the other side of the crowd.

"Say something?" Topher asked. "If you're not interested, that's fine, but tell me."

"You're right," Adelyn said. "Let's at least wait until the imminent danger is over. If we're both alive in three hours, we'll talk."

"I'll take it," Topher said, a smile flickering on his expression. "We're almost there, by the way. You have a plan for what we're going to say?"

Shrugging one shoulder in a deliberately casual gesture, Adelyn said, "I was thinking, 'There's a bomb under the church, also sorry about the bank, also please don't arrest us'."

"That's a good start," Topher said, glancing up at the crowd. "But maybe give it a bit more polish. We—damn."

"What is it?" Adelyn asked, following his gaze.

He didn't have to explain. She spotted Mina right away, standing on a soap crate that she'd dragged up the courthouse steps. She had a bandana over her face, but her voice and posture were distinct, as well as the silver bracelet on her wrist that she'd taken from Adelyn. Mina was shouting slogans to the crowd, her voice unnaturally amplified, and Adelyn had no doubt that the mob was bristling with weapons and gleefully anticipating the moment where the peace officers tried to break up the 'unlawful gathering'. Even without the church bombing, this could turn into a bloodbath in an instant.

"We can sneak around back—" Adelyn started.

Topher shook his head. "My sister sold me out. I think it's time we had words about that."

Adelyn looked over at Mina, watching her rabble rousing nervously. "Are you sure that's a good idea?"

"Nope," Topher said, rotating one arm and bending to the side to stretch a bit. "You go on ahead once I've got their attention."

Biting down on her lip, Adelyn nodded. "Don't get killed."

"My sister wouldn't kill me," Topher said, grinning. "Everyone else might try, but they'll have to work for it."

He walked away from Adelyn at an oblique angle from the crowd, getting some significant distance from her before turning directly towards his sister.

Adelyn put her head down and started walking forward, listening but unwilling to look up and risk being recognized.

Mina was shouting through her amplified voice, rousing the people of the city to rise up and fight against the peace officers. Adelyn didn't check everyone's face to see if she recognized them, but it seemed like much of the crowd were not people she'd seen in the safe house the night before. Mina had, apparently, gathered this crowd organically.

In the middle of her call to action, though, Mina's amplified voice suddenly cut out with a little 'pop' and a barely noticeable shift of the spirit in the air. A second later, a thunder crack of gunfire boomed, and Topher shouted in a voice that was clear and loud even without any magic behind it.

"You locked me in a basement!" he yelled.

Adelyn reached the edge of the crowd, pushing quietly past the far edge.

"Topher?" Mina asked, her tone clearly confused. The next thing she said was drowned out by the murmur of the crowd—based on the tone, it seemed most of them had no idea what was going on.

"Do they know?" Topher shouted. "What you're going to do?"

The timbre had returned to Mina's voice by the time she shouted, "You were going to betray us!"

Nobody was watching Adelyn as she made it around the edge of the crowd. All eyes were on Topher, and if they couldn't see Topher, they were on Mina. Adelyn tried to avoid pushing people out of the way, for fear of someone noticing the rods strapped to her forearms underneath the shirt she wore. It was the only magical tool she had access to besides David's book, and she felt exposed as a result, but it was better than nothing and she wouldn't give them up for a touch more stealth.

"I wanted to talk!" Topher shouted. "I still want to talk!"

"Did you come here straight from the safe house?" Mina asked him. "Then—" Her voice hitched, and Adelyn risked a glance up to see that she was whispering something to a familiar face a few feet away. Brenden nodded, then started pushing through the crowd to leave.

Adelyn made it past the crowd and started walking straight towards the side of the courthouse, trusting Topher's distraction to keep working. When she saw Brenden moving in the same direction though, she hesitated, moving to the side and watching him turn and head down the side street, in the exact same direction Adelyn had been going.

She smiled, following Brenden's path, moving slowly at first. He was fully around the corner, past the sight of the crowd now, and Adelyn started going a little quicker, picking up speed. Once the brick street turned to dirt alleyway she started to jog, then broke into a full run once she was only a few paces away.

Brenden heard her and spun in time to see all of Adelyn hurtling towards him in a charging tackle. Grappling was not her forte, but she was six feet tall and had more formidable muscles backing her up. Brenden was lithe and quick, but any advantage he might have had in agility was not enough to get him out of the way of Adelyn's attack.

They both crashed into the mud with a splash, and Adelyn was up on her knees and had an arm to Brenden's throat before he could scramble away.

"Scream or try to run, I'll blast your ass into the ocean," Adelyn said, trying to put as much force into her bluff as possible.

Brenden nodded, buying it. He hadn't taken the fall well, and seemed a bit woozy as he said, "O—okay!"

"Where are the others?" Adelyn asked. "Shane, Rahk. Where'd they go?"

"Shane's under the docks, I think," Brenden said. "Rahk went to the bridge. Said he wanted to watch those ones blow."

Adelyn swore. She'd been hoping that David wouldn't have to deal with any sorcerers, but that wasn't looking like it would be the case.

"I can't waste time tying you up," Adelyn said. "So I'm

going to let you go. I can't stop you from running, but if you attack me I'll stop you. Okay?"

Brenden blinked. "You're not going to knock me out?"

"I'm no good at that trick," Adelyn admitted, pushing herself up and standing, wiping her hands off on her pants. "I'd threaten you, but we both know I can't blow up your head unless you're pretty close, so I can't stop you from telling Shane where I am." She hoped that the subtle lie would work—she couldn't blow up his head at all, and she wouldn't want to even if she could, but Adelyn would say anything to make herself seem stronger than she really was.

Scrambling backwards, Brenden pushed himself up to his feet, turned, and ran down the side street away from Adelyn and, thankfully, away from the crowd.

Glancing up and down the courthouse wall, Adelyn saw the side door she was looking for. Heavy oak, with a big brass handle.

Perfect.

Adelyn walked up to the door, testing the handle, finding it locked. Unfazed, she pulled David's book of magic signs from her pocket, flipping until she found the right spell, smirking at the irony as she put a hand to the handle and called up spirit.

"Rahk!"

The power flowed out of the book and into the handle of the door, smashing the internal mechanism that would keep the door latched. Trying the handle again, she found that it took a bit of jiggling, but once she'd maneuvered it properly the door swung freely open.

Stepping inside, she saw half a dozen peace officers all staring at her, alongside the witch.

CHAPTER 29

One thing that magic users can only do to themselves, much to the consternation of kings and governments everywhere, is memory erasure.

While it would be incredibly useful to erase the memories of others to protect state secrets, help with embarrassing or otherwise unwanted events in an individual's past, or remove traumatic experiences from people experiencing post-traumatic stress, no wizard or sorceress has ever managed the level of mental precision required to affect memories, let alone remove or modify them. Even the most experienced can only induce hallucinogenic or drug like properties in their subject, and even then only with time to prepare and focus. While this could be helpful for anesthetizing a subject before surgery, or eliciting an appropriate state of mind for interrogation, it doesn't do much that plain, ordinary drugs can't do.

•Informal letter responding to a question about how magic could assist in the running of a nation, taken from the presidential archive in Triom.

. . .

"Uh, hi," Adelyn said, looking around. "You're just who I was looking for."

The half dozen peace officers were staring at her blankly. Not all were fully armed. In fact, two were sitting on a row of benches, in the process of putting on combat boots, and the witch was caught halfway through the process of wrapping two strips of cloth around her hands and wrists.

The officers busy with their boots scrambled to get to their feet, but the witch put out her hand and shook her head.

"If you've come in the back way with ideas of catching us off guard," the witch said, "You'll have to change your plan."

"No, I—" Adelyn started, but she was cut off by a loud boom outside, the roaring thunderclap of Topher's air magic.

"Go handle that," the witch said. "Get the crowd under control. Take their leaders alive. I'm right behind you."

"Ma'am?" one of the officers asked. "Are you sure you can handle her?"

The witch smirked, quirking one eyebrow at Adelyn. "Certainly."

Adelyn swallowed. The witch didn't seem to be fully armed. She was barefoot, wearing trousers and an undershirt, one hand wrapped in cloth, a sweatband ringing her shaved head. She was no less intimidating without her hat or coat, and both she and Adelyn knew that if it came to a fight, Adelyn wouldn't come out on top.

The five other officers hurried out, one of them hopping on one foot as she finished pulling on an unlaced boot.

"I don't want to fight you," Adelyn said, weighing the option of running away. She would have better odds in a fight against Shane than this witch, but neither option was optimistic. Maybe she could talk this fight down without having to win.

"I know," the witch said, facing Adelyn squarely. "You're here to stab us in the back and burn down the courthouse."

"No!" Adelyn said. "I need your help, I came here to talk, and—"

"You came bearing arms because you wanted to talk?" the witch asked, stepping sideways, circling around Adelyn.

Adelyn shook her head, rotating to face the witch. "I needed something to protect myself from the Watched. They're planning something really bad, and I need your help to stop them."

The witch took another step to the side, and Adelyn frowned. On intuition, she glanced in the direction that the witch was edging, and saw that the long black staff the witch used was leaning against the corner of the room, still eight feet away from the witch herself.

Eyes widening, Adelyn leapt for the staff, but before she could grab it the witch barked, *"Jetfell!"* and an ethereal wind caught up the staff and flung it into the witch's waiting hands. Adelyn stumbled and caught herself on the wall, spinning to face her opponent.

"You just want to talk?" the witch sneered, flicking out the staff and calling a word that wreathed the wood in black energy.

Adelyn thought about her options. She didn't have time to go flipping through pages to find the right runes in that book, which left her with precisely one spell to cast. The tools on her arms were too specific for anything else, and unless she could take the staff from the witch, she'd have no offensive options in combat.

Or, that is, she'd have no offensive *magic* in combat.

Kicking off the wall, Adelyn charged towards the witch, only a couple paces away and with as much momentum as she could build in the short space.

It seemed that the witch wasn't expecting this sort of wild attack. Instead of responding with a sweep or strike that Adelyn surely wouldn't have been able to respond to, the witch only sank back into a defensive stance, her magic sword off to one side as she braced for impact.

Adelyn threw herself forward, throwing her shoulder into the charge. The witch accepted the charge, bending her legs and sinking low, absorbing the attack and pushing Adelyn away for an instant, giving the witch time to bring her magic sword into play with a broad sweep.

Throwing power into the runes strapped to her arms, Adelyn raised them and shouted, *"Byndyn ansyr eh-sol!"*

White magic flashed into existence in two long strips, one on each of the wooden bands, and as she struck down the witch's attack, Adelyn brought both forearms down on the black greatsword.

Her tools were not so elegant or refined as the witch's sword, but they were hard and reinforced with the best spell that David could help her make in a few days. When her arms met the blade, spirit met spirit, and the blade was forced down to the ground, flickering black energy repelled from the blinding light of Adelyn's armguards.

For a fraction of a second, Adelyn had an opening. The witch hadn't expected anything that could counter her sword, and her eyes went wide in fear as she saw Adelyn close, but Adelyn had no tools to strike back with, and so she couldn't make anything of the opportunity.

Adelyn threw a heavy kick, but the witch twisted and took it on the side of her leg, yanking away with her sword and raising it back up to a guard. Rather than keep up the close grapple, Adelyn jumped away, nearly tripping over one of the benches as she tried to put space between her and the witch.

As they eyed each other, Adelyn realized she had another advantage—the witch's long sword, deadly as it may be, was cumbersome in such close quarters. The room was only ten feet from side to side, and the staff that the sword grew from was almost five feet long. If the witch went swinging around wildly, she'd have to cut through walls and the ceiling to get a clean swipe at Adelyn.

"I just want to talk!" Adelyn said again, but the witch might not have heard her for all the reaction she gave.

She expected a charge, but instead, the witch spun her staff in her hands, making the black magic vanish and aiming the staff like some massive rifle.

Adelyn felt the power build a heartbeat before a black blob of power came at her, coalescing into existence at the tip of the staff and moving with the speed of a thrown projectile at Adelyn's head. She raised her arms to deflect the blob, barely getting them raised in time, and the white energy protected her against the magic, diffusing and spreading out the energy.

A broad shield would have been better, stinging bits of power still splattered Adelyn's arms, but the attack lacked lethal power.

Unfortunately, the defense had forced her to throw up her arms. As soon as her vision was obscured, the witch had leapt across the room, swinging with her staff, black magic sheathing the wood and forming a blade in the middle of the attack.

Adelyn yelped and threw her right arm in the way, but

the spirit she'd poured into the wooden bar had been depleted, and though the magic kept the blade from cutting her arm off at the elbow, she heard a snapping sound and felt something sharp cut into her flesh.

Dodging back, Adelyn risked a glance at her arm to see how bad the cut was. She was bleeding, but it didn't look too deep, and it would be a source of power to keep her remaining guard charged up.

The witch leapt at her again with another wide strike, targeting Adelyn's protected side, apparently hoping to break the other guard.

"Byndynsryehsol!" Adelyn yelped, the spell coming out in a jumble as she threw up her arm and dumped energy from her blood into the guard. Power flared like an assault on her sixth sense as the witch's blade slammed into Adelyn's arms.

For a moment, all she could see was white, and all she could hear was a loud ringing. She was dimly aware of hot blood moving down her arm in a trickle, and a dull, throbbing pain in her head.

Sitting up, Adelyn saw the witch reeling a few paces away, the sheath of magic around her staff blurry and fading. A second to take stock of herself revealed that spell on Adelyn's arm had gone out as well, and that the other rod had snapped. That explained the shattered fragments of wood had pierced her shirt sleeve and been jammed through the flesh by the impact, as well as the points of blood appearing on her left arm to match the flow on her right.

Another boom echoed outside, and Adelyn knew that she had to get up, but her head was still ringing, the fingers of her right hand felt numb, and when she tried to stand she felt a wave of dizziness that kept her down.

The witch was coming towards her, holding out the staff, chanting a few words that made the inky black blade reform around the wood. It wouldn't be long until the witch was within striking distance.

Digging in her pocket, Adelyn pulled out the pepperbox pistol. The witch had to know how to shield herself, but on the off chance that the witch lacked any shielding tools, Adelyn could get in a lucky shot.

Squeezing the trigger, Adelyn heard a bang several times louder than she'd expected, and felt the gun buck in her hand, powder burning her skin as the pistol misfired and imploded.

Dropping the broken gun in pain and surprise, Adelyn didn't even have the wherewithal to swear in annoyance.

...

David ran down the edge of the riverbank, staying just out of the water. He'd found the river even faster than he'd planned, and was ahead of schedule—there was plenty of time to get to the train.

He could see the bridge up ahead, thirty feet tall and almost three hundred feet wide. Not the largest bridge he'd even seen, not even the largest on the coast for that matter, but still a huge structure. A pair of towers that resembled scaffolding more than anything were built on each side, stacked with pulleys and cable to raise the bridge and allow ships to travel up the river. Past the bridge itself would be a crane for lifting cargo from the ships and moving it to the train station's depot, but David didn't have a good view of that.

A ladder was mercifully hanging from the side, which would let him scale the side easily even with his bad shoulder, and from there he'd get his horse and ride out. Simple.

Unless...

Glancing to the far end of the bridge, David squinted and tried to sharpen his vision. He could see a figure on the far side, standing casually, almost relaxed, but that could be a ploy.

If David had been in charge of the bombing, the first thing he would have done is plant lookouts to stop anyone from sending out a warning. You couldn't send a warning by telegram to a train, someone would have to ride out, and the only way to get across the river quickly was across that bridge. Even if they raised a fuss and drew the attention of the peace officers, the lookout would have a good chance of delaying things and creating enough confusion for the train to arrive unimpeded.

David hesitated. He could try and defuse the bomb, if he could find it, but the only thing more likely than a scout watching for someone crossing the bridge would be a scout watching the bomb itself.

Abandon me, Rahk or Mina might even be guarding the explosives for all I know. David doubted that Shane would be the one watching the bomb, but it was also possible.

Creeping towards the ladder, David tried to think how he could sneak past the guards.

He heard a splash and turned, raising an eyebrow at the river. The splash hadn't been consistent with the general lapping sound of running water, it had sounded more abrupt than that, almost like a stone being dropped from a great height.

Next came a whizzing sound, and a yard away from his feet dirt and gravel were thrown into the air in a shower. David started running as soon as he realized what was happening. Someone with magic was on top of that bridge, and they'd figured out how to muffle gunfire.

...

Adelyn scooted back, trying to get away from the witch. "I just..." She slurred, pushing away on her hands, wincing as she applied pressure to her burned hand. "Want to talk."

The witch rolled her eyes, spinning her mage sword widely. "Talk to the Lords."

Adelyn took another step back, taking the witch's advice and preparing a silent plea to the Lords for some kind of mercy.

I could use an out here, Adelyn thought, glancing up at the ceiling. *If it's not too much trouble.*

"What's going on?" someone shouted from down the hall.

Adelyn breathed out in relief. *Thanks.*

Even so, though, the witch didn't slow her pace or lower her sword. Adelyn stumbled back another step, but her foot slipped and she fell out onto the ground behind her.

"Hey!" the voice shouted again, and Adelyn looked away from the witch to see a woman wearing a rumpled, dirty black uniform and holding a revolver slack in her hand. One pant leg of her outfit was singed grey, and Adelyn recognized her as one of the bank guards. The woman strode over, taking in the scene, looking between the witch and Adelyn. "Gods be, what's going on here?"

The witch continued ignoring her, until the woman raised her pistol and fired it into the floorboards, showering the witch with wood chips.

"Have you lost your wits?" the witch roared, facing the woman.

"I want a damned answer!" the woman shouted back, apparently unintimidated. "I heard an explosion. What happened?"

The witch lowered her sword, jaw tightening as she

yelled her response. "I am a sorceress, operating as an agent of the state! You—"

The woman fired her pistol again. "And I almost died yesterday, and this girl on the ground here saved my life! So I'm going to ask again: What, by Garesh, is going on here?"

Spluttering, Adelyn said, "I came to talk! She started the fight!"

"This witch was at the town hall," the witch said, gesturing to Adelyn. "Fighting with the Watched. She's killed peace officers."

"I didn't kill anyone!" Adelyn said. "I was protecting David."

The woman had an off-kilter stance, and she held her gun off to one side as she stared down the witch. "You've got handcuffs? Take her prisoner."

The witch glared, but conceded, giving Adelyn one last dirty look. "When they need a hangman for you, I'm volunteering." Back up to the bank guard, she said, "Keep her down. I'll be back in a second." Stalking down the hall, she shoved past the guard and walked around a corner.

Once the witch was gone, Adelyn stared up at the bank guard. "I think you're the gutsiest woman I've ever met. You know that gun wouldn't stop her, right?"

"Oh, of course," the woman said, slumping against the wall. "I'm just about pissing myself. But you did drag me out of that fire."

"I don't suppose you'll let me go?" Adelyn asked.

"Did you come here to kill us?" she asked, raising an eyebrow.

Adelyn shook her head. "The Watched are going to blow up the Church of the Divine tonight. I came to warn you, but didn't get the chance before the fighting started."

The woman lowered her pistol, thinking it out. "Abandon me, I'm fired anyways. Hurry."

Standing, Adelyn started to run for the door. She heard the pistol fire a couple times and thought for a moment she'd been tricked, but the shots all went far wide, and she realized that it was a show, to make it seem like the woman had tried to stop Adelyn. It was a paper shield, at best, but it was better than nothing.

"She got away from me!" the bank guard was shouting, as Adelyn slammed the door shut, glanced up and down the hall, and began sprinting towards the front of the courthouse.

Maybe she could get lost in the crowd, and if not, the main thoroughfare would be the fastest way to get to the church. Either way, she wasn't getting the peace officer's help and she had no weapons to fight off Shane.

"Lords?" she asked, looking up at the sky with wry amusement. "I know you just bailed me out, but I could use another hand, if you've got anything up your sleeves."

No help came, so she kept moving into the street.

...

David ran towards the bridge, moving in a zig-zag pattern to avoid the gunfire. He couldn't be sure where the shooter was without taking time to scan the top of the bridge, and standing still to do that would have been a sure-fire way to get hit.

He had to hope that they weren't a crack shot.

Diving through the lattice of beams that held up the train tracks, David rolled forward and kept moving, getting under the structure. The hiss of flying bullets and the splatters of dirt and gravel stopped, and David gave himself a second to breathe. The shelter wouldn't give him long—the sniper was probably already moving to get a better shot.

Still, he had a second to breathe, to plot a way out of the line of fire.

The problem was, the bridge wasn't built to shield washed up veterans from sniper fire, it was built to carry trains over the top and to break apart in the middle and raise up for boats to cross underneath it. There wasn't much structure on the bottom half—just supports on the far sides, nothing that even dipped into the water.

The real shelter would be the train station, thirty feet up and fifty feet away. The only way to get there was to climb, but the ladders on either side of the bridge would leave him a sitting duck to any sharpshooter worth his salt.

David glanced to his side, opposite the way he'd come in.

On the other hand...

...

The street was pandemonium as Adelyn walked out. The crowd hadn't exactly scattered, but it had spread out, with the more wary of the Watched getting their distance, moving far enough away that they could flee should things turn to pure chaos.

She tried to see where Topher had gone off to, but the crowd near the courthouse's entrance was still too thick to see what was happening at its base, and nobody was on the steps leading up.

There was another booming clap of air, accompanied by the thickest part of the crowd pressing back, trying to make room. The siblings were fighting, then, and nobody was willing to try and get between them.

"Peace officers!" Adelyn shouted, trying to get the mob to disperse. "Peace officers are coming!"

That got a murmur from those nearest to her, but

someone flashed a sword through the air and shouted, "Let 'em!"

Gritting her teeth, Adelyn tried to think what might scare them away. "They've got a witch!"

That gave the Watched nearby pause. Peace officers, they could handle, but since Mina was presumably busy at the moment, none of them were willing to take the odds against a witch. Maybe the whole mob could come out on top, but who would be willing to go first in that fight?

Those Watched already on the fence started backing away or leaving, and even some of the more dedicated started to look for quick exits.

Adelyn was starting to think she could get the whole crowd to leave, but a moment later, the courthouse doors flew open and she realized she was out of time.

Five peace officers came out, clad in brilliant white armor, brandishing short-barrelled shotguns with a round, wide chamber that reminded Adelyn of a flat drum. Their armor wasn't a full set of plate, but they had breastplates and heavy padding on their arms and legs, leaving only their faces exposed.

"Get down!" one of the peace officers shouted, pointing his shotgun at the nearest Watched.

Adelyn needn't have bothered dispersing the crowd. The peace officers with shotguns, it seemed, did much of the trick. For all the bluster, nobody wanted to be the first to take a round of buckshot to their chest, and anyone who was thinking of causing trouble quieted down the moment a shotgun was held to their face.

Pushing against the crowd, Adelyn looked over the heads of those who were fleeing, trying to get a view of Topher. The peace officers were forcing those around the courthouse to get on the ground, and after a few moments Adelyn finally got a view of what she was looking for.

Topher was on his back, bleeding from both nostrils, looking dazed and broken. Mina was crouched above him, bandana torn from her face, expression twisted up with frustration and anger as she punched her brother in the nose again.

One of the peace officers came up right behind Mina and pressed against her back with a shotgun. They shouted, "Get on the ground!" and Mina put up her hands and complied, already on her knees, surrendering rather than fighting the peace officers as well.

Topher spotted Adelyn in the crowd and gave her a cock-eyed grin and a thumbs up. She didn't realize what he meant by that, until he slammed a hand against the ground and shot up, diving at his sister's wrist.

Two more peace officers came over, getting between the siblings, hauling them away from one another with considerable effort. In Topher's hand, though, he held a gleaming loop of silver, which he held up triumphantly, then tossed at the crowd in Adelyn's direction.

Adelyn wasn't quick enough to catch the bracelet, but she was able to scoop it up from the ground before anyone else. It was her heat bracelet. She would have preferred the shield bracelet, or even the force bracelet, but any tool was better than nothing.

Not sticking around to face the peace officers herself, Adelyn turned and pushed back into the crowd, running down the street, towards the coast.

...

This is not a good idea, David thought, taking a deep breath. *On the other hand, it is this or stay put and get shot.*

Weighing the options, he narrowly decided to go with his idea.

The lift crane was only fifteen feet away from the bridge. When in operation, there was a complicated system of pulleys and counterweights that allowed the heavy steel cable to lift large cargo crates, but when not in use, the hook and cable were held in place to a large piece of ballast that was set down on the riverbank.

'Ballast' was perhaps too generous a term for it, though—it was a large rock, hewn in a roughly square shape, with a metal loop fixed into the top so that the crane's hook could be attached. Either way, the ballast was David's destination.

No shots were fired while he crossed the fifteen feet to the rock, or if they were, David didn't notice where the bullets landed. He had to take a running leap to grab the top of the stone and pull himself up, and once he was standing on top, he did hear the sound of a bullet kicking up chips of rock next to him.

Here, he had needed to gamble, but his gamble paid off. If the metal loop was pounded into the stone, or screwed in, or permanently affixed in some other way, he would have just made himself a sitting duck. Whether by Divine luck or blessing, though, it was held into place by a simple clasping pin.

Another round sprayed his leg with rock chips, and David didn't waste any more time thanking his Watcher. He grabbed the pin that held the clasp in place, yanked it out, and then pulled the clasp.

Naturally, it stuck. Pulling back, David grabbed the crane's lift cable with his left hand and clinched his brass thumb over the line, leaned back, and kicked at the clasp with the heel of his boot.

The loop came free of the stone, and with nothing holding it down, the tow line shot up without resistance.

Rather, the resistance that existed was negligible. David's weight was nothing next to the several tons of ballast, but the pulley system had been designed to prevent the complete freefall of the counterweights.

The engineers had reasonably assumed that the ballast may fail for one reason or another, and so limited the speed at which the cables could move to about forty feet per second—the speed at which, they had determined, the steel cable could survive coming to a sudden stop. In addition to this, they'd added an extra safety measure—a metal ball, about five feet above the hook itself, that would take the shock of any impact instead of the tow hook.

Clinging to the cable, foot planted on the tow hook, David shot into the air like a rocket, quickly accelerating to the cable's top speed. Had he not locked his thumb in place over the steel line, he likely would have been thrown off and sent tumbling into the river, but the brass prosthetic kept him locked down whether he wanted to be or not.

Not three seconds later, he came to a stop as abrupt as the start had been, nearly being thrown clear again, this time from a height that he wouldn't have survived the fall. His thumb started to shift, but he grabbed tightly with his free hand and held fast, sucking in a panicked breath as he hung there, resisting the urge to look down.

The sniper didn't take long to recover from the shock. David heard a bullet whizz past his head.

Unclipping the hook that was hanging from his belt, David slung the top of it over the metal cable that ran straight down to the base of the crane, amidst all the cargo cases waiting to be unloaded. Grabbing both sides of the blade, he didn't wait around any longer before jumping off the hook and sliding down the wire at a breakneck speed.

He dropped from the hook five feet before he would have slammed into the base of the crane, landing in a heap and twisting his ankle before sprawling out on the ground.

Raising his head, he saw that there were crates on all side of him, blocking off the line of fire from any sharpshooter more than a couple paces away.

Allowing himself a moment to lay back on the ground, David started to laugh.

CHAPTER 30

The legend of Jordan is almost certainly apocryphal, despite being written as a literal story in the book of the Divine. We know this, because of a number of inconsistencies and downright impossibilities in the story.

Firstly, it is unclear why a human sacrifice would be given a sword, or for that matter how he would manage to keep this sword on his person while tied to a pole over the ocean and stripped completely naked. However, even if we assume that he kept it in his grip, this is only the first in a series of many problems.

While ritual sacrifice to thulcuts has been practiced by many cultures throughout history, the idea of thulcuts smelling him because of his perfumes is ridiculous, because as we all know, only one of the thulcut's "noses" can actually smell, and even that only distinguishes between odors in the water.

Additionally, even if he managed to cut off its antennae while riding the creature's back, this would not send any thulcut into a rage of pain unless it had severe deformities with its nervous system, because as any fisher knows, their antennae cannot feel pain.

Finally, if he really was doused in the creature's blood as described in the fifteenth verse, he would have suffered severe acid burns unless it was washed off immediately, which would make his subsequent march through the city rather less heroic.

•*Ichthyologist's paper on the legend of the Divine champion, Jordan.*

DAVID'S HORSE, Ace, wasn't so young as he had once been, but he was a strong mount bred for war, and the animal still had plenty of life left in him as he tore out of the stable, spurred on by a rider desperate to build as much speed as possible as they crossed the bridge.

The handful of Watched posted on the far side of the bridge started as they saw this. They'd been expecting David to try something, but a reckless ride straight across the bridge had not been what they'd been thinking would happen. Ace had made it more than halfway across the bridge before any of them could even raise a call, and then the scramble to get into position left them confused and startled for much longer.

If the crack shot with the rifle got off any shots as the horse rode past his hiding spot, none of the rounds hit, and soon the Watched were mounting their own horses, forced to ride off in pursuit or be left out of range.

Ace couldn't keep up a full gallop like that forever. He'd have to slow down, to rest before too long.

By then, though, hopefully it would be too late to matter.

David watched his horse ride off, hoping he could trust the rider, wishing he hadn't needed to put a stranger in harm's way. They'd start riding away from the tracks before too long, circling back to the city, and David was praying that the Watched would give up pursuit once they realized that the rider wasn't going to warn the train, but there was always the possibility that someone would be feeling vindictive.

Or, worse, they might get off a lucky shot and kill the rider right away, realize they've been tricked, and come around to stop David immediately.

David knew he must have looked a mess when he staggered into the livery stable five minutes earlier, looking up and down the rows for his horse. His gloves were worn almost through at the palms, his shirt was torn from when he jumped the fence to get out of the cargo pen, and all his clothes were soaked through with sweat and spray from the river.

He had guessed that Ace was still there in the stable. His care was paid up for a full month, and even if someone had bothered to note the horse's ownership after the wanted poster with David's face was posted in town, it would make more sense to keep the horse in place and arrest David when he tried to collect, rather than to take Ace off to some other stable as impound.

David had felt, more than heard, the figure walk up behind him, and turned to face the young stable hand a few paces away, holding a pitchfork off to one side. He had a bushy tuft of dark hair, dark skin, and couldn't have been older than sixteen going by his awkward frame and pimpled face.

The stable hand called something at David which he didn't catch, but that was probably something to the effect of 'Who are you?' or 'How did you get in here?'

David had gestured a few signs, hoping by some miracle that the stable hand would understand. He hadn't, but he at least recognized what David was trying to explain. "Can't talk?"

When David had confirmed that with a nod, the boy had snapped his fingers in realization. "You're that guy! From the papers!"

David had guessed that there were wanted posters up, but hadn't realized that they'd been printed in the papers as well. Still, he nodded, seeing no reason to argue the point.

"That was so great!" the stable hand had said, catching David off guard until he asked, "Did'ja really jump off of a flaming train car?"

Blinking in surprise, David had to shift gears in his head and think back to the article that'd been posted when he first arrived in town. *That bit about the car was not in the article...*

He reached for his notepad, then remembered that he didn't have it on him. Raising his hands, he mimed out the act of writing onto his hand, hoping the boy would have something.

"Uh..." he said, confused for a moment. Eyebrows raising, he added, "Oh!" and scrambled to go retrieve the ledger from the front of the stable.

He was back in less than a minute, holding it out and flipping to the back page so David could write in it. The book was heavy and a little awkward to hold in one hand, but David cradled it in the crook of his elbow and wrote out a clumsy note.

'I need to take out my horse. It is a black stallion named 'Ace', I cannot remember the stable number.'

The stable hand read the note and frowned, musing to himself about something, then taking the ledger back and flipping through it.

"I think I remember that," he said. "Ace... here it is. Ace. Stable number..." Trailing off, he looked back up at David. "Oh. You're *that* guy."

Again, David nodded sheepishly. He held out his hands to take back the ledger, but the boy held it away, shaking his head.

"I'm not supposed to tell you where your horse is," he said. "S'the rules."

Sighing, David made the writing gesture again. *Come on, I don't have time for this.*

Realizing David's intent, the boy cautiously handed the ledger back, pointedly turning it again to the back page.

'I had a falling out with those people. They are planning to blow up the bridge. I need to stop the train.'

"Oh," The boy said, eyes widening. "Wow. Anything I can do?"

David knew there was no way for him to get past the Watched safely. Even if he could, if the Watched chased him all the way to the train, there was no way he could convince the engineer to stop—if it looked like a robbery, they would never stop the train and let themselves be robbed. They'd keep chugging along, right up until the bridge blew up beneath them.

If the Watched were all busy chasing him across the coast side, though, nobody would be around to guard the explosives.

It had pained him to send the stable hand out on his horse, even if the boy had been willing and eager to help. He'd given the boy his necklace. It was a stupid token, really, as if the Watchers would truly grant the kid magic in the thirty minutes while he went off to ride. It was a quiet promise, though, as well. If he was sending the boy on a suicide mission, David would never have given him something so precious. The necklace was David's way of saying that he believed the stable hand would return.

Now that he was gone, though, David had to stop

thinking in such morbid terms and get to work. Walking out of the train station, he walked out to the bridge, scanning it up and down, trying to figure out where the bombs would be.

If the Watched were thorough, there were three points that they would have placed the explosives: The pair of rickety towers, with their support lines that kept the bridge upright, and the mount in the center of the bridge, where the two sides latched together when the bridge was in use. Any one of those would likely cause a bridge failure, but all three would leave the bridge completely and utterly destroyed.

David would have to check all three.

Tapping his fingers against the side of his leg, he walked to the first of the towers. A quick inspection led him to a rope ladder in a pile on the ground, the top end frayed like it'd been cut with a saw. The Watched didn't want anyone going up to check on the towers, then, and so they'd cut off the regular path to the top.

Damning them, he looked around for a good place to begin scaling the tower. He settled on an angled support beam, planned his route up, and started climbing.

...

Adelyn saw the church come into view well before she got close. She wasn't too far away, a handful of blocks at most, but the docks were busy with the thickest crowd she'd ever seen.

Peace officers had taken up positions in a wide perimeter around the church, armed with clubs and tall shields. For a moment, Adelyn thought they had blocked off all access to the church, and her heart soared, but once she got closer she saw that they were allowing people through in a thin trickle, only after confirming that the passersby were Divine, and were there to give sacrifice in honor of Eatle's Day.

Adelyn's first thought was to approach, to try and pass herself off as a Divine pilgrim, but she immediately realized that this would end with her arrest. She could hide in a crowd for a while, but she couldn't hide from a peace officer who knew what she looked like.

The church was frustratingly close. She could see it in detail—a tall, gothic structure, with two wide towers built to the left of a squat, long chapel. Dozens, if not hundreds of gods were arrayed in colorful wooden effigies, and Adelyn could see that one of the idols had a fresh set of paint if it wasn't an entirely new statue.

Scanning up and down the glamorous white building, Adelyn didn't see a single thing that wasn't flammable.

Gritting her teeth, Adelyn turned to pace up the dock and think about a plan to get in.

The added security did offer one benefit; the belligerent Watched were nowhere to be seen. Anyone who so much as gave a peace officer the stink eye was firmly asked to leave the area, and if someone tried to start something they were immediately detained and carried off.

Think, she told herself, slapping her forehead as though it would unstick an idea from the corner of her brain. *How can I get to the church? Where would the Watched go?*

It came to her a second later and she turned on her heels, marching up the docks, straight towards Solden's fish shop.

...

David was getting tired of heights. Too many of his recent encounters had left him dangling from high places, a single slip away from falling to his unquestionable doom, and he wasn't fond of it.

Grabbing the top lip of the scaffold tower with his good arm, he heaved up, swinging a leg onto the platform and shimmying a bit until most of his weight was supported, then rolling over and ending on his back, atop the tower.

He took ten seconds to catch his breath before sitting up and looking around. From this vantage point, he had an excellent view of the city, and could see all the way to the coastline, and further after that to the water. It was a beautiful view, which he ignored in his search for the explosives.

There was a heavy steel box sitting on top of the tower, which drew David's immediate attention. Four chains made out of steel rings as thick as David's thumb ran out of the box and over the top of the tower, towards the center of the bridge, and the copper cable running into its side was humming with spirit.

Walking over to the box and giving it a quick examination, David saw that the top was normally held in place with screws, but they'd been sheared off by something. Grabbing it by the lip, he lifted the bronze cover and tossed it to the side, getting a good look at the mechanism inside.

The pulley system, though well-built and powerful, was not complicated. The four steel chains had counterweights that hung down in the middle of the scaffolding, and ran through gear-toothed pulleys in the box. A simple spirit device pressed a locking peg into the pulley that would keep the counterweights from raising the bridge, pulling the pin would raise the bridge.

His attention was drawn by the large wads of jelly that were crammed into the box. A large wad was stuck onto each gearbox and both steel chains, blasting caps visible inside the jelly, and a series of wires were hooked up to a copper wire and a simple mechanical timer.

Not being a demolitions expert, David didn't know if it

was safe to pull the wire out of the explosives, or if that would set off the charges. He could pull the power from the timer—it was a spirit powered device, after all—but for all he knew it was rigged to blow if someone tampered with it.

Fortunately, he didn't need to know. The explosives were stuck in place, but they weren't wired to anything except the timer, and the timer wasn't fastened down at all. One lump at a time, David carefully peeled the explosives out of the box, holding the blobs of translucent matter in the crook of his arm, finally placing the timer atop the pile.

Once done with that task, he unbuckled his belt, letting his pants sag slightly against his waist so that he would have something to tie up the bundle of explosives. It was a simple trick to wad up the entire parcel, cinch the belt tight around the wad, then slip the end of the belt through a loop on his pants and tie that into a crude, stiff granny knot.

Now, he just needed a way to get down, so he could get the bomb far away and go around up the other two spots.

Sighing, David walked back to the corner, swung his legs over the edge, and started the long climb back down.

...

Adelyn almost walked right past the fish shop. It didn't look anything like she remembered. Once stacked with fish and ice, the carts were now empty, those that weren't turned on their sides or smashed to splinters.

Nobody was there selling wares, and the door to the back room had to be held shut with painted yellow tape because the handle and deadbolt had been smashed.

She tried to extend her senses for a moment, feeling out if anyone was inside the building, but all she got was a hazy blur through the broken door. Glancing up and down the dock, she determined that nobody was watching her too obviously, so she peeled off the tape, pulled open the door, and walked inside.

It took her a few steps before the stench of the back room hit her, and it made the old smell of saltwater and fish seem like a pleasant memory. There were still plenty of fish, but nobody had bothered to replace the ice in a couple days, and so the smell had turned rotten. Had Adelyn not known better, she almost might have mistaken the rusty smell of old blood for some other odor, but she knew what had happened in the room.

There were no lights, so she held up her hand and whispered, *"Brenshane."*

A flickering mote of firelight appeared, giving off more heat than it did light. It was the best she could do with the tool she had available, and it let her see the room clearly enough.

The ground had a wide, purple-red stain of blood that had soaked into the floorboards. Gagging, Adelyn forced herself past it, taking the back room's door by the handle and swinging it open, stumbling in and almost falling onto the rug in the next room.

There was a second bloodstain on the far wall, and the smell of dried blood was more prominent here now that the stink of rotting fish was less pronounced. By flickering candlelight, Adelyn pulled up the rug, revealing the trap door that she knew would be there. There wasn't a handle, but she pried it up with her fingernails, and breathed out a sigh of relief that there was still a rope tied to the loop on the inside of the door.

Solden had given Brenden time to escape and covered his tracks, but hadn't had a chance to clean up before she was killed. Adelyn was briefly glad for that, it meant she didn't have to search for the rope. A second later she felt sick with herself for having thought about it that way.

She had no way of covering her tracks or putting the rug back behind herself, so Adelyn didn't even try. She slid over the desk and set one of its legs on top of the trap door so that it wouldn't slam shut and make her lose her grip on the rope, then sat by the hole in the floor, took the rope, and lowered herself into the blackness beneath the docks.

...

After a bit of indecision, David decided to simply drop the explosives into the river. It would be washed out to the ocean, and even if it could still detonate underwater, the power would be contained and it would be unlikely to cause significant collateral damage.

Hopefully.

Holding the bundle out over the edge of the bridge, David loosened his belt and dropped the lumpy mass of explosives into the trickling water below before diving away, dropping flat onto the bridge next to the train rails.

Nothing happened. After ten seconds passed, he tentatively stood, peering down over the edge to see the wad of explosive clay bobbing along in the water, looking innocuous. Once he was certain that the parcel wasn't about to explode, he crouched to grab the lip of the bridge with his good arm, and swung out his legs so that he could climb down.

The explosives on the center of the bridge would be underneath the rails, stuck to whatever steel locking mechanism was in place to hold the bridge together when it wasn't raised.

David was already feeling the burn in his arms by the time he started shimmying under the bridge. His shoulder was aching incessantly, and he damned himself for letting some of his strength go, because he was quickly growing tired from all the climbing.

It was painfully slow. The bridge was perhaps fifty feet wide, and there were steel I-beams placed two feet apart, so to get to the middle he would have to traverse twelve of the beams. Fortunately, the steel beams that formed the structure of the bridge provided easy, wide grips, but even so, it was a chore to grab onto the I-beam with both arms, clinging to the flanges, then moving one leg at a time, his heels and calves providing extra grip and momentary relief to his stiff fingers and burning arms.

The water was babbling twenty feet below him, and for once, he considered that the fall wouldn't be fatal. It would hurt, but unless he lost consciousness, he could probably swim to shore. He wouldn't have the time or strength to get back up and disarm the remaining explosives, but he could survive.

Gritting his teeth, he reached for the next steel beam, heaving himself over. He smelled blood and felt the spirit tingling on his shoulder, and realized he'd reopened the bullet hole that had been stitched shut, but the hot blood just served as a reminder to keep moving.

That's when he heard the foghorn and turned to see the approaching ship.

His swearing was unintelligible, but the meaning was still apparent to anyone who would have cared to listen. Picking up the pace over the complaints of his aching arms, he hauled himself over to the next beam.

Counting the space to the last two, he nodded to himself. *Only two left. I can do that.*

The ship was still several minutes away, and then if he was lucky there would be some more delay in getting the bridge raised. Plenty of time for him to dislodge the bomb, drop it into the river, and climb over the other side.

As he hauled himself to the next beam, he felt the whole bridge tremble, and then felt his heart sink. He wasn't far from the center, but there wasn't going to be time to get away. There wasn't even going to be time for him to pull away the explosives.

Looking up and down, he saw that there were no good places for him to hang on to directly above or below his position. Clinging to the beam wasn't an option, either, his arms would give out long before the bridge got put back down.

There was one thing he could think of, though. As the bridge started to shift, a loud clacking sound rang out one more beam over, as the heavy steel latch was pulled away, leaving the two halves of the bridge disconnected.

The latch was a giant hook, as thick as a man's arm and almost four feet wide. David clung tightly to his beam as the bridge shuddered, but as soon as the rattling stopped and the bridge started to raise up, he all but threw his arms to the last beam between himself and the hook, hauling up and grabbing onto the latch with both hands.

It was possibly one of the most difficult, and certainly the most bizarre, pull-up that he'd ever performed. The hook-shaped latch was still flat against the underside of the bridge, it didn't swing freely or align itself perpendicular to the ground, so as David let his legs go and dangled from it, he had to constantly adjust his grip to hang on.

Raising into the air at a speed of maybe a foot a second, he also had to deal with the fact that the hook was barely too thick to fully wrap his fingers around, and the curved shape made it difficult to get a proper handhold. Even had his arms not been screaming at this point for him to give them a rest, he would have had trouble keeping his grip on the latch.

Biting down so hard it made his teeth hurt, David growled something unintelligible, clamped his eyes shut, and heaved.

A moment later, he had an elbow up over the latch. Not giving in to the temptation to rest, he threw his other arm over, so that he was resting on his armpits. There, he took a few seconds to catch his breath, then he grabbed the top of the latch hook, drug himself up a couple more feet, and kicked his legs up onto the hook.

Finally, for that moment at least, he was safe. The bridge obviously had to lower before the train would pass over it, he would have time to get to the top of the second tower.

And, he noted, looking at the base of the hook as he panted for air and let his arms hang limply by his side, he'd found the second set of explosives. The lumpy bomb was stuck under a metal plate, wedged between the bolts that held the latch in place, a mechanical timer and a spirit battery tied next to it with a length of twine.

He sighed in relief, peeled the bomb away from the bolts, and dropped it into the river below.

CHAPTER 31

Jeremy found the most incredible thing while we were surveying the peninsula islands today. We've gathered that this cave is apparently well known to the locals, who warned us not to go in for fear of angering their gods, but that doesn't make it any less incredible to us, and their gods certainly don't pose any danger.

The cave we are inspecting glows.

Well, not the cave, but the creatures that live inside. Thin strands of some kind of organic matter hang from the ceiling and give off the most beautiful light you've ever seen. It made me feel lightheaded just to look at it for a moment, and I couldn't stay long because my air tank was running low and you have to swim to reach the cavern entrance, but I'm going to go back and try to get a better look at these creatures tonight.

• Surveyor's report notes. Last entry.

THE WATER SEEPED into Adelyn's boots, cold and harsh, refreshing and numbing her at the same time. The water was a black void, colorless, a huge blankness against her sixth sense. It didn't feel like steel or iron, it didn't fuzz or blur the spirit around it, the water seemed indifferent, a giant body that no amount of power could ever sufficiently charge, and so which created a flat, empty space that washed forward and pulled back with the tide as she moved forward.

Adelyn added spirit to her candlelight and whispered a word that sent it up high, floating far above her head. The reinvigorated light let her see a good ways, and cast long, stark shadows off the thick support beams that held the docks up.

If anything, the space looked like a forest. Adelyn was reminded of home, of the time when it had rained for a week and the creek had overflowed. The beams were too neatly placed to resemble a natural forest, but if she squinted and ignored the dock platform above her, she could almost mistake the place for an apple grove.

She started trudging forward through ankle deep water, trying not to think too much of home. Adelyn knew she couldn't afford to lose her nerve, not when she was so close. She wasn't sure how much time she had, but she couldn't imagine it had been close to two hours yet—all she had to do was get back to the church and get rid of the explosives.

It occurred to her as she was walking that, if the Watched had gotten into the church and planted the explosives inside somewhere, she was going to be out of luck. Maybe she could make a hole in the floor and climb up, but she was praying that the Watched had just strapped the explosives to the wooden beams holding up the church.

She was also hoping that the Watched had ran off to hide after planting the bombs, or left a token guard with no sorcerers.

In case not, she pulled the book from her jacket pocket, flipping the pages to find something useful. A rune of force caught her eye, so she stuck a finger on that page and closed the book around it, leaving the tool at the ready should she need to pull it up.

She kept marching forward, looking as much at the docks above her as the path forward. There were no street signs, so she had to look for landmarks—areas where the dock stuck out further to accept ships, and eventually an area with twice again as many support beams and the sound of thousands of footsteps over her.

The candlelight started to fade, so she reinvigorated it, wishing yet again that she had something other than her heat bracelet. It would help if—

"Mina? Is that you? What are you doing down here?"

The voice came from farther down the docks, past where her candlelight could show her. By her voice, it was Ansyr, though Adelyn couldn't be sure. Whoever it was, Adelyn felt stupid for putting a spotlight right over her head, but there was no going back now.

Trying to mimic Mina's accent, Adelyn called back, "Yes! It's me!"

After a confused pause, Ansyr shouted again, though not in response. "It's Adelyn! Go get Shane!"

...

David didn't bother trying to hide as the ship floated by. There was nowhere he could have gone, and he didn't care if they saw him, since they had no way to interfere unless someone on deck had a rifle and a penchant for shooting at strangers.

Someone spotted him and shouted a confused question, so David had happily waved, given them a cheerful whistle, and sent them floating on their way with more questions than answers. Once the boat was past him, he got ready to move, waiting for the bridge to drop.

He didn't have much time to spare. The rest had been enough to give him a little strength back, and the climb was not so exhausting as it had been, but he had to redouble his speed and effort to have a chance at disarming the last bomb in time. Heaving himself to the next beam, and the next, he took in heavy breaths of the salty air and wished that Rahk had decided to bomb somewhere that was easier to get around.

At last, he reached the final beam, reached up the edge of the bridge, and lifted himself back onto something approaching solid ground. Flopping onto his belly, he laid there for a moment, catching his breath, almost not sensing the figure standing over him until a thin silver chain and a series of interlocking silver rings landed in front of his face.

"That was a smart trick," Rahk said from over him, holding his stubby wand in a free hand. "But we caught the kid. Looks like the Watchers didn't feel like giving him a blessing to help him along."

David rolled onto his back, looking up at Rahk. Two people were behind him seated on nearly identical brown horses, wearing bandanas over their faces, and Ace was being led on the end of the rope held by the shorter of the two, nickering in annoyance but not fighting the restraints. Rahk had a bandana on too, but his voice and tone gave his identity away.

"We didn't hurt him," Rahk said. "We're not peace officers, we don't kill kids just because they're inconvenient. It'll take him a while to get back without a horse, but he'll be fine."

Breathing out a sigh of relief, David started to sit up, but Rahk put a foot on his chest and pressed him back down. "You're not a kid, Bren."

'Rahk,' David signed, using the new sign he'd learned. 'Please.'

It was a poor message, something that would've been desperate even if he was sure that Rahk understood him, but he felt a tingle of hope as he said it.

"I like you, Bren," Rahk said. "I wanted this to work, but it's clearly not going to. This is your last chance to walk away. Take your horse, and your necklace. Leave the city by way of the east, never come back, and I'll let you live."

David stared at Rahk, then looked at the two Watched a few paces away. One was holding a rifle in the crook of their arm. They'd be the sharpshooter, then, because the other only had a revolver.

He waved his hand over his head, trying to communicate that he needed a moment to think.

"We don't have long to get off this bridge," Rahk said. "Make your decision. Walk away, or we put a couple bullets in your head and throw you in the river."

David already had his mind made up. There wasn't even a question of what to do, he only had to decide how. Three on one, all of them were armed, and Rahk had magic.

Except... it wasn't truthfully a three on one. The Watched were on sturdy horses, but chances are, they weren't used to combat. Gunfire might spook them, make them run, or at least make it difficult for the Watched to aim. David guessed that the Watched were handy in a fight, but doubted that they were experts in mounted combat.

Ace, on the other hand, wouldn't spook so easily.

Rubbing his hand over his face, David pressed his lips together and whistled three times in short, staccato bursts. Ace bucked suddenly, jerking the shorter Watched back and nearly throwing them from the saddle.

The other Watched jumped in surprise, raising his rifle,

but the horse he was riding saw that its twin was in distress and backed away a few steps, forcing the Watched to take one hand off their rifle and hold themself steady.

Rahk swore and focused spirit into his wand, but David shot his free hand up and grabbed it, draining it of power as they grappled for the weapon. Rahk had the better grip and managed to pull it free, but needed a second to refuel it for a spell, and David used that time to grab his hook, snapping the buckle as he swung it ferociously at Rahk, smacking the flat of the blade on the young sorcerer's hand, sending the wand flying out of his grip.

Rahk grimaced, but before David could get in another attack he diverted spirit into the bracelet around his wrist and shouted, '*Shtap!*'

...

Adelyn ducked behind a beam and killed her light, shrouding the underside of the docks in near perfect darkness. The sun was low to the ground and off to the west, so only the faintest hint of daylight could make it to the man-made cavern along the coast side.

Taking a deep breath, she listened to the shouts and splashes as Watched reacted to her unexpected approach. She couldn't see them, but that meant they also couldn't see her, and that was going to be enormously helpful—Adelyn didn't need to beat them all in a fight, she only had to get past them.

Light appeared from the other side of her pillar, distant motes coming from lamps or maybe torches. Adelyn wasn't sure how far down they were, but it was too far her to accurately hit them with a spell.

Raising the book, she called up the dimmest light she could still read by and hastily flipped through pages, searching for the right runes. She didn't know what she was looking for. Some kind of attack, or a way to distract the Watched so she could run past them, something that would be more effective than heat or fire or bright lights.

Halfway through turning a page, she stopped, considering the bracelet again. She'd made it to be practical and versatile, and though she doubted it would be an effective weapon in the current circumstances, it could still be useful.

Slipping power into her bracelet, feeling herself grow tired with the effort, she whispered out the word. *"Onshane."*

Black tendrils of power spread out around her, spreading out and diffusing into faint wisps as the air went pitch dark around her. The release of spirit made the area under the docks appear more sharp and acute to her sixth sense, as though she'd dropped a bag of flour in a room made of glass.

The spell started deteriorating almost immediately. Saltwater and misty air ate away at her magic hungrily, making it fade in seconds, forcing her to provide a constant supply of spirit, but she only needed the spell to last for a little while.

Pushing away from her beam, she turned and started running towards the voices. Her spell did nothing to mute the sound of her boots as they crashed through the water, but she didn't care about that unless the Watched could aim a rifle based on the splashing footsteps.

"What the—" one of the Watched started to shout, but the oath was cut off by a shout from a voice Adelyn recognized.

"Get back! She's dangerous!"

Shane, Adelyn thought, a pit of concern growing in her chest. He'd be able to feel her plain as day as long as she kept up the spell, but if she dropped the spell, she'd be visible to everyone. She could feel that she was close to the

Watched—one was only ten feet away, close enough that she could have run up and touched them if she wanted to.

Her finger was still stuck in the book, holding the page with the force rune, but force wasn't what she needed.

Instead, she cast her spell again, focusing to tighten its reach and make it more localized around her. *'Onshane byndyn.'*

The darkness closed in around her, leaving her still blind, highlighting her immediate surroundings with a great buzz of spirit.

"She's over there!" Shane shouted, and Adelyn imagined him pointing and flailing right at her. "That dark spot!"

The magic followed her as she stepped forward, making the dark spot shift and glimmer as ocean spray began the work of dissolving it. She'd tightened it and packed more spirit into the condensed spell, so it resisted the water a little better, holding up without needing immediate resupply.

Relying entirely on her sixth sense for navigation, she sprinted towards the nearest of the Watched, stuck out her hand, and called out the spell again, more force in her words as she threw around power like she had an unlimited supply. *'Onshane byndyn!'*

She couldn't see, but instead felt the dark splotch of spirit form in the air around the Watched, blinding them, and making them appear identical to Adelyn. Even Shane wouldn't be able to tell the difference between the two human figures shrouded in magic.

With all the spirit in the air, Adelyn found it almost trivial to feel her surroundings. She was growing exhausted from the magic, but a rush of adrenaline and pride in her idea filled her as she felt her plan working, felt the next Watched and lunged towards them, throwing up a floating ball of darkness that shrouded yet another Watched.

"Abandon me!" someone shouted. "She's killin' them!"

"No!" Shane tried to shout, "It's a trick, don't—"

"I can't see!"

The docks were too echoey, and Adelyn couldn't see which figure Shane's voice was coming from, but she could feel that he was holding spirit ready to cast a spell and so she used that to navigate around him and towards another of the Watched.

There were six people she could feel beneath the docks, not including herself, and fully half of them were surrounded by her black illusion. To her surprise and cheer, another of the figures started running, kicking up wake as they fled at full speed away from the fight.

"Hold on!" Shane shouted, and when nobody responded, he moved and sent out a wave of magic energy. Adelyn couldn't see what he'd done, but it seemed to be some sort of steady ball of power, she guessed it was a light of some kind.

"Shane, I'm blind, I—"

"She's tricking you!" Shane said. "Everyone stop!"

Adelyn froze still, and felt the others do the same. If she moved now, it'd be the same as giving herself up.

"It's sleight of hand," Shane said, walking towards one of the Watched that Adelyn had hit with darkness. "She's just made it seem dark around you. Hold still, I can dispel it, you'll be fine."

There was a slight tingle, and Adelyn felt her spell vanish from existence as Shane sapped it of power. Whoever Adelyn had concealed, they gave a cry of relief.

"Stay put," Shane said. "I'll get you all out of there. We'll see if she's so confident once we bring her into the light."

...

Rahk's spell hit David wide and unfocused, pushing him

into a slide towards the edge of the bridge. Instead of saving himself immediately, though, David swung his hook at Rahk's ankle, sweeping the sorcerer off his feet. Only once that was done did David drop his weapon and frantically claw at the surface of the bridge, feeling his legs slide over the edge and only barely stopping himself from plummeting down to the water.

Flailing his feet, he flopped forward and pulled himself back onto steady ground, but he had to immediately duck and roll to avoid another clumsily aimed spell, sending him too far away from his hook for it to be useful.

A gunshot cracked out, the rifleman having gotten control of his horse well enough to aim, though the round only grazed the back of David's leg. It stung, but compared to the burning in his shoulder, David barely felt the pain.

Rahk slammed force through his silver bracelet, but rather than stop him, David lunged towards the rifleman, taking shelter behind their horse as Rahk carelessly threw out his magic.

The horse whinnied as it took the brunt of the attack, thrown badly off balance. David would have felt a twinge of guilt had so many lives not been at stake, but considering the circumstances he deemed it okay to grab the edge of the saddle and yank down as hard as he could, sending the tottering horse completely off balance.

It fell to the ground, legs kicking wildly and frantically, pinning the rifleman's leg and making him shout in pain.

The other Watched had finally gotten the bright idea to let go of Ace's rope, but Ace had taken to the fight with as much vigor as ever, spinning and bucking and causing a scene that still had the rider's attention.

Snatching the rifle up from the man below him, David

raised and levelled it towards Rahk, chambering a round with practiced smoothness.

Rahk hesitated, his hand raised. "You wouldn't kill me," he said, eyes on the gun.

He was right, but David still held the gun tight. He could shoot Rahk in the arm or leg, but that wouldn't stop him, only give him a strong supply of blood an incentive to get more reckless with his magic.

What's a broken promise next to all those lives?

Killing Rahk wouldn't save anyone, though. Rahk didn't need to die, David had to stop the last set of explosives from detonating.

Gritting his teeth, David roared and threw the rifle at Rahk, charging at him.

Rahk blinked in surprise, threw up his hands, and started to shout a spell. Before he could finish the words, David rammed his bad shoulder up past Rahk's guard, forcing the sorcerer back a couple steps.

Rahk fell backwards over the edge of the bridge, plummeting towards the water below with a look of stunned surprise plain on his face.

David yelled out in pain as he felt the shock of that attack redouble the burning ache in his shoulder, then spun back towards the two Watched, snatching up the rifle from off the ground.

One was still pinned, and the other had only just gotten their horse under control and backed up to a safe distance away from Ace. David pointed the rifle at the seated Watched.

They dropped their revolvers to the ground in a heartbeat. David cautiously walked over to them, kicked both revolvers over the side of the bridge, then chucked the rifle in after it.

Surveying the scene, he hesitated only long enough to scoop up his silver necklace and pocket Rahk's wand before turning to run to the last tower.

...

Adelyn was still concealed, a few paces away, but Shane was going to reveal her any second now. Biting her lip, she took a gamble and pitched her voice high and scared. "Help! I can't—I can't see!"

"You're fine!" Shane shouted, walking straight up to her. "I'll get that magic off you, then—"

Adelyn decided that it was a fine time to resort back to runes of force. Though she was already feeling tired, she sucked the spirit that had been keeping her shrouded in blackness out of the air, slammed that power into the book, and shouted, *"Shtap!"*

Shane never stood a chance. The focused spell hit him in the belly with as much power as Adelyn had been able to manage. She could see her surroundings clearly now, the whole space lit by a stark, bright light that gave off spirit like a radiator, and she used that new clarity to drive a fist into his face.

He groaned, doubling over and clutching at his gut. Adelyn didn't give him a chance to respond. She blasted him again with another spell, less focused but equally as strong, in the chest. And a third, in the belly again, dropping him to the ground where he curled up into a ball in the ankle-deep water, where she kicked him.

Her vision started to go black as she reached for strength to cast a fourth spell. She staggered, spinning around to look at who was still standing.

Four people, and she barely had the strength to stand. Two were still shrouded in blackness, sure, but that would fade soon, and they would be able to resume fighting.

"All of you!" she shouted, waving her head back and forth to look at everyone. "You'd... you'd better run, or I'll kill you all!"

The Watched around her shifted, cautious, but apparently not terrified. Now, in the full view presented by Shane's light, she was no terrifying sorceress, she was just a scared, tired girl.

Ansyr stepped forward, fishing Shane's bronze sword out of the water, holding the weapon out. "No, you won't. You're not strong enough."

Adelyn squinted at Ansyr, then looked up over her head, where Shane's magic light was floating like a tiny sun.

Reaching up towards it, she said, "You're right. I don't have to." Then, she pulled the power out of the light, shrouding the area underneath the docks in total darkness.

CHAPTER 32

I had a patient come in today suffering from fairly mundane injuries, but with the most incredible story.

Local ships pulled him off a piece of driftwood this morning. He had severe lacerations on his arms and legs, and was suffering from malnutrition and dehydration. He claims to be part of the hunting party that went out a week past, the one given up as lost.

According to his testimony, their party was attacked by no less than five thulcuts while making repairs to their ship's mast. He was trapped below deck, though he won't explain why, and narrowly managed to get out only once the deck of the ship was smashed apart.

I believe he is remembering things incorrectly due to stress, though I don't begrudge him that after several days floating with no food or water. According to his claims, the rest of the crew was eaten, but when he was taken by the grasp of one of the thulcuts, it paused and then let him go, even going so far as to keep the other beasts away from him. This is ludicrous, but it does paint a beautiful story.

I fixed his lacerations at a reduced price on account of his trauma, but there's no magical cure for hunger, so for that I sent him to the food cart down the road. He'll be fine, though I expect he's going to give up sailing.

•Excerpt from the journal of Harrington Midsworth, a physician working in Azah.

DAVID HEAVED himself up the side of the far tower, chest rising and falling in deep, rapid gulps of air. He couldn't look at the whole climb, he had to focus on moving up one arm's length at a time, telling himself that if he could make it the next two feet, he would be able to make the rest of the climb.

For a moment, he wondered if this qualified as a lie, and thus break his vow of honesty—he intellectually knew that making it up a couple more feet would not, in fact, make the rest of the climb a breeze. It was motivational rhetoric, not truth. On the other hand, he wasn't speaking the lie aloud, just repeating it in his head, and since he knew that it wasn't the truth, nobody was technically being deceived.

It was a trivial question, but it served as a distraction from the burning in his arms and the shooting pain in his shoulder, and so David threw himself into the meaningless internal debate, gladly taking the chance to focus on anything except the growing exhaustion he felt.

Then, before the dilemma could be resolved, he was at the top. His hand reached the flat platform at the top of the tower, and with a moment of inspired strength he gave one last heave of exertion and pulled himself up.

Rolling onto his back, he gasped for air and watched the clouds. He'd made it. He'd gotten past Rahk, evaded the Watched, and made it to the last point where explosives had been planted. All he had to do was stand, walk two steps to the side, and pluck the bomb out of the gearbox.

Though his limbs were begging him to rest a little longer, David ignored them, instead promising himself rest as soon as his task was done. He rolled over and got onto his knees, then planted a hand on the floorboards and pushed himself up, staggering the last couple steps to the gearbox.

As before, the top wasn't screwed into place or held down, so he grabbed it by the edges and shoved it out of the way, looking at the gears inside.

For a moment, David didn't react, staring down at the gears and chains that were keeping this side of the bridge upright.

No.

He couldn't accept what he saw. He had done everything right. He'd escaped capture, he'd come all this way, he'd worked his body to exhaustion and beaten a sorcerer. He couldn't fail now, and yet there was nothing else he could do.

The explosive jelly had no doubt been put into the gearbox in semisolid lumps around the gears, but that was no longer the case. When the bridge had been raised, the cogs had turned, squeezing the bomb, working it into all the nooks and crannies of the gearbox, with little beads of the jelly strung around the wire and all through the gears. The timer was still intact, tied in place to the side of the box, but the wires that extended from it had been looped and wound around the gears in a hopeless knot.

Given an hour, and the right tools, he might have been able to scrape the jelly out of the gearbox and extract the wires without agitating things or risking detonation, but he didn't have an hour. The timer was ticking down with only a few minutes to go.

There was nothing he could do.

...

The Watched beneath the docks hurried to draw lamps and relight their torches, but it didn't do them any good. Using the spirit she'd taken from Shane's light, Adelyn had shrouded herself in darkness once again, and without Shane around to sense her position, they'd have no chance of finding her.

Adelyn didn't know how much time she had, but she knew there wasn't much. Even so, she didn't have the strength to run, so she waded forward, seeking out with her spirit sense for any obstacles.

The sounds of the Watched were quickly put behind her, as they called out to one another and tried to find Adelyn. First, with ideas of killing her, then, simply out of fear that Adelyn was about to come out of hiding and slaughter the rest of them.

It wasn't even a minute before she could hear the crowd over her head, the sound of thousands of people engaged in a call and response above her. She couldn't hear the orator, but there was presumably a voice leading the crowd, running them through rote, meaningless prayers to a false god.

She rolled her eyes at the prayer, then dispelled the darkness around her, called up a light with the power from her blood, and looked around.

The Watched hadn't even tried to hide the explosives. The first bundle Adelyn saw was tied to a support beam only a couple feet away from her, and she used her knife to cut it free, checking the timer.

Only a couple minutes to go, she thought. *I made it here just in time.*

The looked around, checking for other bombs. She saw three more right away, which she took down equally as easily, though carrying all of them proved awkward as she shuffled from one beam to the next.

In a minute, she took down seven bombs, holding them close to her chest and trying not to feel anxious about holding enough explosive to kill herself fifty times over.

With her free hand, she flipped through the pages of the book, searching for the right kinds of runes. Once she found them, she put the book between her teeth so she could hold it and still use her hand, cutting herself on the back of her arm to get blood for a spell.

Concentrating, she held up the bundle of explosives, said a few words, and sent the whole bundle flying off to sea like it had been shot from a cannon.

That done, she staggered back, leaning against a beam for support. If she'd missed any of the bombs, there hopefully wouldn't be enough to bring down the church.

For now, she decided, she needed to get a little rest, recover some strength. She could close her eyes, for a few moments, then worry about how she was going to get back up to the city and what she'd do from there.

The rest was up to David.

...

David tried to scrape away some of the explosive putty, to mitigate the damage, but he knew it was hopeless before he started. There were barely more than two minutes left on the timer. The best thing to do would be to climb down the tower, take his horse, and run.

Abandon me, he thought. He'd given it his all and still come up short. What good was living to fight another day if he wasn't strong enough to win?

The top of the tower shook slightly and David froze, looking around. He felt the shake a second time, then felt the energy and realized that he wasn't alone. Someone else was coming up the tower.

"Bren!" Rahk shouted, his hand reaching up and grabbing the top of the tower. David thought about trying to kick him off, maybe stomping on his toes to make Rahk fall, but it wouldn't help. There wasn't any point.

Unless...

Walking over, he crouched and took Rahk's hand, hauling him up. It wasn't much of an assistance, as tired as David's arms were, but it was the gesture that mattered more than the help itself. His only hope now was to get Rahk's help, to devise a spell that the young sorcerer could use that would stop the explosion or save the bridge. It was a long shot, but there was no other way.

"Stop, or I'll—" Rahk started, before he realized that David was trying to help him. Confused, he clambered up to the top, looking first at David, then at the gearbox. His clothes were dripping wet, but he seemed otherwise unharmed from his fall into the river.

Please, I need your help, David thought.

"I'm going to stop you," Rahk said, warily stepping away from David, putting some space between them. "Even if you threw away the explosives, I'll destroy the gearbox myself. You got me once, but I won't let you beat me again."

David shook his head, gesturing to the gearbox. Confused, Rahk stepped towards it, glancing inside to see what David was on about. Once he saw the mangled mess of wire and explosive putty, he started to laugh.

"I win!" he exclaimed, grinning broadly. "You can't take out the bomb, and if you try to rip out the timer it'll blow anyways. There's nothing you can do!" He whooped with delight, stepping back and beaming.

Putting up his hand, David took a step forward, doing

his best to stay calm and reasonable. Rahk had to change his mind. There was no other way, not that David could see.

Rahk leaned back and raised his arm, spirit gathering in the bracelet he'd stolen from Adelyn. "Woah, there, Bren. I don't know what you're planning, but I'm getting off this tower before it blows, and you can't really stop me."

Reacting to the spirit on instinct, David sank back, getting ready to dodge or counter Rahk's magic. It was only after Rahk had finished talking that David realized he'd channeled energy into the wand stuck under his belt. A stupid, pointless reflex, one that sapped even more of his flagging strength.

A whistle sounded, shrill and loud. The volume of the whistle made David wince, and when he looked to the source, he saw the train barrelling towards them, maybe a mile away but closing fast.

"That's it," Rahk said. "You're out of time, and if you stick up here you're not long for the world neither."

Before Rahk could turn to climb down and away, David tried one last please. 'Please,' he signed, emphatically and slowly, so that Rahk might understand. 'Rahk, I—'

David froze mid-sign as he felt the spirit in the air shift. A spell hadn't been cast, exactly. To cast a spell, one needed a tool, the focused thoughts of intent, and a spoken word to release the magic.

Despite that, when David said Rahk's name, he had felt something. Focusing on the wand tucked into his belt, he felt that some of the energy had been released, as though by an unfocused, unplanned spell.

Rahk didn't catch what was going on in David's thoughts, but he could tell that the tone had changed. His brow furrowed and he glanced around, putting more energy into his stolen bracelet. He made some kind of threat, a word of warning, but David wasn't paying attention.

Is it possible?

The ability to cast spells was a gift from the Watchers, at least as far as David believed. In that way, each spell was sort of like a prayer, where you had to think of what you wanted, then speak the words to call the spell into being.

Do I think that the Watchers can't understand signs?

Drawing the wand, he stared at it, heart beating a thousand times a second even while his thoughts were locked up and frozen.

He had to try. Putting more power into the wand, he focused on the spell he wanted to create, as though he were a newly blessed sorcerer learning to channel power for the first time.

Moving his hands slowly, he signed out the name again. '*Rahk.*'

Spirit snapped out of the wand, sharp and vibrant, taking shape just as David had imagined. A simple ball of energy that slapped Rahk's hand to the side. Not an attack, but a test of his power, a challenge.

The grin that spread across David's face came from deep inside as he felt the thrill of the spell. The Watchers hadn't abandoned him.

He had *power*.

Rahk was staring at his hand in shock. He'd felt the magic slap him down, but didn't seem to accept it. "Adelyn," he said, looking up sharply and spinning in place to look for her. "She's here, she—"

David shook his head, pointing in the direction of the church. From their vantage point it was just visible on the coast, the tip of the white building poking up over the city's skyline. Rahk raised his head and looked.

"If she went there, she's dead," he said. "But—"

The timing on the explosion couldn't have been done better. Out over the ocean, a plume of water suddenly shot up in a crashing wave, and the sound followed a couple seconds later, a rolling boom that sounded like nothing if not thunder.

The church was still standing, pristine and tall. David's grin only spread wider, even though he had no idea how to defuse the bomb even with magic—his tools were limited, and his time even more so.

Pondering the question, he looked at the timer. Only twenty seconds left. He only knew a couple signs, and didn't have the time to chalk out a complicated rune. The only ink available was his own blood, and—

What did he say?

David looked up at Rahk, shifting his attention to listen to what the sorcerer was saying.

"It's not true," he said, staring at David with an obvious expression of horror. Taking a step back, he said, "It can't be true." Looking behind himself, Rahk saw that he was tottering at the edge of the tower, with no more room behind him.

Returning his gaze to David, he made eye contact for a fleeting second, then took another step backwards.

David stuck out his arms and tried to grab Rahk, but he wasn't fast enough. The sorcerer plummeted over the edge, body flipping in the air as he fell straight towards the tracks below.

Taking a second to remember the right sign, David jumped over the edge after him, throwing power through his necklace and waving the wide, circular sign for *'Ansyr.'*

He wasn't creating a hard barrier, but instead kept his hands spinning in a repeat motion, layering weak shields that slowed his descent by a fraction and then collapsed. The magic felt right in his hands, like embracing an old friend who'd been gone away for too long.

David couldn't savor the joy as he fell, though. He could see Rahk's body on the ground in a heap. Rahk hadn't died on impact, but he had only moments left, and there was nothing David could do to save him.

Five feet from landing, David heard another shrill whistle, an order of magnitude louder and closer than it had been. He didn't spare a glance to the train, he knew it was only seconds away.

Huffing out a breath as he landed, David knelt by Rahk's body, spread out over the train rails. The young sorcerer wasn't moving, but he hadn't yet died, or David would have felt the release of power that accompanied the end of a life.

Wiping a hand on his bloody shirt, David spun around the bridge and slapped down a cheap, bloody circle in one motion. It was a pathetic rune, but David didn't need precision, he only needed power.

Standing, he faced the train. It was five-hundred feet away. David thought it surely would have to be braking, to slow down before entering the train station, but if it was he couldn't tell.

It was four-hundred feet away, then, as David sank back into a fighting stance, planting a heel against Rahk's motionless form.

This has to work, he thought. It was half desperate worry and half prayer as he watched the engine barrel towards him. *You wouldn't give me back my power just so I could end up a splatter of blood and gristle on this bridge.*

Behind him, finally, Rahk died.

David gritted his teeth, feeling the incredible surge of energy. There was no other release of spirit that could compare with the white-hot power, and though David had braced himself for the shock, he still collapsed to his knees as he took that spirit and directed into the bridge, charging up the wooden structure.

As a tool, the bridge was massive and awkward and clunky, like a ship with a sail made of lead. With all the power coursing through it, David had to force his thoughts into order, shutting out all fear and worry so that he could accommodate the force and the magic all at once as he moved his hands in a single, unshakeable sign.

A hundred feet ahead of him, the engine bucked violently as it plowed into the first layer of David's shield. The barrier was strong, stronger than the most powerful shield David could have raised with his necklace, but even so it shattered against the front of the train like brittle glass, barely slowing down the great machine.

The second shield, spaced a foot further ahead, didn't do much more than the first. It shattered and slowed down the train by a fraction as well. The next shield did the same, and the next.

David's vision blurred as he held his hands up, channeling more and more power into the remaining shields. He'd tried to throw it all in one go, but there was so much raw spirit that he couldn't handle the force of it all, and it was going to take every scrap of power available to stop the train.

It was a strange sight. The nose of the train was crumpling in on itself, but there was no reason why that anyone could see. David couldn't even feel the dozens of invisible barriers, his sixth sense was blocked out by the overpowering charge of the bridge that contained Rahk's dying spirit.

The explosion barely registered as important. Shrapnel

blew out in all directions from on top of the tower, and metal shards rained onto David's shoulders, but he couldn't be bothered to care, and he could be bothered even less to notice the chains slipping from their gears and falling, steel links throwing up splinters of wood where they hit the deck of the bridge.

The engine was throwing up sparks as it skidded forward on the tracks, fifty feet away, then forty. The nose had been smashed in so badly that it resembled a crumpled up tin can, and the wheels were no longer turning so much as grinding on the rails, carried forward only by the momentum of the rest of the train behind it.

David tried to get to his feet, to stumble clear of the train and the collapsing bridge, but his arms were lead and his legs seemed to be held to the ground by some unseen force or spell. He could feel the deck shaking as supports, too weak to hold up the bridge on their own, cracked and then broke beneath him. The train was twenty feet away now, metal screeching in a wail that made his ears throb.

The screeching is what did it. David could put up with the pain, the exhaustion, even the inevitable death that was facing him if he stayed on the tracks, but that wailing screech was an assault on his senses that he couldn't abide. It didn't seem fair that, even as he kept the train from plunging into the river, it would conspire to make his last few moments such a torment.

Shouting voicelessly, he found the strength to get to his feet and cover his ears. He almost fell over again as soon as he was up, as the bridge shook beneath him, shifting significantly under his feet. Managing to stay upright by some miracle, David picked a direction to his side and staggered that way, stumbling to the edge of the bridge and letting himself fall.

The landing hurt as he slammed into the river's surface. It looked so inviting, but after a twenty foot fall it was only slightly less solid than a marble floor, and David's tumble over the bridge had sent him into a belly flop towards the water.

After the brief jolt of pain, his body decided that it had had enough and promptly blacked out.

CHAPTER 33

Officer was on duty, managing crowd control after the explosions near the church. Suspect approached them with arms raised, identifying herself as Adelyn Mayweather and surrendering without resistance. When asked to relieve herself of weapons, she handed over a silver bracelet and a book, explaining that they were potential magical weapons.

The attending officer cuffed the suspect and took her to their superior, who then handled transportation to the courthouse jail with an escort of three other officers. The suspect was not belligerent, though she did repeatedly ask about the condition of the train. When questioned, she freely admitted being connected to the rioting around the city, and claims to have averted a bombing plot to destroy the church.

Suspect is being held on charges of murder, attempted murder, grand robbery, destruction of property, and conspiracy against the state. Charges of aiding fugitives were considered but not raised at this time.

•Peace officer report, taken from Azish courthouse archives.

. . .

DAVID COUGHED up a mouthful of salty water and gasped awake, feeling numerous aches and pains rush back into his consciousness. There was someone over him, pressing against his chest to get him breathing.

Shoving them away, David rolled onto all fours, coughing violently to expel more water from his lungs so he could breathe. It took him almost three minutes of intermittent coughing, wheezing, and gasping breaths to get to the point where he didn't feel like he was choking, and then another minute of panting before he felt able to relax.

When he rolled onto his back, he saw that there were a dozen guns all pointed at him, and almost started wheezing again when laughter threatened to bubble up from deep in his chest.

He was lying against the muddy bank of the river, and though it was a poor vantage point, he could see the engine of the train was on its side and smashed beyond use, hanging halfway over the empty space where half of the bridge was normally supposed to be.

Though he hadn't stopped the bombs, he'd managed to save the train.

As he was reveling in victory, David realized that someone was talking to him and tried to focus.

"—destruction of property, attempted murder of god knows how many agents of the state, and conspiracy against the state. Someone cuff him."

David's eyebrows shot up as one of the figures around him approached and grabbed his arms, pulling them behind his back and cuffing them in place. The position made his shoulder ache, and the peace officer didn't seem to mind as they towed him up to his feet.

"You're lucky we bothered saving you at all," one of the

figures said. "But believe me, you're going to wish we'd let you drown."

That was more startling, but David quickly realized the source of confusion. Without context, they wouldn't know that he was there to stop the train from being damaged worse than it had been.

"What, don't you have anything to say for yourself?"

David looked at who had spoken. It was an older man, clearly a peace officer based on his white outfit and silver badge.

He couldn't sign, not with his hands behind his back, so he opened his mouth to show that he had no tongue.

There was a pause at that. Someone said, "Should we get him something to write with?"

"Are you kidding? He's a wizard, that's like handing him a loaded gun."

"But if he can't speak, how's he supposed to cast spells?"

"You saw what he did!"

David shut his eyes and sighed. Though he wanted little more than a few days with a comfortable bed, he could already tell that it was going to be a long, long day.

...

Adelyn pulled at her handcuffs experimentally, testing how much range she had to move them about. They were steel, and bolted to the steel table in front of her, which matched the steel chair and stone blocks that made up her cell. She'd been given linen clothes soaked in saltwater to wear, and though the guard who brought her water to drink hadn't exactly been uncourteous, she felt like she deserved a little better treatment after saving the city.

She hadn't been forced to turn herself in, but she didn't want the news, or the peace officers, to come up with their own version of events as to what happened, so she'd flagged down the first peace officer she saw after coming to the surface and turned herself in. Once they were done bugging their eyes out in surprise, they'd taken her back to the city courthouse, and she'd been locked up in her cell ever since.

She wasn't sure how long it had been. There weren't any windows in her cell. Adelyn had given her version of events several times—leaving out only David's identity as the Blue Flame, and that it was her idea to rob the vault. The first omission was for David's protection, the second was for her own.

"Assholes!" she shouted at the mirror that was placed across from her.

It wasn't the captivity that got to her. The uncomfortable restraints, the lack of sleep, that was all frustrating but tolerable. It was ridiculous that they were treating her like a criminal after she had nearly died while saving the city, but she'd been expecting them to be unreasonable, so it wasn't a surprise.

What pissed her off was that they wouldn't tell her what had happened to David. She had gathered that the train hadn't been completely destroyed, though there was something about a derailment, and not a word of whether David had survived.

The sheriff, Cara, walked inside a minute later, with two cups of coffee. She set one in front of Adelyn, but since Adelyn would have to lean forward awkwardly to take a sip with her hands cuffed to the table, she ignored the drink.

"Let's go over this one more time," Cara said. "From the top."

"We've been over this three times!" Adelyn said. "You tell me how David is, I'll tell you what happened again."

"That's confidential," Cara said, sipping her own coffee. "We're just trying to clear up some details."

"Talk to that bank guard," Adelyn said. "She'll confirm what I'm telling you."

"We've talked to her," Cara said. "She's not the most reliable witness, though, considering she attacked one of our own about half an hour before Watched rebels tried to destroy our church."

"I don't have anything else to tell you, then," Adelyn said. "You've heard my story."

"At least answer me a couple questions," Cara said. "Do you know where your accomplices might have gone to hide?"

"I don't have any idea where David would go," Adelyn said. "The hideout we were staying at wasn't safe for us, because we betrayed the Watched to save your damned town. Remember?"

"I remember," Cara said. "I'm not asking where David would go."

"Then—" Adelyn started. "Topher escaped?"

"I'm trying to establish any hideaways he may have had," Cara said. "I am not saying he or his sister escaped being caught."

Adelyn grinned, sitting back. "They got away!"

She genuinely wasn't sure where Topher would be hiding, but it was a comfort to know that they weren't in custody. Adelyn had a good shot of getting out of this through legal means, but Topher was less likely to be so lucky.

Before the sheriff could continue her line of questioning, there was a knock at the door, and a second later it swung open.

"What is it?" Cara asked, looking back at the man who'd just entered. He wore a neatly pressed suit, nothing like what the peace officers wore, but when he walked in to whisper something to Cara he had such an obvious air of authority that Adelyn had assumed he was Cara's boss.

The sheriff looked up at him angrily. "Are you kidding me?"

Shaking his head, the man said, "I'll be waiting outside."

Glaring, Cara reached to her belt and pulled her ring of keys free. "You're one lucky witch," she said, walking over to Adelyn's side of the table as the man left. "I know this is a trick. I don't know how, but I know it's a trick."

"What's a trick?" Adelyn asked, confused. "What did he say?"

The sheriff scoffed as she leaned in, unlocking Adelyn's cuffs. "You're free to go," she said.

Widening her eyes, Adelyn rubbed at her wrists and tried to figure out if this was some kind of scheme to get her to confess. "You finally decided to believe me?"

"Abandon me," the sheriff growled. "It's over my head."

Brow furrowing, Adelyn got out of the chair. "But, I can leave?"

"Not quite," the sheriff said. "He wants to talk to you first."

Glancing at the door, Adelyn asked, "Who?"

Cara didn't respond. Now that Adelyn was uncuffed, it seemed, her duty as sheriff had ended, so she stormed out of the room, stomping off down the hall.

Adelyn wasn't sure if she should be concerned or relieved. Walking to the door, she pushed it open tentatively and looked around.

The hallway only went one way, so she walked down it. She could hear some voices in the open foyer a ways up ahead, so she walked towards that and tried to hear what was being said.

"... sorry that you had to find out like this."

It wasn't a voice that Adelyn recognized. As she walked in, she saw that the young man in the suit was the speaker, and he was talking to someone in a set of loose linen clothes that matched Adelyn's own.

"David!" Adelyn exclaimed. His back was to her, but she recognized him nonetheless. Even if she didn't recognize his form or posture, his missing thumb was a dead giveaway without a glove to cover it. "You're alive! I—"

David looked over his shoulder at her and she stopped. His eyes were shot red, with tears streaking his face. He rubbed at his face and smiled slightly upon seeing her, but it still wasn't exactly the reunion that Adelyn had imagined.

"What happened?" she asked, directing the question towards David.

David shook his head. 'I have good news,' he said, rubbing the palm of one hand against his cheek to wipe away the tears. 'But not right now.'

"You're free to go," the man said, addressing Adelyn. "As far as the peace officers are concerned, you were acting as an official of the state to destroy the rebel insurgents' gang from the inside. An undercover peace officer, in effect."

"That's not what we—" Adelyn started, before realizing that she should keep her mouth shut. Still, the idea that they were working with the peace officers this whole time felt gross, and the idea that she would be officially listed as their ally made her feel sick. "Why?"

"Because I need David to come with me," the man said. "And he said he wouldn't accept it unless you were released as well."

Adelyn frowned. "What about Topher?"

It was the man's turn to be caught off guard. "Topher?"

"Sorcerer," Adelyn said. "My age. He's—"

"Oh," the man said, looking sheepish. "He doesn't carry

the same immunity, unfortunately. That being said, the first wave of arrests didn't take as much care with him or his sister as they should have. They are at large, and I don't expect they'll be caught."

Adelyn set her jaw. "Okay. What's this about? I know the government doesn't run around handing out alibis for free, even—" leaning in, she added, "Even to someone like David."

"Do you know Sarah Turner?" the man asked, looking at the papers he was holding.

"No," Adelyn said, before blinking. "Wait, yes. That's the person David was trying to contact, before this whole mess started."

Nodding, the man said, "Yes, indeed. We're glad he tried to get in touch, because we've been trying to locate David for a while now, but couldn't place him. Three sorcerers of note for their service in the president's army, including Sarah Turner, were murdered three months ago. We have reason to believe that David might be next."

ACKNOWLEDGMENTS

Cover art by Christopher Kallini
Edited by An Avid Reader Editing